YOUR CHANCE TO GET INTO THE SPY ACADEMY!

JOIN THE GROWING GROUP of readers who've discovered the thrill of Chase when you sign up to get the Olivero Entrance Exam sent straight to your inbox.

Scan the QR code to watch your video invitation and get started on the adventure. Good luck, Recruit!

Acclaim for Staccato Passage

What readers are saying…

"This high-octane sequel to *Nocturne In Ashes* delivers nonstop suspense and intrigue."

~ Reader's Favorite

"A-not-to-be-forgotten story of love, grief and intrigue. Be prepared to be spellbound."

~ Advance Reader

"From the first page to the last, I was drawn into the story and felt like I was a part of it. A must-read for thriller fans!"

~ Advance Reader

"The twists and turns throughout the book kept me turning the pages long into the night. An engaging read you won't want to put down until the last page has been read!"

~ Advance Reader

"With tons of suspense, you can hardly wait to turn the page!"

~ Advance Reader

Get your next Joslyn Chase book free!

But catch up on your sleep now.
Once you start reading,
it'll be *No Rest* for you!

Get the book free when you join
the growing group of readers who've discovered
the thrill of Chase!

Get started now at joslynchase.com
OR
simply scan the QR code below

ALSO BY JOSLYN CHASE

Nocturne in Ashes

Cincher's Waltz

Steadman's Blind

Fastpitch

A Band of Scheming Women

The Tower

The Devil's Trumpet

Falling For The Lost Dutchman

No Rest

What Leads a Man to Murder

Death of a Muse

Duet for Piano & Chisel

STACCATO PASSAGE

A RILEY FORTE SUSPENSE THRILLER

JOSLYN CHASE

PARAQUEL PRESS

Library of Congress Control Number: 2024906511

Publisher's Cataloging-in-Publication Data
Names: Chase, Joslyn.
Title: Staccato passage : a Riley Forte suspense thriller / Joslyn Chase.
Description: University Place, WA : Paraquel Press, 2024. | Series : Riley Forte suspense thrillers ; book 2.
Identifiers: LCCN 2024906511| ISBN 9781952647147 (pbk.)| ISBN 9781952647154 (ebook)
Subjects: LCSH: Spies – Training of – Fiction. | Terrorism – Prevention – Fiction. | Pianists – Fiction. |Spy stories. | Bavaria (Germany)– Fiction. |BISAC: FICTION / Thrillers / Espionage. | FICTION / Thrillers / Terrorism. | FICTION / Women.
Classification: LCC PS3603.H37 S73 2024 (print) | DDC 813 C--dc23
LC record available at https://lccn.loc.gov/2024906511

Prologue

Mid-morning.

The sun shone golden on the wide spread of evergreens seven thousand feet below, gilding and lifting them like jewels from dusty velvet, making the lush pools of shadow sink in contrast. Purring vibrations from the sturdy little four-seat Sundowner filled the cabin, muffled by the headset she wore and the woman at the controls smiled, remembering the days when she had to drop a quarter into a motel bed to get that kind of relaxation.

To the east, the waters of the Atlantic Ocean sparkled deep blue, edged by a rind of white Brazilian beaches along the coast. She glanced at her companion in the seat beside her and gestured toward the distant expanse.

Speaking into the headset mic, she said, "Maybe we can go sailing this afternoon."

He gave her a look, waggled his head. "I'd prefer a leisurely lunch and a nap."

She laughed. "Oh ye of little adventure."

"Little adventure?" Leaning close, he sent her an air kiss. "Just being with you is the adventure of a lifetime."

She gave his knee a squeeze and checked the gauges. Everything looked fine. Everything was—

Bang!

The plane shuddered and bucked with a sickening shriek of metal.

The explosion had come from the engine compartment, and it sent a plume of greasy black smoke billowing across the Sundowner's wrap-around windshield, shrouding visibility, throwing a dark cloud over the little plane.

The woman pilot screamed, then clamped her teeth together, holding tight to the yoke. The smoke blew off, leaving behind a grimy film and enough light for her to see the control panel.

All zeroes.

The needle on every gauge lay flat at the bottom of its range.

She tore off her headset and heard the last thing she wanted to hear.

Silence.

The engine was gone.

Next to her, the man had gone sickly pale. He said nothing, but his lips worked soundlessly and his hands dug into his thighs, the knuckles white as bone.

Fumes crept into the cabin, choking and nauseating. The woman stared out at the thick, endless field of tiny, distant pines and eucalyptus, approaching too fast. Relentless.

She gripped the yoke, pulling up, willing the plane to rally and rise. But the controls that had always felt so responsive, so alive under her fingers, now felt cold and dead.

Wings, and the dynamics of flight, kept them aloft. For now.

Despite that knowledge and her experience, she wrestled the panicky notion that they were dead and falling like a brick in the sky. Going down hard and fast.

She fought to keep the nose up, to force the plane into a long, slow turn, buying time. She needed a break. A meadow, a clearing, something to aim for.

There was nothing.

With a desperate burst of hope, she tried starting the engine again.

No use.

The woman tried feathering the controls, straining to eke some altitude out of the plane, slowing its descent.

Nothing responded. Nothing worked.

Heart booming, she peered out the windshield. The looming pines still appeared tiny, but they were close enough now to see stony projections, stark cliffs and diamond-hard rock formations thrusting up between them.

The woman blinked. Sweat dripped into her eyes, stinging.

Beside her, the man let out a series of strangled sobs. She heard frantic breaths—harsh and wheezing—and realized they were her own. She swallowed hard, struggling for control, but felt the fight seeping out of her like air from a spent balloon.

With shaking hands, she activated the GPS emergency beacon and tried the radio.

Static.

It didn't matter. None of it mattered anymore.

The trees grew large, a black sea reaching up to swallow the broken Sundowner.

———

From his vantage point at the top of the highest hill, John Harrigan watched the plane go down.

He followed its decline with his binoculars, noting with interest how the wings sheared off as it hit the inexorable wall of Brazilian forest and how abruptly it came to rest against a jagged crest of rock.

The day was fine, almost too hot for his taste. Screwing the cap off a thermos, he took a long draught of cold water, feeling the chill trace through his chest, tasting the slight metallic tang.

His radio hissed and he picked up.

"The charge went off exactly as planned," Haagen told him. "And she activated the GPS beacon."

"Good," John said. "Move in, and have the ambulance standing by. I'll meet you at the hospital."

He didn't hurry as he hiked back to the road where his car waited. Rescue operations took time. His people would have to traverse difficult territory to retrieve the plane crash victims. He could afford to linger.

The heat of the day brought out the smell of pine resin, heavy in the dry air of the Rio Grande do Sul. Not so much different from the forests around Seattle where he'd grown up.

Where he'd blossomed.

The woodlands were full of tiny sounds—insects, birds, an occasional rustling breeze. As he trekked through the carpet of pine needles, John heard another sound, a sort of frenzied sniffling. He slowed his steps, approaching cautiously. He'd once met a bear cub in the Washington woods, and that hadn't turned out well.

The noise came from a small deer, a young doe, caught in a jumble of vines. The creature stamped her hind feet as John came near, eyes wide and roving with fear. John watched her struggle, all alone in the big, bad forest.

Coming closer, he saw the doe's front hooves had become entangled in a trailing mass of vines. A slice of the knife could free the creature.

Reaching for his pocketknife, John opened the Damascus steel blade. Slowly, carefully, he stepped nearer, speaking soothingly, reassuringly. The deer snorted, rearing back, trying frantically to get away before he reached her.

He laid a hand gently on her neck, feeling the pulse beat beneath his palm, her life in his hands. He waited until she went still, until her heartbeat matched his own. Then he leaned in and made a swift cut.

The animal was free.

He watched her bound away, clumsy in her haste, the sound of her flurried escape reaching him for whole seconds after she'd disappeared from view. He knelt in the dirt, touching the place where she'd been. A thrill shuddered through him.

Rising to his feet, he folded the knife. Sun-dappled leaves quivered in the eucalyptus breeze as he tucked it back into his pocket.

He walked on.

As he neared the hospital, John watched the ambulance arrive, saw his men jump out and wheel in two gurneys, each carrying a sheet-swathed figure. He met Haagen in the corridor and they rode the elevator down to the basement together.

"Did she make it?" John asked.

"She's hurt bad, but I think she'll recover." Haagen lifted the sheet off the body on the gurney. The woman pilot lay still and cold, traces of fear frozen on her face. She was dead.

"Good," John said, offering a grim smile. "Let's get her into surgery."

In the basement, they were met by another of John's men, dressed as a morgue attendant. He stood beside a third gurney with another sheet-covered form. This one sedated but breathing.

The man swapped gurneys with Haagen. Without a word, the attendant began wheeling the DOA crash victims to the morgue.

John watched him for a moment, then returned to the elevator, followed by Haagen steering the newly-acquired gurney. Upstairs, the eminent Dr. Daniel Bernardo awaited their arrival. He was prepped for surgery and John had supplied the nurses and an anesthesiologist.

A discreet team he could trust.

Dr. Bernardo didn't know the name of his patient. Nor did he want to. He understood that the less he knew, the greater his chances of survival.

John was confident the good doctor would keep silent, a silence guaranteed by the continued wellbeing of his wife and three daughters.

In addition, the money he was being paid would provide critical funding for his medical school to stay open, giving hope to the poor people of his home region.

John knew very well how to find the beating pulse, how to wield a knife.

And precisely when.

The operating theater allowed him to watch from above as Dr. Bernardo raised the scalpel and made his first cut, working from a photograph on the table beside him. They had discussed the changes he would make to the ears, the cheekbones, the shape of the chin.

The skilled surgeon would create a new woman, fashioned in the likeness of the expired pilot. And John would use her. He'd mentor her.

He would teach her how to fly.

1

A HUNDRED FEET OFF the ground, Riley clung to a narrow crevice of rock.

Heart pounding against the sun-heated stone, she wedged her hand into a crack running vertically along its rough surface. The fleshy part of her palm lodged in the constricted space, allowing her to pull herself another twelve or thirteen inches up the cliff. With her knee angled outward, she found a place to cram her toe sideways into the crack and turned her foot, pushing upward, increasing her progress.

Careful not to look down, knowing how dizzy, how shaky, that made her feel, she concentrated on the stretch ahead. But squinting upward, she saw an endless expanse of sheer rock, broken only by the jagged crack. No end in sight.

A wave of nausea washed over her. The energy reserve she'd tried so hard to foster drained away as if someone had pulled a plug.

She couldn't move.

Her legs trembled uncontrollably and her hands ached. Sweat poured down from her hairline, bringing the taste of salt and coconut sunscreen but she didn't dare lift a hand to wipe it clear.

"My foot's stuck!" she shouted, feeling the rise of panic.

Far below, her partner, Christopher Neville, held her lifeline, belaying her. "Rotate your knee, Riley," he called. "Reverse the movement."

His steady voice calmed her. Pulling in a shuddering breath, Riley angled her knee, returning her foot to its sideways position. With a jiggle, she pulled her shoe free but lost her balance. Gasping, she thrust her hand deeper into the crack and felt the pressure of her weight pulling against her wrist and palm.

It hurt.

Gritting her teeth, she jammed her foot back into the crack. "Why are we doing this, Chris?"

She heard the petulance in her voice, but felt it justified. Why had he brought her here? Chris was a friend, and a fellow concert pianist.

Except, his career was blossoming, growing, whereas hers...

Pushing the sour thought aside, Riley yelled, "What are we supposed to be gaining from this? You value your hands as much as I do."

His voice floated up to her and she heard the smile in his words. "Exhilaration! Inspiration! As needful to feed our souls as to school our fingers, Riley. Your playing will be the better for it. I promise."

"Not if I snap them off in this horrid crack," she muttered.

A shadow flitted by on her right, a bird making a clacking sound. It perched somewhere out of her range of vision and continued to scold.

"Are you done?" Chris asked.

Riley lifted her chin, straining her eyes against the sun, looking again for the top of the climb. Still not seeing it.

She closed her eyes and swallowed hard, thinking of Jim. Thinking of Tanner.

She still missed them so much.

The image of a face shimmered across her mind—the man who'd taken her husband and child from her—and she let it come. It was a rare moment when she allowed herself to think about him. He had been her friend, taking care of her, encouraging her. He'd taught her to kayak, told her the secret of crickets.

And betrayed every trust she'd ever placed in him.

He was dead now too, but the shadow of evil under which he'd crouched still loomed. It was still out there.

Riley moved her head, rubbing her face against her sleeve, trying to wipe away the sweat stinging her eyes. She raised her chin again, but the top of her climb had not materialized. It was no clearer to her now.

Dragging in a deep breath, she shouted down to Chris. "No! I'm moving on."

Reaching above her, she jammed a hand into the crack and turned her thumb, securing her grasp. She levered herself up, hand over hand, moving her feet up by intervals. Determined. Single-minded. Making progress.

And then, for a fraction of a second, she failed to keep the exhaustion at bay, letting it shatter her concentration, sap her energy. She wavered and her foot skidded down the rock, losing its purchase. She gasped as her hand slipped from the crevice, flailing and finding nothing.

She fell.

Her stomach lurched as she swung back and spun in the air, held by the rope and safe enough, but with the crush of defeat washing over her.

Shaking, exhausted, she finished her descent and slumped in the shade cast by the towering rock, working to catch her breath.

"You did good, Riley," Chris said, passing her a water bottle. "It's better than the gym, right? A lot more fun."

She gulped the water, still blessedly cool in the insulated flask. "I'll reserve judgment on that for now. Maybe I'll feel better in hindsight."

"Of course you will. I know you, Riley."

Did he? Did she even know herself? It felt like she'd lost everything she'd ever fought to keep. Was there really any point in looking for something new?

A crescendo of chords jangled from the bag beside her. Even out here, in the thin air of the Cascades, her phone picked up a signal. She saw who was calling and answered, feeling the stir of curiosity.

"Riley, it's Devin Wright."

Wright was the founder and CEO of Olivero Security, a firm providing private protection and investigative services to clients around the world. He'd been angling to recruit Riley for the better part of a year and she'd finally signed on, making it official.

"I know we talked about sending you out to the academy in June," he said, "but..."

He paused, and Riley pictured him running his hands through the thinning hair on top of his head as she'd seen him do on previous occasions.

"Things are happening, Riley. I don't know how closely you've been watching the news." A beat passed. She said nothing. "We're moving your training forward. You leave day after tomorrow."

The stirring curiosity in her gut churned into anxiety. "What? So soon?"

"My secretary will email your instructions and travel itinerary."

Riley's tongue felt thick in her throat. "I don't know what—"

"Riley," Wright interrupted her. "You are important to us. To our mission and the values we hold dear."

She said nothing.

"I wouldn't be calling you to come in early like this," he continued, "if I didn't feel some urgency." A pause. "You can do this."

Her chest felt tight, making it hard to draw breath. Inside her stomach, something moved, slow and greasy. She felt sick with trepidation, and another sensation she couldn't identify.

She thought it might be excitement.

She gripped the phone in her chalky hand, pressing it against the side of her face.

"Yes, sir," she said.

She ended the call and took several steps back from the cliff, moving on uneven ground tufted with scrubby brush. Shading her eyes, she looked up. From here, she could see the top of the rocky precipice.

From here, it looked reachable.

A surge of nervous energy rushed through her as she packed her climbing gear into a canvas duffle, making her feel light-headed and anxious to get home.

"That's it for today," she told Chris. "I've got to get going."

2

Rush hour traffic in Seattle.

Rick hated being on the road at this time of day. The fumes, the noise, the stop and go.

Whenever he could, he avoided the snarl of vehicles vying for pavement, their erratic movements sometimes unpredictable and downright foolish. He hated the squeeze, the feeling of being hemmed in.

He had good reason.

Barely seven months ago he'd been literally sandwiched between two cars on this stretch of freeway, trapped in a crushed metal cage during the worst disaster Seattle had ever seen. The memory of it left him feeling queasy.

Gritting his teeth, he pressed on, watching for his exit and taking it with a sigh of relief. Watery sunlight spilled down from the eastern sky, painting a stripe across the newspaper on the seat beside him. The paper was folded to reveal a news story on page two.

The article wasn't surprising. Little surprised Rick when it came to the news of the day. Murder, arson, terrorism. Kidnapping, sex trafficking, conspiracies. All of it was too prevalent, too disheartening.

But something about the owner of a local jewelry chain being arrested for homicide and selling stolen merchandise disturbed him beyond the usual. It was the part where the reporter had interviewed the man's nephew.

"I guess I never really knew him," the nephew said. "I haven't seen him in years, but I wouldn't have believed he'd do something like this."

A common enough sentiment among friends and family of apprehended wrong-doers, but in this instance it touched an ominous chord at the back of Rick's mind, not letting go.

He turned off on a side road, following its shaded curves beneath towering evergreens. He was always amazed by how quickly the feel could go from urban congestion to rustic tranquility in the outlying areas of the city.

Olivero Security, a private, high-end and under-the-radar investigative firm, had its headquarters in a tucked away spot, giving it the ambiance of a mountain retreat. Rick enjoyed the effect—found it somehow both calming and energizing—and he relished the work he did for the firm.

It made him feel effective and useful in the world.

The complex spread out over a dozen acres and included three main structures joined by breezeways and several outbuildings. The muted gray exteriors with forest green trim blended well into the landscape, giving the place a harmonious feel while still maintaining a business-like impression.

To the outside world, the company simply ran a crack team of private investigators and bodyguards. To those who knew, Olivero's scope encompassed so much more and ran so much deeper.

Rick pulled his Mustang in next to a copper-colored Mini and set the parking brake. Scooping up his messenger bag, he shoved the newspaper inside and hustled for the building's entrance, breathing in the pine-scented air.

Inside, he headed straight for Devin Wright's office. Wright was the founder and chief executive officer of Olivero Security. He'd poured everything he had—money, time, energy, integrity, personal commitment—into the company, and was rightly proud of what he'd built, ever vigilant to safeguard it.

More than a full-time job.

"Right on time, Rick," Wright greeted him. "Let's get started."

The chief's face was grim, almost gray beneath the sparse hair at his temples. Rick took a seat at the conference table between a large, well-tanned man and a diminutive woman in a green dress. The woman, a top-notch analyst named Sophie Alvarez, had a copy of the morning paper on the table in front of her. It lay open at the same article Rick had flagged.

Wright paced the room, hands folded together beneath his chin. "I have some startling news," he announced. Halting, he pivoted, pinning the assorted group around the table with his eyes. "Hugh Jenkins turned up yesterday."

Rick took in the gasps and raised eyebrows, but he didn't know anything about Hugh Jenkins.

"Alive?" someone asked.

Wright dropped into his chair at the head of the table. "Barely."

Directing his attention to Rick, the newbie of the group, he explained. "Hugh Jenkins is an agent we sent undercover in Argentina a few years back. He disappeared, presumed dead."

Turning back to the table at large, he said, "Hugh showed up at one of our safe houses in Costa Rica. My man there, James Holloway, tells me he was sick, exhausted. He'd been kept in a sort of prison camp and subjected to hard labor. Somehow, he managed to escape."

"Is he okay?" asked Daniel Escobar, the man at Rick's side, one of the best IT investigative specialists in the country. Wright didn't answer his question directly.

"Holloway said Hugh could barely talk, but he had some incredible things to say. A lot of it he picked up in the prison camp—"

"Of dubious validity, then," Daniel stated.

"But disturbing nonetheless," Wright continued. "Anyone here ever seen the movie *The Princess Bride?*"

Everyone had.

"Anyone here ever heard of a criminal puppet master called The Cincher?"

Frederick Yates, head of the Personnel Department, snorted. "Cincher is a myth, chief."

Nods around the table agreed with him.

"So I always thought as well," Wright said. "I may be re-evaluating that position. According to Hugh, The Cincher leads an international criminal syndicate called The Knot. And according to Hugh, it's a position of power passed down from one mastermind to the next, much like the Dread Pirate Roberts in *The Princess Bride.*"

Rick looked around at the group. Most faces held skepticism or even scorn. He thought his own face must look the same. It was an improbable idea.

Ramona Reed adjusted her glasses, looking doubtfully at Wright over their rims.

"Sounds far-fetched, Devin."

A former DARPA scientist, she headed up the Research and Development arm of the company. She wore her graying, thick blonde hair piled haphazardly atop her head, secured by a pencil. Every time Rick saw her he had to fight an urge to pull out the pencil and watch the hair tumble down around her shoulders.

"I would concur," Wright said. "Except that someone killed Hugh to keep him from saying anything more."

A small, shocked silence fell over the room.

"What happened?" Sophie asked.

"Hugh told Holloway about Cincher and The Knot, said they were involved in coordinated attacks around the world—targeted robberies, terrorist actions, orchestrations of rioting and looting. A tangled network of powerful, well-funded mischief makers."

Wright gestured to the newspaper in front of Sophie Alvarez. "I wonder if you've been thinking what I've been thinking. Hugh suggested part of The Knot organization specializes in placing imposters in key positions by secretly replacing players with their own people."

"Creepy," Ramona said. "Like *Invasion of the Body Snatchers.*"

"A bit like that maybe, but before Holloway could get any details, he was called away for an important phone call."

"Oh no," Daniel said. "I see where this is going."

"Yes," Wright confirmed. "It was a ploy. When Holloway returned, Hugh was choking on his own tongue."

"How did it happen?" Rick asked.

"I spoke to a witness who saw a nurse bring Hugh a cup of tea. A few sips into it, Hugh was dead and the nurse had disappeared."

"Damn." Daniel slumped back in his chair. "We need more information." He pointed to the newspaper. "What's the deal?"

"It may be nothing," Sophie said.

"It probably *is* nothing," Rick piped up. "But I had the same idea when I read the story. A jewelry store owner arrested for homicide and trafficking in stolen merchandise. The jeweler had no close friends or family. The report quotes a nephew hadn't seen the man in years, but swears he acted out of character."

"Almost as if it wasn't even the same guy," Sophie agreed.

"I highly doubt this jeweler has anything to do with The Knot," Wright said. "But it caught my attention as the *kind* of situation we need to be thinking about—where key people can be subbed out for doubles and no one the wiser. Apparently, it's worked before for The Knot, and if it ain't broke…"

"It's a sinister idea," Ramona said. She turned to Frederick. "I'm very sorry to hear about Hugh. I know he was a particular friend of yours."

"Yes, from way back. I recruited him."

Rick was used to seeing Frederick brimming with vitality, always smiling and full of bonhomie. The man now looked like a popped paper bag, wrinkled and flat.

"That's all, everyone," Wright said. "I just wanted to pass on Hugh's information. He paid a high cost to get it to us."

Murmured agreement rippled around the room as people rose to leave.

"Rick?" Chief Wright motioned him back into his chair. "I'd like you to stay."

When the room had emptied, Wright closed the door and pulled a chair close to Rick, leaning forward, hands clasped, elbows on knees. He grimaced.

"I had some of my operatives in Europe dig a little deeper on this Cincher thing. It appears there may be some truth to this Dread Pirate Roberts type of passage. They're saying a new guy has recently taken command. By all accounts, a more brutal and innovative leader than his predecessor."

Rick shifted in his seat. Bad news, of course, but it didn't explain why Wright was telling him, specifically. The chief paused, something delicate and unsaid suspended in the air between them. Rick wished he'd just take a breath and say it.

"There's some indication that Cincher could be the man we know as John Harrigan."

Now Rick wished he hadn't said it.

"Are you going to tell Riley?" he asked.

Riley Forte was not only a good friend, but Rick had been the one to recruit her. Like Frederick had recruited Hugh Jenkins.

"I'm sending her to the academy in Bavaria tomorrow. I haven't decided whether or not to tell her our suspicions about Cincher. That's why I wanted to talk to you."

"I thought her training was scheduled for June."

"It was."

"Then why now?"

"Two reasons. First, I don't want to delay any longer on getting her the skills she needs to protect herself and to be useful to us."

"And the second reason?" Rick asked.

"The second reason is that she'll be safer at the academy, surrounded by some of our best people than most anywhere I can think of."

Rick nodded. He saw the logic.

"But are you going to tell her about John?" he asked again. "She survived his attack. She's seen his face. She's definitely a person of interest to him. And if he is this Cincher..."

"I know." Wright straightened in his chair, balled his fists in his lap. "I just don't think she needs the added stress right now. She'll be somewhat insulated at the academy and she'll be concentrating on her training."

"Yes..." Rick said, letting the word hang.

"And," Wright continued, "as an added measure, I'm sending you in as an instructor. To be there on the premises for her. Watching over her."

"Okay, good."

Chief Wright stood and straightened his tie.

"Go pack a bag, Rick. You leave in three hours."

3

Taz Salih stared through the glass, sweat breaking out beneath his gas mask.

Two canisters, nestled in a clear acrylic holder, waited beyond the unbreakable glass. Two canisters, more deadly than anything he'd ever encountered.

Over the years, his work had brought him face to face with some of the most lethal substances known to man. Here, operating in Nuremberg, he was part of an underground laboratory team tasked with engineering a new, particularly vicious variant of Sarin gas. Commissioned by an ultra-secret international research committee, the project was intended to provide data useful in the prevention and defense against chemical attack.

But Taz had recognized in it another potential.

In his eyes, the nerve agent had become a calling card. A way to send a message of terror and awe.

Beside him, Aludra tapped at her mobile phone, focusing and resizing the image sent from Raul's screen in the van outside. Their control center and getaway car.

A chill passed along the back of Taz's neck, partly due to the frigid temperature in the lab and partly due to the cocktail of dread and elation that coursed through his veins. He threw a nervous glance behind him. The low, constant hum of the ventilation system provided camouflage for the tiny noises he and Aludra might make, but they would also muffle the sound of someone approaching.

They were still alone.

Taz had used his credentials to get through the gate while Aludra and Marcos huddled in the trunk of his car, shielded from backscatter x-ray detection by a lead blanket stolen from the radiology lab. At 3:00 am, the facility was deserted, other than a periodic sweep of armed patrols.

But Taz knew a tactical team was kept on standby in a small barracks at the back of the property.

While Marcos kept watch at the lab's entrance, Aludra brought the high-resolution image of Dr. Klossner's eye into sharp focus. She looked at Taz and crossed her gloved fingers in a bid for luck.

Taz watched her place the screen of her phone in front of the retinal scanner which controlled the lock protecting the canisters. They'd tested this method with good results, but this was the only time that really mattered. He held his breath.

Nothing happened.

Taz trembled through four long empty seconds before the lock finally clicked, releasing with a faint whooshing sound. He snatched one of the canisters, gripping it hard to calm his shaking hands. Aludra seized the second canister.

Their eyes met through the gas masks they wore and Taz saw her excitement and triumph, echoing the emotions rocketing through his own breast. He snapped open the airtight titanium case designed to carry the canisters and pressed the one he held into the foam-lined space, feeling it settle into place.

An alarm blared, shrill and sudden, shattering the silence of the lab into a thousand dangerous pieces. Pulse throbbing in his eardrums, Taz nearly dropped the case. Fumbling it open, he held it out for Aludra's canister, but she was running to Marcos at the door, still holding the vessel of toxic gas cradled to her chest.

Raul's voice rasped in his earpiece. "Trouble's coming. Get out."

Marcos, armed with a rifle, nosed into the hallway, clearing it and motioning them forward. Taz ran, his heart pounding, Aludra at his heels. Before they'd gone five meters, four uniformed gunmen turned the corner and fired.

Marcos shot back. The clattering racket filled the corridor, multiplied by the canyon-like walls, a torrent of noise and confusion. Taz saw two of their attackers go down and then Marcos spun, hit in the chest.

He fell.

His rifle skittered on the tile and Taz made a grab for it, but was driven back by a rain of gunfire. He retreated into the lab and Aludra slammed the door, locking them inside.

"That will hold them for thirty seconds," she said. "No longer. What do we do now?"

"There's another door. On the other side of this divider. Help me!"

Taz shoved the carrying case under his arm and struggled with the locking mechanism holding the accordion divider in place. He knew it hadn't been used in years and it didn't want to budge. Aludra still clung to her canister, using her free hand to claw at the divider.

It did no good.

The door to the lab burst open with a crack like a rifle shot, spilling men into the room.

"Halt!" one of them shouted. *"Nicht bewegen!"*

Taz gave a final tug on the lock and it popped open, creating an instant gap three inches wide. As he punched his fist into the breach, straining to push the divider along its rusty track, one of the tac team men leaped forward and dragged Aludra back, pulling off her gas mask.

Taz turned, saw the grim, determined look on Aludra's face. He screamed, "No!"

Before anyone could stop her, Aludra sprang the cap on the canister, breaking the seal. A slight hiss, as if she'd popped the top on a can of soda, was the only perceptible indicator that something had happened.

The gas was invisible and odorless.

Taz watched in horror as Aludra doubled over, vomiting onto the immaculate tile floor of the lab. She collapsed, writhing with the effort to breathe but unable to do so. The two men dropped beside her.

A pool of urine spread from beneath one of them, reaching to Aludra's flailing legs, soaking her pants.

It was too late. Too late for him to do anything, even if he'd known of something to do.

He gripped the case and ran.

"Raul!" He shouted into his mouthpiece, reaching out to the last remaining member of his team. "Raul, can you hear me? Aludra and Marcos are down. I'm alone now, heading to the rendezvous. Meet me there."

He heard only a crackle, then silence.

Taz burst out of the building. Raul was blown. His bridges were burned. He'd have to think on the fly as he ran.

His car was no good. He wouldn't get three blocks in it. But he remembered a little-used gate at the far end of the research complex. A rugged galvanized steel turnstile. You could get out that way, but not in.

That worked for him.

Keeping to the shadows, Taz made his way to the turnstile and crouched low, scanning the area. He saw no one.

The longer he waited, the more time lab security would have to summon men and implement a planned response. Once outside the gate, he could get his hands on another car and proceed with the contingency plan put in place by the man in charge.

Someone they called The Cincher.

Taz grasped the handle of the titanium case and sprinted for the gate.

4

RILEY LET HER SHOULDERS relax and pull back, opening her posture and feeling the tension release as her fingers moved across the keyboard of her piano. She finished running through the scales and Hanon exercises that had honed her technique over years of practice. They were no problem for her to execute with precision, even when her mind was a million miles away. Muscle memory prevailed and her fingers found the keys without conscious thought.

But she owed more than thoughtless automatic movement to her performance pieces.

Natural sunlight poured through the high clerestory windows above the mahogany grand piano, burnishing its varnish to a glowing, translucent red. Riley loved the piano and normally she cherished the time she spent with it, letting her fingers dance over the keys, delighting in their rich and mellow tone.

But very little about today felt normal.

She dug into a Mendelssohn *agitato,* felt the heaviness in her forearms bringing out the depth and volume of the tempestuous music. It suited her mood and she let it roar beneath her fingers, filling the room, feeding her irritated, restless temper.

Pressing her lips together, she tasted the peppermint of her favorite lip balm, savoring the subtle burning sensation as she rolled through the last crashing chords of the Mendelssohn. She sat for a moment on the bench, eyes closed, breathing deeply in and out, before turning her attention to the Bach Prelude she'd been studying. She started working through the complicated fingering, trying to find the patience and focus the task required.

And failing.

She pushed away from the piano in frustration. On her way into the kitchen for a glass of water, she indulged in a primal scream, letting it echo around the house where she lived. Alone.

How had her life become this fragile, this empty? Less than three years ago, she'd had a husband, a son. She had a promising concert career and a bulldog agent helping to make it happen. She was on track for the life she'd always dreamed of.

And somehow, it had all derailed.

She'd lost Jim and Tanner in a horrendous fire, set by a man she'd believed to be her friend.

Her ability to perform had shattered, robbing her of everything she had left and plunging her into a deep mire of depression. It had taken the better part of two years and every ounce of courage she had to thrash free from that sucking hole.

She'd struggled to rebuild her career through slow, painful effort, believing it could be her lifeline, a slender thread to happiness.

Only to have her comeback tour destroyed by a spurting volcano and a fiendish killer.

And now, out of these ashes, she'd been given a small burning ember of hope.

But could she do it? Did she have the grit, the stamina, to do what Devin Wright and his Olivero agency expected of her?

They wanted her to go undercover, to use her identity as a concert pianist to move in certain circles and gain access to key people and locations. They wanted her to uncover secret information, to pass along messages and critical communications.

They wanted her to be a spy.

She'd spent enough time with Rick, with Chief Wright, and inside the annals of the agency to be convinced their values coincided with her own, that they supported the cause of freedom and justice.

But could she accomplish what they asked of her?

Would it be enough?

Could she build a new life with substance and meaning sufficiently deep to bring her—if not happiness—a sense of fulfillment?

Riley looked down at the glass of water in her hands. She didn't remember pouring it. Tipping the tumbler, she gulped the water, nearly choking as her throat closed, thick with tears.

She slammed the glass down on the granite countertop, watching a crack spread up from the heavy base to the delicate rim. Dragging in a ragged breath, she straightened her spine and lifted her chin, standing with eyes closed, feeling the cool of the tile spread across the soles of her bare feet.

Just breathing.

She was made of rugged material. She had steel in her DNA.

She reached for it now.

Her great-great-grandfather had gone down on the Titanic, still playing with the orchestra as frantic passengers stormed the life boats.

As a young man, her granddad—Zach Riley, for whom she was named—had traveled with the USO, giving battle zone performances during WWII. More than once, he'd been wounded in the course of his duty but that hadn't stopped him from returning.

Her own parents had braved hazardous situations to bring music where it was most needed and Riley had once or twice gone with them. She'd played charity concerts in war-torn nations and to benefit the victims of the September 11th attack and other terrorist actions.

Not only could she do this, she *needed* to do this. She needed to rise above the forces crushing her down. To make something meaningful of her life.

To honor those who had gone before, and give hope to those yet to come.

Hell, yes!

She would ace her spy school training and become the best damn agent Olivero ever produced.

Riley shook herself and headed for the bedroom. She pulled a suitcase out of the closet and opened it on the bed, making sure it still contained the large laundry bag she used as a hamper for dirty clothes while traveling.

She pulled blouses from hangers, took down folded pairs of pants from the overhead shelf, arranging them on the bed for packing. Tossing toiletries into the zippered compartment, she wondered what kind of shoes she ought to bring.

She paused, absently running her fingers over the hard, pebbled surface of the suitcase while her mind wandered. Lifting her shoulders, she pulled in a deep, cleansing breath, letting the oxygen flow through her, willing herself into serenity. Into strength.

She'd faced her fear and anger, made peace with it and chosen to use it as an impetus rather than an obstacle. Yet her heart continued to beat with a trace of agitation. There was still something niggling at her and she knew she'd have to take it out and examine it before she'd truly be ready to go.

Nate.

Over the past months, the police detective she'd teamed up with to catch a killer, had become a significant part of her life. She and Nate had grown close and in some ways she'd come to depend on him—his cheery optimism, his talent for having fun, his expertise and encouragement. They were friends.

And maybe something more.

But he had a daughter, Sammy. And an ex-wife named Marilyn. Marilyn wanted them to be a family again, and Riley knew Nate wanted that too. She couldn't blame him.

Family was everything.

She and Nate had talked about it, but left things between them up in the air. One way or the other, Riley would have preferred to settle the situation before she left.

She couldn't help feeling that by the time she got back, Nate would be lost to her.

Just one more precious part of her life...gone.

5

ANTON FORST TRUDGED UP the wide, dusty mountain trail. The spring air was cool, not yet warmed by the rising sun, and it nipped at the lobes of his ears below the knit cap he wore. The scent of insect repellent traveled with him, overpowering the fragrant budding wildflowers growing thick along both sides of the trail. He'd rubbed the bug spray over every exposed inch of skin, hating the smell and feel of it.

Hating what mosquito bites did to him even more.

As he walked, his hiking boots crunched on loose pebbles and stones, sending them skittering across the dirt. A noise from behind made him turn his head and he watched a mountain biker pedal up the path. A native Berliner, Forst was used to the German enthusiasm for cycling through nature but found it more prevalent here, in Bavaria, than anywhere else he'd lived.

While he applauded the practice in theory, at times it posed a potential hazard for him.

Like now.

However, at the turnoff up to the Rauher Kulm, a long-dormant volcano, the rider continued on, leaving the path less traveled by free and clear. As Forst started up its rocky incline, he understood why. It was more suited to a mountain goat than a bicycle.

Fortunately, he didn't need to follow it to the top. Using an app on his phone, he clocked off half a kilometer and found a faintly delineated trail, following it into thick pine and oak coverage as he'd instructed his contact to do.

The man was there, waiting for him.

'Were you followed?" Forst asked. "Did anyone see you come?"

"No, I made certain of it."

Forst studied the man, judging his sincerity, his competency, measuring the look and stature of him. Weighing it against certain data points and details.

He would do.

"Have you brought all your documents as I instructed?" Forst asked, holding out his hand to receive them.

"They're all here," the man said. "My passport, driving license, birth records, social security and residency cards."

Forst opened the packet and checked that everything was in order. "And you've told no one about this?" he asked.

The man laughed bitterly. "Who would I tell?" he said. "I no longer have colleagues. My family is gone. My last friend left months ago. Everyone believes I am scum."

Yes, they would. After the rumors and allegations of extreme sexual deviancy and child pornography Forst had engineered and strategically planted, destroying the man's career as a schoolteacher. His wife deserted him soon after, leaving him desperate and ready to grasp at the chance for a new beginning when Forst offered it.

As he had. Confidentially. In the guise of a friend.

"Good. Are you ready, then?" Forst asked.

"More than you can possibly know."

Forst stepped closer, running a finger along the man's jawline, lifting a hank of hair off his forehead.

"We'll have to make some changes to your appearance," he said, edging behind the man.

With swift, practiced movements, Forst wrapped one arm around the narrow chest, using his other arm to grasp and wrench the head in one sharp, abrupt motion, breaking the man's neck.

The crack of it echoed in the silence of the forest.

The body flopped heavily at Forst's feet. He kicked it over so that it fell supine, the pale face staring blank-eyed at the lacework of branches overhead. He searched through the pockets, removing everything, even the lint. He took off the shoes and socks, checking them carefully. In his experience, people often hid important items in their footwear.

Concealing the body under a pile of brown, crackling leaves, Forst surveyed the area and made sure it was ready for his disposal team. They would move in after dark.

He scooped up the packet of documents, tucking it inside his jacket, and made his way through the trees and foliage. Back to the rugged path, this time leading him down the basalt mountain.

A nice payday awaited him, but he had work yet to do. Running a service such as his—securing new identities for hunted criminals—was indeed lucrative. But also demanding and dangerous.

Some days, his work never ended.

As he neared the place where his car was parked, well back and hidden from the road, his mobile phone rang. He picked up.

"Forst."

"You got one coming in hot. The lab gig in Nürnberg didn't go off as planned."

"Only one?"

"Marcos and the girl are down. Police nabbed Raul."

Forst swore. "Not good," he said. "What about the chemical? Did they get it?"

"That's unclear at this point."

Forst ground his teeth and stared off into the trees. "This guy coming in," he asked, "is he the one? The one with the key?"

"Yeah, he's the one. Cincher said to take care of him until the next op. And make sure his exfil docs are ready to go."

"I copy," Forst said, ending the call.

He had one more important appointment that took precedence even over these orders. He'd take care of it before returning to base and preparing to receive the fugitive.

Letting himself into the car, he started the engine and pulled out onto the narrow, winding road. He used one hand to rub at the knot forming along the base of his neck.

It was going to be one of those days.

6

—·—

LIESL SAUNDERS DESCENDED THE staircase from the apartment where she lived with her son and parents and entered the mezzanine surrounding the lobby of the Swanhilde convention center. Like she did every morning, she stopped and pinched herself.

Literally.

Astounded, amazed, and so utterly grateful to be living and working in this spectacular place.

The sun coming in the eastern windows tinted the massive towering fireplace that served as the lobby centerpiece, turning its stones to pale gold. Liesl stood at the balcony rail, flanked by enormous picture windows, and gazed out over the rolling fields and forests of the Upper Palatinate, spread like a patchwork quilt over the surrounding hillsides. Deep greens and rich browns alternated with squares of bright yellow rapeseed just coming into bloom.

Breathtaking.

From here, she could see two more basalt mountains in the distance, little sisters to the one on which the Swanhilde center was built. All part of a long-extinct chain of volcanic fissures. An old but still functioning church sat atop one of the sisters. The other was crowned by the ruins of a castle dating back to the Middle Ages and destroyed

35

during the Second Margrave War. She'd hiked to the top and been as enchanted by that vista as the one laid out before her now.

Here, on her basalt mountain, the Swanhilde Sammelplatz had pride of place, a small private convention center which hosted anything from family reunions and weddings to diplomatic talks and peace summits.

Like the one she was organizing now.

Leaders from seven Eastern European countries, lately torn by high-tension relations, would be meeting to discuss and negotiate arrangements between their governments, with an eye toward cooperation and greater transparency.

General expectations for the outcome were optimistic. But, like anything political, that optimism rested on a knife edge and could teeter one way or the other into disaster.

Her job depended on the smooth and successful completion of the summit.

Liesl heard the snap of a heavy door closing and the click of heels on the polished marble of the floor below her. Margaret Vonnegut, the facilities manager, moved into view, running her hand along the surfaces of the lobby counters and furniture, checking for dust and seeming satisfied with her inspection.

"*Guten Morgen*," Liesl called down to her.

Margaret turned, looking up, squinting against the streaming sunlight. "*Morgen*, Liesl. Were you able to finish those estimates for the banquet?"

"Oh, yes. I did them last night and they look good. I left the file in my apartment, but I'll bring it down to your office."

"Thanks. Just leave it with Gisa."

Liesl turned and climbed the stairs, re-entering her apartment, still scented with the morning coffee and breakfast rolls. Her parents, Peter and Ingrid, sat at the table with her son, Max, the remnants of the meal laid out before them.

"Mama," Max said, surprise and delight spreading across his face. "Are you home?"

Liesl felt the familiar wrench at her heart, the surge of fierce love she often knew when looking at her child. She drank in his simple, open and honest face, made a bit owl-like by the glasses he wore and the blinking hazel eyes behind them.

He was fourteen years old, but Down's Syndrome made him seem much younger. His father had left shortly after the boy's second birthday, unable to deal with the child's condition or his own disappointment. Max and Liesl had seen him only a handful of times since. She thanked God her parents, patient and kind, were there to help care for her son.

She smoothed the hair over Max's forehead, planting a kiss there. "No, I'm not home yet," she told him. "I only forgot something and had to come back."

Liesl noticed the empty place at the table, the coffee grown cold, rolls and butter untouched.

"Julia's not up yet?" she asked.

Her father looked exasperated but said nothing. Ingrid shook her head. "Not yet. I think I'll go rouse her. She needs to eat and sleep on a regular schedule."

About a month ago, Liesl's sister, Julia, had come to stay. Straight out of a drug rehab program. They were all determined to keep her with them until she'd solidly recovered, but their worry over her and the disruption to the regular flow of their routine imposed a strain.

Just another layer on top of the stress Liesl already bore in connection with the imminent peace talks.

The head of the corporation who owned the Swanhilde Sammelplatz had made it clear to Liesl that she'd been hired on a trial basis. She and her family could live in one of the apartments attached to the center and she'd draw a good salary and a generous benefit package.

But if her event planning skills didn't hold up to the challenges of an international peace summit, they'd all be sent packing.

Message received.

Liesl delivered the file to Margaret's office, leaving it with her secretary. In her own office, she greeted her assistant, Joseph, and got right to work checking details and confirming the arrangements she'd made for the success of the summit.

After a busy few hours, the phone on her desk buzzed. She stood and stretched, pressing a hand to the small of her back, easing the ball of tension that always seemed to settle there. She pressed a button on the phone, putting Joseph through on speaker.

"Frau Saunders," he said, his voice sounding nasal over the wire, "Anton Forst is here for your eleven o'clock appointment."

7

Riley wrapped her hands around the mug of steaming tea, breathing in the vapors of lavender and mint, letting them and the warmth of the cup soothe the wrestle in her chest. Her cell phone alarm clock still showed seventeen minutes before it was set to go off, but Riley hadn't needed the reminder.

She was wired to go.

Canceling the alarm, she stared out the window at the pink, iridescent fingers of dawn stretching up from the eastern skyline. Her packed suitcase and carry-on waited beside the front door, ready for Chris to haul out to the car when he came to take her to the airport. The thought set her heart thumping again and she gulped the tea, burning her tongue and the roof of her mouth.

Her phone jangled and she snatched it up.

Rick. She hit the green button.

"Hope I didn't wake you, Riley, but I figured you'd be up by now."

"I'm up," she confirmed. "Been up most of the night, to be honest."

Rick laughed. "Perfectly understandable. I hope it's as much excitement as nerves. This will be good for you, Riley. And I'm not just saying that as your recruiter."

Riley sucked in a long breath, let it fill the cramped corners of her lungs. "I know," she said, exhaling. "I'm sure you're right. I am excited. And nervous."

"Well, I'm here ahead of you, paving the way. I just got off the plane and someone from the academy is picking me up. I'll be here waiting when you arrive."

"Thanks, Rick. I can't tell you how much better I feel, knowing you're going to be there with me."

"I'm pretty happy about it, too. See you soon."

Riley moved her finger over the end call button, but before she tapped, Rick spoke again.

"Oh, Riley, one more thing. Give me a call as soon as you get to Germany."

"Okay."

"I want to see you first thing when you arrive at the academy. I'd like to be the one to show you around and introduce you to Stanley Edwards, the director."

Riley smiled. His dedicated enthusiasm was one of the things she loved about Rick.

"I promise," she told him. "I'll ask for you first thing."

"Great. Enjoy your flight, Riley. And get some rest."

Riley ended the call and went to the kitchen where she swallowed the last of her tea and rinsed the cup, finding herself grateful for good friends. Rick had been that for her since the day they'd met. And Nate, too.

Regardless of how that turned out.

Riley used the bathroom and brushed her teeth, smoothing on some of the peppermint lip balm she relied upon. Almost to the point of addiction.

She returned to the living room just as a swinging flash of headlights danced across the dim walls, signaling Chris's arrival in the driveway. Riley pulled on a light jacket, trying to quell the shaking of her hands, and grabbed her house key from its shelf near the door.

Time to go.

8

Liesl crossed the hardwood floor of her office, the sound of her pumps intermittently loud and then muffled by the Oriental style rug that stretched beneath her desk to the window beyond. At the door, she paused and smoothed her hair before gripping the knob and pulling it open. She stepped into the anteroom and greeted the man waiting in an upholstered chair.

He wore charcoal gray slacks and a polo shirt the color of a winter sea. His head was well-proportioned and shaved very smooth, as was his face. No facial hair beyond a rather bushy set of eyebrows. He sat with legs crossed, looking relaxed, confident, and professional.

An attractive man. His author bio and photograph had given her no reason to expect any different, and she found herself hoping he'd grant her request.

"Mr. Forst," she said, extending her hand, "thank you so much for coming."

She'd suggested they meet at a coffee shop in the village, but he'd insisted on making the trip up the mountain to the Sammelplatz.

"I welcome the opportunity to see this place," he said. "I'll admit, I've been curious. Writers are like that, you know," he said with a wry twinkle.

"Let's walk, then," Liesl said. "I'll show you around."

As she led him back to the impressive lobby, she said, "I was delighted to discover that we have a published author—a naturalist—for a neighbor. That must be fascinating work."

"I enjoy it. You know, I feel like there's something I should—"

"Oh, look!" Liesel said, pointing out the plate glass window. "There's a peregrine falcon."

They stood side by side, watching the falcon soar across the cloudless spring sky, Liesl feeling inordinately proud that she'd been able to offer such a sight. She pointed out the two basalt mountains, but he'd know all about those already. He'd be more interested in specifics relating to the convention center.

"The stone for the fireplace," she said, sweeping her arm to encompass the massive structure and feeling foolishly like a game show hostess, "was taken from a local quarry." She refrained from mentioning that the quarry had originated as part of a Nazi labor camp.

"And the wooden sled you see suspended there," she continued, "is reputed to have been the boyhood toy of Levi Strauss before he emigrated to America and started his famous blue jeans company."

"Very interesting indeed, Ms. Saunders."

Forst paused. "I hope you won't think me crude for asking," he said, "but can you take me into the bowels of the place? The parts guests don't normally see? That's what I would find most intriguing."

She hesitated. "The center doesn't have any secret passageways or priest's holes that I'm aware of."

He laughed. "I'm not asking for anything so fantastic as that. Just the ordinary inner workings."

"You mean, like the kitchens? The storage closets and maintenance rooms?"

"Ah, yes," he said. "That's exactly what I mean. I want to see the guts of the place, and in turn I'll be more than happy to accept your invitation."

"My invitation?"

"The reason you asked me here, Ms. Saunders. I suspect you were going to ask me to take your guests on a small walking tour. Much like we're doing now, except that I'd be showing them the area's flowers and explaining the birds and bees. So to speak."

Liesl felt a rush of blood to her face. "Well, yes. That is what I was going to ask you."

"Say no more then. Just let me know when you'd like me to appear."

"Thank you, Mr. Forst."

"Please, call me Anton. And may I call you Liesl?"

"Yes, of course."

"Excellent." He took a step closer. "Now might be a good time for me to let you know—"

"Oh, marvelous," she said, interrupting him at the familiar click of heels on marble. "Here's Margaret Vonnegut. She's the facilities manager for the center. Let's see if she'll go with us into the basement. She's far more knowledgeable about that part of the building than I am."

Half an hour later, after traipsing through the cramped and dusty lower levels of the convention center, they climbed back into the light of day and Liesl felt relief flood through her. She'd never suffered from claustrophobia, but the atmosphere below had felt oppressive to her, and somehow sinister.

She didn't understand how someone could be so absorbed by the minute details of plumbing and ventilation. But Anton Forst looked wholly satisfied as they stood together on the flagstone terrace, breathing the fresh air.

Liesl was about to excuse herself and get back to the office, when movement caught her eye and she turned to see Julia coming toward them. She cringed inwardly, taking in her sister's ratty denim jeans and heavy eye makeup, afraid it might dent the competent, professional image she wanted to project for the center.

Her slight dismay intensified as Julia came closer, and then closer. Completely invading Anton Forst's personal space.

She wrapped her arms around him and kissed him on the mouth.

Shock zapped through Liesl like an electric wave. She stared.

"I'm sorry, Liesl," Anton said, grinning at her over her sister's head. "I've been trying to tell you."

Julia turned. "Don't look so surprised, Sis. We've been seeing each other for weeks."

9

—·—

Taz drove the side streets of Nuremberg, avoiding the main thoroughfares where he occasionally caught sight of patrol cars out looking for him and the lethal canister he carried.

He kept his speed moderate, reining in the urge to press the gas pedal to the floormat. Pulling in deep, even breaths, he struggled to bring the frantic beating of his heart under control, to think clearly.

Steering around a corner, he came upon a row of white and orange barriers blocking his way, the asphalt beyond broken into chunks of rubble. A sign pointed out the *Umleitung*—detour. The route would take him back into the central stream of traffic.

He cursed, but didn't stop moving, not wanting to call attention to himself. He drove an older model Mercedes, pale yellow. Well able to blend in with the other cars on the road, easy to hotwire. As an added benefit, it had rolled off the assembly line well before the age of GPS tracking systems, making it difficult to trace by modern means. The titanium case was stowed under the passenger seat, out of sight but readily findable in even the most cursory search.

In his pocket, he carried a knife.

He merged the Mercedes into the flow of traffic, wiping beads of moisture from his forehead, smelling the sour tang of his sweat. The growls and squeals of engines and brakes seemed to him suddenly deafening. He rolled up the window, using the hand crank. Very old school.

Congestion thickened, traffic slowed. Something up ahead was creating a delay. Taz swallowed hard, sitting tall in his seat to peer over the tops of the cars in front of him, his view blocked by a work van several yards ahead. As he rolled forward, a break in the *Stau* allowed him to catch a glimpse of what was causing the stoppage.

A road block.

Manned by a crowd of *Polizei,* their cars parked at angles along the road, creating an automotive gauntlet. They were checking ID documents at each car going through.

An electric *zing* of fear whipped through him. He signaled, turning off at the next street, going wherever it took him, trying to think. He needed a new identity, and ironically he was headed directly to the man who could get it for him. But in order to get there, he needed a new ID. Catch 22.

Think.

There would be other road blocks, and no real way to predict when he might be expected to produce identification. There had to be a solution for him, at least something stopgap, something temporary yet effective. Where could he find a passport, a driving license good enough to get him past a road block and through every checkpoint on his way to the contact Cincher had arranged?

His hands on the steering wheel shook and he clamped them down hard, letting out of moan of frustration. Where was he? He cast his gaze about, looking for a street sign, and found one. It said *Flughafen.*

The airport.

Nuremberg had an international airport, much smaller than the one in Munich, but perhaps adequate for his needs. This time of day, there would be an influx of arrivals, people looking for taxis, searching for their rides. People coming from every part of the world and carrying their passports.

Taz followed the signs to the airport, turning into the lane for arrival pickup. He cruised slowly, reminded of his teenage years, trolling the main drag for pretty girls willing to take a chance with a stranger. Only now, he was looking for a familiar face—one as close to his own as he could find.

He pulled even with a likely candidate, dark haired and olive skinned. Shorter than he was, but Taz didn't think he could afford to be overly picky. He braked and leaned over, cranking down the passenger window. The man looked his way but before Taz could make his pitch, a woman ran forward, folding her arms around him and leading him away.

Taz nudged the car forward, eyes roving over the moving crowd, seeking, praying. A dozen meters ahead, he saw another possible and pulled closer to the curb. The man turned, saw he was being scrutinized. He raised his hand in a tentative wave and approached Taz's open window.

"You my ride to the conference center?" he asked.

Taz nodded, gesturing for the man to get into the car. His look-alike sported a cleaner shave than Taz himself liked to wear, but scored fairly well on many points of comparison. The man opened the rear door and slung a large duffle bag onto the back seat before sliding in next to Taz and proffering a hand.

"Mike Martinez," he said. "Thanks for the ride."

"No problem," Taz said, checking his mirror and pulling into the line of cars heading away from the airport.

He felt the hard, metallic lump of the knife in his pocket. Now all he had to do was keep his eye open for a lonely stretch of road.

10

— · —

Rick slouched in the passenger seat of the old Mercedes Benz, massaging the back of his neck. It had been a long flight, but he was used to the trans-Atlantic journey and was usually able to catch a few winks.

This time, he had not.

The fussing baby in the seat behind him had accounted for part of the reason, but the anxiety which rumbled through him on a low-level hum, keeping him on edge, bore the real brunt for the restless flight.

He was worried about Riley. About Cincher's possible interest in her. About a shadowy, powerful figure in a position to do a lot of harm.

To those he cared for, and the world at large.

There was a lot to worry about. And now, as his driver navigated the roundabout at the airport exit and headed toward the outskirts of the city, Rick registered a new blip on his radar. Something else that was bothering him.

The driver hadn't responded with the appropriate phrase.

Under Chief Wright's instructions, Rick had switched to his cover persona once he'd cleared customs. He was not on covert assignment, but as part of the training environment of the academy, all students and personnel operated under alternate IDs, posing as conference attendees while outside the boundaries of the school.

His alias was Michael Martinez.

At least he'd remembered that much, but he should have waited for the driver to respond by assuring him the conference was running on time.

Riley, too, had received an alternate identity and he hoped she'd observe her instructions better than he had. Rick gave himself a mental slap. He could blame it on exhaustion, but he couldn't excuse it. It had been a reckless lapse. The type that could lead to disaster.

Why hadn't the driver given the pass phrase? Like Rick, was he excessively tired? Had he grown cavalier about the regulations, willing to snub procedure when he felt like it?

Or was there a more dire reason?

Rick watched the fields and industrial buildings pass by, feigning interest in the landscape but using the opportunity to study the man at the wheel in short, targeted glances. His complexion was dusky, his dark hair thick, eyes hooded. A well-trimmed beard and mustache disguised the lower contours of his face and his ears were small, tucked tightly against the sides of his head.

Every item of clothing he wore was black and nondescript. No brand labels apparent, no distinguishing attributes. Not that different from what Rick himself was wearing.

They approached a traffic light where a left turn would take them into the city. The driver turned right.

"Got an errand to run?" Rick asked. "You're going the wrong way."

"No errands," the man said. "There was a traffic accident, a three kilometer *Stau*. I know another way."

Could the man be legit? They were heading in the general direction of the academy, but the road was rural and passed through tiny villages along the way, slowing them down. Weighed against the clog of an accident and the resulting traffic jam, it might make sense.

The driver slowed, veering to the right, taking them down an even narrower, more isolated road. A prickle of apprehension danced along the back of Rick's scalp. He no longer doubted his suspicions. His moment of carelessness had put him in a bad position, getting worse by the moment.

He considered his options. He carried no weapon, other than the training in his head and hands. If the man believed Rick had swallowed his story whole, he might be able to count on the element of surprise.

But Rick sensed from the way the driver gripped the wheel and the short, nervous darts of his tongue along his upper lip, that the man was poised for action and had maneuvered the Mercedes into a remote spot to carry it out.

Once, in a training exercise, Rick had jumped out of a moving car. His clothes had been shredded to ribbons and he'd collected a dozen bumps and bruises and a wicked case of road rash, but all in all, it hadn't been too bad. He remembered the admonitions of his trainer—look for a good landing spot, leap at an angle perpendicular to the car's movement, tuck and roll.

He rehearsed it in his head, watching the surroundings for a soft spot, thinking he saw one coming up. He reminded himself to open the car door as wide as possible before jumping, and he grabbed the handle, jacking it upward, hard and fast.

The door flew open.

Before Rick could so much as bunch his muscles for the launch, the driver had him by the arm, yanking him hard away from the door. Rick fought back, trying to free himself, no longer concerned with finding a soft landing pad. He just wanted to get out of the car.

It felt like a death trap.

The man no longer held the wheel. Both his hands latched onto Rick, one gouging into his left forearm, the other gripping his hair, tearing it from the roots. They wrestled.

The car shot off the road and down an embankment, bucking and bouncing, shaking Rick and his deceitful companion like the last two Milk Duds in a little yellow box. It hurtled down the slope and rammed into a boulder, putting an instant stop to their descent.

Rick saw the end coming and raised his arms to shield his head, using the driver's hand in his hair to further cushion the coming blow. The last thing he heard was the snap of bone as they both hit the dashboard.

And nothing more.

11

RILEY TRIED TO SUPPRESS a yawn but it persisted and she gave in, letting her mouth go wide and her eyes crinkle shut. Stretching her legs, she pressed back against the head rest, enjoying the gentle flow of warm air from the heater vent.

At the wheel of the car, Christopher Neville yawned too, proving the contagion theory. He accompanied the yawn with a protracted growl that spanned the scale, sounding like a vocal exercise. Riley thought it probably was one.

"Did you get any sleep at all?" he asked her.

"A smidgen. A skosh. A wee tiny bit," Riley said.

"I think what you're trying to say is none at all."

Riley smiled. "Pretty much."

"Grab a good long nap while you're crossing the Atlantic," Chris advised.

"That's the plan," Riley said, though she doubted it would happen. She'd never been able to let go and sleep soundly surrounded by strangers.

The Sea-Tac airport thrived on early mornings, its busiest time of day. Even at 6 am, the traffic on I-5 flowed in a thick continuous

54

stream, but Chris was an expert driver, unruffled and ruthless. He delivered her to the departure lane with time to spare.

Inside the big glass doors, Riley squinted against the harsh lights high overhead, a bright contrast to the dim gray of the Seattle morning. She stood in line at the Delta counter, listening to the muted conversations of her fellow travelers, and checked one large suitcase stuffed with ordinary items.

She figured she'd have some shopping to do once she arrived in Germany. Unschooled as she was in undercover work, she suspected the role required more dark-colored clothing and gum-soled shoes. Maybe a balaclava or two.

She endured the stress and tedium of the security checkpoint and found her gate, spotting an empty chair. Taking a step toward it, she was nearly run down by a flurry of airline personnel—pilot and co-pilot followed by a gaggle of flight attendants, heels clacking on tile as they zoomed by, creating a slipstream strong enough to dislodge the boarding pass from Riley's fingers.

It fluttered to the floor and she bent to retrieve it, but was beaten to the task by an elderly gentleman wearing a dark blue suit and paisley tie. She stared at the graying strands of hair pasted across his pale scalp, feeling grateful but a bit embarrassed. He scrabbled for the paper, scissoring it between his fingers, and straightened with a grimace, one hand pressed to his back.

"Here you go, Miss," he said, passing her the slip of paper with a shaky hand. "You don't want to go losing that."

"No," she agreed, smiling. "Thank you."

"My pleasure."

He gave her a genteel nod, his blue eyes magnified slightly by the thick lenses of his wire-rimmed glasses, and shuffled back to his seat. The chair Riley had been heading for was now taken. She went in search of another and had barely settled into it when boarding calls began.

Once on the plane, with her carry-on securely stowed in the overhead compartment, Riley let herself relax a bit. She was on her way. At this point, most everything was out of her hands. The plane would take off, the plane would land. The flight attendants would serve drinks and, since it was a nine-hour trip, presumably a meal.

She didn't have a lot of control over what happened for the next stretch of time, nor would she have to make any earth-shaking decisions. There was something freeing in accepting that.

And also something vaguely disturbing.

Flying meant relinquishing control, placing your life in the hands of strangers more than thirty thousand feet above the ground. Nowhere to run to, nowhere to hide if things went bad.

Utterly terrifying, if you let yourself think about it too long.

So she didn't.

She thought about Rick instead. She'd been elated to find that he would be at the academy when she arrived. Having him there during her training would be a huge boon and a big boost to her confidence level. Just knowing she had a friend on hand would go a long way to helping her succeed.

Reaching into her bag, she pulled out a Lee Child paperback and settled into her seat, letting herself escape into someone else's problems.

12

—•—

THE MAN CALLED CINCHER closed his eyes, shutting out the clamor around him, listening to the calming voice in his head, letting it mesmerize him.

Breathe in...breathe out.

Feel the power in you. Feel the power in your mind. Feel the power in your body.

You are bigger than your mind. You are bigger than your body.

You encompass the world.

He let the exhale carry him deeper, back through years, through decades. To his days in the modest house outside Tacoma.

In those days, he wandered the woods alone, digging worms for bait and fishing in the cool, delicate air of morning, reeling in tiny wriggling fish, not worth keeping. He let them flop and twitch in the dirt before pulling them off the hook and throwing them back into the water, watching the splash and ripple.

Spreading, reaching out.

Disappearing.

From a *Boy's Life* magazine, he'd learned to make a slingshot. A flipper, they called it. He found a forked branch, peeled the bark off it and whittled the rough edges until it was smooth. With a pock-

57

etknife—the first one he ever owned—he carved notches, one high on each prong.

He used latex surgical tubing to create the sling, threading it through a scrap of leather for the pouch and securing it to the notches.

It was a thing of beauty.

He tested his flipper with rocks of varying size, shape, and texture until he'd dialed in his technique, setting up rows of empty soda cans and shooting them down, listening to the *ping* as the rocks made contact.

When a black crow flew down to peck among the fallen cans, he'd picked up a rock to shoo it away and stopped with his arm raised, a new idea entering his brain. Fitting the stone into the pouch, he'd aimed and let fly, killing the bird with one shot.

A stab of remorse hit him at once. He hadn't wanted to approach the dead creature, but morbid curiosity won out in the end. Creeping close, he'd poked the blood-spattered feathers with a stick, captivated by the crushed skull, the sightless, staring eye.

He'd had nightmares that night and tried for several days to drive the thought of the dead bird from his mind. The flipper lay abandoned at the back of a dresser drawer. Guilt, revulsion, and a crawling sort of dread haunted him.

But he was also taken by an odd exhilaration, which he tried to tamp down and push away. As the days passed, the remorse took up less space in his mind and curiosity, mixed with a strange sense of excitement, took its place.

He didn't want to kill another bird. A different idea had taken root in his mind, growing there like a thorny vine until he could no longer ignore it.

He rode his bike half a mile to Timmy Norton's house. Timmy wasn't his friend. A grade ahead, Timmy hung with an older crowd, and was not a very nice boy.

"What do you want?" Timmy had asked him.

"Bet you can't kill a bird with my slingshot."

"Bet you I can."

In the field next door, he watched the older boy launch rock after rock, finally shooting down a sparrow. He felt no remorse this time, only an elation, a sizzle in his blood as he watched Timmy stamp on the dead bird, breaking its neck.

Timmy handed back the slingshot, a scornful smirk on his face. But he had another question for Timmy.

"How about a cat?"

They'd graduated to dogs by May of that year, 1980. When Mount St. Helens erupted, he'd watched the ashfall cover his neighborhood, frightened yet fascinated. He took in every bit of news coverage his parents would allow. The massive, unbridled power of the volcano held him in thrall and set something blooming inside him.

He watched hordes of people moving en masse, in terror, helpless in the face of disaster and ordered about by government officials. He felt a thrill, a hunger for that magnitude of power.

He'd been nine years old.

He'd covered a lot of ground since then. Reflecting on his associates at play across the globe, wielding more sophisticated versions of his childhood slingshot, Cincher felt a surge of satisfaction. He had people working for him, doing his bidding, on six of the seven continents.

He did, indeed, encompass the world.

What's more, his potential for growth inspired and amazed him. He was exploring new vistas, discovering some of the best-kept secrets of the ages. That was part of his reason for establishing a base camp in Bavaria and moving certain branches of his operation to the region.

The other part had to do with Riley Forte.

In his mind, Riley was a loose and fascinating thread. He'd failed to kill her when he had the chance and at the time, he'd been enraged.

Now, he was intrigued.

She'd seen him, been able to identify him to the authorities, made him a fugitive. She'd caused him a great deal of trouble, but she'd opened up a new set of rewarding opportunities as well.

And, thanks to her, he was now a much better-looking man. His teeth, once slightly bucked and mildly yellow were now straight and pleasingly white. His hair implants had taken root nicely and he'd had a modest medical procedure done on his nose. He was astonished at the difference it made to his appearance.

She hadn't even recognized him.

Of course, he was traveling in disguise. A talent he'd cultivated over the years and become remarkably adept at practicing. Many people didn't realize the art went a lot deeper than wigs and makeup. You had to *become* your alter ego.

When he'd bent down to retrieve Riley's boarding pass, he'd actually felt his spine crack. It ached. He moved in a shuffle because the ravages of age had racked him, seizing his muscles and compressing his bones. Even now, he was uncomfortable in the seat, shifting, trying to find the best sort of relief an old man could hope for on the long flight ahead.

The real challenge was in being able to instantly shed a disguise if the situation called for it. He could do that too.

A flight attendant captured his attention, an older woman with marvelous bone structure and deplorable skin. She asked his drink preference and he accepted a cup of coffee with a tiny napkin and an even smaller packet of cookies.

As he munched, he stared at the seat in front of him. Or rather, at the woman occupying it. Riley had appeared quite tired to him. He hoped she was able to get some rest during the transit. In fact, she might be sleeping now.

As the auburn-haired head turned toward the window and Riley slumped in her seat, a thick curl fell against the wall of the plane, sliding silkily down within his reach. He felt like a schoolboy, tempted to yank the pigtail of the girl sitting at the desk in front of him.

But he had a better idea.

Rummaging in his carry-on bag, stashed beneath Riley's very seat, Cincher removed the sewing kit he always kept on hand. It had saved him in many an emergency and included a lot of extras not found in a standard-issue kit. The tiny pair of folding scissors was small enough to pass muster through security.

But big enough to do the job he had in mind.

Cincher glanced around. The flight had not been fully booked and many of the seats were empty, including the one next to him. The man in the aisle seat sat with eyes closed, a pair of noise-canceling headphones fastened over his ears. A couple across the aisle were looking out the window, apparently absorbed in the scenery. No one paid him any attention.

Quickly and carefully, Cincher made the cut, securing for himself a lock of Riley's hair. He curled it around his finger and pushed it down inside a tiny ziplock bag, another of the useful items in his souped-up sewing kit.

He shoved the carry-on back under the seat and cradled his head on a dainty airline pillow, cramming it against the window and fidgeting around until he found a position that would allow him to drift off.

It tickled him to be this close to Riley, close enough to touch, and she hadn't a clue. No notion at all that he was there. It pleased and amused him to be sleeping with her, in a manner of speaking. She was near enough to be his bed partner.

He closed his eyes.

Breathe in...breathe out.

Feel the power in you. Feel the power in your mind. Feel the power in your body.

You are bigger than your mind. You are bigger than your body.

You encompass the world.

13

THE PATH TO THE riding stable followed a slight decline, leading to a shallow dip below the Sammelplatz. Liesl surveyed the surroundings, making notes as she walked. In her quest to ensure that everything would be perfect for the summit, she made a regular tour of the entire property covering the twenty-acre spread at the top of the mountain.

The bright shimmering morning had clouded over into afternoon and a hazy blanket lay over the sky, blunting the direct rays of sunlight into something softer. She met the sharp, unmistakeable smell of horses as she passed through the gate and moved along the fringe of pines that bowered the stable.

It was a small well-built structure of wood, stone and plaster, with room for a dozen horses though it currently housed only half that number. The horses were expensive to keep, but popular with many of the guests, so for now, horseback riding continued to be part of the Sammelplatz experience. Liesl liked being able to offer the option.

The outer wall of the building featured a painted mural of a Leder-hosen-clad man on horseback, as was the custom in Bavaria. Over the years, some of the paint and plaster had chipped away, but that only made the place appear more picturesque. It was a favorite spot for taking photos.

Inside, Liesl spoke to the two grooms and riding instructor, getting assurances that all was well and ready to accommodate the summit guests when they arrived. Liesl walked the stalls, patting the velvet noses of the inquisitive horses, greeting them by name. The earthy odors of straw and horse manure hung in the air, present but not overpowering. Just right for enhancing the charm of the experience.

Satisfied, she left the stable and continued her inspection, turning toward the trout pond. As she walked, she wrestled with her mixed feelings about Julia. Her sister had brought down a lot of pain and trouble upon the family in the past, but Liesl loved her with a stubborn fierceness.

She'd been so pleased to secure this position here at the Sammelplatz, and so relieved that she could offer Julia a haven to come to after leaving the rehab clinic. She believed the fresh air, healthy environment, and the support of family were just what Julia needed to stay on the path of recovery. Though Julia could be irritating and quarrelsome, Liesl thought things had been going well.

Now, she was not so sure.

Why had Julia kept her relationship with Anton Forst a secret? Clearly, she'd been meeting him without the family's knowledge. Was he supplying her with drugs? Could Julia be using again?

The thought wrenched at Liesl. Certainly, Julia had been secretive in the past. In fact, there was a period of years after she'd left home that Liesl knew nothing about and Julia refused to enlighten her, leaving the abyss open to Liesl's worst imaginings.

When Julia returned, she'd seemed so different from the big sister Liesl remembered. Almost like a stranger. But the memories of their time together, the bonds they'd forged as young girls, sustained and fed Liesl's devotion and she was so grateful to welcome Julia back into the arms of the family.

She had a lot of unanswered questions, but her sister was vulnerable. Liesl knew that much. Was Forst taking advantage of her?

Reaching the trout pond with its little wooden fishing hut, Liesl checked that all was in order. There would be free time during the summit for guests to socialize and enjoy a variety of recreational opportunities. Including fishing, though Liesl had never understood the sport's appeal.

As she started back toward the main buildings, Liesl struggled with another disturbing thought. She worried that her misgivings about Forst might be partly due to jealousy. As much as she hated to admit it, she had been attracted to Anton Forst from the moment she'd read his author bio and seen his photograph.

She'd initially enjoyed her time with him, though she'd lost some of that enthusiasm once they'd entered the bowels of the building, as he'd referred to them. She remembered the slightly sinister ambience of the place, though surely the setting can't have produced it. It was merely the basement of a large facility, without personality.

Had her uneasy feelings come from Anton himself?

Thinking back to the moment her sister had arrived on the scene and made the bombshell announcement that they'd been seeing each other for weeks, Liesl remembered the chill that had run through her at the look in Anton's eyes. It had seemed somehow...predatory.

Imagination only, or a trick of the sunlight. It was crazy to think that the author of the bee books might mean harm to her family. Yet, Liesl couldn't shake her suspicions.

Arriving back at her office, she went to her desk and pulled off her shoes, digging her toes into the pile of the Oriental rug. She swiveled back and forth in her chair, grappling with her conscience, then she lifted the handset of her desk phone. Her assistant answered.

"Joseph," she said, "please get me Dieter Voigt on the line."

14

—·—

RILEY'S CHIN HIT HER chest and she jerked awake, heart racing.

It was only turbulence, a bit of atmospheric disturbance, but she felt disoriented and disturbed. She couldn't remember dreaming—was surprised that she'd slept at all—but she felt a vague sense of disquiet and knew her unconscious thoughts had been less than pleasant.

The plane continued to buck gently and Riley heard a *ding* as the seatbelt light came on and the pilot made an announcement requesting passengers to remain fastened in their seats. She realized she needed the restroom and now that she couldn't use it, the need became urgent.

She suppressed it, tried to think about something else. She was anxious about the academy, there was no denying it. But she was also looking forward to the challenge, the new experiences. She welcomed the chance to acquire a new sense of purpose in her life and a new set of friends.

At last, the seatbelt light winked out and Riley's seatmate rose, heading for the restroom. He was a good-looking blond man, at least a decade younger than her, dressed in jeans and an unbuttoned button-down over a T-shirt. Riley was glad she hadn't had to bother him and squeeze past his legs. On the other hand, now he was ahead of her in the line and she really had to go.

She stood, knees slightly bent to absorb the occasional bumps that continued to brush the plane, and was relieved to hear the sudden rushing sound of an airline flush. As the door opened, her seatmate gallantly waved her ahead and she shut herself into the tiny cubicle, grateful that chivalry was not dead.

Returning to her seat, Riley noticed that the passenger directly behind her was the polite elderly gentleman who'd picked up her fallen boarding pass. He appeared to be sleeping, his hands crossed over his little paunch of a stomach, rising and falling with even regularity.

Had he been awake, Riley would never have examined him so closely, but she wasn't ready to sit down again. She stood, stretching and applying a layer of lip balm, watching the old man sleep. Like most people of a certain age, he had liver spots on his hands and one in particular caught her attention. It was shaped like an almost perfect fermata—a curved arch with a dot beneath it—the musical symbol giving control of a note's duration to the musician.

Giving him license to hold it as long as he felt like it.

She pushed her bag back under the seat in front of her and sat, buckling her lap belt. She realized she should have noticed the man before, when she got on the plane. In fact, she should be noticing everyone around her. That's one skill she'd been told to work on—observation. She should pay more attention to everything around her, all the time. Both Rick and Nate had given her examples of how their situational awareness had saved them in circumstances past.

Riley focused her attention on the couple across the aisle, noting the elongated shape of his ears and how attentive he seemed to the woman next to him. Riley made mental notes about what they were wearing, about how the woman's hairline formed an unusual frame around her face, about the large gold ring on the man's right pinky finger.

She didn't believe they were in any way criminal or dangerous, but for a moment she pretended they were. She played through half a dozen scenarios in her head, casting the couple with nefarious intent. How would she react? What could she do? How could she prepare?

These were the kinds of things she hoped to learn about at the academy, among other sorts of skills. Her seatmate returned, giving her a smile. Their mutual trip to the bathroom had raised the level of their social awareness. He buckled in and turned his head, meeting her gaze.

"Is this your first trip to Europe?" he asked.

Riley hadn't counted the number of times she'd been to the continent, but knew she'd need all her fingers and toes. "No, I've been before," she said. "Your first time?"

"Yes, and I'm not going to lie—I'm pretty thrilled about it."

"Great, I wish you a happy trip."

"Thanks, and you as well."

He seemed reluctant to let the conversation drop. "Where are you going?" he asked, then flushed. "I mean, if I'm not being too nosy."

She laughed, but she hadn't thought about how to answer. She would have to go through a similar grill at passport control, so why not make this a practice run?

"I'm a musician. I'm attending a conference in Germany."

"Ah, right. The birthplace of Beethoven, Mozart—so many of the greats."

Riley didn't mention that both Beethoven and Mozart had been born in Austria. She understood his point. "*Genau*," she said.

He looked blank and she explained, "In German, that's how you agree with someone. *Genau* means exactly right."

"Oh, thanks. *Genau.*" He let a moment pass, then, "How long will you be in Germany?"

Riley felt a little niggle at the back of her mind. Was he probing for information or just making conversation? Did he find her attractive or did he have an ulterior motive for wanting to know more about her plans?

"I'm not sure yet," she told him. "I'm playing it by ear."

"Oh good pun," he said. "Music humor."

She nodded and reached for her paperback novel, opening it and hoping he'd take the hint. He did, letting her read in peace. But she found her attention wandering from the page as she played back over their exchange. How sad that she should be suspicious about something so human and innocent.

It was all part of the price she was paying. She hoped it would be worth the cost.

15

Taz Salih woke in agony, draped across the buckled dashboard of the old Mercedes.

The pain in his broken hand seemed to shriek with a voice of its own and his head ached with a deep thudding torment. Blood filled his mouth and he spat it out, disgusted by the tinny taste it left behind.

He tried to move but that was a mistake. He felt shattered in so many places and fear flooded over him, sharp and terrible.

He needed help.

Taz moved his head slowly, carefully, to look at the man he'd picked up from the airport, the one who had caused this disaster. He sprawled halfway out the open door, unmoving, bathed in the deep maroon of darkening blood. But Taz thought he saw the stranger's chest rise and fall, indicating he was still alive.

A situation he intended to remedy.

The late afternoon sun hung heavy and low in the sky, cloaking the scene in shadow. Taz squinted into the gloom, saw that the car had lodged against a boulder at the bottom of a ravine. He imagined it would be invisible from the road.

It seemed hard to breathe. Air. He needed more air.

The crank for the window was missing, broken off in the strife of the crash. Taz fumbled with a metal pull-up handle, managed to crack the door open. He pushed it wider with his foot and let the air wash over him, bringing a fleeting bit of relief.

Shifting in his seat, he strained to dig the mobile burner from the pocket of his pants, screaming with the pain of it. At last he held the phone in his hand, but now a shifting fog covered his brain, scrambling his thoughts. He stared at the phone stupidly, trying to remember why he wanted it.

He pulled in a shaky breath and struggled to grasp and order the half-formed ideas in his head. A number came to him, hazy at first then firming into something real. He tapped the number on his phone.

A man answered. "Forst."

Taz wheezed, tried to speak, but produced only a feeble croak. He cleared his throat and tried again. "Cincher said you were expecting me."

"Are you the one with the key?"

"Yes, I have it."

"And the chemical? Did you get it?"

Taz hesitated, decided to explain later why he only had one of the canisters.

"Yes, it's here. But there's been an accident. I need you to pick me up."

Silence stretched for so long that Taz feared the man would refuse. Finally, he said, "Where are you?"

Taz described his location as clearly as he could.

"I think I know the stretch of road you're talking about. I'm on my way."

"Good, and one more thing. Bring a doctor."

Taz heard a beep and the call ended. He wasn't sure Forst had heard his final request. Letting out a long anguished groan, he cradled his injured hand in his lap. He was alone now, with only a man on death's doorstep for a companion.

Gritting his teeth, ignoring the pain, he reached for the stranger.

16

Liesl paced her office, shoes off, dictating notes into her phone. She liked the contrasting feels of the hardwood and the softer carpet as she alternately crossed over them. Outside the open window, the buzz of a gas-powered lawn trimmer floated on the cooling breeze of a late afternoon, scenting her office with the smell of fresh cut grass.

She'd instructed the grounds crew to make sure every detail of the landscape was in order for the summit and she had every sign they were meeting her expectations. Every day, deliveries of supplies arrived and the pieces of her planning puzzle were falling into place. Liesl dared to hope the event would be a grand success.

Her desk phone rang and she picked up the line.

"I have Dieter Voigt on the line," Joseph said. "He's waiting to speak with you."

"Thank you, Joseph."

Voigt was a private investigator Liesl sometimes used to vet visitors to the facility or for background information about prospective employees or suppliers. She liked the man and trusted his competency.

"Dieter, thanks for returning my call. I want you to do some digging into a man named Anton Forst. He's a naturalist, writes books about wildflowers and the insects that love them."

"Hmm. That name rings a bell but I can't think why."

Liesl paused, hesitant about mentioning drugs, but her anxiety over Julia prevailed. "I want to know if he has anything to do with illicit substances. Dealing or importing. That sort of thing."

"Hang tight," Dieter told her. "I'll run a check and get back to you."

Liesl hung up the phone and sat to put her shoes on. It was time to call it a day. She looked forward to Max's darling face as he greeted her, and her parents' solicitous interest in her day's activities. And she wanted to see Julia and get a feel for how her sister was doing.

She closed out her computer files and straightened her desk. Just before she turned to go, she noticed the philodendron on the credenza looking parched, its leaves curling in the setting sun. Filling a cup from the bathroom tap, she carried it back to the office, arriving just as the phone on her desk began to ring.

"Liesl, it's Dieter."

"That was quick."

"Yes, I work fast. My preliminary screening didn't turn up anything related to drugs, but..."

"But what?"

"This may not mean anything, and I'd have to do some more checking, but Forst's name did come up in connection with a hench-man from a high-profile terrorist group."

Shock hit Liesl in the pit of her stomach. She sank into the desk chair. "Terrorist?"

"Yes, well, the association is tenuous. I can dig deeper but it might get dicey. Do you want me to continue?"

Liesl swallowed hard. "Yes, definitely. It's personal this time, Dieter. The man is dating my sister."

The investigator's voice took on a note of concern. "I'm sorry to hear that, Liesl. I'll do what I can but it may take me some time."

"Right. I understand. Thank you, Dieter."

Liesl dropped the phone, letting it clatter into its cradle. The satisfaction she'd felt over her preparations for the summit dissolved, leaving a sickly taste in her mouth. Her skin crawled with the thought that she might have let a viper into the midst of her family.

Though, truth be told, he'd already found his way inside before she even knew the man's name. She couldn't bring this up to Julia without some kind of evidence. Julia would scorn anything less than concrete.

Dieter had said it would take him time, but Liesl didn't have a lot of time. Guests for the summit would be arriving in less than a week. She needed this dealt with before they checked in and became her responsibility.

She thought about the amenities available to her at the Sammelplatz—tennis courts, riding stables, the indoor pool. Rising from the desk, Liesl grabbed her handbag and headed for the apartment. She needed to talk to Julia, swap some sisterly chit chat and make a suggestion.

She thought Julia should invite Anton over for a swim.

17

RILEY STOOD ON THE curb, flanked by her suitcase and carry-on. The crisp morning breeze swirled through a tiny pile of leaves and litter, sending pieces of it skittering across the pavement in front of her. A young man in a knit beanie boogied past, blasting music from a handheld device. As he stopped near her, the driving beat was blotted out by the roar of an airliner taking off.

An elderly couple vacated the bench behind her, but Riley was too nervous to sit. Her flight had touched down just after ten o'clock the night before and after clearing customs, Riley had walked across to the airport hotel and checked in under the name Janice Fairmont.

She was now officially undercover.

A seasoned traveler, this was the first time she'd used a false name and faked documents and she was experiencing a mixed cocktail of feelings. It was part fulfillment of a fantasy, fun and exciting. But she found that aspect being eclipsed by guilt, misgivings, and a touch of fear.

She comforted herself by remembering that once she'd mastered the technique, she wouldn't need to resort to it again. The whole point of recruiting her had been to use her true identity as a touring concert pianist to get her into certain circles and locations.

This was just a necessary part of her training.

She'd been told not to rent a car, that most of her time would be spent at the academy and for the few instances when she needed to leave, a motor pool was available. Rick had said he'd send a driver to pick her up from the airport. She checked the time on her phone. Her ride was late.

She'd tried phoning Rick last night after landing, but the call went straight to voicemail. Same again earlier this morning. She was about to try a third time when a car pulled to the curb and a petite Asian woman wearing a dark green business suit climbed out from behind the wheel.

"Ms. Fairmont?" she asked, offering her hand.

A flicker of panic washed over Riley as she tried to remember the pass phrases.

"Yes, I'm Janice Fairmont," she began, shaking the woman's hand. "Is the conference proceeding as scheduled?"

The woman smiled. "Call me Miko. Yes, the conference is running right on time."

Together, they loaded the luggage in the trunk and Riley got into the car, energized by a sudden burst of confidence. She felt an instant ease and liking for this Miko. The next chapter of her life was beginning and her doubts dissipated under the influence of excitement.

As they left the airport behind, Miko made small talk, asking about her flight and her stay at the hotel. Riley wanted to ask about things at the academy but didn't know how much she was allowed to discuss. So instead, she talked about Nuremberg.

"I'm a concert pianist," she told Miko. "Years ago, during a tour, I went to the Nuremberg Christmas market. Spectacular. I still have the pyramid windmill I bought from there. But somehow, the thing I remember most is that awful rabbit."

"Rabbit? Oh, you must mean the Dürer Hare. Yes, it is rather horrifying, isn't it?

Riley shuddered, remembering how she'd felt, standing there in front of the giant yellow-eyed sculpture. At first, it had simply looked like a massive dead hare, but on closer inspection, she'd perceived the smaller demonic-looking rabbits seeming to crawl out from around it, like maggots on a carcass. She'd almost missed the lifeless human hand extending from beneath it all, a silent unheeded plea for help.

"What about the Nazi Rally Grounds?" Miko asked. "Have you been there?"

"No. I've been fortunate to travel and I've been to a great many cities, but I'm usually so booked with rehearsals and appearances and performances that I've missed a lot of what there is to see." She looked out the window at the passing shops and houses, the people on bicycles and walking on the streets. "I regret that."

"Well," Miko said, giving her a wink, "you may yet get a chance to visit the Rally Grounds." She sobered. "But I warn you—it's a chilling experience. You'll be standing on the very spot where Hitler finally succeeded in winning the people over to his cause."

"I've been to Dachau, Auschwitz, and Birkenau," Riley said. "I've felt the ghosts of monsters."

"Then you have an idea what I mean."

"Yes."

Miko merged onto the *Autobahn* and accelerated, passing a series of semi trucks before returning to the right lane. Three speeding cars in succession whizzed by on the inside lane, disappearing rapidly into the distance ahead. Riley had forgotten how fast traffic can move in Germany.

She noticed several signs pointing to *Praha*, the Czech name for Prague, and realized how close she was to one of her favorite cities.

"You're very far east here, aren't you?" she asked Miko.

"Oh yes, the academy is only ten or fifteen miles from the Czech border, as the crow flies. Perhaps you'll get a chance to visit."

"I'd like that."

Twenty minutes passed, mostly in comfortable silence as Riley stared out the window. They left the *Autobahn* for a narrower highway and then an even narrower winding country road. On the horizon, Riley saw a strange-looking hill popping up from the mostly flat landscape.

"What's that?" she asked.

"That's Parkstein," Miko said. "A small basalt mountain formed from a volcanic fissure."

"It's a volcano?"

"Don't worry. It hasn't been active for thousands of years. There are a number of those volcanic mountains in the area. The *conference center*," she said, raising an eyebrow, "is situated at the foot of one of them."

A chill slithered down Riley's spine. She couldn't believe she'd left the shadow of Mt. Rainier and traveled across a continent and an ocean just to settle beneath another volcano. She'd barely survived the last one.

"They're pretty awesome to see up close," Miko continued. "The molten lava cooled into these fascinating hexagonal tubular formations. Like the Giant's Causeway in Ireland. Have you been there?"

"It's on my bucket list," Riley said.

Miko slowed the car and pointed.

"Okay, we're just about there. This is the turnoff."

Riley watched with interest as they passed through a small storybook village, probably not looking drastically different than it had a hundred years ago. Pots of geraniums hung from carved wooden balcony rails, spilling pink and red blossoms. She caught glimpses of inner courtyards paved with cobblestone and bordered by weathered wood and stone houses and barns. Altogether charming.

"There's a *Milchtankstelle,*" Miko said, pointing to an open-sided shed with what appeared to be a vending machine inside.

"What is it?" Riley asked.

"It's kind of fun. You can buy a bottle there or bring your own and you put it under the tap and get fresh milk. Organic, unpasteurized."

"Wow, seriously?"

"Cross my heart. This one also has local honey and homemade chocolates you can get from the vending machine. You'll have to try it out sometime, but not now. I'm sure you're anxious to settle in."

Miko turned into a gateway and entered a code on a keypad. The sturdy metal gate rumbled open and they drove through.

"All this is part of the academy training grounds," Miko said. "And I can call it that, now that we're inside the gate. I'm Matsui Haruko, by the way. My real name. And yours?"

"Riley Forte."

Matsui gave her a look from under wrinkled brows. "No, really," she said.

"Really. That is my name."

"A concert pianist named Forte."

"Just one of the many ways I knew we were supposed to be together when I met my husband. James Forte."

"Okay," Matsui shrugged. "Over there, you can see the ropes course and PT yard, and beyond it, the shooting range. You'll be getting real familiar with all of that. In fact, you'll get to know every inch of this place before your training's over. We use it all."

"What do *you* do here?" Riley asked.

"Me?" Matsui grinned. "I'm the explosives instructor."

She pulled the car into a large garage filled with battered vehicles. "The motor pool. You'll use these in your driving course."

Matsui popped the trunk and hauled out Riley's suitcase, which must have weighed almost as much as she did, but she made it look effortless. Riley wheeled her carry-on, following her new friend, and stepped through the front door of the academy.

She realized she'd been expecting something like a vacation resort, but that illusion was instantly wiped away. The place was unapologetically utilitarian. Not ugly, but clearly designed for functionality rather than aesthetic appeal. It was more like a college dorm with leanings toward a military barracks vibe.

A scarred wooden counter stretched the length of the reception hall, and behind it a bank of gray metal filing cabinets lined the cream-painted wall. A gaunt, solemn-faced man stood beside the counter, awaiting their arrival. He held out a large manila envelope to Riley.

"Your welcome packet," Matsui explained. "There's information about the academy, a map of the property, your training agenda and a schedule for mealtimes, assemblies and such." Glancing at her watch, she said, "I'll see you later, Riley. I'm teaching a class in five minutes, so I've got to run. This is Luther. He can show you to your room and help you get settled in."

Matsui hurried to a pair of elevator doors and jabbed the UP button. The door on the right opened immediately and she rushed in, waving goodbye.

"But wait!" Riley called after her. "I'm supposed to call Rick Jimenez as soon as I arrive. He wants to give me the tour."

Matsui's face went blank and then, as the elevator door began to close, took on an expression Riley couldn't interpret. The explosives instructor took a hesitant step forward, her mouth open as if she would speak, but Riley watched the thick metal door slide shut with a mechanical whir, cutting off anything the woman might have wanted to say.

"Come," Luther said. "I will take you to your room."

He seized her suitcase and started down a corridor, covering the distance quickly with his long legs. Riley jogged to keep up with him. "I need to get in contact with Rick Jimenez," she told him. "He's a new instructor here. Do you know him?"

He didn't answer. Riley tried her sparse and rusty German. "*Entschuldigung, sprechen Sie Englisch?*"

"I will take you to Frau Hill," he said, "after we drop off your bags."

Riley sighed, only now realizing how much she wanted to see Rick's friendly face and be with someone familiar. Soon. Maybe Frau Hill could help with that.

Luther opened a door with a keycard, handing it to her afterward. She barely glanced at the small room he led her into. Time enough for that later. She left the luggage and ran after Luther. He forsook the elevator and took four flights of stairs to the top of the building.

Emerging into a hallway, he indicated a row of straight-backed wooden chairs. "Rest here," he said, disappearing inside a doorway. Riley fell onto one of the chairs, working to catch her breath before being ushered into...whatever.

Barely two minutes passed before a blonde woman rushed out with Luther on her heels. He stalked away without another word, while the woman tucked Riley's hand inside both her own, squeezing gently. The hands were cool and smooth, meant to welcome and comfort, but Riley felt trapped inside them. She pulled away.

"My dear," the woman said, "I'm Paula Hill, assistant director here at the academy. I'm so sorry your friend Rick couldn't be here to meet you. Please come in."

She led Riley past a small antechamber and directly into her office beyond, closing the door behind them. Gesturing for Riley to sit, Paula Hill perched on the edge of her desk. She took off her glasses and put them aside, tucking a stray lock of hair behind one ear with a trembling hand.

Riley saw the older woman's eyes were pouched and red-rimmed. The misgivings of her morning flooded back, all her doubts about being here suddenly magnified.

"I'm sorry," Hill said again. "We're all a bit shocked right now. We just found out this morning that Rick was in an accident on his way to the academy."

A stab of alarm shuddered through Riley, hitting her in the gut. "Is he all right? What happened?"

Hill paused and Riley heard her draw in a deep breath.

"I'm so sorry, Riley. He didn't survive the accident. Rick is dead."

18

Riley sat stunned, her world going fuzzy around her. A sensation like a sudden roller coaster drop hit her in the stomach and she understood why people always wanted to deliver a shock to someone sitting down.

Every sound in the room seemed suddenly amplified, falling harsh on her ears. The breeze coming through the open balcony door. The rustle of papers on Paula Hill's desk. The monotonous, discordant tinkle of a wind chime coming from somewhere outside.

Swallowing hard, Riley forced down a lump of nausea in her throat and focused her gaze on the woman's face, wanting to deny, to disbelieve. But Paula Hill's face was deadly sincere, filled with concern and regret.

Riley's tongue felt dry, glued to the roof of her mouth. She worked to loosen it, to form the dreadful words she didn't want to speak.

"What happened?" she asked at last.

Hill shook her head. "I'm afraid we don't know much about it at this point."

"But you must know something!" Riley heard her voice spiraling up in pitch and tried to rein it in, to get a hold on her anger and bewilderment, but failed.

"What happened?" she said again. "Tell me what happened. It can't be true. It isn't true!"

The last words echoed in her ears, petulant and childish. She, a grown woman who'd endured the death of her husband and son and already learned the hard fact that life goes on, was screeching like a nine-year old.

She clamped her lips together and pulled in a deep breath through her nose.

"I'm sorry," she said.

Hill left the desk and sat beside her, this time laying one of her cool hands on Riley's shoulder. "It's the shock," she said. "Let me make you some tea."

Riley nodded. "Do you have herbal?"

"Chamomile or raspberry?"

"Chamomile, please."

While Hill brewed the tea, Riley stared around the office, not really seeing anything her eyes passed over. How could Rick be gone? She'd just spoken with him. He'd always impressed her as so vital, so alive. How could he have been snuffed out in a flash while she was flying over the ocean, completely unaware?

A soft double-knock sounded on the door and a mocha-skinned African man entered. His expression was grave yet so filled with compassion that Riley was afraid to look at him. Hill brought her the cup of tea on a saucer.

"Riley, this is our director, Stanley Edwards," she said. "Stan, meet Riley Forte."

He took Riley's hand, bowing over it, and spoke in a low, rich tone touched by an accent she thought might be Kenyan.

"I am so sorry about Rick," he said. "I understand he was a good friend."

Dangerously close to losing it, Riley gulped a mouthful of hot tea, letting it burn down her throat, focusing on the pain. After a moment, she was able to glance at him and nod her thanks.

"Nevertheless, we are glad you are here and hope you'll choose to stay. We'll do all we can to help you."

"About that," Hill told him, "I understand you've put her in a room with Colette. Surely she'd be more comfortable in a room of her own?"

"Or perhaps not," he said. "There are no single rooms available at the moment, and she might find solace in the companionship of another soul."

"Yes," Hill said, "but...Colette?"

Why were they discussing her as if she wasn't there in the room with them? Riley realized it might be because she almost wasn't. She felt so ephemeral, wispy and insubstantial. Time to get her feet back on the ground.

She shook herself and gulped another mouthful of hot tea. Raising her chin, she said, "Can you tell me what happened to Rick, Director Edwards?"

He looked rueful and Riley saw a glance pass between him and Paula Hill, a glance that held something unspoken, something he wasn't willing to say.

"All we really know right now is that when our man arrived to pick him up, he was gone. Somehow, he ended up in another car, and that car crashed on the side of a remote country road outside of Nuremberg."

"Was there anyone else in the car?"

"No, he was alone."

"I don't understand," Riley said. "He called me from the airport and said he was waiting for his ride."

The director shook his head. "We just don't know what happened, Riley, but we're investigating."

"Aren't there surveillance cameras at the airport that might help?"

"Yes, of course. We'll take a look at those, and more." He paused. "You must be exhausted."

"Yes, I'd like to freshen up and rest. I think I'll go to my room now."

"Certainly," Edwards said. "You just missed lunch but I can have a tray sent to your room."

Riley had no interest in trying to eat, but she mustered a weak smile for the director. "Thank you."

She took the stairs down to her room, striking the ground solidly with her feet, feeling the vibrations travel through her, achingly real and present.

Hard facts can hurt, but they remind us we're alive.

In the room, Riley sat cross-legged on her bed, back against the wall. The beds were European-style, mattresses fitted with a sheet and topped by a folded white duvet and fluffy down pillow. Riley had always appreciated the simple luxury and how easy it was to make the bed.

Despite the easiness of it, her roommate's duvet lay crumpled across the bed, the pillow mashed into a twist of linen. Riley stared at it as she dialed Chief Wright's number in Seattle, hardly caring that it was four o'clock in the morning on the American west coast.

He picked up on the first ring. "Riley! Are you okay?"

Her throat closed and it was a moment before she could force the words out. "Yes, I'm okay, Chief." She hugged herself, rocking on the bed. "I'm okay. You heard about Rick?"

"Yes, of course and I'm so sorry, Riley. I can't tell you how much..."

"I know." Her chest felt tight. "Do you know what happened?" she asked.

"We're trying to piece it together, but it's not making a whole lot of sense yet."

"Something doesn't feel right to me," Riley said. "Why didn't Rick wait for his ride from the academy? What's going on? I feel like people here aren't telling me everything."

"Maybe they're not. Maybe they think they can spare you some pain."

"What if it's more than that? What if they're hiding something?"

"That seems unlikely, Riley, but I'm not going to discount your intuition. Your knack for insight is part of why I recruited you in the first place."

He paused. "I'll tell you this—I called Tillo Zimmermann, head of the local crime unit. He said the car was a burnt-out shell when they got to it. They identified Rick by the singed remains of his wallet and one of our people from the academy went out to identify the body. We're waiting on DNA confirmation."

"Fire?" Riley said. "Was it arson?"

"Zimmermann said they're investigating the possibility. There are a lot of questions, Riley. I ought to order you back on the next flight, but—"

"No," she said. "I want to stay here. At least until I find out what happened."

"Don't go digging into things, Riley. It could get dangerous and you're not trained for it. Yet. Stay and get a start on your training. Be on hand, observe, but don't dig."

"What if I find something worth digging into?"

"Call me. I'm working on getting someone you know from our Seattle unit out there to support you, but there's a lot of trouble brewing around the world just now and our resources are stretched extraordinarily thin. You're our boots on the ground for now, but keep those boots out of harm's way. Understood?"

"Yes, I understand." Riley pinched the bridge of her nose, trying to stave off a headache. "Does Bobbi know yet?" she asked. Bobbi was Rick's girlfriend and Riley thought things had been getting pretty close to a marriage proposal.

"I was waiting until a decent hour to call her. No point in ruining her day before she even gets out of bed."

"Right. I'll do the same and then call Nate."

Even though Nate was not officially a part of Olivero, his close associations with several members and his involvement in the serial killer case that had brought Riley into it, meant he had a lot of friends in the organization.

"Good," Wright said. "Thanks, Riley. For all of it."

Riley ended the call and hugged her knees to her chest. Wright had told her to steer clear of trouble, but if she was honest with herself, she had to acknowledge she might not be able to do that. Something felt wrong about the whole situation—something beyond the absolute wrongness of Rick's death.

If she could find out what it was, she would.

Right now, it felt like that's about all she had left to live for.

19

Forst stood against the wall of the farmhouse bedroom, warming his hands on a steaming cup of coffee. It had been a long, sleepless night fraught with risk, and they weren't out of the woods yet. He watched the doctor, a man he knew only as Müller, work over Taz Salih—cleaning and stitching a head wound, wrapping a sprained wrist and splinting a broken finger.

The room was silent other than the clank of instruments and the swish and drip of water in the basin. Müller, a doctor on Cincher's payroll, was a humorless man of few words. Forst had been relieved when he'd announced the injuries were not as bad as they'd first appeared.

"With time, he'll mend," Müller said.

"In a week's time," Forst asked, "how far will he have mended?"

The doctor gave him a baleful stare. "Enough," was his only answer.

The injured fugitive remained in a nebulous state of consciousness, moving in and out of awareness, as yet unable to piece together a single sentence about what had happened to him.

"You speak of his body," Forst said. "What about his brain? Will he be able to function?"

91

The doctor finished taping a bandage and rose, gathering his things. "All you need is a pulse," he said.

Presumably, the doctor knew what Cincher expected of Salih a week hence and felt he'd be up to the task. Welcome news, but Forst knew the dangers involved in harboring the incapacitated fugitive and he wasn't happy about it.

Still, it couldn't be helped. Cincher had commanded it. Forst would do his best to nurse the man back to health—or as close to it as they could get by the end of a very busy week.

The doctor left the room and Forst dropped into the bedside chair, sipping at the coffee, wrinkling his nose at the antiseptic smell of the bandages and dressings swathing the man before him. He let his head nod, drowsing fitfully as he thought through what had happened the night before, hoping he'd handled the situation in a way Cincher would approve.

The last of the light had been melting from the western sky when he'd reached the stretch of road Taz Salih had described on the phone. The heavens stretched overhead, a dark gray void waiting like a backdrop for stars and moonlight to sprinkle its length, and the night was eerily silent.

He'd driven his modified SUV slowly along the deserted country road, looking for the gouging tire tracks or broken branches that might indicate where the man's car had gone off track.

Müller, in the seat beside him, had peered out the opposite window. It wasn't the first time they'd worked together and Forst was glad to have help with the unpleasant task, even that of the taciturn doctor.

"Slow down," Müller said. "I see something."

Forst braked the SUV to a crawl and watched the doctor shine a torch into the damaged foliage. It glinted off something pale and metallic. He saw the ruins of a yellow car, slanted at an alarming angle on the uneven ground, the Mercedes ornament winking at him like an eye.

He pulled to the shoulder and switched off the engine, a rush of dread shivering through him as he steeled himself for a nasty experience.

He smelled gasoline, but he knew an explosion needed a lot of hot gas in a confined space. The Mercedes had been dormant and cooling for almost two hours. It wasn't an exploding car he feared.

It was what he might find inside the car.

Salih had told him he had the chemical, and presumably it was inside a protective container. But in a collision like this one, a breach might have occurred, damaging the seal, releasing the chemical in a slow, deadly leak. If Salih was wounded and covered in vomit, Forst meant to light a match and get far and fast away, Cincher's plans be damned.

Grabbing another torch from the glove compartment, he trailed behind the doctor clambering down to the broken car, happy to let the other man go first. Like a canary into a coal mine.

He was halfway down the incline when Müller called out, "We got two guys here. They don't look good."

Two guys? He'd been made to understand the four-person team was down to one man. Two killed in action, one taken into custody. Who was the extra guy?

"Are they breathing?" he asked.

A moment passed. "Both alive, but unconscious. One of them breathing his last, I wager."

Forst swore, unsure what to do. Finally, he said, "My orders are to get Taz Salih, and that's who I'm getting. The other guy is out of luck."

By this time, he'd arrived at the car, figuring it was safe enough. "Check the pockets for ID."

The man Müller was searching began to moan. Forst shut his ears to it.

"Okay, this is our guy," he said, flipping through the wallet he'd extracted from one of the injured men. "How do we move him?"

"Have to use the stretcher and hope we don't injure his spine," Müller said. "This guy's ID says Michael Martinez. Mean anything to you?"

"No. Leave him. Let's get Salih out of here."

Forst tramped back up the hill for a blanket and the stretcher, while Müller opened his bag and did what he could for Taz Salih. Back at the wreck, they carefully moved the blood-smeared broken man to the blanket-covered stretcher. Müller continued to minister to him while Forst searched the car, looking for the case containing the illicit designer nerve agent Salih had helped create.

Beneath the passenger seat, he found a metal carrying case and gingerly pulled it out. It appeared undamaged, but there was no way he was going to open it to see if the canisters were intact. This had to be the chemical. He carried it to the SUV and wrapped it inside a thick, plastic garbage bag, securing it with the seatbelt, like a child.

He returned to help the doctor transport his patient on the stretcher. The SUV was customized with a ventilated concealed compartment large enough to hold a man. Forst had often utilized it for the purpose.

"They've still got road blocks up and patrols out looking," he said. "I'm not willing to risk leaving him in the open. He's got to go in the box."

Müller scowled, but gave a reluctant nod. Using the blanket as a sling, they maneuvered Salih into the space and closed the cover over him.

"Stay here," Forst told Müller. "I'll be right back and then we're getting out of here fast."

He sidestepped once more down the steep-sided ditch, sliding on loose stones, skinning the heel of one hand. The eerie silence of the night closed around him, amplifying the sound of his own panting breath.

When he reached the car, he realized that the remaining injured man had stopped moaning. He lay still and Forst recognized the glaze in his eyes. Michael Martinez— whoever he'd been—was no more.

Forst sniffed the air. Much of the spilled fuel would have soaked into the dirt or evaporated, but there would be enough to fulfill his purpose. The Mercedes was old and contained a lot of foam and plastic manufactured before fire-retardant became a hard and fast regulation.

Pulling a paper book of matches from his pocket, he lit the bunch of them with his pocket lighter and watched the hungry tongues of flame lick toward his fingers.

Then he flung the burning wad beneath the car, letting it drink from the gasoline-soaked earth and find the dripping fountain of fuel, following it upward into the heart of the car.

Scrambling up the hill, he'd started the SUV and sped away down the dark country road, watching the glow in his rearview mirror.

Yes, Cincher ought to be happy with the way he handled the situation.

He hoped.

At any rate, it was time to report in.

Forst made the call and waited to hear Cincher's voice.

"I've got him," Forst said.

"Yes, Müller's already given me his report."

Forst might have known the doctor would beat him to it, but he was glad he wouldn't need to go into the medical details.

"And the nerve agent?" Cincher asked.

Forst hesitated. He still hadn't opened the titanium box containing the chemical.

"I have the case right here."

"I didn't ask about the case, Forst. Do you have eyes on the canisters?"

Forst hesitated.

"You're afraid to open it," Cincher said.

"Hell yes!"

Cincher laughed. "That's because you're smart. I like that about you, Forst." A pause. "You know what I'd like even more?"

Forst swallowed. "I'll open it."

"Go ahead," Cincher said. "I'll wait."

Forst retrieved the plastic-wrapped package from the corner of the room and made a decision. He was not going to peel back the layers like a timid virgin on his wedding night. If he was going in, he was going in bold.

He pulled the case from the plastic and placed it on top. Rolling the dials on the combination lock to the numbers he'd been given in advance, he heard the clasps spring open with a metallic pop. Without giving himself a chance to back out, he lifted the lid and stared down at the contents of the case.

"There's only one here," he said into the phone.

"One canister? Why?"

"I don't know. Salih hasn't been conscious or coherent long enough to tell me what happened."

"Find out as soon as you can."

"Understood."

"He has the key," Cincher said. "Make sure he stays alive."

"I will." Forst cleared his throat. "I've been invited for a swim at the Sammelplatz this afternoon," he said.

"Great. Be your charming self. Take some photos. Send them to me."

"Will do," Forst said, but Cincher had already broken the connection.

20

CINCHER ENDED THE CALL with Anton Forst.

He tucked the phone into an interior pocket of the down vest he wore and continued his trek up the stony mountain path, feeling the jagged rocks beneath his feet even through the thick soles of his hiking boots. As he moved among the stands of pine, maple, and oak, he heard the *drip* and occasional *plop* of melting snow as the season warmed into spring.

The day was crystal clear, giving him a breathtaking view of the *Schlafende Hexe*, a double-sided peak named for its resemblance to a sleeping witch. He pulled a deep, cleansing breath into his lungs, feeling them expand, enjoying the rush of oxygen, imagining it spreading to every part of him.

Like his own expanding hold on the world.

He was not well-pleased with the progress of the peace summit operation. While it was only one of many ongoing maneuvers, it held a special interest for him and he'd deployed several of his key people to facilitate its success. His appetite for a triumphant outcome prickled in his gut, stoking his anticipation.

Among the many great pleasures it would bring him was how it would affect Riley and the Olivero agency. So close—just a few short miles from the summit's location—and yet they were oblivious. It delighted him to think about it, to contemplate their shock, their inevitable feelings of futility when the summit was struck by disaster.

Olivero's under-the-radar training base was no secret to him. He'd been keeping tabs on Olivero for years, but he'd been astonished to learn that Wright had recruited his very own Riley after her involvement in apprehending a serial killer.

A serial killer who'd bumbled and butchered over many years, a wonder he'd never been caught. Disorganized and fuzzy in purpose, Cincher had found him and raised his work to a whole new level, focusing his tenacity to a laser point. It had been child's play to get inside that one's head and redirect his energies.

They weren't all so easy to manipulate.

Cincher thought back to those early days with Timmy. He'd been a burnout, a disappointment, unable to make the leap from cats and dogs to anything more complex. Cincher had moved on, turning his attention elsewhere.

By the time he'd reached junior high, he was spending much of his time researching, learning from the masters—Machiavelli, Octavian, von Bismarck, Stalin, Hitler. He studied their techniques, practicing what he learned in subtle ways on his classmates and family.

His keen interest in human behavior combined with his years of research to produce a pleasing ability, one he wielded and honed as he followed another passion of his—how the earth itself worked.

He earned a Bachelor of Science degree in Geology, and a master's in Volcanology. Volcanoes had always fascinated him and he was thrilled to discover that Olivero's Bavarian spy school lay at the foot of a volcanic structure, however dormant. And then, when he learned

Wright would be sending Riley to that very place, Cincher had shifted the focus of his own interests to the area.

And been richly rewarded.

He'd ordered Forst to move a branch of his operation to a nearby location in the peaceful countryside of the Upper Palatinate—a *Hof*, or farmhouse just outside the boundaries of the Olivero property. The high walls and enclosed courtyard made a perfect haven for the man to conduct his covert business.

Cincher himself had established a base somewhat south of the area, but close enough to keep his finger on Riley's pulse.

With a little help from his friends.

Forst had facilitated the insertion of a mole, poking a finger neatly inside Olivero and its environs. More than one, in fact, though each was ignorant of the other.

Cincher heard a screeching cry overhead and squinted against the sun, watching a large bird soar with outstretched wings, marveling at the majesty of it.

A golden eagle, bird of prey.

He stopped to drink from his canteen, wiping a sheen of sweat from his forehead before pressing on, feeling the muscles in his legs strain against the upward climb, the stones pressing into his feet.

Not for the first time, he reflected how much better it was that he hadn't killed Riley Forte. Knowing she was alive and nearby made his life so much more meaningful, so much more exciting.

He wouldn't have missed it for the world.

21

Dr. Vadim Novak lay in misery between the sheets of his bed, groaning and fighting the deepest well of regret he'd ever faced in his life. He had made a colossal mistake, and one from which it seemed impossible to escape.

For the past three weeks—ever since he'd moved into the discreetly situated research compound on the western border of the Czech Republic—he'd become increasingly uneasy. And this afternoon, against his better judgment, he'd opened Pandora's box, unleashing the host of nightmares which tormented him now. In a cold sweat, he stared at the ceiling, remembering with sharp recrimination his foolish anticipation on the day he'd first met Dr. Mitchell Anderson.

Amid the first signs of spring, Vadim had arrived at the facility mid-morning, parked his car and walked to the security gate, a flutter of eagerness in the pit of his stomach. He'd waited at the tall metal gate under the stern gaze of the guard who'd announced his arrival to Dr. Anderson via handheld radio. The guard wore a dark, nondescript uniform and peaked hat, a rifle slung over one shoulder, his posture poised and alert as if Vadim might attack at any moment.

The morning was fine, though chilly, with clear skies overhead and the faint chatter of birdsong drifting over from the fringe of birch and pine surrounding the property. A hint of breeze stirred the air, sending goosebumps prickling along the backs of his arms.

Coils of razor wire stretched away along the top of the high chain link fence, glinting in the sunlight. While Vadim deplored the prison-like appearance it gave to the laboratory and grounds beyond, he recognized the need for protection and privacy from those who didn't understand the important work going on inside the fence.

From the time he'd first heard about Dr. Mitchell Anderson's little-known private research facility in his beloved Czech homeland, Vadim had hoped to tour the lab and meet the brain behind the project. As a man of science, trained in psychotherapy, Vadim had been impressed by Dr. Anderson's grasp of the subject, catching a glimpse of promise in the treatment of behavioral disorders.

Thanks to the experimental work being conducted inside the laboratory.

Vadim had been thrilled to receive Dr. Anderson's invitation to come and see, to ask questions and explore possibilities. And he'd been frankly astounded at the suggestion that he might join the research team if he liked what he saw.

The gate screeched open and Vadim stood face to face with Anderson, reaching to meet his outstretched hand as he stepped onto the laboratory grounds.

"Ah, my dear colleague," Anderson said. "It is a pleasure to welcome you to my facility. Please come along, I'm excited to show you around and tell you about our work here."

Vadim murmured his thanks, but Anderson hardly seemed to notice as he strode briskly down a concrete walkway, pulling Vadim along in the wake of his enthusiasm. They toured a three-story building where Vadim saw an impressive array of separate labs, experiment rooms, and a vast storage system for preserving records and results.

Anderson pointed out a second building as a dormitory, living quarters for the doctors, orderlies, and administrative staff. He took Vadim inside and showed him into a small but beautifully appointed apartment complete with kitchenette and compact laundry room.

"This is where you'll stay," he said, "if you decide to join my research team."

Vadim stared, hardly able to believe that only a short time ago, he'd first learned about Dr. Anderson's critical work in behavioral therapy and wished to be a part of it. And now, he was standing in its midst, his dream within reach.

Without waiting for a response, Anderson whisked him away again, back outside and across a quad to a structure housing a cafeteria on the first floor and a library above.

"Let's continue our discussion over lunch," he suggested.

As they crossed the large square of grass, Vadim pointed to the building on the remaining side of the quad, one they hadn't yet visited. "What is that building for?" he asked.

Anderson, without slowing his brisk pace, said, "That's where we house the subjects who volunteer for human testing. They get their own dormitory space."

"Where do they come from?"

"We source from many different areas to get a statistically viable population."

"Oh, of course." Vadim nodded, acknowledging the wisdom in that.

Inside the cafeteria, the air was scented with the rich, meaty aroma of goulash and Vadim's mouth watered. He realized it was after noon and he was hungry after the substantial amount of walking they'd put in throughout the morning. However, Anderson didn't stop in the cafeteria, but led him upstairs to a private dining room where a server waited with plates of goulash and bread dumplings kept warm under silver domes.

As they ate, Anderson talked about some of the successful experiments conducted by his team and how they contributed to the body of scientific advances in treating psychological disorders.

"I am supremely interested in observing human impulses, temptations, and motivations," he told Vadim. "And to learn from the behavior that results from certain, controlled sets of circumstances designed to test such aspects of the psyche."

Vadim nodded. "Yes, a fascinating line of research."

"The Milgram experiment," Anderson continued, referencing the work done by Stanley Milgram at Yale in the 1960s, "laid a foundation for one branch of our studies here. But the test subjects administering the shocks and those receiving the shocks were strangers to one another. I'm interested in determining what would happen between friends put in a similar situation. I think this is a valid line to pursue."

Vadim swallowed a mouthful of spicy beef, considering the premise. "I agree, it is interesting. But I see difficulties in constructing an experiment with effective parameters for testing the hypothesis."

Anderson waved a hand in the air as if chopping through such difficulties. "I'm convinced it can be done. The type of breakthrough we need can come only from reaching farther, risking more than those who've tried and failed in the past."

Vadim paused. He wiped his mouth with a thick damask napkin and took a sip from his goblet of red wine. "You are surely aware that Hitler's people did research along these lines?"

Anderson scowled. "Yes, but let's not hold ourselves hostage to that man's failings. How can we help people if we don't understand what motivates them?"

Vadim opened his mouth to speak, but Anderson rushed on. "Bah! I am not speaking of the psychopath or patients with sociopathic leanings. I am talking about ordinary people. I am in search of the anomaly—chemical, emotional, or biological—that predisposes one person to behave more ruthlessly than others."

"Yes," Vadim said slowly. "I can see the value in that."

"Quite right." Anderson smiled. "Let us raise a toast."

He poured more wine. "To science," he said, lifting his glass.

"To science."

The server came, clearing the table and leaving a slender slice of chocolate layered torte for each of them.

"Splendid meal, Dr. Anderson," Vadim said. "Thank you very much. For lunch, and of course for the fascinating tour of your facility."

"I'm pleased you enjoyed it." Leaning back in his chair, Anderson studied Vadim until he felt like an experimental subject himself.

"So," his host said at last. "May I welcome you to my team, Dr. Novak?"

When he'd left the hotel that morning to visit the lab, Vadim had every intention of accepting such an invitation should it be offered. Now, a vague stir of unrest swirled inside him, settling in the pit of his stomach.

However, as he considered the extensive and pristine laboratory facility, the exciting work being done, and the potential good that could come of it, he quelled his misgivings and thought about the neat, comfortable apartment waiting for him in the building next door.

It was all too good to pass up.

"I would be honored to join your team," Vadim had said.

It was the mistake of a lifetime.

Tortured by the memory, Vadim twisted in the sheets, now hot from his fevered writhing. He was trying, with every ounce of energy he could muster, to forget what he'd seen inside that other building. The one where Dr. Anderson housed his human test subjects.

Volunteers, he'd called them, but Vadim suspected their presence here was anything but voluntary.

And now he had to accept that the hopes and expectations he'd had for the work he would do here were just as illusory.

Biting the inside of his cheek until it bled bitter into his throat, Vadim fell into a tormented sleep.

22

RILEY'S ROOM AT THE academy was on the ground floor. She didn't have the kind of views she'd glimpsed from assistant director Hill's balcony, but she did have a small patio outside a large German-style window.

She loved the ingenuity of a German window, how it could open from the top to let air circulate while keeping out the rain, or swing wide like a door. Riley worked the handle to make it function like a door and stepped onto the concrete pad outside, greeted by the mild air of a spring afternoon.

Her eyes felt heavy and filled with grit, even after she'd washed her face with a nubby cloth and hot water, almost steaming out of the faucet. A small basket of toiletries rested on the bathroom counter and Riley had smoothed rosemary-scented lotion over her hands and forearms, breathing deeply, letting the fragrance soothe some of the anxiety from her before she picked up the phone.

It was now barely six a.m. Pacific time as she settled onto a patio chair, but Riley understood she couldn't put it off any longer. Nate had to know, and he wouldn't thank her for delaying the news. With fingers that felt like lead, she dialed his number and waited several long seconds for him to pick up.

"Riley, sorry—I was in the shower. How was your flight? Are you settling in?"

"Nate," she said, her voice cracking. She couldn't continue.

"What's wrong? Are you okay?"

She bit her lip. Hard. "I'm fine. It's Rick, Nate. He's dead."

Silence crossed the line for several seconds, then Nate said, "What happened?"

"No one seems to know exactly, but I'm not leaving here until I find out."

"What are you talking about, Riley?"

She drew a deep breath. "Rick called me right after he landed in Nuremberg. He said someone from the academy was picking him up. That was the last time I talked to him. When his ride from the academy arrived, Rick had vanished."

"So he's missing."

"No, Nate. His body was found several hours later, in a burned-out car."

"Burned-out? How can they even be sure it was Rick?"

"Police were able to recover ID in his pocket for Michael Martinez—Rick's operational alias—and the academy sent someone to identify the body. They're waiting on DNA confirmation."

"Oh."

Riley waited for Nate to make all the painful connections and arrive at the plain, hard reality that their friend was gone. But as the seconds passed, she realized she hadn't truly accepted it herself. It just couldn't be.

"Riley, I'm so sorry. I hate that you're out there alone. Do you want me to come?"

So much. So, so much.

"No, Nate. I'm okay."

"I've already put in for leave. I have a week off starting tomor-row."

"I know, but you're going camping with your family."

Another stretch of silence.

"Riley, I—"

A knock sounded at the door. Riley stood up.

"There's someone here, Nate. I'm fine, really. I have to go. Have fun with your family."

She hit the button to end the call. She hadn't meant for that last part to come out sounding snide, but she was afraid it had. She really did hope he could enjoy the trip with his ex-wife and daughter.

She really did wish him all the best. Even if that didn't include a life with her.

Angry with herself, Riley opened the door to admit a tall, thin woman in a chef's cap and apron, carrying a tray. Without being invited in, she walked to the small table and deposited the tray, turning to regard Riley with sharp dark eyes, like a bird's.

"Is there anything else you require?" the cook asked in a clipped German accent.

The words were solicitous but the piercing eyes made Riley feel she was under inspection and not measuring up. She glanced at the tray without caring what it contained.

"Nein, danke. Alles passt."

The cook left and Riley dropped into one of the table's two chairs. She opened the manila packet Luther had given her and pulled out a sheaf of papers. Scanning the pages without really taking in any of the information, Riley tried to eat a bite of the panini on her plate. Her throat closed around the ham and cheese, nearly choking her.

Abandoning the meal, Riley tried to focus on the packet, unable to latch onto a single paragraph long enough to process meaning from it. Pushing back from the table, she changed her flats for a pair of sneakers and fled out the window onto the grounds of the academy.

Less than thirty yards from the building, she found a woodland trail and let it swallow her in shadow as she ran.

23

Nate stood, wrapped in a towel, numb and dripping on the bedroom carpet. He let the phone fall from his nerveless fingers onto the unmade bed. Beyond the closed blinds, the dawn made a gray square of his window, emitting a dull, pewter-colored glow that resonated with Nate's own consciousness.

Everything was changing.

Life *is* change, and that had often felt like a good thing. But not today.

Today, he felt totally inadequate. No good to Riley, no good to his own family. No good to his dead friend and former partner on the force.

What the hell had happened?

A stubborn denial rose within him, he felt his jaw harden. This couldn't be real. He couldn't help clinging to the hope that it was all a horrible mistake.

He ripped the towel from his hips and rubbed it back and forth across his shoulders with clenched fists, feeling the textured fabric rake his skin.

He dressed and ran a comb through his hair. This was his last day on the job before taking Marilyn and Sammi on a camping trip, and they'd all been looking forward to it. His ex-wife had been making supreme efforts of late to patch old wounds and make them a family again. Nate, too, felt a strong tug to get back to the way things were.

But life is change.

Deep down, a part of him believed it couldn't be done, that he might not even want to go there again. He'd moved on. They all had.

And there was Riley.

As much as he cared about Marilyn, he loved the way he felt with Riley. They were comfortable together, in sync. Yet he found her fascinating and challenging. He was endlessly amazed by the depth of her and touched by her compassion.

Now, with the news of Rick's death, the stone in his chest took on fresh weight, sinking to deeper levels. He ground his teeth and let out a primal groan as he pulled his jacket off a peg and grabbed his keys, heading out the door.

He felt he owed it to Sammi and Marilyn to try again and to really give it his all. He'd made a commitment to do so. And he would.

He'd keep his grief to himself rather than ruin the camping trip. He'd give everything he could to his daughter, to the woman he'd once taken as his wife. They would enjoy each other's company and build some great memories for the years to come.

But as he started the car and steered through the neighborhood, he couldn't help worrying about Riley.

Would she really be okay out there on her own?

24

LIESL STOOD CONCEALED BEHIND a pillar in the breezeway that linked the Sammelplatz lobby to the indoor pool. The air here felt a little dank and smelled faintly of chemicals, despite a gentle wind coming through the open windows of the pool area.

Beyond the glass walls, the sky shone like an azure dome cupped over the mountain. It was the kind of day Liesl drew strength from, recharging her batteries and nourishing her soul. But she couldn't enjoy it, couldn't embrace it.

She was far too nervous.

Forst and Julia sat on wicker lawn chairs, sipping tall glasses of pineapple juice. Both were wearing swimsuits and Liesl knew Forst had used one of the cabanas to change out of his clothes. She hovered behind the pillar, watching and waiting, chewing her fingernails to the nub.

Just as she'd decided it would never happen, her sister rose with a shout of laughter and dove into the deep end of the pool. Forst followed her in, staying under so long that Liesl worried he wasn't coming up. When he did, it was to push Julia under.

With the two of them shouting and splashing, engaged in water-play, Liesl edged into the pool area, keeping to the shadowy perimeter until she reached the row of six cabanas. Quickly, she opened doors until she found the one draped with Forst's pants and shirt, his shoes neatly placed beneath the bench seat.

She let herself in and closed the door with trembling hands. The sound of splashing and laughter continued, but how long could it last? Liesl had noticed that Forst kept his phone with him. It lay on the table now, next to the pool, beyond her reach.

The phone was out, so that left the wallet. Stooping, she dug into his pants pocket, extracting a folded wallet of tooled leather. She opened it to reveal a German driving license with Forst's name and photograph and a selection of credit cards, also in his name. A thick layer of euro bills was stuffed into a divider behind those.

Nothing else.

She stood, feeling sick to her stomach. This was stupid. What had she hoped to gain by this foolish and risky ploy? In frustration, she closed the wallet. Then opened it and looked again.

Removing the stack of euros, she spread the wallet wide, peering closely at the leather interior. And there it was. A slender slit, almost invisible. A hidden compartment.

Excited now, Liesl stuck two fingers down inside the wallet and worked to remove a single card from the slit. As she pulled it free with shaking hands, it slipped out of her grasp and onto the floor. Nearly moaning from anxiety, she plucked it up and laid it on the bench. Sliding her phone out of her pocket, she struggled to hold her hands steady as she snapped several photographs, capturing both sides of the card.

It was another *Führerschein*, a driving license. The face in the photograph was Forst's, but the name was different. Moritz Schiller.

Not daring to spend another second than necessary, Liesl replaced the card. She didn't remember which side had been face up and desperately hoped it wouldn't matter. She pushed the wad of euros into place and folded the wallet shut.

As she snatched up the pants, she heard Forst's voice at the door. He was right there!

In horror, she watched the doorknob turn. There was nowhere to hide in this small, contained space. Biting her lip, she crouched and waited for her doom.

"Quitter!" Julia called out, laughing. "Can't hack being beaten by a girl."

The knob finished its rotation and the door snicked open.

Heart pounding furiously, Liesl watched Forst turn his head to shout something back.

"Beaten? I'll show you beaten."

His hand fell away from the doorknob as he stalked back to the pool to defend his honor. Liesl melted onto the bench, knees shaking so badly she could no longer stand. She crammed the wallet into his pants pocket and draped the pants as she'd seen them when she'd entered the cabana.

In her frenzied haste, she kicked one of Forst's shoes. It hit the wall with a smack.

Silence from the pool.

Nearly immobilized by terror, Liesl stared through the two-inch crack of the opened door. Forst and Julia were at the shallow end of the pool, fused in a hot embrace, kissing.

She hurriedly placed the shoe next to its partner and crept from the cabana. Before she reached the end of the row, she heard movement in the water.

They were coming out.

She'd never make it to the exit without being seen. As she reached the final cabana, she turned and wedged herself into the shadows of the corner it formed with the wall, partially hidden by a potted palm. She watched Forst and her sister leave the water and come dripping to the table where they toweled off.

Dread hit Liesl's stomach as she realized she was trapped. She'd have to stay where she was, not more than fifteen feet away, frozen and hoping they wouldn't look over and notice her crouching there as they finished their leisurely visit.

They didn't sit, however, but used the towels in a seductive sort of dance that ended with them retreating to the cabana for more privacy.

Liesl didn't want to think about what they meant to do in that cramped, uncomfortable space. And right now, she didn't care.

On wobbling legs, she made her escape.

25

Riley stood in front of the fogged mirror, tugging a comb through her wet hair, attacking the tangles with savage satisfaction, almost relishing the pain. If only the knots inside her could be worked out with such a straightforward approach, the pain dealt with and left behind.

Biting her lip, she switched her blow dryer to a 220 volt setting and plugged it into the wall using an adaptor. With a brush, she absently styled her hair, still feeling numb despite her run on the forest trail and the hot shower afterward. As she pulled the brush through the hair at the back of her head, she felt a thinness there and frowned.

Switching off the dryer, she fingered the tresses falling against her back, finding a hank several inches shorter than the rest of her hair, sheered off at a blunt angle.

Odd. How could that have happened?

It hardly seemed important. She shrugged it off and put the hair dryer away in a cabinet beside the sink, smoothing on a layer of lip balm and a brush of powder as a knock sounded at the door. Her legs felt heavy, unwilling to move beneath the millstone at her heart, and she was tempted to ignore the summons.

117

Rick would not have wanted this torpor, this dejection for her. He'd been excited for her to join the Olivero team, to embark on this new chapter of her life. He believed she would find great purpose and fulfillment from her investigative work and she'd begun to believe it herself.

Now she felt that belief crumbling.

Scowling at herself in the mirror, she hunched her shoulders and let them fall, willing herself to rally, to find that bar of inner strength she'd found and clung to more than once before in her life.

Making her feet move, she trudged to the door of her room and opened it to find Matsui standing in the corridor, a look of concern on her delicate features.

"Riley, I'm so sorry! I should have told you about Rick, prepared you for the shock, but I didn't realize you knew him. No one told me you were friends."

Riley stepped back and motioned the worried explosives expert into the room. "It wouldn't have made it any easier for me to hear," she said. "Nothing would have. I still can't believe it."

Matsui grasped one of Riley's hands, squeezing gently, her brows wrinkled above a pair of caramel brown, almond-shaped eyes. "Is there anything I can do for you?"

Riley's chest ached as she drew in a deep breath and straightened her spine. "You can show me around and help me get settled."

"You're staying?"

Swallowing hard, Riley nodded. "Yes. I think I need to stay. I need to work hard on something new, keep my brain occupied, be around people." She didn't add that if she went home, it would be to an empty house and the prospect of an empty life.

Olivero—Rick's hope for her—represented her best chance to honor his memory.

"Right," Matsui said, nodding sympathetically. "Absolutely. I'm happy to help any way I can."

Together, they walked back to the lobby area where Riley had first entered. "The first two floors of this building comprise the dormitory for trainees," Matsui told her, spreading her arms to point down the two corridors forming wings off either side of a lounge area dotted with brightly colored sofas and chairs in dark red, teal, and cornflower blue.

"Sometimes we have a game night here," she continued. "A lot of fun, but watch out—some of us tend to get a little overly competitive."

"Are you speaking for yourself?" Riley asked.

Matsui gave her a demure smile. "What can I say? I'm used to winning."

She gestured upwards with her thumb. "The instructors and staff are housed on the next two levels, and the top floor is for the administrative offices."

"Right. Luther took me up to Paula Hill's office after I arrived."

"So you've met Paula?"

"Yes, and Director Edwards."

"Excellent. I like Edwards, and I think he does a good job running the place."

She walked toward a set of glass doors leading out the far side of the lobby and pushed through, letting in a rush of air that fluttered the papers tacked up on a nearby corkboard. Outside, the late afternoon sun still held enough warmth to feel good on Riley's upturned face. She paused a moment to stand with eyes closed, feeling the ground beneath her feet, reminding herself life could still be good, assuring herself it would be.

A faint twittering of birds floated on the air, coming from the rows of fruit trees flanking the concrete walkway, their tiny buds just beginning to show. Though nothing blossomed yet on the spindly branches, Riley smelled a sweetness on the breeze. The promise of spring.

Without opening her eyes, Riley felt Matsui come to stand next to her and was grateful when the woman didn't speak, just waited, letting the quiet moments pass until Riley sighed and said. "Okay, what's next?"

Matsui lifted an arm, gesturing to the small mountain rising just a short distance away to the north. "Remember the dormant volcanoes we talked about? That's the largest of them. There's a facility at the top, a kind of elite gathering place called the Swanhilde Sammelplatz. Once or twice in the past, Olivero has provided services for high profile meetings there."

"Why not more often?"

"I think those were special circumstances. They do their own thing, hire their own security, and we maintain our cover here as just another conference center." Matsui paused, pursing her lips. "Actually, I heard they've got some bigwigs coming in soon for some kind of peace summit."

"Really?"

"Yeah, you might catch a glimpse of a limousine entourage passing on the road outside the gate, but you won't have time to even think about what goes on at the top of the mountain. You'll have your hands full down here."

She pointed toward a large field and a sprawl of buildings about a hundred meters off. "There's the fitness course, the gym, and the shooting range. And that," she said swiveling to gesture at a building set well apart from the others, "is my wheelhouse."

Riley squinted at the plain, boxy building. "The bomb factory?"

"Officially, it's called the Explosives Shed, but your description is apt."

She grinned. "You've already seen the Motor Pool. That's where you'll go for your tactical mobility instruction. Let's head over to the classrooms now. We've got something special for you over there."

On the opposite side of the courtyard, a building in the same Bavarian style as the dormitory rose three stories tall, ringed by wood-railed balconies hung with pots of pink geraniums. Matsui held the door open and gestured Riley inside.

"Take a moment to look over the directory," Matsui advised. "Get an idea of where everything is."

Riley studied the map posted at the entrance, taking in the location of Basic Field Skills, Cryptology, Psychology, History, Communications, and other subjects related to the work done by Olivero operatives. She was surprised to feel a burst of anticipation, coupled with a grim determination to put her time here to good use.

"And now for something you'll really like," Matsui said, winking. She led Riley down a hallway to a set of double doors at the end of it. Pushing them open, Matsui flipped on the light switch, waving her arms like a game show hostess. "Ta dah!"

Riley walked forward, delighted by the sight of a polished ebony baby grand piano.

"It's probably not what you're used to," Matsui said, "but Chief Wright insisted we get a piano so you can stay in practice. You have two hours daily blocked out on your schedule. Is that enough?"

Riley lifted a shoulder. "It will have to do. I'm here to focus on learning other skills. I can't spend eight hours a day at the piano."

"Is that how much you usually practice?"

"More, sometimes, if I'm preparing for a concert."

"That's positively...athletic."

"And burns an astonishing amount of calories," Riley added, smiling.

"Do you want to play now?"

"With every fiber of my soul."

Matsui came close, wrapping Riley in a gentle hug. "I'll leave you to it then. Is there anything else you need?"

Shaking her head, Riley sank onto the piano bench, adjusting it to her height and running her fingers up and down the keyboard in a tinkling chromatic scale. She launched into a Beethoven sonata and when she thought to look up, Matsui was gone.

For an hour, Riley lost herself in the music, the best kind of therapy. She played through sad laments, furious agitatos, and ended with some jazz by a modern composer she liked, Christos Tsitsaros.

When she headed back to her room, some of the heaviness had lifted off her chest. She used her keycard to let herself in and found a stunningly beautiful young black woman staring with distaste at the congealed remains of her uneaten lunch, still on the table.

"Sorry about the mess," Riley said. "You must be Colette."

"And you must be Riley," her roommate said, a trace of French accent in her high, clear voice. "Do not worry about the mess. I will ask someone from the kitchen to pick it up."

The girl studied Riley, a puzzling mix of expressions passing over her face—sorrow and compassion followed by austerity, the lovely dark eyes growing distant. "I am sorry your friend Rick has been killed," she said, a little stiffly.

"Did you know him?" Riley asked.

"Not well, but we'd met."

Riley tried to interpret the girl's tone, her stilted body language, wondering if she was reading hostility where none existed. Wondering if that kind of thing would be included in her training.

"How long have you been here at the academy?" she asked.

"I am doing deep training," Colette replied. "It takes many months. I have been here for nearly a year."

Riley felt her eyebrows go up. "It must feel like a second home to you by now."

"Yes."

Riley sensed the woman wanted to say more, but instead she slipped her feet into a pair of ballerina flats and went into the bathroom, running the water as she washed her hands.

"It's time for dinner," she announced. "Shall we go?"

The cafeteria where meals were served was at the end of the corridor, not far from the room they shared, sparing the need for conversation as they covered the short distance. Inside, Colette showed her where to grab a tray and move down the line to choose what she wanted to eat.

"Pasta with chicken tonight—it's a good option, and the salad bar is passable, too."

An appealing aroma filled the spacious room and Riley realized she was hungry. Ravenous, in fact. She filled her tray and followed Colette to a table, not sure the girl welcomed her company but hoping they could become friends.

As she settled into place and lifted her fork, she caught sight of Paula Hill at a table across the room. The assistant director's gaze was locked on Colette, a frown twisting her lips. She saw Riley's attention on her and smiled before turning away to chat with her table mates. The interchange was brief, completely ordinary, yet it left Riley with the distinct impression that Hill was displeased at seeing her and Colette together.

As she ate, Riley thought about how the woman had protested over the two of them sharing a room and wondered if it was her imagination or a notion with some substance. And if her instinct was accurate, what lay beneath it?

These strange undercurrents disturbed her, making her feel wretched and uneasy. More than ever she missed Rick and wished he were there to brace her up.

Riley's throat tightened and she found it hard to swallow the bits of salad and chicken she was pushing around on her plate. Feeling thoroughly alone and completely out of place, she forced herself to finish her dinner so she could go to bed and, with luck, to the blessed oblivion of sleep.

What had ever made her think she could succeed here in the wild world of spycraft?

26

DR. VADIM NOVAK STOOD at the bank of windows overlooking the testing room and watched the group of subjects below, a queasy feeling rising in his rib cage. He didn't like the direction his experiments were taking him, and each day seemed to bring something new to dismay him further.

The harsh light, striking down from overhead with a merciless, all-searching beam, washed over the test subjects and the man administering the protocol, bleaching the color from the room. Novak observed, making notes. No noises penetrated the sound-proofed walls and windows. He'd switched off the speakers after the screaming began.

He'd been so eager to launch this project after accepting Dr. Anderson's invitation to join his team of researchers. He had high expectations for what could be done with the resources provided by Anderson and his lab. The potential for mining valuable insights that could make a real difference in the lives of individuals, families, and whole societies had excited and motivated him greatly.

His initial enthusiasm wore off shortly after moving into the facility.

In the room below him, the administrator, a man known only to him as Raptor, concluded the experiment. Orderlies clad in hospital scrubs arrived to clean up the mess and transport the subjects back to their rooms. Or their cells, as Novak now understood them to be.

He finished notating his observations and wrote a summary for his report. Capping his pen, he rubbed at the base of his neck, hoping to curtail the headache and nausea rolling in on him like a storm. He rose from the desk and placed the clipboard inside his bag, summoning the energy to carry him out the door and down the steps to the ground floor.

Outside, he caught the peaty smell of freshly turned earth, warmed by the afternoon sun but growing cold now as evening closed in. Dark shapes swooped in the trees beyond the chain link and razor wire of the facility's perimeter, bats intent on catching their fill of supper.

During that first tour with Dr. Anderson, Novak had understood the need for protection and privacy, recognizing that certain security measures were necessary to guard against those who might break in and disrupt the important work going on inside the fence.

Now he realized that the facility had the appearance of a prison because that's what it was.

He, and the rest of the inmates lived and breathed on Anderson's orders, carrying out his instructions. Those who didn't, ceased to live and breathe. The sudden disappearance of belligerent subjects had not escaped Novak's notice, and he had little doubt about their fate.

"Doctor Novak, how are you this fine evening?"

Novak flinched. He hadn't heard the man approaching from behind. Bile rose in his throat, and he swallowed it down, turning to nod a cursory greeting.

"I'm well, Dr. Anderson. And you?"

Novak knew he fared the best chance at survival inside this hell hole by showing deference to the despotic doctor, playing his game. Inside, where Anderson couldn't see, he plotted, planned, and thirsted for deliverance.

"Oh, I'm feeling marvelous today, Novak. Simply splendid. And your test session this afternoon—are you seeing the sort of results we expected?"

"Yes, doctor. I'm certain Raptor has no idea he is the actual test subject. His reactions are just what we predicted."

"You mean, he administered the test without compunction."

"So it appeared. There was no hesitation."

"Excellent! Thank you, Novak. Carry on."

Anderson turned off on a tangent, heading toward the cafeteria. Novak continued on to the apartment he'd been allotted in the dormitory, moving as quickly as he could, hoping to make it to the toilet before he threw up.

27

CINCHER PAUSED OUTSIDE THE door to the cafeteria, watching Novak hurry toward his quarters. The psychotherapist's face had been practically green. He was definitely not adapting to the course of this project as Cincher—or Dr. Anderson, as he was known here at the lab—had anticipated.

Nevertheless, the results Novak produced were pleasing. It was a pity he'd soon be terminated. Cincher knew the signs, saw into the man's soul. He would escape these walls one way or another. Cincher only hoped to squeeze the best bits out of the good doctor before he did.

He entered the cafeteria and was immediately assaulted by the smell of boiled cabbage. Suppressing his distaste, he moved among the tables where his staff sat eating bundles of minced meat rolled in cabbage leaves and steeped in a spicy tomato sauce. A favorite among the natives, but a dish he avoided at all costs.

With a pleasant half-smile fixed on his lips, he nodded a greeting to a pair of cafeteria attendants and made his way upstairs to his private dining room where a steak, medium-rare, and grilled vegetables awaited him, along with a fine cabernet.

As he ate alone, wiping the juice from his chin with a thick damask napkin, he reflected on his day, on this compound full of people subject to his command—only one of several similar facilities. He thought about the many plans he had in place and the myriad methods of discord he held at his disposal.

With a deep sense of satisfaction, he lifted a small brass bell in the table's center and shook it briefly, sending out a dissonant metallic jangle. A server appeared and Cincher signaled for dessert.

28

Anton Forst stood over the stove, stirring a pot of simmering soup. A fragrant vapor rose from the bubbling pot, redolent of onion, celery, and chicken, stoking his appetite. Placing the wooden spoon aside, he gnawed on a crusty bread roll as he walked to the window and stared out at the tree-lined field beside the Hof, cast in shadows thrown by the setting sun.

A black cat stalked some small unlucky creature among the withered stubble, remnants of the winter harvest. From a nearby perch, a dove cooed, sounding mournful and reminding Forst how lonely this isolated farmhouse could feel. Which was a good thing.

Isolation was a safety measure where his business was concerned.

He was alone with Taz Salih tonight. The doctor had been called away to tend another patient and had declared the escaped terrorist's condition stable and improving. Earlier in the day, Salih had woken and tried to speak, though his shaky sentences were still garbled and intermittent and the effort had exhausted him, sending him back to sleep.

In Forst's mind, questions and doubts were arising about the injured terrorist. Cincher had called with disturbing information about the man who'd died in the crash. Why did Salih have an American with known connections to a private security firm in the car? What had really happened back at the lab in Nuremberg?

As soon as the soup was ready, Forst would try feeding him and getting some answers, though it irked him to play nursemaid. Downing the last bite of his roll with a draught of beer, he wiped the foam from his lips with a sour-smelling dish towel, grimaced in disgust and tossed the stiffened fabric into a corner. Outside, the cat pounced and ran off triumphant, something wriggling in its mouth.

With a fork, Forst speared a piece of celery from the bubbling pot and blew on it before popping it into his mouth. Judging it to be tender enough, he switched off the burner and fetched two bowls, ladling soup into them and watching the steam rise to the ceiling. Bowls in hand, Forst pushed the bedroom door open with his foot and stepped inside.

The bed was empty.

Spluttering a curse, he plunked the bowls down on a cluttered dresser, sloshing soup onto the scratched wooden surface. Hurrying back to the kitchen and down the hall, he checked the bathroom and the other bedroom but Taz Salih was in neither.

He found the man on the back porch, fumbling with the latch that would let him out into the garden. Salih looked up, saw him coming and scrabbled more frantically at the gate. Forst grabbed him by the wrist and pushed him into a wicker chair. A pouf of dust flew up from the dirty cushion.

"You're okay. You're safe here," he said, making his tone loud and matter-of-fact.

"No," the fugitive said, his voice wavering, eyes wide and darting. "I should be...in a hospital. Why are you...keeping me here?"

"In a hospital," Forst said, "you'd be cuffed to the bed rails, waiting on a one-way ticket to prison. You're hiding, Salih. That's why you're here. Hiding and healing. You have a job to do."

The man went still. Forst saw something wake in his eyes. "Do you remember?" he asked.

Forst waited, listening to the harried breathing get slower and quieter, but Salih didn't answer. The wild scramble had clearly cost him and he slumped in the chair, eyelids drooping once again.

"What happened at the lab, Salih?" Forst prompted. "Why did you bring only one canister?"

Silence from the wicker chair.

Forst squatted in front of the man, poking him in the gut. "Where's the other canister, Salih?"

Nothing, other than a low moan.

"You had a man in the car with you," Forst pressed. "Why?" He gave the man a shake. "What were you doing with an American spy?"

Salih's eyes opened, rolling in his head. "A spy? No...no spy. I found him...at the airport."

"For what purpose, Salih?" He paused, then leaned closed and shouted, "Why?"

Salih drooped, gave no response. Forst had his doubts whether the terrorist would be able to carry out the function for which Cincher had engaged him. The operation was mere days away.

Still, if he was the only one who had the key...

Rising, Forst grasped Salih and pulled him from the chair, grunting as he took the man's weight and half dragged, half carried him back to bed. Settling into the pillow, Salih's eyes closed and his breath fell into the even rhythm of sleep, but Forst took perverse pleasure from squeezing his shoulder until the man groaned and tried to shrug free, his forehead rumpling with the pain.

Forst maintained the pressure, even increasing it, making sure he had the invalid's attention.

"One thing, Salih," he said. "One thing I have to know right here, right now."

He leaned close, bringing his lips just inches from Salih's ear. "Do you have the key?"

The man's eyes sagged shut again, but Forst pressed his thumb, digging into the tender flesh around the scapula. "Do you have it?"

Salih's eyes flew open and he cringed under Forst's fingers. "I...have...the key," he gasped.

Forst released his grip and the man flopped against the pillow, his face as pale as the sheet.

"Good," Forst said and sat back to eat his soup.

29

LIESL HURRIED ALONG THE bridle path, straining her eyes in the twilight, stumbling a little on the uneven surface. Her heart felt heavy in her chest as she looked around, making sure she was alone, dreading what she had to do.

A breeze, stiffening in the cool of evening, brushed the back of her neck, bringing out a prickle of goosebumps down both arms. The stable lay in a pool of shadow below her and Liesl heard a gentle neigh from one of the horses. She thought it was the dapple gray she'd patted yesterday on her visit to the stalls.

During the long dinner, she'd struggled to appear normal and cheerful, to smile and pass the peas, all the while planning the casual excuse she would make after dessert, how she'd escape to a quiet place and make this wretched phone call.

She didn't want to tell Dieter what she'd done, how she'd snooped in Anton Forst's wallet, how close she'd come to getting caught.

And what she'd found.

Part of her wished she'd never done it, that her suspicions about Anton weren't gaining weight like a fat man on a binge. The other part of her was screaming to do something—to pull her head out of the sand and fight to keep her family safe.

She couldn't go to Julia with this little bit of knowledge. By itself, a driver's license with an alternate name didn't mean much and confronted with it, Anton would undoubtedly explain it away with ease. She knew her sister—she needed stronger proof before Julia would pay her any attention.

Meanwhile, she felt compelled to move in secrecy rather than declaring open war. That's what had drawn her out to the stables, with no one but the horses to hear the call. She gripped the phone and dialed.

"Dieter, do you have a moment?"

She told him about the picture ID she'd found in Forst's wallet, bearing the name Moritz Schiller.

"I'm sending you the photos I took. Please find out everything you can about this man my sister is with."

"Of course, I will." Dieter hesitated. "Liesl, I don't quite know how to ask this, but I think it would help me if I knew more about Julia and her...vulnerabilities."

Liesl swallowed and rubbed a hand across her forehead. "Yes, I realize that—"

She broke off, taking a moment to organize her thoughts, to let the unpleasant memories rise to the surface.

"Julia was brilliant in school, and so popular. Mama and Papa—all of us—expected her to end up as Chancellor. Or Bürgermeister, at the very least. But after she went off to university...she changed."

"How so?"

"Julia and I had always been close, as sisters, but she stopped returning my calls, stopped coming home for weekends. And then, the year before she was due to graduate, she did come home for the holidays. And she brought her boyfriend."

Liesl shivered, remembering Florian. Leonardo DiCaprio handsome, except for his eyes which were shuttered and secret and made her feel as if they'd suck the very soul out of her if she looked directly into them. He seemed to have some kind of hold over Julia, too, and it had taken Liesl most of the Christmas vacation to work out that it was drugs.

"By then," she told Dieter, "Julia was an addict and Florian, her supplier. She never graduated from university. Instead, she disappeared and we heard nothing from her for more than three years. We have no idea where she was during that time or what she got up to. She's never spoken about it."

"When did she come back?"

"About three months ago, she showed up here at the Sammelplatz, clean and sober and asking for our help to stay that way. Of course, we took her in."

"But you, yourself, had only been at the Sammelplatz for a short while, correct?"

"*Genau*. About six weeks. I was just starting to feel comfortable in my work when she arrived. It was...an adjustment." Liesl felt a stab of frustration. "I really thought Julia was doing well, but now I fear it might be like that Christmas vacation all over again. Please Dieter, help me find out what Anton Forst is up to."

A moment of silence passed while Liesl listened to the whispering branches in the tall pines above her head. A noise like a brittle snap came from the forest to her left and she shifted her gaze, squinting into the darkness. She thought she saw movement, a darker shadow beneath the trees, but nothing more happened as she watched.

"Men like Forst," Dieter was saying, reclaiming her attention, "they smell vulnerability. They're hunters, and they're drawn to victims—people who have been used before. Easy prey."

"That's what I'm afraid of," Liesl said, trying to keep the quaver out of her voice. "I'm sure he's planning to use Julia somehow. Help me find out how, Dieter. Help me stop him."

"I'm on it, Liesl. Try and get some rest."

"I will. Thanks, and *Gute Nacht.*"

Liesl ended the call and hurried up the hill to the Sammelplatz, shivering outright now and glancing behind her every few seconds, afraid someone—Anton Forst?—might step into the rising moonlight and follow. Outside the door to the lobby, she stopped and peered along the path she had taken, lit now by a faint, silvery glow.

She saw no one.

30

BUTTERFLIES STIRRED THE CONTENTS of Riley's stomach as she settled at a table near the window and stared out at the early sun painting stripes on the dark green of the pines and the pale trunks of birch trees swaying gently in the morning air.

She opened her notebook and clicked a ballpoint pen, anxious for something to do with her hands. Her training was about to officially begin, and her nervous excitement almost overrode her grief. The raw, sharp pain of it still echoed in her chest and she welcomed the chance to forget it momentarily, knowing Rick would approve that intention.

A large man with curly brown hair pulled out the chair beside her, making it screech across the tile floor. Riley cringed at the noise and mustered a smile for her classmate. He blew on a steaming cup of coffee, sending out a cloud of fragrant vapor as he returned her smile.

"Here we are," he said, "Spycraft 101. Are you as green as I am?"

"Several shades greener, I suspect," Riley told him. "Only a few months ago I never would have dreamed of doing anything like this."

"Really? I've been dreaming about it for years."

"What's your background? Military? Police force?"

"Army MP. Yours?"

"I'm a musician."

He laughed and took a sip of his coffee. Riley watched the realization dawn on him, amused by the startled look on his face.

"Oh, you weren't joking," he sputtered.

"No, I wasn't."

"Okay...interesting." He paused. "My wife plays the guitar. She even used to tour with a band but I can't imagine..." He trailed off, a thoughtful look crossing his features. "Ah, maybe."

"It's a different skill set," Riley agreed, "but I hope I can be useful."

She glanced around at the other tables. Only four more students were in attendance as the instructor entered and greeted the class with a chipper English accent. He was tall, with ginger hair and a slight paunch hanging an inch or two over the belt line, and wore a pair of wire-rimmed glasses.

"Good morning, recruits," he said, plunking a thick sheaf of files onto the lectern and stepping away to beam at his students. He strolled slowly among the tables, peering closely at each trainee, and Riley thought he spent an extra bit of time inspecting her. She wondered what conclusions he'd drawn.

"I'm Professor Simon Martel," he continued, "and I am pleased to be giving your orientation today, starting you down the exciting and challenging track ahead. You will also be seeing me in your history and cryptology courses since those are my specialties."

Riley made a note of his name and the subjects he taught.

"You may, of course, take notes if it helps you to learn the material," Martel continued, "but you won't be allowed to take those notes off the premises and you'll be instructed to destroy them before you leave the academy. Sorry," he said, with an apologetic look at Riley. "The nature of the beast."

Riley decided to be more selective about the notes she took. She put the pen down and focused on the professor.

"Let me point out another ground rule," he said. "Here, on the property, we use our real names and identities, except in the case of training exercises where your alias is required. You must get used to switching personas. Any time you leave the boundaries of the academy during your training—for whatever reason—you will maintain your alternate identity, including all the backstory details, which I suggest you memorize backwards and forwards. Any questions?"

No one spoke up, so Martel went on. "Most of you will have arrived here via the Nuremberg airport, so you've seen at least the outskirts of the city. At various points in your training, you will go out on field trips to certain points of interest in the region—Flossenburg concentration camp, the Grafenwöhr military base, and the city of Nuremberg, to name a few.

"No other city in Germany is more intertwined with the Nazi legacy than Nuremberg. At the Nazi Rally Grounds, you can stand in the exact spot where Hitler whipped the crowds into a frenzy with his propaganda. It is a sobering experience and a reminder of our mission here at Olivero—to preserve freedoms, justice, and human dignity. It's the reason Director Wright chose to build a training center in this location."

Riley's throat swelled and she swallowed hard. Outside the window, a group of recruits in gym shorts jogged past on their way to the fitness course, led by a well-muscled blond man. It should have been Rick. She was still struggling so hard with the idea that he was gone.

"The name Olivero," Martel said, "is derived from the words "olive" and "arrow," and pertains to the Great Seal of the United States, which depicts an eagle with thirteen arrows in one talon and an olive branch bearing thirteen olives, in the other.

"The olive branch signifies peace. The arrows, war. We pursue our objectives through peaceful means, whenever possible. And when countries resort to war, we operate within that framework toward our same stated objectives, with an eye toward restoring peace."

A woman at the table opposite Riley raised her hand, catching Martel's attention.

"Yes?" he prompted.

"You're British," she said. "I'm from Argentina, and I've met others here from around the world. If Olivero is an international firm, why use the seal of the United States to inspire its name and mission?"

Martel nodded. "Fair question, and the easy answer is that Devin Wright, Olivero's founder and CEO is an American, drawing on what he knows and believes in. But I think there's a deeper answer, too. Let me see if I can put it into words."

Martel walked to the front of the room and hoisted himself to sit on the corner of a large wooden desk. He let his head hang down for a moment, then lifted his face to the room.

"I think we can all agree America's had its problems and downfalls through the decades of its existence. It's not a perfect nation by any means, but Director Wright believes that—at its best—it was the closest thing to a perfect union the earth has known."

He took off his glasses and began polishing them with his shirt. "You may have heard the story about Benjamin Franklin as he walked out of Independence Hall after the Constitutional Convention of 1787. A woman shouted out, 'What have we got, Doctor? A republic or a monarchy?' and his reply—'A republic, if you can keep it, madam.'"

Martel tugged at his shirt front, freeing a larger piece with which to polish his lenses. "America's founding fathers created the closest thing to a perfect governing instrument they could fashion, but they knew it would erode with time, that its precepts would have to be protected and the cost might be high.

"Olivero's mission statement is modeled after that constitution because Wright believes its values surpass all borders and embrace all mankind. It's a worthy standard to aim for."

He replaced his glasses and peered down at the Argentinian woman. "Does that answer your question?"

"I think so. Put another way—we're all in this together, reaching for ideals that, if properly implemented, would benefit all nations."

"*Genau*, as they say here in Deutschland. Which is another element of the Great Seal—e pluribus unum. Out of many, one. Unity is an important part of our mission at Olivero."

He rose from his perch on the desk and brushed his hands down the front of his trousers. "Thus ends our history lesson for today, and now if you'll head down the hallway to Chief Bateman, she'll give you a fascinating lecture on secret operations and send you off to complete your first practical exercise. The dead drop."

The class members stood and moved toward the door but Professor Martel said, "Ms. Forte, would you mind staying for a moment? I'd like a word."

Her table mate raised his eyebrows. "First day of class and you're already in trouble," he teased in a whisper. "Good going, Ms. Forte."

Holding her notebook to her chest with crossed arms, Riley stood, waiting.

"I'm sorry for your loss," Martel said, his forehead creased and shiny beneath his thinning ginger hair. "I knew Rick well and liked him a lot."

"Thank you, sir."

He tilted his head. "He spoke about you, you know. He told me how you helped close in on that Seattle serial killer, how good you are with identifying and interpreting patterns—in music, in behavior, in history."

Riley felt her cheeks go warm. "It's something I've been doing all my life."

"Marvelous. I think you'll do very well in my cryptology class. Very well indeed. I look forward to working with you."

Riley didn't know what to say. "Thank you, sir," she replied again.

"Off you go, then. You'll enjoy the dead drop."

Maybe.

If she didn't drop dead.

31

—·—

CLUTCHING A CLIPBOARD TO his chest, Vadim hurried across the quad and out to the exercise field where Dr. Anderson stood waiting. Beads of dew from the grass moistened his socks and the cuffs of his trousers but the rising sun of a fine spring day would soon dry them out.

Vadim let his gaze travel beyond the razor wire to the line of forest with its sprinkling of wildflowers, purple lupine, creamy Edelweiss, and small golden blooms he couldn't put a name to. As he had many times before, he reflected dismally on the contrast between the serene and lovely surroundings outside the fence and what went on within its confines.

He dreaded to think what today's activities might hold.

As he neared the edge of the field, Anderson beckoned to him impatiently. "The vans will arrive at any moment, Novak," he called. "I want to catch you up to speed."

Reaching Anderson's side, Vadim stopped and stood rigid, waiting to receive his instructions.

"You may relax somewhat," Anderson said, giving him a smile. "The weather is pleasant, and today we will have fun. In a moment,

144

a batch of prospective test subjects will be arriving. Raptor will take them through some exercises and let them play."

Anderson gestured to the field beyond and Vadim saw it had been set up for various activities—a bean bag toss, horseshoes, a volleyball net, a soccer ball and a set of goals.

"You will observe their interactions and make notes about what you see. After lunch, you will administer a questionnaire to the subjects which will determine their eligibility for our program."

Vadim waited, but Anderson said nothing more.

"That's it?" Vadim asked.

Anderson spread his hands, palms up. "That's it. So you see, it will be an easy day for you."

The distant rumble of a motor caught Vadim's attention and he turned toward the compound's entrance to watch two dark blue vans roll through the gate and start along the perimeter road flanking the field. They drew up and stopped where Raptor stood to meet them.

Eight men from each van climbed out and stood in a line while Raptor checked them against a list. He spoke to them, and though Vadim was too far away to hear the words, the meaning was clear as he gestured toward the field, smiled, and patted several of the men on the back. The group trotted off and began tossing balls and bean bags, laughing and shouting as they competed. After checking through a folder of paperwork on a nearby table, Raptor ran to join them.

Vadim sat in a small stand of bleachers beside the field. He watched the men—presumably strangers when they'd boarded the vans at the start of the day—loosen up and fall into a sort of camaraderie, as men will when given a nice day and a ball to kick around.

He made his notes, feeling increasingly uneasy as he remembered Anderson's obsession with learning how subjects were able to inflict pain on those they viewed as friends. He feared today's activities were meant to lay the groundwork for such a set of experiments.

As horrified as he was by the notion, he didn't dare speak out against it. Last week, a fellow doctor, Martin Branislav, had protested against one of Anderson's procedures. In the dawning light of the following morning, Vadim had watched two orderlies carry a sheet-covered stretcher to the heavily wooded rear of the property and Branislav was never seen or mentioned again.

The men ran and kicked and tossed for the better part of three hours before Raptor blew a whistle and ordered the group to wash up before lunch. Grinning and bantering, the men shuffled into the cafeteria and piled their plates with meat and vegetables. Filling both sides of a long table in the center of the dining room, they broke bread together, Raptor among them, sharing their goodwill.

Vadim continued to observe and make notes, consciously registering that a shared meal was a ritual sign of friendship. He suspected this lunch figured into the parameters of today's test, though Anderson had assured him they were simply having fun while screening potential subjects for future testing.

As these dark thoughts churned in Vadim's mind, Anderson came by his table to hand off a stack of questionnaires for the afternoon. He glanced over the pages, noting the strangeness of many of the questions.

"What would you do if you found a dead body in a hotel room?"

"Forced to choose, would you rather be alive and alone or die with a group of friends?"

"If a convicted criminal about to be executed in an electric chair has a heart attack, should he be saved?"

"Have you ever felt strongly inclined to jump off a cliff or other highly elevated spot?"

Though he saw how answering such questions might provide some insight into a patient's personality and thought processes, Vadim suspected Anderson derived a sadistic sort of pleasure from messing with the minds of his subjects, making them sweat over their answers.

When the men had finished eating, Raptor herded them back across the field to a small brick outbuilding Vadim had never been in before. He saw it consisted of a single room, bright with sunlight spilling in through a row of windows along the front of the structure. Four round tables, each with four chairs, provided space for the men while Raptor paced among them, squeezing shoulders and patting backs.

Vadim passed out the questionnaires and distributed pencils, explaining that the questions should be answered as honestly as possible. What he really wanted to tell them was to run, to get away from this place while they could. The words bubbled several times to the tip of his tongue, but he swallowed them down where they pitched and roiled in his stomach.

Pencils scratched on paper as the men wrote out their names at the top of the page and began answering questions. The door opened and Anderson poked his head in. He gazed around at the subjects, approval on his face, and gestured to Vadim to join him outside.

"What do you think?" he asked. "Are they a good group? What did you observe about their interactions—with each other and especially with Raptor?"

Vadim hesitated. To him it had seemed the men liked Raptor and felt at ease with him. Maybe even counted him a friend in the making. He didn't want to admit this to Anderson, but the man had seen for himself. He knew.

Before he could reply, movement caught his eye and he turned to watch Raptor leave the little building and shut the heavy steel door behind him. Taking a key from his pocket, he locked the door and glanced at Dr. Anderson who nodded back. Opening a metal panel on the side of the building, Raptor activated a switch. Vadim's heart lurched inside his ribcage as a horrible feeling of unreality settled over him.

Anderson joined Raptor where he stood looking in at the windows. Vadim held back, but even from his slightly removed stance, he could see men swinging chairs at the unbreakable glass, hear the thuds as they bounced ineffectively away.

He could see the agonized faces, the scrabbling hands, the bodies writhing as Anderson and Raptor watched with interest.

With a cry of despair, Vadim turned and vomited into the grass.

32

"Over here, Dad—I hit the jackpot!"

Nate clambered over a log, half-rotted and covered with slimy moss. The air smelled rich with damp earth, things growing, coming to life in the warmth of spring.

He grinned at his daughter, giving her a thumbs up as he made his way to her side.

"Good work, Sammi," he said, surveying the pile of deadfall branches that would fuel their campfire. "Let's grab a bunch of this and get back to camp. Your mom's waiting to stoke the fire and cook up some hobo stew."

"And hot chocolate?"

"Could be. Did you pack the hot chocolate?"

"That was your job, Dad." She stopped gathering sticks and glared at him with an exasperated expression so much like his ex-wife's it wrenched his heart. "Don't tell me you forgot," she scolded.

"Okay, I won't tell you."

She stared accusingly. "Daddy, *did* you forget the hot chocolate?"

"Come on, Pumpkin—I'm only teasing you. Don't drop your load of firewood." He stooped to help her. "There'll be plenty of hot chocolate."

She tried to maintain her stern gaze on him, but it melted into a delighted smile. "Good, because it's gonna be chilly tonight. Chill—ee."

Laden with armfuls of broken branches, they made their way back to camp.

"Just in time," Marilyn called when she caught sight of them. "The foil packets are ready. Now we just need some nice embers to tuck around them."

"Your wish is my command," Nate said, adding a few chunks he'd taken from the fallen log to the fire, feeding it with smaller tinder.

As he worked, he tried to keep his mind there, in the moment, spending time and making memories with Sammi and Marilyn, to hide the ache dragging at him like a heavy weight. Rick had been one of his closest friends. In the short time they'd known each other, they'd become almost like brothers. He just couldn't believe they'd never go hiking, sailing, or simply shoot the breeze ever again.

Gone. In an instant.

And what about Riley? Not only had she also lost a good friend, but she was now suddenly alone in a foreign country in a completely new and stressful situation. She'd been counting on Rick to be there for her to lean on. This had to be taking a terrific toll on her.

He took a step back from the fire and gave a mighty roar, grabbing Sammi and swinging her around until she was laughing hysterically. He put her down and hugged her close, pulling Marilyn into their embrace. The three of them snuggled together, Sammi still giggling.

If he could freeze this moment and stay inside it forever—would he? He loved them both so much. Sammi owned his heart entirely and Marilyn.... He knew it had been difficult for her, being married to a policeman. It's a tough life, and when he'd made detective and started working grisly homicides, it had affected both of them in ways that stressed the relationship beyond bearing.

Could they repair it? Nate thought they both wanted to, but would that be enough?

And, in his most honest moments with himself, he wasn't sure he could quell the feelings he had for Riley. Part of him thought it would be a travesty to do so. She was a beautiful person, with a need to be loved and so much to give.

Why did life have to be so achingly complicated?

"I think there's time for a few ghost stories around the fire before dinner's ready," he said, letting go of his two camping companions and dropping into a canvas chair. The sky was darkening overhead, the pine boughs and bare branches of early spring rustling in a faint, whistling wind. The perfect backdrop for the kind of scary tales he knew Sammi adored.

He told the story of "Duffy's Jacket," one of her favorites, and followed it up with one from his own boyhood about "The Viper." Sammi loved screaming at the appointed moments and when Marilyn handed her a Styrofoam cup of hot chocolate, the look on her face said she was in camping heaven.

A mouthwatering aroma rose from the fire and Nate realized the pangs in his gut were at least partially due to hunger. With a stick, he raked the foil packets of hobo stew from the coals and Sammi said grace while they waited for the packets to cool enough to handle.

The stew made a fun and hardy meal, roasted almost to perfection, with only a few bits of potato that hadn't cooked all the way through. By the time they'd eaten and cleaned up, Sammi was nodding and Nate tucked her into her pink princess sleeping bag, kissing the top of her slightly grubby head.

"G'night, ladybug."

"G'night, Dad."

She rolled over and snuggled deeper into her pink cocoon. "Thanks for the hot chocolate. I knew you wouldn't forget."

Nate zipped the tent shut and joined Marilyn fireside. They held hands and stared into the mesmerizing flames. Nate wondered what she was thinking, wondered if he dared ask or it that would open a door he wasn't ready to go through.

He thought about how much they used to love singing together, but he didn't feel like singing a rousing campfire song. Instead, he found himself voicing lines from Cohen's Hallelujah, closing his eyes and feeling the mournful melody resonating in his soul, bringing him close to tears.

Marilyn cupped a fire-warmed hand under his chin and lifted his head, covering his lips with her own. The kiss was long and gentle, not rising to the level of passion but not canceling out the promise of it either. After, they huddled together, watching the fire die down.

Nate tried to stifle a yawn, but Marilyn said, "It's time for bed."

She looked pointedly at Nate's tent, set yards away from the one he'd put up for her and Sammi. "I could join you," she said, "tuck you in."

Nate smiled, brushing his hand down her cheek, caressing her collarbone. "It's not that the idea doesn't appeal to me, Marilyn," he said. "It's just that I'm not sure either one of us is ready for that. And we can't leave Sammi alone, unguarded."

She sighed. "You're right, of course. Blame it on the moonlight."

He pulled her close, holding her for a long time before releasing her and stepping away.

"I'll douse the fire," he said, and grabbed a pail, heading for the small brook near the camp site.

When he got back and poured the bucket of water over the embers, sending a billow of steam into the chilled air, she was gone.

Nate climbed into his tent, shivering, alone.

And miserable.

33

RILEY RUSHED DOWN THE hallway, the hushed and rhythmic sound of her soft-soled shoes swishing on the tile like a jazz drummer with a brush. The walls, striped by the morning sun streaming in through a high set of windows, were painted pale green, and a faint resinous odor suggested the paint was fairly fresh.

A small bubble of anticipation rose within her and she realized she was excited to be moments away from some real, hands-on spy training. Her little talk with Professor Martel had taken less than two minutes, but as she stepped into the classroom, things were already underway.

"Ms. Forte, over here at table two with Mr. Korolev, if you please."

Riley took her seat next to a clean-shaven blond man with blue eyes that made her think of Frank Sinatra. He gave her a curt nod before returning his attention to the woman in charge.

The instructor, a former CIA chief, was a tall middle-aged woman in a burgundy pantsuit, her dark hair pulled back in a long ponytail that hung almost to her waist. Riley noticed she wore sensible shoes, the kind a person could run in, if occasion called for it. That made her smile. On TV, women spies and cops always seemed to wear spiky high heels and Riley had always thought it a ridiculous, dangerous, and unlikely choice.

"For those of you new to the academy," the teacher announced, "your table mate will be your handler and mentor throughout this course. Pay attention and learn everything you can from them. Somewhere down the road, you will become handlers for new students coming in."

"My name is Victoria Bateman. You may call me Chief, and by the end of the week, I'll be calling you by your first names." She walked to the white board at the front of the classroom and wrote the word INFORMATION with a black marker.

"We are in the information age, people. Info is king. My job is to teach you how to pass or receive information covertly. A lot goes into running a secret operation. In later lectures we'll talk about trailing a suspect, evading a tail, and a whole lot more. Today, we'll focus on a single topic."

Underneath the word INFORMATION, she used a red marker to write DEAD. Pausing, she lifted an eyebrow and half turned, making sure she had everyone's attention before writing DROP.

"More spies are caught servicing dead drops or changing batteries in surveillance devices than by any other means," she said, facing the twelve students in the classroom. "Learn the proper techniques. Do not forget them. Do not let yourself become complacent."

She tossed the marker onto the tray where it skidded and came to rest against the eraser. "So, what exactly *is* a dead drop?"

Riley's Argentinian cohort popped a hand up and spoke. "It's a way to pass information between two people without having to actually meet in person."

"Okay, good. The dead drop itself is a container or small hiding place located in an area commonly accessible to the public. As you say, it's used to pass information—and sometimes other items—without physical contact."

The curly-haired man who'd shared her table during orientation, piped up with a question. "You pointed out that we're in the information age. Everything's digital now. Why would we even bother with using a physical dead drop?"

"Good observation. Any ideas as to why we still use the dead drop?" she threw the question out for everyone's consideration.

Riley raised and lowered her hand.

"Yes, go ahead."

"Maybe because it's *not* digital. It's disconnected from technology, so it doesn't leave a digital fingerprint or open itself to the vulnerabilities of a computer network."

"Very good, Riley. It's old school, but it has its advantages. And there may be times when you need to pass something physical—like cash or medicine—that can't be sent through digital means. Sometimes the dead drop is your best option, and the mechanics of it are very simple. Step one, sender hides the message in the agreed upon location. Step two, sender signals to indicate a message has been delivered. Step three, receiver recovers the message."

She folded her arms and scowled at the class. "Simple. But not always easy. And—as I mentioned before—potentially deadly. Let's talk about the form your information might take. Thoughts?"

Answers flew up around the room—flash drives, microdots, computer chips, postcards, newspapers with secret ciphers, coded messages written in invisible ink.

"Okay, so the possibilities are endless, right? Limited only by the imagination and creativity of the agents involved. Does anyone here" Chief asked, "know who Robert Baden-Powell was?"

Surprised, Riley said, "Wasn't he the founder of the Boy Scouts?"

"Yes, he was. And that's what he's best-known for. But he had an early military career in intelligence-gathering." She began pacing at the front of the classroom, warming to her subject.

"During one mission, he posed as an entomologist while he spied out details of enemy fortresses in the Balkans. He then incorporated his findings into his sketches. The veins on a butterfly's wing depicted the plan of fortifications, while the spots indicated the size and positions of artillery. The veins in the drawing of a leaf laid out a schematic of enemy trenches. Quite ingenious, really. The sketches are rather good."

Pausing, she pulled her ponytail forward so that it cascaded over her shoulder, thick and shiny in the morning light through the window. "As you can see, information can be concealed by a wide variety of methods. Let's turn our attention to the dead drop itself. What kinds of receptacles might work best?"

Again, the students responded with a spate of ideas—fake rock, magnetic capsule, buried box, birdhouse, metal tube, waterproof pouches.

"Clearly, you've all indulged in your share of spy novels and Hollywood movies," the Chief said, "but you might be surprised to hear about one of the most successful dead drops used by the CIA. It's not very glamorous."

Grimacing, she reached into her desk and held a large rodent up by its tail. "No one wants to touch a dead rat. No one would imagine it to hold anything of value. It can lie, unmolested, for days. Weeks, even."

Riley couldn't keep the distaste from showing on her face and the Chief nodded her way. "Exactly. So, someone had the idea to take a dead rat to the taxidermist where it was doctored up with a hidden pouch and dipped in Tabasco sauce to discourage animal predators from running off with it. Thereafter, it served a long and honorable second life as a CIA dead drop, facilitating the passage of critical information."

Laughter rippled across the room, evaporating quickly as the chief continued. "Information may come in all manner of formats, but how do you protect it once you've got it?"

No one spoke up right away so she went on. "Quick solutions include tucking into the armpit or a bra, if you come equipped with one. Sometimes pushing the message down into a shoe might suffice, or inside a pocket created by a fake layer of skin. The annals of spy history hold a few more elaborate and unusual methods, such as inside an artificial eyeball or a rectal capsule. There's even a legend about one spy using a fake scrotum."

Another bout of amusement passed through the room, but Chief Bateman's expression was solemn as she spoke her next words.

"Always have a plausible reason to be in the area," she said. "In case you're challenged. Like Baden-Powell and his butterfly sketches. And never forget to be vigilant."

Pacing the room again, she said, "Keep any communications you may receive at your dead drops secret and secure. As you learn how to decrypt different types of secret messages in Professor Martel's class, they will function as practice exercises, giving you some practical experience in deciphering."

She clasped her hands together and beamed at her students. "It's time. Huddle with your handlers, they'll brief you on your first covert op. Good luck."

34

Liesel slit the paper wrapping on the package from the printer, sliding the sharp letter opener with precision along the seam. She unfolded the paper layers to reveal the printed cards beneath, elegant lettering on cream gilt-edged card stock. Running her fingers over the slightly rough texture, she read the top card in the stack.

Wilkommen
Herr Doktor & Frau Vlasov
Hoffnung und Frieden

She wrinkled her nose. The cards gave off a faint chemical odor, but she was pleased with their appearance. Tucking the bundle of welcome cards into her basket, along with the small gift bags for each attendee at the peace summit, she grabbed her clipboard and slipped her feet back into her flat-heeled pumps.

Stepping into the outer office, she saw Joseph was busy on the phone, a frown creasing his forehead. She lifted the basket and nodded her head toward the door, letting him know where she'd be, then headed to the opposite wing where most of the guests would be quartered.

Liesl loved the spacious solitude of the Sammelplatz when it was empty, though she realized too much downtime for the place would signal its death, and the end of her pleasant tenancy. Besides, the hubbub of the facility when occupied only made these peaceful moments all the sweeter.

Consulting her clipboard, she delivered the welcome cards and gift bags to each of the rooms in the wing, pausing to check that all looked in order. As she left the final room and started back toward her office, a figure rounded the corner, coming toward her.

It was Anton Forst.

A chill ran through her as she realized no one else was near. She was alone with a man she was becoming increasingly frightened of and who had no business wandering these halls. His face, as he approached, held a slightly amused expression.

"Surprised to see me, Liesl?"

"Frankly, I am. What are you doing here?"

"I came to pick up Julia. We have a date."

"You're in the wrong part of the building, as I'm sure you're aware."

He blocked the corridor and Liesl came to a stop three feet from the man, determined not to show her growing apprehension.

"Why don't you like me, Liesl?" he asked. "I so hoped we'd get along well."

"Don't we? I think we do."

He gave a wry chuckle, shaking his head and moving a step closer. "Your opinion is important to me. Really, it is."

Grasping her forearm, he said, "I want to show you something."

He began pulling her down the corridor, away from the heart of the Sammelplatz and the other occupants of the building. Liesl suddenly found it hard to breathe as she fought down a burst of alarm.

"Let me go, Forst. I'm working. I have things to do."

"This won't take but a moment. I promise."

They reached the vestibule leading to the parking lot and Forst marched her through the set of double doors. Liesl debated frantically whether to keep her cool or start screaming, and as he pulled her toward his SUV, parked at the edge of the lot, she pulled in a lungful of air, ready to screech her loudest.

"Okay," he said, letting go. The air went out of her in a startled breath. "Tell me what you think about this."

Reaching into the glove compartment of the SUV, he extracted a blue velvet box and opened it to reveal a string of small pearls with a delicate gold filigreed clasp.

"Will Julia like it, do you think? Too much? Too soon? You're a woman, Liesl, and she's your sister. Tell me if this is a good idea."

Liesl's legs felt rubbery, as if they would buckle beneath her if she didn't sit down soon. She stared at the pearls, at his anxious face, and felt dizzy. Had she built up a boogeyman where none existed? Did her persecution of Forst's character stem from some inner jealousy or resentment?

Was she crazy?

"I think it's beautiful," she told him. "Julia is sure to love it. But I would suggest waiting for a significant event to give her such a gift. Her birthday, for example."

"October? Really?"

"Really. That's my advice. Now I absolutely do have to get back to work."

She walked toward the entrance, trying not to stumble, feeling his eyes on her back. Working to control her breathing, to smooth it out and slow it down, she struggled to get a grip. She would stop worrying about Forst for the moment and wait until she heard back from Dieter with more information.

Then she'd worry.

35

RILEY'S HANDLER REGARDED HER doubtfully, his smooth face giving him the look of a twenty-year old, but fine lines around his eyes suggested he might be closer to forty.

"You're a pianist?" he asked.

Riley tried not to bristle at his dismissive tone. "Yes," she told him, "but I have enough brain cells to qualify me for a few additional pursuits."

The wrinkles around his eyes deepened and his lips twisted, lifting at the corners into an appraising smile.

"So I see. Good."

He held out his hand and she shook it, making her grip firm.

"Okay, let's get right to work," he said. I am Ilya Korolev, and this," he spread a large, creased piece of paper on the table in front of them, "is a map of Weiden. That's where our dead drop is located."

His English was good, with only the trace of a Russian accent. His expression was very serious as he showed her several photographs of the site, a path running alongside a narrow canal in a park-like setting. She saw a bench below a tree with a unique, twisted arrangement of branches, and next to it, a variety of shrub Riley had come to know as *Hagebutte* in Germany, rose hip in America.

Ilya pointed to one of the photos. "Here's a closeup of the dead drop container itself. It's a metal tube with a screw top I buried under that bush in the middle of the night. The top sticks out above the ground. You can almost reach it while sitting on the bench. Just wait until no one's in sight and then screw the top off, deposit your info and pick up anything left there for you."

Riley studied the photos, suddenly feeling less confident about her ability to do this.

"Take a book or a sketchpad as your excuse for being there. When the coast is clear, leave me something. It doesn't matter what it is—that's not the point of the exercise. It's the procedure you need to practice."

He suddenly gave her a smoldering look, a spark of humor in his Sinatra eyes. "Write me a love letter," he suggested, smiling.

Riley smiled back, feeling a little more encouraged.

"The drop is here," Ilya continued, circling a spot on the map with a pencil. "Of course, if this wasn't your first rookie exercise, you'd have to memorize and destroy the map and photos. But this time, you get to keep them. Look them over. Any questions?"

"Yes. What's our signal for message delivered?"

"Ah, an important point. But we've got something even more vital to discuss."

"What's that?"

"Our duress signal in case things go wrong. For example, if you get caught and they try to use you to get to me."

"Or vice versa."

"Or vice versa," he agreed. "Look here." He used the pencil to make a check mark on the map. "This post," he indicated a telephone pole in the photos, "is near the start of the path. Make a chalk mark like this one if you've left something for me and all is well."

He reversed the mark on the paper, drawing it like a left-handed person might. "This is our duress signal. Make this backwards mark if you need to warn me off. And if you're on your way to the dead drop and see this mark from me, just keep walking. Stay casual. Someone will be watching you."

A chill ran over Riley. Was she really going to do this with her life? It wasn't a game, but a deadly serious business with very high stakes.

It was a question she'd wrestled with many times before. In the end, she always felt like it was the right course for the remains of her life, so altered from what she'd always imagined it would be.

"Okay," she said. "How do I get to Weiden?"

"Borrow something from the motor pool," Ilya told her. "And don't use GPS—your movements can be tracked. Go old school, stick to the map, and don't get lost."

Riley was just old enough to remember navigating before the age of global positioning, watching her parents do it on road trips and helping when they let her.

"Find the dead drop," Ilya said, "and leave me something. Go for a coffee. Come back after an hour and see what I left for you." He grinned, then his face quickly sobered. "But don't forget the check marks."

"I won't, Ilya. Thank you."

He pressed a stick of chalk into her hand. "Good luck, Recruit."

At the motor pool, Riley was given a slightly battered Volkswagen with a faded blue paint job. Before she started the engine, she took a moment to familiarize herself with the map and decide on a route. She scrawled a note for Ilya on a page from her notebook:

Roses are red
Violets are not
Thanks for teaching me
How not to get caught

As she entered the city of Weiden and traffic thickened around her, she started to feel claustrophobic, longing to be out on the open road again. She'd given herself landmarks to watch for and felt relieved to recognize a couple of them. She was on the right track.

The road wound past the marketplace and pedestrian zone, crossing over the canal Ilya had shown her on the map. Riley looked for a parking place and was fortunate to find one in front of an Indian restaurant, right on the street where she could jump in the car and head out fast, without the fuss and constrictions of a parking garage.

Her hands holding the notebook to her chest were shaking, but she made herself stroll casually along the path beside the *Flutkanal*. She passed the telephone pole, noting a few nails pounded into its scarred surface, but no chalk marks. Ahead, she identified the bench she'd seen in the photos, set apart by the distinctive tree branches above and *Hagebutte* bush beside it.

It was occupied by a young mother with a baby carriage. Riley passed, glancing at the sleeping baby and giving the woman a slight smile. She sank onto the next bench and let her head drop back, face up to the sun, willing her neck and shoulder muscles to relax.

After a moment, she opened her notebook, turned to a fresh page and began sketching the interesting tree and the flowing water of the canal beside it. Ten minutes passed as the mother drank from a paper cup of coffee and the baby began to cry. After they moved on, Riley took their place on the bench and continued her sketching, hoping no one would ever have reason to see her artwork.

Riley tried to appear casual as she glanced under the shrub and caught sight of the dead drop's lid protruding slightly above the ground, about three inches in diameter. When the path was deserted, Riley quickly crouched and unscrewed it, reaching inside.

Her fingers met paper and she pulled forth a folded index card. Without opening it, she thrust it down the front of her shirt, securing it in her bra, and replaced it with the poem she'd written for Ilya. Glancing around to make sure she was still alone, she screwed the cap back onto the metal tube, her fingers shaking so badly that she had to try three times before she lined up the threads correctly.

Realizing she'd been holding her breath, she let it out, and tried to quell her trembling. An elderly couple walking a Scottish Terrier had entered the path on the opposite side of the canal, and twenty yards behind them, a man in a gray coat, a black beanie pulled low over his forehead. The couple smiled at her as she passed. The man ignored her.

Before reaching the main street, Riley took the chalk from her pocket and quickly made a check mark on the post, as instructed. She turned left and entered under an archway into the pedestrian zone.

Finding a bakery with tables and chairs on the sidewalk, she bought a slice of *Apfelstrudel* and sat at a tiny round table and nibbled while she watched shoppers moving among the storefronts. She waited for her heartbeat to return to normal, assuring herself she'd done well, it was all right.

After finishing her pastry, she spent another half hour wandering the square, taking pictures of the lovely flowerbeds, the church, the statues. When she gauged enough time had passed, she turned her steps back toward the canal and entered the path.

She'd taken only a dozen steps when she was able to discern a chalk mark on the telephone pole, next to the one she herself had made.

A backward check mark.

Her stomach flipped, threatening to jettison the apple strudel, and her knees turned to water. Trying not to falter or stumble, she maintained her pace and walked past the dead drop, all the while keeping her eyes turned toward the gurgling water in the canal as if fascinated by its passage.

She found a back entrance into the pedestrian zone, stopped to buy some postcards, and continued to circle around to where her car was parked. She'd studiously avoided looking behind her, not wanting to appear worried about it. But now, as she passed under the archway onto the main road, she glanced back and felt her veins go icy.

Not ten yards behind her was the man in the gray coat and black beanie.

36

Full-blown panic hit Riley like a hammer across the skull. She didn't stop to think—couldn't think—just instinctively shifted into flight mode and sprinted the few remaining yards to the blue Volkswagen, digging the fob from her pocket as she ran.

Cranking the key, she ground frantically at the ignition until the engine fired. In her side mirror, she watched the man in the beanie signal to an oncoming car, a black BMW. He ran across the street to meet it and as he jumped inside, she pulled out into traffic and sped away from the city center with no idea where she was headed.

Her tires squealed as she veered through a roundabout. The black BMW would have had to find a spot to turn around on the narrow, crowded street, buying her maybe thirty seconds, at best. She tried to steady her breathing and suddenly, without warning, burst out laughing.

This was only an exercise!

She was hightailing it out of town for no good reason and, in fact, she must have imagined the man in the beanie was following her. She didn't see him now.

What a fool she was! She'd gotten so caught up in the theoretical challenges of the operation that she'd lost sight of reality.

But what if this was part of the exercise? A test?

She checked the rearview mirror again and saw the black BMW pulling ahead and passing, about four cars behind. Despite her reasoned lecture to herself, a sizzle of adrenaline shot through her and she pressed down again on the accelerator.

The late afternoon sun was sinking behind a blanket of clouds, creating a somber backdrop to the countryside as Riley left the city behind. Now that she needed woodland, cornfields, some kind of cover, there were only empty, rolling pastures with an open vista for miles ahead. There were still two cars between her and the black BMW, kept there by virtue of the narrow two-lane road and a stream of traffic passing in the opposite direction.

Off to the left ahead, she saw a town on a hill. Lacking a forest in which to hide, maybe the twisting streets of a town would give her an opportunity to lose her tail. She made the left turn and put on speed, feeling another jolt of alarm as the BMW turned and followed.

She entered the town about a hundred yards ahead of her pursuers and took random turns until she was certain she was out of sight. She crested the hill and saw forest at the far side of the scattered houses. Rushing down to it, she turned off onto a dirt trail probably reserved for tractors, her heart pounding like a manic church bell.

She drove about a quarter mile then doused the lights and took a moment to catch her breath while she thought about what to do next. Exercise or not, her next action came to her clearly enough. Popping the car's cigarette lighter, she rolled the map into a cone and lit it. Climbing out of the car, she carried the photos Ilya had given her and found a flat rock, laying them out and burning each until it was unrecognizable.

By that time the map was nothing but a stub of char with only a lick of flame left. She fished in her bra and brought out the folded card she'd retrieved from the dead drop.

"Stop!"

Riley froze, blinded by the sudden glare of a powerful flashlight. She tucked the card into the back pocket of her jeans and raised her arms.

"Enough, Riley," came a voice from the darkness. "You did great." A pause. "For a pianist."

It was Ilya. Another man stepped up beside him, no longer wearing the beanie, his bald head shiny in the light of the torch.

"Hell's bells woman," he said, betraying a bit of Irish lilt. "You gave us a good chase. And destroyed every bit of actionable intelligence, as well," he said, gesturing to the remains of the burnt photographs.

"Extra points for that, Riley," Ilya said. "I'll make a note of it in my report." He grinned, giving her a thumbs up. "If we leave now, we'll make it back in time for dinner—you've earned it. Do you know the way?"

Riley shook her head. "I haven't a clue."

"Follow us, then. We know a short cut."

37

FORST UNLOCKED THE HEAVY door to the basement. He pushed it inward and winced at the loud, drawn-out creak it made, not wanting to wake the fugitive sleeping down the hall. Taz Salih was gaining strength, staying lucid for longer periods, and had even come to the table for lunch, though he'd tired quickly and said little. Forst's expectations for the job ahead began to look up.

Peering down into the basement stairwell, he wrinkled his nose. It was dark and smelled of mildew, a throwback to the days when anyone descending the staircase would carry a lantern or candle. The basement itself had electricity but inexplicably, the stairwell had been neglected in the modern rewiring. Forst had offered the housing inspector a sizeable bribe to overlook *der Keller*.

The real reason he hadn't wanted the man to descend into the basement had more to do with the machines and equipment he kept there than with the lack of proper lighting. The basement featured three rooms branching off from a central area. One of the rooms housed a photographic studio, complete with lights, reflectors, backdrops, and racks of clothing and accessories in a variety of sizes.

Another room held a series of drawing tables with bright lamps attached. Each of these had works in progress clipped to them. This was where Forst crafted documents with meticulous care, turning out products virtually indistinguishable from their authentic counterparts.

The third room was filled with machines. Photocopiers and scanners, alongside a four-color printing press. An embossing machine sat next to one of his favorite toys, his newest acquisition. It was a seventy-two character printing machine for use with plastic card stock and EMV chips supplied by a contact in Switzerland. A credit card creator.

The basement's central area had a long counter set up with computer workstations, a small bank of file cabinets, and several heavy-duty shredders plugged in and ready to go at a moment's notice. A ceramic-glazed *Kachelofen* flanked by a metal basket filled with split logs took up a corner of the space.

As Forst worked, he couldn't keep his mind from thoughts of Liesl, remembering her growing dismay as he'd gripped her arm and pulled her out of the Sammelplatz toward his car, her eyes growing wider, filling with terror. He shouldn't have teased her like that, but *bei Himmel* she was fun to toy with.

When Cincher had ordered him to find a way inside the workings of the Sammelplatz, he'd planned to seduce one of the sisters. By chance, he'd met Julia first and she'd made it so easy, practically offering herself up on a platter. It seemed the perfect opportunity, and he'd taken it.

Now, he wished he'd waited and made Liesl his target instead. She was such a pretty thing, with a sweetness and innocence more enticing to him than Julia's brash, sensual nature. The seduction was all part of the job, but there was no reason he shouldn't enjoy it along the way.

Forst moved to the counter beneath a grimy basement window and interrupted the screensaver on his laptop. He entered the password, still thinking about the sisters at the Sammelplatz while he waited for his email inbox to flash up on the screen.

Weeding out the unimportant items, he worked his way down the unopened mail, responding where necessary. A subject line caught his eye.

For your consideration.

No information about the sender.

He hesitated, hand hovering over the delete command, then clicked to open the email. No greeting. No words of any kind. The email held only pictures, three of them, and they made the skin on the back of his neck prickle.

Reflexively, he spun around, making sure he was alone in the room. Taz Salih, still groggy and mostly incoherent, continued to spend most hours of the day in bed, though he sometimes walked slowly up and down on the patio when the sun shone warm on the flagstones. Forst had fed him broth and fried potatoes for lunch, leaving him to drowse on the pillow as daylight dwindled.

Assuring himself no one lurked in the basement shadows, he returned his attention to the anonymous email and the damning photos it contained. They were dark, a little difficult to make out, yet what they showed was unmistakable. He well remembered the night they must have been taken, the sky filled with scudding clouds that obscured the moonlight, hindering him in his task but giving him cover as well.

Or so he'd imagined.

The first photograph showed a man gripping a shovel, his face glowing slightly in the light of an electric torch, sheened with sweat. Beside him rested a bulky bag, undefined in the gloom, and at the bottom edge of the photo, just seen by the lamplight, were the curling fingers of an upturned human hand, lying limp on the dirt.

The second photo was a closeup of the bag, now identifiable as a canvas duffle, partially unzipped, the corner of one stack of banded bills showing through the gap, limned by the light of the torch.

The third photo had been taken after he, Forst, had finished digging the hole and was dragging the dead man—a client named Holtz—into it, both their faces visible and recognizable. He spluttered an oath, pounding the table hard enough to make the laptop jump.

Someone wanted to show they owned him. If word got out about what he'd done, his business would be destroyed and he'd be lying at the bottom of a quarry with his neck broken.

He had a few ideas about who his secret tormentor might be. Only a very limited list of select persons were in a position to catch him out like this. If Cincher knew what he'd done, he'd be dead already. So that left...

He thought about that night, how he'd departed the farmhouse with Holtz, poised to implement his plan for a new identity and a new life for the man. But a demon greed had seized him when the client zipped open the duffle, giving Forst a glimpse of the precious contents. He realized everyone connected to the client now believed Holtz to be dead. For all intents and purposes, the man no longer existed.

It hadn't been the bundles of cash that had swayed him. It was the gleam of gold. Bars, rich as golden slabs of chocolate, stamped and beautiful, shining and delectable as they slid against each other with a cold, silken clink.

Irresistible.

Never before had he stepped out of line, betraying Cincher's orders, and never again. But he was very good at making people disappear. He had simply put his talent to use on his own behalf. It had been easy.

Or so it had seemed.

Now, thinking back to the time, he started connecting the dots. Only a week prior to that fateful night, he'd smuggled a woman into the country according to Cincher's instructions, and provided an identity package that would allow her to integrate into her chosen community. His arrangements had worked to perfection, but now it appeared he'd been paving the way for his own destruction.

Surely, she was the sender of this nasty, unexpected bundle. She was on the spot and was the type to do it. If that was the case, she had a lever over him. But he had a stick.

He knew who she was and where to find her. She ought to be very careful.

Very careful indeed.

38

·—

DURING THE DRIVE BACK to the academy, Riley worked to let go of the tension in her neck and shoulders, drawing in deep breaths, letting them out slowly and trying not to think about Rick or Nate or any of the messy parts of her crazy life.

Ilya made it easy for her to follow him, driving at a moderate speed and slowing down to let her catch up anytime road conditions led to her falling behind. She relaxed enough to switch on the radio and find a station playing a mix of German and American songs from decades past.

As she drove toward the garage, she caught sight of Matsui stooped over a patch of earth furrowed into brown rows dotted with sprouts of green. She returned the Volkswagen to the motor pool, thanked Ilya for his help, and walked across tufts of grass to greet the explosives instructor.

"What are you growing there?" she asked.

"I'm hoping for a good salad bowl, come July. Lettuces, peppers, tomatoes, cucumbers, red onions, carrots, radishes. Probably a few more I'm forgetting to mention."

"Fantastic! Is this part of your job or a labor of love?"

"It's my favorite way to unwind at the end of the day. How'd the dead drop go?" Matsui asked, grinning.

"Good. I think." Riley paused, wondering about the wisdom of what she was about to ask. "What can you tell me about assistant director Hill?"

Matsui sat back on her heels, regarding Riley with curiosity. "Is this part of your job or a labor of love?"

Riley laughed. "I'm not sure, on both counts. I just really want to know more about the woman and how she came to be here."

"Well, I don't know a lot about her except that she came highly recommended and that she took a leave of absence before coming here. She'd had some trauma in her life and—"

She broke off, her attention caught by a man cantering up on horseback. She hailed him and he drew near, reining in the horse, a handsome chestnut. Riley realized she was staring at the rider in the saddle and felt a blush rise on her cheeks. He was strikingly attractive, with the Teutonic good looks of a German folk hero, appearing as natural on the horse as a god in his chariot.

Matsui gave her an amused glance. "Riley, this is Gideon Schmidt. He teaches our martial arts and personal defense classes. Gideon, meet Riley Forte, concert pianist and spy in training."

The man dismounted and came to shake Riley's hand, gripping hers firmly without crushing it. "I'm very happy to meet you, Riley. *Sprechen Sie Deutsch?*"

"Not really. *Ein bisschen.*"

"Shame. You must learn."

He smiled and Riley felt her knees go weak. Swinging himself back into the saddle, he said, "Ladies, I take my leave. I wish you *Schönen Abend noch.*"

He rode off, silhouetted against the sunset. Riley laughed. "How storybook is that?" she said.

"Right? But I assure you, Riley—he's the real deal. The man knows his stuff and he's very dedicated to his work."

As horse and rider disappeared into the distance, Riley remembered what they'd been discussing before Gideon's arrival.

"You said Hill experienced some trauma before coming here," she said, hoping to resume their conversation. "Do you know what happened?"

"Not the details, but she was in some kind of accident. Her husband was killed and she was badly injured, took some time off to recover."

Riley remembered the woman's initial warmth toward her and wondered if it was inspired by their shared tragedy, each of them losing a life companion.

"Have you ever noticed anything...off...about her?"

"What do you mean?"

Riley hesitated, not knowing how to put her thoughts into words. Finally, she said, "I arrived here to find out one of my best friends had been killed. I'm just starting to realize how much I'd depended on his being here for me."

She paused to swallow and clear her throat.

"I know denial of the facts is not unheard of in such a situation, but I just can't believe he's gone. I don't want to accept it and maybe that's why I feel like there's more to this than what I'm being told. I'm just looking for answers."

"And you think Hill might have those answers?"

Riley shrugged, frustrated. "I have no idea, but I get a funny vibe from her, and I have a hunch I'm not alone."

"Well, she's never made me feel all warm and fuzzy, but I can't believe she—"

Matsui stopped, tipping her head thoughtfully. "I did think it was a little strange that she was the one who went to identify Rick's body."

"Strange how?"

"Strange because she's only been with us for a few months. I don't think she even knew Rick."

Riley stared at Matsui's face, shadowed in the dim of twilight. The woman rose and brushed off the seat of her pants, gathering her gardening things.

"Be careful, Riley. You're a tiny seed just beginning to sprout. Don't let the weeds get to you."

She handed Riley a basket of tools to carry, giving her shoulder a friendly squeeze.

"Let's go eat."

39

THE DINING HALL WAS warm and smelled of grilled meat and spices from the fajita bar spread along the serving counter. Riley finished loading her tray and moved among the tables, looking for a place to sit. She spotted her roommate, Colette, at a round table in the corner with a few empty spots, and their eyes met. Colette looked away and raised a fork to her lips, her face expressionless.

Matsui came off the line and nudged Riley with her tray. "Let's sit over here," she said, leading the way to a long table filled with faces all becoming more familiar to Riley, some of them in her cohort.

"Too bad we missed out on the guacamole," Matsui complained.

"Early bird gets the worm," Riley's Argentinian classmate said, raising her eyebrows and digging into a small mountain of mashed avocado.

"You can keep the worms. Just give me some of that guac."

The woman relented, laughing, and pushed her plate to the center of the table. Matsui helped herself to a spoonful of the guacamole and Riley followed suit, nodding her thanks.

As they ate, Riley felt herself relaxing, soothed by the normal surrounding sounds of chatter, silverware clinking, liquid pouring from pitcher to glass. If not for the shadow of Rick's death and the stress and uncertainty of the future, she could really be enjoying this experience. She decided to try, at least for that moment, to forget about the doubts that nagged at her.

But as the cafeteria cleared, leaving only a few stragglers, including assistant director Paula Hill, Riley knew she couldn't let the opportunity pass to speak to the woman alone. She approached and dropped into a chair next to Hill. The assistant director looked up from her paperwork and peered over her glasses at Riley.

"Hello, Ms. Forte. I hope you're feeling somewhat better than the last time we spoke. I've been meaning to check in with you, but I..." She waved her hand over the folders spread across the table. "I'm sorry. It's no excuse. How are you?"

"I'm fine, but I have a question about Rick's death."

Riley sensed a moment of hesitation, but the smile Hill turned on her appeared genuine and sympathetic. "Of course. I'll be happy to tell you all I can."

Riley drew a breath, deciding to jump right in. "I understand you were the one who identified Rick's body at the morgue and I want to know why. I thought you didn't even know Rick."

Hill's eyelids fluttered. She looked surprised. "I don't know why you thought that. I did know Rick. We met last year at a conference for law enforcement officials and we spent some time together. I didn't know him well, but I liked him and I realize we lost a good man, Riley. I'm very sorry it happened."

Riley studied the woman's face. She looked sincere. Riley let her gaze wander to the next table where the tall, thin cook who'd delivered her lunch on that first awful day was filling salt shakers and swiping a cloth over the table's surface. Before she could think of anything to say, Hill spoke again.

"I don't want to upset you, Riley, but it really didn't matter who we sent to identify the body. It was a mere formality. The body was burnt beyond recognition. I was simply there to represent the firm. Rick's ID was determined from credentials in his wallet and will be confirmed from DNA analysis. We're still waiting on the results, but there's really no doubt." She hesitated. "I'm sorry, Riley. I know it's hard to accept."

It was hard to accept. It didn't make any sense. Why had Rick been in that car? What had happened? Riley felt something hard and stubborn rise within her, along with a few more questions she wanted answered. She opened her mouth to speak, but Hill cut her off, turning to the lingering cook.

"Move along, Hilde," she said, irritation quivering in her voice. "You've been wiping that table long enough to strip the varnish off it. We're having a private conversation here."

The cook straightened from the table, her expression cold and full of reproach. She stalked off to the kitchen with one swift backward glance from her sharp bird-like eyes.

"Don't worry, Riley. There's really nothing she can say to anyone. All the local nationals who work here sign strict confidentiality agreements. What happens at Olivero, stays at Olivero. Still, I hate to see snooping where it doesn't belong."

Riley thought she detected a slight inflection in Hill's tone as she uttered that last sentence, and wondered if it had been aimed at her. Regardless, she chose to press a bit further.

"I'd like to know more about my roommate, Colette. What can you tell me about her?"

Hill's eyes hardened and her nostrils flared slightly. "Absolutely nothing," she said. "It's up to each of our recruits how much—or how little—they reveal about themselves here at the academy. If you're curious, you should ask Colette. Is there anything else you require? I really must return to my work."

"Yes, one more thing. How do I get an appointment with Director Edwards? I'd really like to speak with him."

Hill shook her head. "I'm sorry, Riley. He's extraordinarily busy right now. I've seen his schedule and I assure you there are no gaps. I can provide any help you need. Just let me know."

Riley thanked the woman and made the short trip down the hall to her room. Colette wasn't there, so Riley sat at the little table and looked at the notes she'd scrawled while on the phone with Chief Wright after learning about Rick's accident.

He said he'd contacted the head of the local crime unit, a man named Tillo Zimmermann, who was in charge of the investigation. Riley plugged in her laptop, activated her VPN, and connected to the academy's wi-fi, running a quick search to find contact information for Zimmermann.

Grateful that most people in Germany seemed to speak passable English, she was able to connect with Inspector Zimmermann after only a few moments' wait. She explained her relationship to Rick and her business in the area, keeping to the cover story she'd been given, feeling nervous about using the pretense with an officer of the law.

"I'm not sure how to explain my problem, Inspector," she told him. "I'm having trouble accepting that my friend is dead. I'd really like to come down to the station and see him for myself."

A pause while Zimmermann cleared his throat. "No, Frau Forte," he said, "I really don't think you would like that. I assure you it would be unpleasant in the extreme."

A hard lump rose in Riley's throat and she swallowed repeatedly, forcing it down. She'd identified burned bodies before. Her husband and son had died in a fire. Looking at what remained of them had been a nightmare experience, but it had provided a degree of closure, however harsh.

"I'm prepared for that," Riley told him.

Another moment of silence then Zimmermann said, "I'm sorry, Frau Forte. You must not come. It's not possible for you to see him now. We are running tests, making official inquiries. You understand."

"No, I'm afraid I don't understand—that's just it. The situation, as it's been described to me, doesn't make sense."

"Please," Zimmermann said, "let us conduct our investigation and we will tell you everything we have found. Then it will make sense. Let us do our job, Frau Forte. And now, I really must go. Auf Wiedersehen."

Riley slumped in the chair, exhausted after the ups and downs of her long, challenging day. At least she'd passed the dead drop exercise, accomplishing something useful. Suddenly, she remembered the message she'd scooped out of the dead drop receptacle. Chief Bateman had said to keep all communications as practical exercises in decryption.

Digging the printed card from her back pocket, she unfolded it and smoothed it on the table in front of her. It held a series of letters, grouped like words:

JNYJLTND MNO FQ RDL VK IZEBQQ HF MUXSJNEX

It looked like it could be a cryptogram, like the ones in the puzzle books she'd been doing since her mom hooked her as a kid. Noticing a number of J's, she tried substituting J for E, but nothing clicked into place for her.

She tried using the double Q as a double L, but immediately recognized it as an unlikely choice, since that would make FQ a two-letter word ending in L. Double S was more probable, but that led her nowhere because the FQ would become AS or IS, or possibly US. Which would make the HF into a two-letter word ending in A, or I, or U. Again, not likely.

She thought about plugging in a double E or double O in place of the Q's. That seemed logical, as it would make the FQ into a two-letter word ending in E or O. But she got no further than that.

She considered looking at RDL as the word THE, but that would make L into E, which seemed unlikely, considering there was only a single other instance of an L in the message.

There were no additional double letters to lend a clue, no identical endings that might be ING or TION. Frustrated, she tucked the card into a pocket of her laptop case. She had a lot to learn about ciphers, codes, and secret communications. Soon, she would gain the skill to crack this message but for now, she was so tired she could barely think straight anymore.

Riley brushed her teeth, pulled on a pair of pajamas, and climbed into bed, switching off the lamp on her night table. With the turmoil in her brain, she expected to toss and turn, wasting an hour of her sleep time.

She was blessedly wrong.

40

Liesl walked the marble floor with Gunther, head of security for the Sammelplatz, cringing a little at the clattering racket her heels made on the floor in comparison to his crepe-soled shoes. Dusk had fallen, knocking out the natural light and turning the windows opaque, obscuring the spectacular view she so loved to see.

The lobby was lit, instead, by soft yellow bulbs spreading their glow like melting butter. Liesl thought their golden tone imparted warmth and comfort to the guests better than the harsh, white bulbs favored by her predecessor. That seemed important to her, especially when the guests were concerned with making peace agreements.

"I understand you've hired a few extra hands for the duration of the summit," she said to Gunther. "I think that's wise. It looks like you've got the security arrangements well-covered. Is there anything else you need from me?"

"*Nein, Frau Saunders. Alles gut.*"

"Very well, then. I'm late for dinner, so I'll say goodnight. Let me know if you need help with anything—the guests will be arriving the day after tomorrow and I want everything ready for a successful event."

"*Naturlich. Guten Abend.*"

Inside the apartment, Liesl was met by warmth and the aroma of *Sauerbraten,* sending a surge of gratitude shimmering through her. She was so blessed to have her parents living with her, taking good care of her and Max. And Julia.

Max ran to hug her as she entered the dining room. "Mama," he exclaimed, clasping his hands to his chest, "you're home now."

"Yes, my darling. I'm home now." Touched by his delight, she kissed his cheek and smoothed the cowlick that always made the hair stand up on the crown of his head.

Dinner was delicious, the mood around the table genial and light-hearted. Even Julia had only nice things to say and kept Max entertained with jokes and riddles from a book she'd found in the Sammelplatz's book exchange.

She cupped Max's face in her hands and said, "A teddy bear took his date out for dinner, but he skipped dessert."

Max grinned. He loved teddy bears.

"Ask me why he skipped dessert, Max."

Max started giggling and it was infectious. Liesl couldn't help joining in and pretty soon everyone at the table was laughing. Max could hardly get the words out, but he managed to sputter, "Why did the teddy bear skip dessert?"

"Because he was stuffed!" Julia shouted.

Liesl saw the change in Max's face as he understood the joke and broke into a new fit of laughter, his enjoyment enhancing her own. While he continued to marvel over the joke, Julia lowered her voice and waggled her eyebrows in a Groucho Marx impression. "Here's one for the grownups," she said. "A truism for the well-mannered family to think about—if you don't go to people's funerals, they won't come to yours."

Liesl watched her father convulse with laughter, almost choking on a bite of *Sauerbraten* and needing a good whack on the back from her mother. He raised his glass to Julia and took a sip before letting out another guffaw.

When the meal was finished, Liesl insisted on cleaning up. "Dinner was lovely, Mama," she said. "I'll clear the table and wash the dishes. Max will help me, right Snickerdoodle?"

"Right!" Max agreed, always eager to chip in.

"I'll help too," Julia added. "You deserve to put your feet up, Mama. Relax with some television."

"I will, thank you all."

Liesl stacked the dirty plates and carried them to the kitchen where Julia was filling the sink with hot, soapy water. Max stood ready with a dish towel.

"Reminds me of old times," Liesl said. "Remember when Mama used to make us wash the dishes together and it took six times longer than it should have."

"Yes, because you were lazy."

"I was not lazy! We goofed off, making beards out of the bubbles and singing into the spoons, playing air guitar with the pots and pans like we were rocks stars."

Julia scooped a handful of suds from the sink and smeared it across her chin. "Like this?" she asked.

Max shrieked with laughter, reaching into the sink to create his own bubble beard. Julia grabbed a ladle and used it like a microphone, belting out a Bon Jovi classic while gravy dripped on the floor.

A bittersweet twinge of nostalgia rippled through Liesl as she watched her son and her sister vamp and play. She understood this was a moment she would hold in her heart for years to come.

When the kitchen was finally clean and the leftovers stored away in the refrigerator, Liesl sent Max off to take a bath and get ready for bed.

"Thank you, Julia," she said, giving her sister a hug. "You're good with Max. He really likes you. I'm glad you're here so he can get to know you."

Julia returned the squeeze. "Me too."

As Julia pulled away from their embrace, Liesl resisted, keeping hold of her sister for a moment longer. "Julia," she said, working to make her tone even, non-judgmental. "How well do you really know Anton Forst?"

She felt Julia stiffen. "Why do you ask?" she said, her tone cool, their kitchen camaraderie over. "Is it any of your business?"

"Well, yes. I think it is my business. The Sammelplatz is my responsibility now. It's my job to organize events and keep everyone safe."

Julia frowned, her forehead creasing and turning pink. "What are you suggesting, Liesl? That Anton is a threat to your precious place here?"

"I'm not saying that. I just..." Liesl pulled in a deep breath, letting it out in a frustrated sigh. "I just feel like he may be hiding something from you. Something that could hurt you."

Julia stared, her eyes hard. "You're jealous," she said. "You were always jealous of me and nothing's changed, has it, Liesl?"

"I'm not jealous. I just...care about what happens to you."

"You don't care," Julia sneered. "You just want to ruin things for me. You can't bear that I might have found a little happiness at last."

"No! Julia, that's not it. I do care. I want you to be happy."

"Then stay out of my business. And if you want to be a part of my life, accept that Anton is a part of it, too."

Liesl watched helplessly as Julia swept out of the kitchen, leaving it cold and empty, the mirth of moments before dissolved like the bubbles in the sink.

41

—·—

RILEY ROSE TO CONSCIOUSNESS, swimming through the last dregs of her unremembered dream. She didn't open her eyes, just lay unmoving in the warmth of the bed, sensing the pale light of morning on her closed eyelids.

Her first coherent thought was dismay that she hadn't woken to an alarm. Then she remembered it was Sunday, typically observed at the academy as a day of rest.

And that brought the next thought crashing over her with brutal force. Squeezing her eyes tighter shut against the bleak wrench of pain that descended over her, she shifted in the bed, turning away from the window, curling into a ball.

It was Tanner's birthday.

He would have been nine years old.

Her sweet boy, a marvel growing before her eyes, blooming into a surprisingly unique little person with recognizable components inherited from Jim or herself, but undeniably distinct. His own little man.

Achingly irreplaceable.

Hugging herself, Riley reached for the happy memories. Tanner, grinning at her as he proudly held up a two-pound trout, his first ever catch. Jim and Tanner rolling in the grass, wrestling after a Fourth of July picnic, the three of them sprawling later on the blanket, watching the dazzle of fireworks sparkling overhead.

Tanner, his darling, pudgy four-year-old fingers on the keys of her piano, playing his first Beethoven piece as she taught him the Air from Little Russia theme, his feet swinging below the bench, a foot off the floor.

As she did every year on his birthday, and plenty of other days as well, she bid the good times to flood over her, holding the memories, letting them grow until she felt able to sit up, straighten her spine, and face the future.

She still missed both of them so much.

The dining hall was sparsely populated when she arrived. She chose a fruit cup and two poached eggs on toast, eating alone at the same table where she'd spoken with assistant director Hill. Afterward, she spent an hour in the chapel, reading scripture, meditating. Praying.

There were no formal services offered at the academy chapel. It was a non-denominational space intended to foster peace and impart spiritual strength to all who entered. Riley was both surprised and heartened to see that the chapel benches held more comers than had the tables in the cafeteria. The atmosphere was one of quiet reverence, and it was precisely what Riley needed to continue her healing.

After her time in the chapel, she headed to the classroom building to implement the last piece in her self-prescribed therapy program. In the piano room, she lost herself, forgot her pain, as she let her fingers wander the keys, creating, inviting, simply living inside the vibrations of sound as they echoed around the room.

At last, she was ready to work, to apply herself to the new piece of music she was learning. She found the composition challenging to play, especially the bridging movement, because it demanded a smooth, connected legato in the right hand, combined with a simultaneous and sharply detached staccato in the left hand. The contrast between the two articulations created an interesting, compelling passage that both fascinated and frustrated Riley, but there was no question it was the genius of the piece.

Riley struggled to master the technique. She played through the section with each hand separately, working out a fingering strategy so she could execute the complicated rhythms and smooth notes of the right hand without fracturing the legato phrases.

And then, after breaking the demanding left-hand staccato passage into manageable bits and patiently working through the transitions, she was able to perform the part without error.

But when she played the section with both hands together, the whole thing broke down.

At last, defeated and feeling the gloom rolling back in on her, Riley returned to the main building. On impulse, she took the stairs up to the administrative floor, running hard, throwing herself up the steps, and stopping at the top to let her heart pound, rushing the blood throughout her body.

She let the tension drain away as her pulse settled down to normal. Maybe the Director would be in his office. Maybe he'd have time for her without a schedule full of appointments. She only wanted a moment.

She knocked at the outer door and was surprised to hear someone invite her to come in. Opening the door, she saw a trim young woman at the desk in the antechamber. She was dressed in jeans and a red sweatshirt, perched on a corner of the desk, a cell phone in her hand.

"One moment," she said into the phone, then, "Hello, you must be one of our new arrivals. We don't normally hold office hours on Sunday."

"Oh, I realize that," Riley said. "I just...I wondered if I might catch Director Edwards here. I only need—"

"I'm sorry, he's out of town," the woman said. "I'm Marta, by the way."

"Riley. When will he be back?"

Marta gave an apologetic shrug. "I don't always know. Perhaps Assistant Director Hill can help?"

Riley let her shoulders slump and Marta quickly said, "I'm sure she can help. She stepped out, but she's certain to be back soon."

Glancing down at the phone in her hand, Marta said, "Why don't you wait in her office?" which Riley took to mean she wanted privacy to finish her call.

On the verge of thanking Marta and leaving, Riley smiled instead and entered Hill's office. Closing the door behind her, she felt her heartbeat rev again at what she was about to do. Hands shaking, she rifled quickly through the papers on the desk, looking for anything connected to Rick or his death.

Her face felt hot with shame. This was not something she was used to doing. Pausing, she set her jaw and challenged herself to get over it. This is what she was there for—learning to ferret out information someone else wants hidden. She was convinced there was something here to find.

Nothing on the desk caught her attention. She turned to stare at the locked file cabinets, lifting the rug to see a safe set into the floor. All things she expected to see in the office of the leader in a security firm.

She picked up a framed photo from a walnut credenza and studied the picture—Paula Hill with a man, both casually dressed, their arms entwined, smiles on their faces, a row of beach umbrellas in the background. Turning the frame over, she examined the paper backing, smooth except for a slight buckling at one corner where the adhesive had worn away.

Or been tampered with.

Running her finger over the brown paper, she felt a tiny raised edge, barely perceptible. Pushing gently with her fingernail, she nudged at the anomaly, rewarded by the peeping of a thin, dark-colored data chip emerging from the hidey hole.

Elation rushed through her veins, followed by an immediate stab of panic as she heard voices outside the door. Shoving the data chip back into its slot, she replaced the photo on the credenza and dropped onto the same sofa where she'd received the news of Rick's death.

Half a second before Hill opened the door and stepped into her office.

"Riley," she said, sounding more resigned than annoyed. "I didn't expect we'd meet again so soon. What can I do for you today?"

"I'm sorry to keep bothering you. Only...I wondered if you'd learned anything more about the accident and fire. I just don't understand what happened."

"None of us really do, Riley." Hill sighed. She carried a cup of steaming coffee, its aroma filling the room. Placing it on her desk, she said, "We may never have all the answers, but if I learn anything more I will certainly let you know, Riley."

"Thank you. I'll go now."

Riley walked down the stairs, slowly this time, and let herself out onto the grounds. The difficult day had almost passed, the sun hanging low in the western sky and mostly blocked by the fringe of forest, a few beams breaking through. Fingers of light. Poking. Seeking.

In the distance, silhouetted against the sinking sun, Riley caught a glimpse of a man on horseback. Surely Gideon Schmidt. He had a talent for it, appearing in romantic fashion like a storybook character. Could he possibly be for real?

Moving quickly, Riley entered the path into the woods and walked along it, her brain fizzing. She broke into a loose jog for a minute or two then slowed to a walk, finally stopping to stretch, the worst of her nervous energy stripped away.

As she had before, she wished she could enjoy this experience, embrace her training, devote herself fully to this new chapter of her life. But she couldn't fight off the doubts or stem the flow of questions, and now she added a new one to the list.

Why would someone with access to any number of secure hiding places use an old standby like the backing of a picture frame?

Unless she had something to hide from the others who had access to her office—like the Director.

She turned, beginning the short walk back to the dormitory. As she drew near the edge of the woods, she saw a figure, dark against the side of the building. Someone slender, moving furtively.

As she watched, the figure crept along the student patios, keeping behind the half-walls that divided them. Pausing beside one of the patios, the figure moved around the divider and pushed open the window, slipping inside.

A moment later, the room lit up as the light came on and Riley saw two things that surprised her.

The room was her own.

And the figure who'd crept into it like a cat burglar was her roommate, Colette.

42

Nate stood in the driveway and watched Marilyn's midnight blue Tahoe pull away from the curb, engine growling. Sammi's wistful face stared at him from the window, a pale oval framed by a tangle of dark gold tresses, her breath misting on the glass. The image of it haunted him long after they'd turned the corner and disappeared.

A cool breeze feathered through the row of spruce lining the driveway, releasing a fresh scent as he bent and hefted his backpack. Letting himself into the cramped garage, he hummed tunelessly as he put away the camping gear and entered the house. He'd tried to make a good weekend for Sammi—and he thought he'd succeeded—but she needed more than that from him.

More than just a part-time dad.

That had been Marilyn's complaint when they were married, that he was so often unavailable when they needed him. And she was right. He'd pointed out that certain jobs, like being a cop, require more than a 9 to 5 commitment, that he had no control over when a bad guy decides to be bad.

To which she retorted that he could have chosen another profession, no one had forced him to be a cop. To which he countered that she chose to marry him, no one had forced her to walk down the aisle.

And so it went.

Inside, the house smelled stale. Nate opened some windows to let in a cross-current of air, then took out the garbage, something he should have done before leaving for the weekend. He wanted a quick shower but decided to try calling Riley first. It was drawing near midnight where she was. If he didn't call now, he'd have to wait until tomorrow, and he really wanted to know how she was holding up.

He dialed her number, but it went straight to voice mail. He waited five minutes, thumbing through a stack of mail on the counter, before trying again. After a third failed attempt, he got in the shower and tried to wash away the worry growing on him like a second skin.

When he emerged from the steamy bathroom, he forced himself to admit it was too late to try calling again, but he had to talk to someone about what was going on. Would Devin Wright take his call on a late Sunday afternoon?

He would.

"Have you heard from Riley?" Nate asked after their exchange of polite formalities.

"I haven't spoken with her over the past two days, but I have someone at the academy keeping an eye on her. She's grieving, she's anxious, she's upset about what happened and wants more answers than she's getting, but essentially, she's okay, Nate. I hope you'll stop worrying about her."

"I wish I could, sir. The more I think about it, the more I'm convinced she's right—that there's more underlying Rick's death than a simple accident."

"You mean, a simple accident compounded by engine explosion and a fire burning away all indications of what really happened and why Rick was in the car in the first place?"

"Yes, exactly. That's what I mean."

"I understand your concerns. I share them, and I have people looking into it. Video footage from the airport shows Rick getting willingly into the car. He doesn't appear to be coerced at all. Puzzling."

"Will you keep me in the loop about what you find?"

"Absolutely, Nate."

"And you'll let me know if there's anything I can do to help?"

"Of course."

Nate ended the call and let the phone fall into his lap as he gazed out the window, listening to the first spate of raindrops splash against the screen, bringing the distinctive scent of ozone. With a growing sense of unease, he watched the line of spruce trees flanking the driveway as they twisted and writhed in the rising wind, surrounded by increasing darkness.

And couldn't help feeling their condition was eerily similar to his own.

43

RILEY GRITTED HER TEETH as she guided an old-model BMW over the muddy, rutted track, bumping and bouncing through a series of potholes forcing her to slow down. A deep ditch flanked the road on one side, thick woods on the other, limiting her way forward.

Keeping a grip on her nerves, she squinted ahead into the darkness looming beyond the twin beams of thin illumination from the headlamps, her hands sweaty on the wheel. The only sounds were the growl of the motor and groans from the suspension system, not loud, but magnified by her anxiety.

She'd spent the afternoon in classroom instruction for this tactical driving exercise, learning the techniques and best practices for tailing, evading, and dealing with sticky road situations. Now she was taking that theoretical knowledge and putting it into action.

She didn't feel at all ready.

An elaborate network of roads and narrow tracks ran through a practice course covering nearly a hundred acres on the Olivero property, currently populated by marauding groups of instructors in the guise of drug runners, terrorists, and general baddies. During her classroom instruction, Riley had been given a map to memorize before being sent off for dinner.

Now, after dark, it was time to begin her mission.

She was tasked with making it to the "border" and getting across successfully. She was to carry her alias documents and stick to her cover story without fail. The clam chowder she'd eaten in the cafeteria sloshed in her stomach, making her wish she'd kept to the soda crackers and left the soup alone.

In the dim light ahead, she saw a signpost marking the crossroads and turned off onto a paved road leading to the improvised border. This lane felt narrower, with trees crowding in from both sides, giving Riley the uneasy feeling of being trapped. It seemed to run on forever. As she began to wonder if she'd made a wrong turn, the glint of headlights flashed in her rear view mirror.

Another car was behind her, closing the distance between them fast.

She rounded a curve in the road and saw two cars parked on the pavement ahead, blocking her path. A jolt of alarm shot through Riley and she fought to stay calm, to remember this was a test.

Pulling in a shaky breath, she looked at the cars ahead. They were parked nose to tail across the road, exactly as depicted in the video and written exam from the classroom instruction. Riley immediately knew what to do.

In theory.

It had been easy on paper, but her mouth went dry as the headlights behind her drew nearer and the stationary cars ahead grew large. She had only two options—slam on the brakes or do what she'd been taught to do.

Tensing, she aimed the frame rail of the BMW, which she judged to run roughly like an extension of her left leg, directly at the rear wheel axle of the car in front of her and mashed down on the accelerator.

With a shriek of ruined metal, the BMW smashed into the car, sweeping it out of the way like a cumbersome gate thrown open. Jarred but unhurt, Riley shot through the gap and kept driving, her heart racing like mad as she watched the lights fade out of view behind her.

Eyes blurring with sudden tears, she dabbed them away with her sleeve and felt some of the tension lift off her almost like magic. Sitting taller in her seat, she actually smiled.

She'd made it past her first roadblock.

Driving on, she came to an unmarked "T" in the road. She hadn't been allowed to bring her map, part of the point being to test her memory and instinct. Turning right, she guided the BMW along a winding road. She arrived at a bridge and crossed it with caution, recognizing it as a choke point, but she met no opposition and continued on unhindered.

The moon had risen, its silvery light splashing at random intervals through the dark weave of overhanging branches as she made her way down the wooded roadway. Steering around a wide curve, she saw an orange and white barrier stretching across the road ahead, and beside it the familiar *Umleitung* sign designating a detour.

The sign indicated a turnoff down a dirt road. Misgivings rose in Riley's chest and she braked, bringing the car to a stop while she debated whether to follow the detour or turn back. Her internal compass told her she was headed toward the border. Turning back and taking the left branch at the "T" would take her in the opposite direction.

On the other hand, these roads were not laid out in neat rows and columns. Like the medieval era cities and surroundings they were meant to represent, they twisted and wound around in all directions. Perhaps following the road back the way she came would eventually lead her to the academy's border checkpoint.

In the end, she decided to follow the detour, expecting it to lead her into another obstacle designed to test her mettle and grasp of the classroom material. Letting her foot off the brake, she entered the dirt track, peering hard into the darkness, alert for any signs of trouble.

About a hundred yards later, the road came to an abrupt end. A U-shaped brick wall enclosed the cul-de-sac, and before Riley even recognized what was happening, masked men began launching themselves over the wall, thumping hard on the BMW's hood and banging on the windshield, screaming in a language Riley didn't understand.

Heart lurching inside her chest, hands shaking, coherent thought shredded to rags in her panicked brain, Riley watched as the hoodlums pounded on the windows and pried at the door handles. Swallowing hard, she checked the rear view mirror and saw that none of her tormentors were behind the car.

Shifting into reverse, she punched the gas and broke free from the knot of masked men. She kept moving fast, gaining enough distance to skid the car into a three-point turn and blow dust speeding away. Trying to steady her breathing, she arrived back at the main road and saw that both the barrier and the detour signs had been removed.

She'd passed the second part of the test.

Blood still pumping fast through her veins, she turned right and continued toward the border, rehearsing the details of her alternate

ID and backstory, knowing she'd need to have all of it down cold at the checkpoint.

Shivering, she realized she was chilled, her store of energy running low after the adrenaline spikes of the last half hour. She needed to call on her reserves, lift her chin, show some stamina. She recognized this danger point from her concert performance experience. That moment when the end seemed in sight, when success seemed achievable—that was when she was prone to stumble.

That was when she gave in to doubt.

Ahead, the trees wore a halo of light and Riley knew she was nearing the border. Leaving the cover of the forest, she approached the gap in a long stretch of chain link fence topped by coils of barbed wire. The Olivero team had done a good job making it look authentic, flooded with harsh lighting and stern-faced guards in drab uniforms, carrying weapons.

Slowly, she zig-zagged through the arrangement of concrete barriers, pulling up at the guardhouse as directed by one of the guards. She lowered her window and offered her passport. The man leafed through the document, studying the pages and peering at her face.

He leaned down, almost thrusting his chin through the window. "What is your business in the Allterra republic?" he demanded.

Allterra was their made-up name representing any nation, a placeholder for whatever region she might be called to serve in.

"I'm a musician," Riley said. "I'm researching the folk music of your country for a book I'm writing."

He narrowed his eyes and barked something at her in a foreign language she couldn't identify.

"I don't understand what you're asking. Could you repeat that in English?"

"Wait here."

Taking her passport, the man disappeared into the tiny guardhouse where he conferred with his fellows. One of them came out and walked around the BMW, cupping his hands around his face to stare into the windows.

Coming around to face Riley, he said, "You will open your trunk, please."

Riley searched for a button or lever to pop the trunk but couldn't find one. She opened her door to get out, and the guard shoved it hard with his knee, slamming it closed.

"Do not exit your vehicle. Do not attempt to drive on."

Shocked, Riley realized she was being handled and her concerns about getting through the checkpoint multiplied as the guard reached into the car and pulled a knob beside the air vent. Riley heard a *thunk* as the trunk lock released.

She sat frozen, afraid to do anything that would further arouse their suspicion. After a moment, the man rummaging through the trunk came around to her window, pinching a small plastic bag filled with white powder between the gloved fingers of his right hand.

"This is part of your musician's equipment, yes?"

Riley swallowed, shaking her head. "No. That is not mine. I've never seen it before and I have no knowledge concerning it."

"You say you are a musician wanting to come into my country, but I see no guitar, no violin, no instruments, no music stands, nothing that backs up your story."

"I'm a pianist," Riley said. "It's a difficult instrument to transport in the trunk of a car."

He regarded her with stony eyes. "So you say."

The first guard came out of the shack, carrying her passport. The other man held up the bag of powder.

"It is as you suspected. I found this in the trunk."

"It is not mine," Riley protested. "I didn't put it there."

"What are you saying? Are you suggesting *I* put it there?" asked the man with the powder.

"I'm not saying anything," Riley said and closed her lips.

She sat still in the car while the two men, along with four others, milled around the BMW and pawed through the items in the trunk. Riley had no idea what was back there and decided that should be part of her pre-trip inspection from now on—making sure what she carried with her matched the story she told.

But the question remained, nagging at her, taunting her. Had the man really found the powder in the trunk, or had he planted it there himself?

At last, the first guard returned her passport, giving her a sour look. "You may go. But," he said, indicating the bag of powder, "you may not bring such things into our country. You cannot have it back."

Riley took the passport and nodded her understanding. Firing the engine, she drove forward, thrilled to be leaving the checkpoint. Trembling with the release of tension, she watched for a road that would take her back to the main compound. Instead, she saw a man standing at the side of the road, waving a white handkerchief, the international distress signal.

Would tonight's test never end? Riley slowed, pulling to the side of the road. She lowered the passenger window and the man leaned his head inside, long dirty strands of gray hair falling forward over his face. He wore glasses and a bristly white mustache. In the gloom of the night, his features were undefined and Riley wondered if he was one of the instructors she knew, working in disguise, probably getting a kick out of this.

"*Danke, Fraulein,*" the man said, his accent that of the local Bavarians. "It is lucky you came along. My bicycle is *kaputt.* Please can you drive me to the gate? It is only a kilometer down the road," he pointed, "but I hurt my ankle in the fall. The walk would not do me good."

Feverishly, Riley considered her options. Was she supposed to refuse, not expose herself to potential danger? Or was this contact a deliberate connection, designed to pass her vital information which she would lose out on by skipping the opportunity?

It seemed unlikely the bicyclist was simply what he pretended to be. Not at this time of night. Not inside the boundaries of the academy. No, this had to be part of her test.

But what was she meant to do?

Sighing, she popped the door lock. "Get in."

"*Danke.*"

The man smelled of stale sweat and Riley left the window down. The night air was not chilly enough to worry over it during the short drive to the edge of the Olivero property. Her passenger spent his time inspecting the injured ankle, clucking over it like a mother hen. Riley had not realized there were gates on the far reaches of the compound, leading out into local communities, and she was curious about their purpose.

"Do you work here?" she asked.

"I am working here today," he answered as Riley drew up to the gate. His German accent had disappeared. "Well done, Ms. Forte. You may give this to your instructor for extra credit."

He passed her a token, a thick coin about two inches in diameter, depicting a rope tied into a complicated-looking knot on one side and a globe of the world on the opposite side.

"Now go get some rest," he told her. "You look exhausted."

"I am," Riley admitted. "I'm so glad that's over."

"Over?" The man smiled. In the darkness, she couldn't see his eyes or much of his face except his white teeth bared beneath the mustache. "This is only the beginning, Riley."

He climbed out of the car and walked to the gate, no limp evident in his step. Punching a code into the keypad, he let himself out of the gate and disappeared into the night.

Riley watched, rubbing her thumb across the ridges of the coin he'd given her, trying to ignore the chill building inside her stomach.

44

IN THE DARKNESS OF her room, Riley lay motionless under the warmth of the feather duvet, aware of the absolute quiet from the bed across the room, occupied by Colette. A gentle snoring, the rustling of the bedclothes as she shifted position—these were the things Riley wanted to hear, what she was listening for. These were the things that would allow her to relax, unwind a little.

Instead, silence.

Riley wondered if Colette was lying there, waiting for the same signals from her. Tension hung in the air, making sleep an unlikely prospect in the immediate future.

Many matters of concern pressed on Riley as she squeezed her eyes shut and concentrated on breathing deeply and evenly. Not least was the reaction from her tactical driving instructor when she'd shown him the coin she'd received from the mysterious bicyclist.

As she'd suspected, he knew nothing about it, and she didn't enlighten him. Now, more than ever, she needed to speak with Director Edwards, who was still out of town. Instead, she'd called Chief Wright in Washington and been told he was in a meeting.

She hadn't left a message.

Twenty minutes passed and Riley was just beginning to drift mentally, wisps of dreams floating at the edge of her consciousness, when she became aware of stealthy noises in the room.

Colette was on the move.

Riley watched through slitted eyelids as her roommate dressed quickly and threw a dark-colored hooded cloak over herself before slipping out into the hallway. The door clicked softly shut and Riley leapt from bed and hastily pulled on a pair of jeans and a sweater.

As she bent over to tie her sneakers, she caught a glimpse of a cloaked figure outside the window, moving down the path and into the forest. Grabbing her jacket and cell phone, Riley eased open the window to follow and understood why Colette had chosen to exit through the hallway.

The wind grabbed the door, rattling the glass and whistling into the room. The night had grown wild, ragged clouds scudding past a subdued moon, wind whipping the branches of the fruit trees in the courtyard and the oaks and pines of the forest, making them creak and whine.

Riley hurried up the open path, anxious to gain the cover afforded by the woods ahead and not wanting to lose her quarry. Just hours previously, in her morning class, she'd been instructed how to tail a subject and how to evade a follower.

She'd had no notion she'd be putting those tips to use so soon.

As she entered the woods, her visibility diminished in the deepened gloom. She hadn't brought a flashlight and wouldn't have used one anyway. Moving carefully along the path, she waited for her eyes to adjust, hoping to catch sight of the cloaked figure ahead.

She saw no one.

Picking up speed, she peered right and left into the foliage as she passed down the trail, and fifty yards ahead was rewarded by a flash of light and movement to her left. She froze, straining her eyes into the darkness.

A narrow path, less defined than the one she was on, angled away on a slight incline. Riley turned to follow it, taking care not to step on dry sticks or kick rocks as she drew closer to the dark shape moving ahead, led by the dim light of a small electric torch.

It was Colette.

Keeping a good distance between them, Riley followed. At length, Colette reached the boundary of the Olivero property. The path led to a gate, similar to the one used by the bogus bicyclist. Riley estimated they'd walked more than half a mile from the dormitory building.

As she watched, Colette entered a code on the electronic keypad and passed through, the metal gate clanking shut behind her. Riley stood behind a screen of trees as the hooded figure melted into the forest beyond and disappeared.

She shivered. The jacket she'd thrown around her did little to stop the wind's piercing grasp though she raised the hood and tied it beneath her chin. The boughs overhead swayed and dipped in a restless dance, a branch of pine needles reaching to brush against her arm.

What now?

She could turn back, climb into bed, and try to get some sleep. Or she could punch in the code she'd been given for the front gate, on the chance that it might activate all the gates on the property.

She might be able to get out that way. But would she be able to get back in?

She wasn't sure where she was now, in relation to the main road and the front entrance to the academy. It was dark, it was cold, and suddenly she felt exhausted enough to sleep for a week.

Yet, could Colette's clandestine activities have something to do with what had happened to Rick?

She had to find out.

Leaving the shelter of the trees, she ran to the keypad and entered the six-digit code she'd used at the main entrance. The gate swung open on well-oiled hinges and without giving herself time to reconsider, Riley slipped through the gap and into the woods on the other side.

Hoping she hadn't lost Colette's trail, she found an opening in the brush and plunged onto the outline of a path, half-overgrown with ferns and tangling scrub. Riley knew stinging nettle grew prolifically in the area and hoped she wasn't traipsing into it now.

Moving silently was impossible, but the wind's moaning voice helped drown out the sounds of her passage. She didn't encounter Colette, but soon came upon a small cluster of buildings—house, woodshed, barn—surrounding a central courtyard, what the Germans called a *Hof.*

Could Colette be inside?

A chink of light showed through a crack in the shutters, guttering as people moved across its beam inside the house. Somewhere nearby, a dog barked for a full minute and then all was quiet except for the wind.

What could Colette be doing here? Why was she so hostile? The compulsion to seek answers drove Riley toward the shuttered window, creeping cautiously, terrified of being caught, terrified of being attacked by the dog.

And, possibly, terrified of the truth.

The dog remained silent as she drew up to the side of the house, positioning herself to peer through a gap in the wooden shutters. Inside, she saw a bald man standing in front of the fireplace, drinking beer from a stein.

And beside him, with her back to the window, was Colette, warming her hands before the crackling flames. As Riley watched, the woman pushed the hood back from her face and shrugged out of her dark covering.

Riley gasped.

The figure she'd followed through the woods and out the gate was not her roommate, Colette.

It was Olivero's assistant director, Paula Hill.

<h1 style="text-align:center">45</h1>

Frozen with shock, Riley stared transfixed at the woman now clearly lit by the leaping flames in the fireplace, wondering what sort of alchemy had transformed one hooded figure into another. She realized she must have lost Colette during her initial plunge into the forest and picked up Hill's trail by strange accident.

And it had led her here.

What was this place? Who was the bald man now speaking with sullen face and wild gesturing to Paula Hill? Frightened and bewildered as she was, Riley knew she had to find out.

The wind plucked at her own hood and rattled the window panes behind the shutters, making it difficult to hear anything through the glass. Riley pressed her ear to the wooden covering, listening to the strident tones, struggling to make out the words but catching only shreds of the vocal exchange.

"...her mobile...asking too many questions," Riley heard, recognizing Hill's voice. "...your clumsy handling of the crash site."

"Clumsy!" came the man's shouted reply, followed by more words lost to the wind.

A sharp gust whipped along the plastered side of the house, and then a lull so that Riley heard Hill clearly say, "Why did you burn the car? You've triggered a full-blown investigation and now Cincher's pet is poking into it."

Riley swallowed hard. She'd been right in believing there was more to Rick's death than a simple accident. Here was the man who'd set fire to the car. But why? And who was Cincher?

The man was speaking again, his louder tones easier to pick up despite the wind's renewed racket. "...damaging evidence...find nothing useful...Zimmermann will keep the risk of exposure low."

Riley groaned. Zimmermann, the head of the local crime unit who'd refused to let her see Rick's body, was apparently involved, meaning she couldn't turn to the police for help. The notion so distracted her that she nearly missed the bald man's next words. But as they registered on her consciousness, a chill settled over her heart.

"...agent...Jimenez...dead and soon buried."

Rick.

Hill's reply was swallowed in the wind and several moments passed before the buffeting died down and Riley heard her say, "You have no choice, Forst. You'll meet my demands or those photos go to Cincher."

The man growled in reply and Riley peered through a crack in the shutter to see that he'd backed Hill against the stone wall of the hearth. Hill's face was painted with a sneer, her hands drawn up into claws and poised as if she would scratch his eyes out if he pushed her one more inch.

The silent tableau continued for several seconds before the man released his grip on Hill and stepped back. It suddenly occurred to Riley that she ought to try taking some photos. Maybe Wright could identify the man from a picture.

Fumbling her phone from her jacket pocket, Riley wondered if she dared ease the device up under the shutter. She doubted the camera would pick up much of value pressed against the crack as her eye had been.

As she carefully pulled on the thin weathered wood, making a gap for the phone to slide into, Riley heard a few more snippets of speech from the two inside.

"...make sure your patient is able..." Hill said. "...come through with his part."

And the man's response, "...could get messy."

Riley sensed the interchange was coming to a close. Crouching below the window, she pushed her phone into the space she'd made and snapped a series of blind shots, hoping they'd yield something worth the pain and risk.

Withdrawing her hands, she fled into the cover of thick shadow thrown by the tall pines. Not waiting to see if she was being pursued, she hurried along the choked path back to the gate marking the entrance onto the Olivero property and bit back a whimper as she punched the code into the keypad.

Faint with relief as the gate swung open, Riley squeezed through the opening and followed the trail until it merged with the main path back to the center where her bed awaited. She was more than ready for it now.

Peering through the glass of her window, she saw that Colette was still absent, so she stepped in and undressed quickly, slipping into her pajamas and rolling into bed, pulling the duvet close around her. She lay shivering until the warmth of her body spread to the coverlet. Eyes drooping, wanting nothing more than to fall into dreamless sleep, she stared instead at the ceiling and tossed thoughts feverishly in her head.

What should she do? Who could she trust? Could she even make a private phone call or was her phone compromised?

Assistant Director Hill had adroitly cut off all her attempts to speak with Director Edwards. That suggested to Riley that he was not part of Hill's evil plan, whatever it might be. She would try harder to get a moment alone with him.

She heard a noise outside the door and snuggled into the pillow, closing her eyes as a slice of dim light crossed the carpet then disappeared as the door closed. Colette moved quietly in the room, hanging her cloak on a peg and sliding out of her shoes as Riley watched through her lashes.

The last thing Riley remembered was the sound of Colette brushing her teeth in the bathroom as the dark hands of sleep reached out and grabbed her at last.

46

Dr. Vadim Novak crept from the shelter of a row of spruce trees and moved quickly over the grass to a small stand of oak and elm, melting against the rough bark of their trunks. A wisp of night breeze feathered through the branches, sighing softly like a woman over bittersweet memories.

He'd timed his movements with those of the moon, waiting for the inky fall of darkness before the moon's silver rising. Vadim was aware of only one guard tower on the compound, situated near the front entrance, but he knew teams of sentries with dogs patrolled at random intervals, putting his attempt at moving undetected on a par with a roll of the dice.

A risk he was more than ready to take.

Dressed head to toe in black, he intended to gain the cover of the wooded area on the backside of the property and proceed to the perimeter fence. Moving awkwardly due to the rolled carpet beneath his coat, he broke from the copse and ran to the outer fringes of pine, breathing out a sigh of relief as their needled boughs closed in around him.

From the far side of the compound, he heard a dog bark insistently. The sound raised the hairs along the back of his neck, but he told himself it was a positive sign. The animal was calling attention away from his position, creating a welcome distraction.

A good omen.

Navigating in the dark, he pressed through the trunks and underbrush of the woods, moving instinctively toward the outer fence. When, after ten minutes of forward progress the chain link and razor wire failed to appear, Vadim began to worry he was walking in circles. The moon was on the rise and would soon be high enough to potentially cause him problems.

Pressing on through the blackness, he stumbled on a downed tree branch and fell onto a mound of soft earth, his outstretched hands sinking into the loose crumbles of dirt. A stench wafted up from the soil he'd disturbed, fetid and sweet, making him gag. Half rising, his dark-adjusted eyes took in the series of earthen heaps scattered randomly in a rough clearing among the trees.

Dr. Anderson's graveyard.

Heart pounding, he scrambled up and staggered away, brushing the palms of his hands against his overcoat, fighting the nausea that rose in his throat. In the distance, he heard the barking dogs, still a ways off but moving in his direction.

Gritting his teeth, he pushed himself forward and at last found the fence, standing twenty yards from the cover of the woods. He felt dangerously exposed as he left the sheltering trees to meet it. Unbuttoning his coat, he let the heavy rug fall free and rolled it open. With a grunt, he hurled it up, draping it across the fence to cushion his way over the razor wire.

And climbed.

The cuff of his coat caught in the wire and he tore it free with a gasp of near panic. The rug was both help and hindrance, giving him nothing easy to hold onto as he scrambled over the top and fell to the other side, landing heavily on his shoulder and knocking the breath from his lungs.

Pulling himself to his feet, he brushed dirt and leaves from his pants and shook all his limbs. Everything seemed to be in working order, though he suspected he'd pay a price in pain for his tumble in the days to come.

Meaning to remove the rug and hide it among the trees, he tugged at the bulky fabric but it clung stubbornly to the sharp coiled wire. Not willing to spend time working it free, Vadim abandoned the carpet and fled into the ebony darkness of the forest beyond the fence.

He moved carefully. The rising moon would now be his friend, and he waited for it with longing. His first rudimentary plans for escape had included circling back to the parking lot where he'd left his car upon arrival at the facility, naively thinking he could use it for weekend forays into nearby towns and villages. In his first fevered attempts at planning, he'd meant to use his little Volvo to get him far and fast away from Anderson's grasp.

But a brief reconnaissance had shown him the car was gone. As sure a sign as any that Anderson never intended to let him leave the compound again.

A thrill of triumph rushed through him as he realized he'd foiled Anderson's expectation on that count, at least. But he was on foot, moving slowly, and Anderson had dogs.

He knew of a man, perhaps a dozen miles distant, who represented his best hope, though they'd never met. A former operative and well-known authority on criminal conspiracies, this man was the most likely to believe Vadim's fantastic story. The most likely to help him.

That's where he was headed.

47

—·—

THE MAN CALLED CINCHER braked the Alfa Romeo, listening to the engine growl as if sharing his impatience. Caught behind a lumbering semi truck, he drummed his fingers on the steering wheel as several cars shot past in the left lane. Then, pressing the accelerator, he cut away into a small gap left by a silver BMW and barreled south down the A93.

Glancing at his watch, he gauged another thirty minutes to Salzburg, and by that time the morning rush hour traffic would be thinning, easing his way through the city. All traces of pink had disappeared from the eastern sky, replaced by a crystalline blue without a wisp of cloud. Miles Davis played through the speakers, the beautiful melancholy trumpet tones perfectly matching Cincher's mood.

As he drove, he contemplated his current pet project, its culmination just days away. The strategic disruption of a peace summit at the top of a dormant volcano. Thinking about it roused pleasant memories of a distant volcano on another continent and how it had erupted so gloriously in concert with his own desires. As if acting as his accomplice.

Cincher craved knowledge of the earth's inner workings, burned with a yearning to harness and control its power. That spectacular eruption had planted in him the hope, the expectation, that he might find a way—at least in part—to achieve his aim. He wanted to rule the world, the actual planet, as no man had since Jesus walked the earth.

Thoughts of the volcano led to thoughts of Riley. He wondered how she was enjoying her training, how well she was learning and embracing the techniques of her new trade. He hoped she was seizing the opportunity to expand on her considerable talents, adding a phalanx of new skills to her remarkable repertoire.

He planned to present her with some interesting challenges, spice up her curriculum, put her to the test.

In fact, he'd already begun.

His phone rang and he hit a button, muting the music and bringing the voice of his caller into the car, one of his guards at the Czech research facility.

"Sir, Dr. Novak has escaped."

Cincher ground his teeth and switched lanes, passing another truck. "Details," he commanded.

"Novak didn't show up for his first scheduled session. He wasn't in his room or the cafeteria. We searched the grounds and found a rug thrown over the fence at the far end of the compound. He's gone."

Cincher said nothing.

"Sir, do you want us to—"

"No. I'll handle it."

Ending the call, Cincher took the next exit and reentered the autobahn going the opposite direction, shifting without conscious thought around traffic as he sped north. How long ago had Novak climbed the fence? Where would he go once he got outside the compound?

The Alfa Romeo hummed over the pavement, meeting his every demand as he pushed her hard, streaking past a blur of slower vehicles. He tightened his hands on the steering wheel as the obvious answer came to him.

Novak would make his way to Jan Eichel. The man's residence was only thirteen miles outside the compound and he was certain Novak knew about it. That's where he would go.

Cincher calculated the time and distance. He was maybe four hours away. Closer to three, if he maintained his current speed for most of the trip. Novak was so much closer. But he was on foot. With too many variables up in the air to make a sound prediction, Cincher knew one thing.

He wanted to get there first.

48

RILEY WOKE LATER THAN usual, bleary-eyed after her late night and feeling a little sore. Colette was already gone, her bed neatly made this time, so Riley had the bathroom to herself as she quickly showered and dressed. Swiping her towel across the fogged mirror, she stared at her reflection as she wrestled again over what to do about her discovery, as if her mirrored self might offer wisdom beyond her own.

She was among the last of the breakfast group in the dining room and hurried through a plate of over-cooked eggs and dried out cantaloupe, with the smell of bacon lingering to tell her what she'd missed. Her phone chimed out as she swallowed the last bite and wiped her fingers with a paper napkin. The screen identified the caller as Chief Wright, ringing in from Seattle, and Riley's heart rate quickened as she picked up.

"Any news?" she asked. "About Rick?"

"Not much from this end, Riley." A pause. "I called to see how you're doing."

"We need to talk," she told him. "But I'm not certain this phone is secure. I'm sending you some photos. The quality is not great, but see if you can ID the man."

Wright's voice was stern as he spoke again. "Riley, what are you doing? I'm afraid you're getting in deeper than I ever intended. I'd like to put you on a plane tonight, get you home."

"No," she said. "I can't go now. I have to know what's going on and I think I can help find out. I need to tell you what I saw and heard last night."

"Riley, please—"

"Chief Wright, I need to do this." She let a beat pass before adding, "Help me."

He sighed. "If you're determined to stay, then I need to arm you with a lot more knowledge than you currently have. And Riley," he warned, "you're not going to like what you hear."

"I'm ready," she assured him. "But I'm due in my first explosives class right now."

"Yes, I know. You'll get your first instructions in bomb making and breaking this morning, but it won't be what you expect. Report for class, Riley. We'll talk soon."

Leaving her breakfast tray on the table, Riley rushed out the dormitory and along the walkway leading to the classroom building. The buds on the fruit trees were beginning to open, blossoming like popcorn on the spindly branches and releasing a faint, sweet perfume into the warm morning air.

Hurrying down the hall to the EOD classroom, Riley stopped when she saw the sheet of paper taped to the door. A message in red marker said: "Explosives class postponed until tomorrow. Use the time to study for your exams."

And beneath that, in letters underlined three times: "Come in, Riley."

Mystified, Riley opened the door and found Matsui at the desk, red marker in hand, grading papers. She looked up and smiled. "You ready for a field trip?"

Riley stood, a little out of breath from her mad rush to get to class on time, the surprise at finding it canceled, and the personal summons in red. "Sure," she said. "Can we swing by my room to pick up my purse?"

"I think we can work that in. Let's go."

Once in the car with Matsui behind the wheel, Riley said, "Where are we going?"

Matsui passed through the main gate and turned onto the road, heading east. "We'll get to that," she said, "but there's something you need to do first." She handed Riley a cell phone. "I got you a new mobile. It's clean. Chief Wright's on speed dial. Call him."

Riley felt her head spinning a little. Things were happening so fast. Wright had said they'd talk soon, and he was certainly a man of his word. She hit the button and he answered right away.

"Okay, Riley. Tell me what's going on" he ordered.

She told him about following the figure through the woods and finding out it was Paula Hill, assistant director of the academy. She related as much as she could remember about the conversation she'd overheard between Hill and the man in the *Hof,* including their reference to Zimmermann, head of the local crime unit, and the bald man's part in setting fire to the car.

"And," she added, swallowing the lump in her throat, "they confirmed that Agent Rick Jimenez is dead and soon to be buried. Hill is somehow involved in Rick's death, Chief Wright, just as I suspected.

And they're not finished. There's more to their plan but I couldn't hear much or make sense of the little bits I did hear."

Wright listened without interrupting. When she finished, there was a silence before he said, "Don't share this with anyone else, Riley. I think you're safest if no one knows you're aware of Hill's involvement. I'm moving pieces into place to protect you and manage the situation. In the meantime, please lay low. Do not put yourself in more danger. What you did was risky."

"Isn't it the sort of thing you sent me here to learn?"

Laughing, he said, "You make a fair point." His voice sobered. "But I sent you there to be well-trained before going into the field. You are jumping the gun."

He paused. "But then, this isn't the first time you've done that, is it Riley? It's what brought you to our attention in the first place."

She said nothing, and Wright ended the call with another admonition to keep her head down and be careful. Riley dropped the new phone into her purse and turned sideways in her seat to face Matsui. Clearly, Wright trusted his explosives instructor and Riley's instinct led her to do the same. It felt good to be with someone she could rely on.

"And now, listen up," Matsui told her. "We've got an hour drive ahead, so you're getting a personal preview of tomorrow's class material. Your first lesson in bombs."

Riley wanted to ask again where they were going, but as Matsui began speaking, she found herself caught up in the woman's enthusiastic lecture. Settling into her seat, she leaned her head back and listened.

"A bomb is essentially a simple device," Matsui said. "A chemical process of combining certain substances in specific proportions. In most cases, the components only become dangerous once the switch is activated."

She looked at Riley to see if she understood. "An open switch allows you to safely assemble the parts. But activate the switch, close the circuit, and you've got *kaboom!*"

Twitching, Riley said, "I doubt I'll ever have to face a bomb during my concert tours, Matsui. Much less, have to make one."

"Ah, but you never know, do you? That's the nature of field work. You have to be ready for anything."

Matsui signaled and made a turn, a little too sharp and a little too fast. Riley fought to stay upright in her seat.

"Sorry," Matsui said. She glanced at Riley with an apologetic grin. "Most people," she continued, "don't realize how prevalent explosives are in everyday life. You may not realize, but we've got little bombs going off in front of us right now. That's what makes the car go—explosions of gasoline in the engine's cylinders push down the pistons and turn the crankshaft."

"Okay," Riley said, "but those aren't bombs."

"Think outside the box, MacGyver. They could be, with some modifications. We're surrounded by materials that can be made to explode. Ever heard about a grain silo explosion? Wheat flour, under the right conditions, is flammable. Same with coal dust. And do you know what kind of purchase often leads us to catch a budding bomb maker?"

Riley thought. "Fertilizer."

"Correct. Fertilizer full of nitrates." Matsui held up a finger to emphasize her next point. "But not only are explosive substances found in abundance—so are potential switches. Alarm clocks, kitchen timers, the little thingy you attach to your sprinkler system to turn the water on and off, or your lights so burglars will think you're at home."

Matsui's brow wrinkled as she maneuvered the car around a tractor, but she continued her subject with undampened zeal. "A bomb can be triggered by a coffee machine, a toaster, a barometer when a predetermined altitude is reached. Or fixed to a motion sensor. The fashion nowadays is to use a cell phone, but there are a hundred other options. Really, it's only limited by the fiendish bomb maker's imagination."

Riley stared at her friend, unsure whether to be impressed or horrified. "You are certainly passionate about the deadly art of bomb making, Matsui," she said.

Matsui bobbed her head in definitive agreement. "It's a fascinating field. Bombs are not just a way to blow things up," she said. "They're a riddle. A puzzle. A window into the soul of their creator and an indicator of what he thinks of others.

"The way someone designs an explosive device," she went on, "says something about his opinions and expectations of the intended recipients. His victims, or in many cases, those tasked with stopping his destruction."

"The bomb squad," Riley said.

"Right. He is thinking of the bomb squad while constructing his device, pitting himself against them, predicting what they'll do and how they'll react to his creation, working to stay one step ahead of them."

"Were you on a bomb squad, Matsui?"

"The best," she said. "NYPD. That's where I learned everything I know about bombs." She hesitated. "And that's where I got this." She peeled back the sleeve over her right arm to show Riley a wicked, disfiguring scar where a palm-sized piece of flesh was missing just below the elbow.

"Oh, Matsui!"

"Score one for the bomber," Matsui replied. "But I'm alive, so score a dozen points for me."

Riley felt a sting of tears but blinked them away, inspired by her friend's courage, her determination to continue down a path that had dealt her that kind of blow. "Will you tell me where we're going?" she asked.

"We are going to Czech, to visit a retired operative, an old friend of Chief Wright's. This man is an authority on conspiracies, and a specialist regarding one in particular—an organization known as The Knot. No one outside the organization itself knows more about The Knot and how it operates. I think you'll be very interested to hear what he has to say."

A chill flickered through Riley. She remembered the coin passed to her by the mysterious bicyclist, the knot on one side, the world on the other. She'd forgotten to mention that strange interaction to Wright. With sudden certainty, she understood that The Knot—for some unknown reason—was aware of her.

It was time to repay the favor.

49

RILEY STRAIGHTENED IN HER seat and looked around as Matsui slowed the car, turning into a narrow lane thick with woods on both sides. She realized she'd been so absorbed in the explosive expert's talk of bombs that she hadn't noticed crossing the border from Germany into the Czech Republic. They'd traveled off the autobahn, passing through villages on smaller roads, and the transition would have been indicated by a simple sign rather than a well-marked checkpoint.

Still, she chided herself for failing, once again, to be observant and aware of her surroundings. It was a habit she must cultivate. They rounded a bend and Matsui pulled up to an iron gate set in a high stone wall. She leaned out the window and pushed a button, activating the intercom system.

A buzzer sounded and she spoke into the mic. "Matsui Haruko and Riley Forte," she announced. "We're here to see Professor Eichel. Devin Wright made the appointment."

Riley expected the gate to swing open. Instead, an elderly man walked out from the ivy-covered house beyond, moving at a dignified pace as he traversed the pebbled drive. A full minute passed before the crunch of gravel beneath his feet grew audible and he inserted a large old-fashioned key into the lock and waved them onto the property.

Matsui drove on, leaving the butler to make the return trip as she steered around the circular driveway and parked the car. By the time she'd stepped onto the gravel, shaken out the kinks, and collected her purse, Riley heard the man's footsteps once again.

"The professor is waiting for you," he said. "In the library. Follow me."

Riley stared around her as they entered the house. From the outside, it had appeared ordinary in the extreme, a plain and boxy brick structure overgrown with vines. Stepping inside was like entering a miracle of illusion. The walls and ceiling seemed to open up, pulling out into a larger space than could be contained by the outward dimensions.

And that space was filled with wonders.

Antique clocks and radios, a vintage jukebox, a 1930's model Harley Davidson parked in the corner. Model airplanes suspended from the ceiling. A wide array of medieval weapons. Framed maps from every age of the world's progression. Relics gathered from Egypt, India, South America. Ships in bottles and shrunken heads. Riley tried not to gape.

The butler led them up a curving staircase and along a wide hallway graced by a royal red runner. The abundant collection of knickknacks, souvenirs, and memorabilia continued. Ushered into the library, she stopped and stared at the shelves that seemed to rise upward forever, tier upon tier of books, to the glass ceiling at the top. She thought about Willy Wonka's wonderful chocolate factory, with its glass elevator, and decided Professor Eichel's house contained a similar trove of treats and treasures.

"Please come in and make yourselves comfortable."

Riley turned to see a thin man dressed in a periwinkle blue cardigan and gray corduroy slacks. Wisps of fine white hair rose from various spots on his shiny scalp, but the salt-and-pepper mustache perched above his lip was thick and luxurious, as if proclaiming he could grow hair where he really wanted it. He smiled and waved his hands toward a grouping of chairs and sofas in the center of the amazing room.

Riley dropped into a velvet armchair while Matsui went to the professor, giving him a brief squeeze and a peck on the cheek where he remained seated. Riley noted the walker next to his chair, the tremor in his hands, and deduced that Professor Eichel was not a well man.

"It's good to see you again, Jan," Matsui told him.

"And you, my dear." He peered at Riley. "Who have you brought with you?" he asked.

Matsui made the introductions and the professor's gaze sharpened, but he only said, "Ah."

The butler arrived with a tray of lemonade and a plate of thin, delicate wafers that melted like butter on her tongue when Riley tried one.

"Devin instructed me to tell you about The Knot," Eichel said, "and I'll do my best to hit the salient points. There's more to know than I can tell in one sitting. And far more than you can tolerate," he added grimly.

"I feel certain the roots of the organization could be traced back to Cain," he continued. "Since man's first steps on this planet there have been secret sects dedicated to serving evil and destroying the agency of mankind. The Knot is just another iteration, but a treacherous one indeed."

Eichel's gaze wandered to the wall of books. "No one really knows when or where The Knot began, but the leadership has been passed down from one dastardly hand to another for at least a hundred years."

"Like the mafia," Matsui suggested.

A frown formed between the professor's eyes. "But a good deal more insidious," he said. "Organizations like the mafia operate for profit and power within their own realm. Those inside The Knot want money and power also, but they don't stop there. Something within them demands the destruction of the human spirit, the enslaving of the soul."

Riley shivered, putting down her glass as if the chill came from the ice inside it.

"The Knot has access to unlimited funds, channeled from a vast variety of sources—drugs, prostitution and pornography, human trafficking, political corruption, and a host of well-meaning but deluded donors who buy into the facade of one propaganda scheme or another. It's frightening to contemplate the amount and degree of conflict caused by The Knot, and the number of world leaders who are simply puppets under The Knot's control."

Riley saw the look of horror on Matsui's face and knew it must match her own. "That's atrocious," she said, hearing the quiver in her own voice.

"I'm sorry to say, it gets worse," Eichel went on. He really did look sorry, his face tinged yellow now and lined with sorrow. "The current leader of The Knot is financing a series of research and testing centers in several areas of the world. He is interested in human psychology and the art of manipulation and has been furthering the work done by evil scientists from ages past."

"Like Hitler, you mean," Matsui said.

Eichel nodded. "And others." He hesitated. "The latest information I have also suggests he is researching and developing instruments to harness the power of the earth itself. I am exceedingly disturbed by reports that he is working to produce a weapon more powerful than the world has ever known. It's rumored to be able to control the weather and cause earthquakes, tsunamis, and other natural disasters."

A wave of nausea broke over Riley and she swallowed hard. "Could it trigger a volcanic eruption?" she asked.

Eichel looked at her, compassion in his eyes. "My dear, I don't know. Perhaps the reports are exaggerated or the rumors false. I am an old man now. I spend my time here, in my library, while others gather the data and explore the field. I can only infer from what they bring me."

Riley hardly heard him. She was remembering a man called John, to whom she'd turned in a moment of dire need, trusting him to help her. He'd lulled her in, played the hero, and then turned her world upside down and nearly strangled the life out of her.

In the aftermath of Rainier's eruption, people said he was responsible for saving thousands of lives. Others said he manipulated the public and caused a panic. Riley knew the truth—he was a liar and a murderer. As insane as it sounded, was it possible that he'd somehow caused the eruption?

She turned her gaze on Professor Eichel. "Do you know the identity of this leader of The Knot?"

Looking more miserable than ever, he met her eyes, his own crinkled with pain. "He's called the Cincher," he said. "But I believe you know him as John."

50

LIESL LEFT HER APARTMENT, Max's kiss still warm on her cheek, and walked along the mezzanine, peering down over the railing. The lovely view from the lobby's enormous windows which had never failed to lift her spirits and prepare her for the day, left her strangely flat this morning.

She was anxious about the summit, but a deeper concern stemmed from being at odds with Julia. Since the disastrous dish washing incident, they'd hardly spoken to each other and Liesl worried that her sister's frequent absences signaled time spent with Anton Forst and his unsavory influence.

Entering the office, she exchanged *Guten Morgens* with Joseph and sank into her chair, kicking off her pumps beneath the desk. Scrunching her stockinged toes in the pile of the rug, she allowed herself a moment to brood before picking up the phone and dialing Dieter's number.

"Liesl," he greeted her, "I was going to call later this morning."

"Why? What have you found?"

A small silence passed before he said, "I'm afraid I haven't found anything. My sources have dried up and the fellow I spoke with earlier left yesterday on an impromptu vacation. No one knows where he went, and he's not answering his phone."

Liesl pinched the bridge of her nose. "I don't know what to do, Dieter. This just keeps getting worse and worse."

"I'm so sorry, Liesl. I wish I had something brilliant to offer, but..."

"No, it's okay. I appreciate your efforts."

"May I ask," Dieter said, "if you've expressed your concerns to your security team? You should put them in the picture."

Liesl sighed. "You're right. I'll speak with Gunther right away. Thanks, Dieter."

She ended the call and squeezed her toes hard against the nubby fabric of the rug, pulling in a deep breath and curling her hands into fists at the same time. She held steady for ten seconds then exhaled and let the tension drain out of her fingers and feet. Slipping back into her shoes, she rose from the desk and went in search of her head of security.

She dreaded the thought of airing her family's dirty laundry among the staff but felt an increasing need to let Gunther know her concerns.

The first of the guests were scheduled to check in this evening.

51

ARRIVING BACK AT THE academy with Matsui, Riley felt too keyed up even for the piano. She needed a wider space to absorb the waves of tension radiating through her. Changing into a running suit and shoes, she jogged past Matsui's garden, heading away from the forest to a path across the open pasture.

Reaching it, she ran hard, feeling her feet connect with the earth, somehow soothed by their rhythmic pounding. The late afternoon was clouding over, turning gray, and the smell of wet soil permeated the air from freshly plowed and planted fields.

Ahead, Riley saw Gideon Schmidt, the German martial arts instructor, on his horse. She hailed him, realizing he might be able to supply some information about the *Hof* and its occupants. He turned the horse and came near but didn't dismount, looking down at her with an expressionless face.

Riley felt a momentary confusion. Had she done something to offend him? His attitude toward her seemed distinctly altered from his gallant greeting the first time they'd met. Suddenly unsure what to say, she began with, "I saw you last night."

Gideon's expression changed from mild derision to borderline hostility, his eyes narrowing suspiciously, jawline going hard. Baffled,

Riley cast about for some way to neutralize the growing coldness in the air between them.

"You were riding against the sunset," she said. "You and your horse looked magnificent." She gestured toward the horse. "Such a noble and beautiful animal. What's his name?"

Her tack had been the right one. His face transformed, melting into a smile as he slid from the saddle and brought his horse to meet her.

"He's called Maximus."

Riley rubbed the snuffling velvet nose and laughed when Maximus pushed gently against her palm.

"He wants a carrot," Gideon told her.

"I wish I had one for him." She hesitated, then said casually, "Where do you live, Gideon?"

He flung an arm to the west. "In a village over the hill, about five kilometers."

"Have you been there long?"

"Since I was a child. I live with my grandparents still. They need help taking care of the place."

Riley wanted to ask more about his family, but feared that might reawaken his earlier disdain. Instead, she moved on to her main objective.

"Outside of your village, does anyone else live over that way?"

He looked at her curiously, but seemed willing enough to answer. "Only a writer, some kind of naturalist. He keeps to himself, but I sometimes see him out walking."

"A writer? Really? What kind of books does he write?"

Gideon shrugged. "I really can't say. Books about nature, I suppose."

"Does he often get visitors?"

His lips twitched and a note of mockery entered his voice as he said, "You may be surprised to discover that I don't keep tabs on my neighbors, Riley."

She smiled. "Actually, I am a bit surprised. Aren't you a teacher in a school for spies?"

Laughing, he put his foot in the stirrup and swung up into the saddle. "I am," he admitted. "But intelligence gathering is not my strong suit. I'm only here to teach defense courses."

He nodded a farewell and signaled Maximus into a fast trot, leaving Riley to stare after him.

"And that's what I really need to learn," she said to the empty field. "How to defend myself against an enemy I can't even see."

52

Vadim followed the butler up a curving staircase, scarcely noticing the lavish assortment of ornaments adorning the walls, suspended from the ceiling, and resting on every tabletop. His legs trembled violently enough to make him wonder if each step he mounted would be his defeat. Scratched from brambles, stung by nettle, weak with hunger and thirst, he nevertheless felt tremendous relief at having reached his goal. The house of Professor Jan Eichel.

The one man both accessible and in a position to believe his incredible report.

The butler threw open the door and held it wide. "A visitor for you, Professor. A Dr. Vadim Novak."

The old man in the damask armchair didn't rise, but waved a trembling hand in welcome, motioning Vadim onto the adjacent sofa. "Please sit, you look absolutely exhausted." He turned to the butler. "Find something in the kitchen for the good doctor. He needs nourishment." With a glance at Vadim, he added, "And a stiff drink."

Vadim sank onto the sofa, feeling the warmth and softness of its support, almost giddy with the release of tension. "Thank you, Professor Eichel. You are providing a much needed refuge for a most desperate man."

"Please, call me Jan. Unburden yourself, my dear man. Tell me what has made you so desperate."

With an effort to keep his voice reasoned and in control, Vadim told the professor how he'd been seduced into Anderson's mad research compound and the horrendous experiments he'd been forced to conduct, without regard for human life and suffering.

While he spoke, the butler returned with a tray of sandwiches and a large whiskey. The smell of chicken and cranberry sparked his appetite and his stomach roared. A moment previously, his nausea was such that he would never eat again. But now, with shaking hands, Vadim lifted a sandwich, chewing and swallowing past the lump in his throat. After several bites and a few sips of whiskey, he felt calmer and able to continue his story.

"Anderson is determined to find fool-proof methods of brain-washing and manipulation. I believe," he hesitated, knowing what he intended to say sounded extreme and irrational. "I believe he is planning to create an army of soldiers who will obey his every command without question."

The professor studied him closely, then nodded as if satisfied. "Yes, your story is credible to me. A very dangerous man, this Dr. Anderson. Surely an alias. Do you have any idea of his real identity?"

Vadim shook his head. "I know him only as Anderson, though I am sure you are right. No man would commit such heinous crimes in his own name."

Eichel stared at him a moment longer, then made a clucking, disapproving noise in his throat. "Ach, you must rest, my friend. We can speak more about it tomorrow."

Summoning the butler with a tinkling bell, Eichel ordered a bedroom prepared and soon Vadim was stretching out beneath the cool smoothness of clean sheets, covered by the weight and warmth of a heavy quilt. The horrors of the last weeks dropped away as he fell into a deep and dreamless oblivion.

53

Nate flattened the empty pizza box and shoved it down into the curbside recycling bin, nestling it among the sour-smelling milk cartons and yogurt containers. The Seattle morning had been damp and drizzly and the afternoon continued along the same theme. Cold rain slicked the driveway and passing cars sent up rooster tails of dirty water, splashing the sidewalk and the back of Nate's pants as he trudged back toward the house.

Disgusted, he dried the dripping hem of his pants with a dish towel and stared out the window at the line of soggy, drooping evergreens. He still had five days of leave time to kill. He'd cleaned out the refrigerator, changed the oil in the car, and finished binge-watching episodes of *White Collar*. Nothing he did took his mind off the three ladies in his life—Sammi, Marilyn, and Riley—and his quandary surrounding them.

Finally, he did what he'd been itching to do all day. He picked up the phone and called Devin Wright.

"I'm going to Germany," he told the Olivero chief. "Short of abducting me, you really can't stop it happening, so let's work together, Devin."

"As a matter of fact," Wright replied, "I'm relieved to hear it. Riley's uncovered a mole at the academy and I'm a little worried about her."

"A mole? Who?"

"My assistant director at the academy, Paula Hill, has been working for the wrong side." A pause, then Wright said, "I'm sorry, Nate. She was involved in Rick's death."

"What! How?"

"I don't know yet."

So, Riley's in real danger," Nate said, pounding a fist on the table in front of him.

"Hill doesn't know Riley's onto her," Wright assured him. "If she keeps her head down, she'll be okay until I can get a team in there to handle the situation."

Nate stood, pacing the kitchen floor, his fist still clenched at his side. "How soon will that be?"

"There are complications, Nate. They won't arrive before Friday."

"I can get there sooner. I'm taking the first flight I can find."

"Agreed. Thanks," Wright said. "But Nate, you're just there to keep Riley safe, okay? I don't want the two of you taking on Hill and her gang."

"She has a gang?"

Wright hesitated. "Riley sent me pictures of a man working with Hill. We were able to identify him as Moritz Schiller, currently using the alias Anton Forst. He is suspected of running a high-end service for wanted criminals, providing them with fresh identities and documents, some forged but many of them genuine."

"Stolen from their rightful owners?" Nate asked.

"Unfortunately, yes. We believe Forst steals not only their identities, but their lives. He murders innocent people and clears the way for terrorists, traffickers, and drug lords to step into their place. Sometimes even drastically altering their appearance with plastic surgery."

Queasy from a combination of anxiety and the greasy pizza he'd eaten earlier, Nate said, "How did Riley find out about Hill and this guy?"

Wright coughed. "I'll let her tell you about that. She did say," he added, "that they were discussing plans for some kind of operation. She couldn't make out the details."

"Any idea what they might be plotting?"

A pause. "Actually, I have an inkling about a possible target. Did you know there's an event center at the top of the mountain where the academy is located?"

"Not until now," Nate said.

"There hasn't been a lot of publicity about this—they're trying to keep it under the radar—but several leaders from eastern European countries are meeting there this week for peace talks."

"Hmm, and you think that might have something to do with Hill's plans?"

"I think it's worth looking into."

"Wonderful," Nate said, anger roiling in his gut. He never should have encouraged Riley to sign up for this. "Anything else you want to tell me?" he asked.

"No," Wright said. "But there's one last thing I *should* tell you."

Nate let out a growl. "What?"

"We think this man, Anton Forst, is connected with The Knot, the criminal organization run by Cincher."

"You mean—"
"Yes, Nate. I mean the man who tried to kill Riley last October."

54

VADIM FELT A PRICKLE on the side of his neck, a brief sting like the bite of a mosquito, and slapped at the spot as he rose to consciousness. He opened his eyes and pushed up onto an elbow. The room was dark and he was still very tired. Closing his eyes again, he sank back onto the pillow and was almost asleep when the light came on, a harsh contrast to the blessed dimness.

Holding a hand up against the glare, he blinked and saw Professor Eichel standing beside the bed.

"I'm so sorry to disturb you, Dr. Novak," Eichel said, "but there's someone here who would like to join you."

As he watched, the butler entered the room, dragging an elderly man dressed in a blue sweater and gray corduroy pants. He appeared to be dead, his neck twisted at a fantastic angle, head flopping with each of the butler's steps. Dismayed, Vadim struggled to sit up but found he couldn't move.

"Ah, yes," Eichel said. "By now, you've discovered that you are paralyzed. That is due to the injection of succinylcholine I administered just moments ago." Stepping aside, he turned to the butler and gave a sweeping motion with his hand, inviting him to advance with the sagging body.

The butler turned back the coverlet and hoisted the body into the bed, arranging it beside Vadim, draping one of the corpse's arms around his shoulder. As he finished, Eichel stepped forward and doused Vadim liberally with liquid from a large glass bottle, soaking his clothes and the sheets beneath him. Vadim recognized the distinctive odor of cyclohexane.

Struggling to move, to scream, to do anything, Vadim could only produce a feeble whimper.

"What's that you say?" Eichel taunted, cupping a hand to his ear. "Did you have something more you wanted to tell me about the evil Dr. Anderson?"

Eichel laughed. Reaching a hand to his face, he peeled off the grizzled eyebrows and luxuriant mustache. Vadim stared, watching helplessly as Anderson revealed himself, contempt showing in his every move. Vadim understood he was now sharing the bed with the real Jan Eichel.

Anderson lit a cigarette, releasing a mouthful of smoke as he stared down at the entwined couple in the bed.

"You really should be more careful," he said. "A distinguished scientist such as yourself should know better than to spill chemicals on his clothing. It can be quite dangerous."

Taking a final puff on the cigarette, Anderson held it poised as he added, "Especially if you're going to smoke in bed."

He flicked the cigarette onto the sheets and flames rose up before Vadim's eyes, wavering, stretching, growing. They obscured his vision, producing black clouds of acrid smoke.

Searing pain engulfed him.

His thoughts flickered, guttering like the flames, taking him back to those men locked in the brick building with the unbreakable windows. Like them, he must bow to the vicious, ugly truth.

There was no escape.

55

—·—

Riley woke to the sound of her phone vibrating on the bedside table.

Snatching it up, she rolled into a sitting position and looked across to her roommate's bed. Colette was stirring beneath the duvet, one slender ebony leg stretching out to test the air. Riley took the phone with her into the bathroom and shut the door.

"Riley, this is Director Edwards."

At last. Riley sank onto the closed lid of the toilet, so relieved to hear his voice.

"Thank goodness," she said. "I've been—"

"Don't say anything," he interrupted. "Put on your sweatsuit and go jogging on the woodland trail. We'll meet accidentally."

The call ended and Riley stared at the phone, her heart rate rising. Moving quickly, she brushed her teeth and hair and pulled on her running clothes, tying her shoes as Colette slipped past without a word and disappeared into the bathroom.

Outside, the morning was draped in fog, giving the stretch of forest a haunted appearance. Riley took a moment to stretch, for the sake of her muscles and to add authenticity to her run, if anyone was watching. The air smelled damp and slightly spicy as she began a loose jog into the trees, listening and alert for anything she might encounter on what promised to be another unusual day.

Just beyond a point where her path crossed with another trail, she caught sight of a figure in a navy blue jogging suit coming toward her. Director Edwards greeted her, wiping his face on a white towel hung around his neck.

"Riley! How nice to see you again. I trust you've settled in by now?"

She slowed to walk beside him. "Yes, Director Edwards. I'm learning my way. And thank you so much for supplying me with a piano. I can't tell you how much that means to me."

"Call me Stan," he said. "And it's my pleasure to make sure you have a piano to play. I'd love to hear you practice sometime, if that's all right."

"Of course."

He was leading her by the elbow, steering her onto the intersecting path. "We can speak freely here," he told her. "And there is much we need to discuss. I hardly know where to begin."

Riley knew where she wanted to begin. "Your assistant director, Paula Hill, is a traitor," she said. "I followed—"

"Yes, Chief Wright told me what you did. We'll circle back to that, Riley. First, however, I must share a sad piece of news."

His voice, with its faint Kenyan accent, held a note of sorrow and Riley steeled herself for another shock. "I received word early this morning," Edwards continued, "of a house fire over the border in the Czech Republic. A house you visited just yesterday."

A sudden heaviness settled over Riley's chest. "Oh no. The professor, is he all right?"

"Professor Eichel burned to death in his bed," Edwards said. "The butler was found at the bottom of the stairs with a broken neck. Local authorities have concluded that the fire was caused by Eichel smoking in bed. They think the butler was running to the aid of his master when he tripped and fell. A tragic ending all around."

"But that's not what really happened," Riley said, and then felt foolish for stating the obvious.

"No. There was another man in the bed with Eichel. We are working now to identify him and piece together how he got there."

Stunned, Riley struggled to accept this new development as a horrifying thought occurred to her. In anguish, she stopped walking and gripped the director by the shoulders. "Did Professor Eichel die because of me? Did my visit bring this upon him?"

"No, Riley. You must not think that. This was in no way your fault."

Stepping back, she covered her face with her hands and felt Edwards move closer, his voice low and soothing, just beside her ear.

"There are wicked people at work here, Riley. You did not spawn them and you do not inspire them. They march under different orders."

She let her hands drop and he continued. "You, me, those of us who embrace and believe in light and goodness—however trite that may sound—we do what we can to defeat their efforts and protect the innocent. That is what you are here to do."

Riley stared at the ground beneath her feet, the path scattered with pine needles, and lifted her chin. "I know you're right," she said. "It just seems so impossible sometimes."

Edwards grunted. "Perhaps it is," he said. "But does that mean we should step back and do nothing?"

He paused. "This man Eichel told you about—the Cincher—is clever and determined, with a finely-tuned ability to make men dance at his command."

"And with unlimited resources, apparently," Riley said, remembering Professor Eichel's report. "Are we the only ones opposing him?"

"By no means," Edwards assured her.

"Who else?" Riley demanded.

"I know several good people, from a variety of agencies, who've stood against The Knot. People of character, with integrity and brains."

"What results have they achieved?"

Edwards sighed but didn't speak.

"Tell me."

The director started walking again and Riley stayed beside him. "Last year, a British journalist wrote a headline article," he said, "exposing The Knot's connection with terrorist activities in Europe and Asia, leading to dozens of arrests and destroying two powerful sub-organizations."

"Okay, that's encouraging. What's the journalist doing now?"

They walked several steps before Edwards said, "Two days after the article went to press, the journalist was found in an alley, stabbed through the heart. The murderer was never caught."

Riley bit down on her lip, tasting blood. She knew this road she'd chosen to travel was hazardous and rife with risk. As difficult as it was for her to hear what the director was telling her, she needed to prove to herself that she wasn't burying her head in the sand. She would be more useful to Olivero, and to herself, if she went in clear-eyed.

"I want to know more," she told Edwards as they continued along the path.

"I personally knew an international banker who helped us, and firms like ours, to trace and circumvent funding sources for The Knot. Thanks to her help, we were able to shut down multiple streams of income the organization relied upon to carry out their deeds."

"And?" Riley prompted. "What happened to the banker?"

"Dead," Edwards admitted. "Infected with an engineered disease custom-designed to attack her respiratory system. We still don't know how the pathogens were introduced."

Riley kicked a pine cone, sending it bouncing off the thick trunk of a towering fir tree.

"The details of this are still classified, Riley, but I can tell you that the president of an unnamed South American country who denied agents of The Knot passage through his nation's airways died in his bathtub. The cause of death is still undetermined. The medical examiner described the body as shrunken and burned from the inside out, as though a wave of electrical energy of incredible power had passed through it. He'd never seen anything like it."

"All right," Riley said. "That's enough. You've given me a pretty clear picture. We can do some good, but the price of our progress is likely to be very high indeed." She stopped walking and turned to face Edwards, meeting his eye. "So why do I still feel like going forward?"

His smile was tinged with sadness as he replied, "Because that's who you are, Riley. Rick saw that in you. Chief Wright recognized it, too. You are one of us. Those who must fight or we can't live."

"Or can't live, because we fight," Riley said.

The director lifted his arms in acknowledgment. "The dilemma of the two-edged sword."

They resumed walking, their steps making almost no noise on the carpeted soil of the trail. After a moment, Edwards said, "There's something else I must tell you, Riley. Those photos you sent to Wright—he's identified your mystery man. He uses a number of aliases, but is now going under the name Anton Forst, a supposed writer and authority on insects and pollinating plants."

"He and Paula Hill are plotting something," Riley said. "I couldn't hear the details, but I got the sense it's going down soon."

"Wright is sending a team to take Forst and Hill into custody and deliver them to the proper authorities, along with any evidence we can gather. But that," he said, his voice stern, "is not your job, Riley. Let the specialists handle it. You need to stay out of Hill's way. Is that understood?"

"Yes," Riley replied. "I do understand."

And she did.

56

THE MAN KNOWN AS Cincher cut into the thick steak on his plate, cooked so medium rare it showed bloody raw at the center. He chewed slowly, letting the slightly charred flavor permeate his senses, enjoying the melting texture and satisfying mouthfeel before swallowing the meat and taking a sip of dark pinot noir.

He held the glass up, letting the afternoon light filter through the wine, burnishing it to a glowing cherry red. He'd not expected to return to his private dining room at the Czech compound so soon, but Novak's escape had altered his plans.

It had all worked out for the good.

He'd hoped the reluctant doctor would last several more weeks. His work had been exceptional, though Cincher had seen the quality decline steadily over his time at the facility. Beyond that, his observations of Novak himself provided him with interesting insights and some real moments of pleasure.

He regretted having to dispatch the doctor so prematurely, but the silver lining came with getting rid of Eichel at the same time. It was something he'd meant to do for a long while, but never got around to. The man, in his retirement, caused little harm and it tickled Cincher to know he was there, ineffectually gathering news and data, deploying his chess pieces, always one move behind.

It was almost a pity he was gone, but there were always those who would step in to replace him. An unending supply of well-intentioned people, every one of them human. Every one of them with vulnerabilities, flaws, weaknesses to be discovered and exploited.

Ah, the joys of life.

Cincher put down his glass of wine and sliced off another bloody bite of steak.

57

RILEY SAT AT THE table in her room, notes spread out around her, still feeling a fuzzy sense of unreality from the disturbing events unfolding at an alarming rate. She had no scheduled classes for the afternoon and was supposed to be studying for upcoming exams and practicals. But she couldn't even begin to concentrate, her mind flooding with flashes of memory, fragments of a bewildering and terrifying puzzle she couldn't piece together.

From outside, she heard faint shouts and an occasional whistle from the soccer field where a group of recruits played a game of football. Through the window, she had a glimpse of a corner of the field, the motion never failing to catch her eye and pull her attention away from her notes every time the game action moved into that corner.

Too tense, too distracted to study, she thought about visiting the piano room. This would be her usual method for dealing with most any mental dilemma. But memories from her last session there, trying to work through the challenging staccato passage and meeting only frustration, steered her away from that option.

It too closely felt like a metaphor for what she was going through now—trying to balance frenetic leaps of unpredictable movement with the methodical acquisition of fresh skills to create the strong, resilient fabric of a new life for herself.

Instead, she opened her laptop case and extracted the coded message she'd retrieved from the dead drop. Unfolding the paper, she stared at the odd collection of letters. How long before she'd be able to decrypt the message? Would it be included in her exams? Was she really up to the challenge?

She tried again to apply familiar techniques to the cipher, even applying all 26 permutations of the alphabet, but got nowhere. This was useless. She was accomplishing nothing of value sitting here in her room.

Motion from the field caught her eye again, and she saw assistant director Hill on the sidelines, speaking with the instructor. Edwards had warned her to steer clear of Paula Hill, and she intended to comply. But knowing where Hill was, meant she also knew where Hill wasn't.

Putting on her sneakers, Riley left the room and headed for the woods. She wanted only to get a look at the *Hof* in the daylight. As she moved through the trees, she touched their trunks and budding branches, marveling over the miracle of spring.

It fascinated her how the evergreens maintained their needled fronds year round while the maples, birch, oaks, and myriad other species changed their plumage with the seasons. Their boughs were sparse now, but would soon be lush with new growth, green leaves as big as her hand. Stepping among them, feeling them tower over her, brought her back to her childhood and long summer days spent playing outdoors and often ending, in the twilight, with her favorite game, dubbed Spy Catcher.

This was her neighborhood's version of hide-and-seek and few of the resident kids could resist its appeal. Spreading out in the fringe of woods that bordered the block, the spies melted into the trees or took cover behind the shrubs and flowerbeds of nearby yards as the hot pursuit began. Those captured joined the catchers, so the game became ever more tense for the remaining spies until only a solitary spy remained.

Riley remembered that had often been her. She'd had absolutely no idea, at the time, how much her life would come to resemble the game. She hoped she could become as good at it now as she had been in those long ago childhood days. When time ran out, she wanted to be able to tag base and shout, "Home free!"

Arriving at the gate, she made sure she remembered the new set of six digits, just distributed that morning. The entry code for the gate changed weekly and no one was allowed to write the numbers down. For Riley, accustomed to memorizing whole scores of music—a coded language of another type—this was not a problem.

Letting herself through the gate, she moved cautiously among the foliage. In the strife of her stormy nighttime flight, the distance from the gate to the *Hof* had seemed to stretch for a mile at least. Riley was surprised to realize it was a small fraction of that distance. She came upon the house with its little group of outbuildings after pushing through the woods for maybe two hundred yards.

Careful to stay well back, under the shaded cover of the trees, Riley stared at the *Hof,* taking in details of the layout, the window and door arrangement, the implements in the surrounding garden, the dusty black Mercedes parked on the dirt beside the front door, at an angle making it impossible to see the license plate. She didn't know if observation skills would be part of her upcoming exams, but this seemed to be the sort of study she could conduct in her current state.

Wondering about the dog she'd heard in the night, she peered around but saw no animal, no water bowl, no sign of a dog in the courtyard. Then, as she watched, the front door opened and a man in a long coat exited the house and slid into the car.

He wore a cloth cap pulled low, and it all happened so fast that Riley couldn't be certain she was looking at the bald man she'd seen arguing with Hill. Anton Forst. The Mercedes rumbled to life and Riley kicked herself as it disappeared around a bend in the lane. She hadn't taken note of the plate number.

In a quandary of indecision, Riley rubbed a hand over her forehead. If that had been Forst, and not a visitor to the house, then the *Hof* might be empty now, presenting a perfect opportunity to move in a little closer and explore. She wanted to at least get another peek through the windows, which now stood unshuttered.

Swallowing hard, she made a decision and stepped forward, moving carefully toward the house, keeping her eyes and ears open to warning signals. Arriving at the same window she'd used on her previous visit, she peered cautiously inside, taking in the fireplace, now devoid of flame, and a large wooden table, littered with evidence of a recent meal.

Creeping quietly along the side of the house, she looked in at the next window and saw a bedroom, a rumpled pillow and duvet atop the empty bed, the door closed to the rest of the house. A bit further along, the walls of the house recessed to create a covered patio bounded by a wire fence almost invisible within a coil of growing vines.

Riley stood against the side of the house, peeking around the wall to see a set of patio furniture, dingy and weathered. Beyond that, a large slider window gave access to the house, flanked by a similar window so that, together, they offered an unimpeded view into the interior. A living room spanned the width of the windows, with an enormous and elaborately carved wooden *Schrank* running the entire length of the back wall.

A brown leather couch, with matching chairs and end tables topped by lamps, took up the center of the room. Riley was relieved to find all of them unoccupied. A low coffee table was spread with large sheets of paper, some of them appearing to be blueprints and maps. Riley's heart, already pounding wildly in her chest, gave a leap and picked up the pace.

Those papers could be the key to learning what Forst and Hill were plotting. The voice of reason told her to turn around and get out of there quick. But standing there, so close to knowing, so close to getting a glimpse into what had gotten Rick killed...

She couldn't leave it alone.

Looking again to make sure no one was inside, Riley moved to the wire fence and found the gate, nearly engulfed in twining, spindly branches. Running her hand along the side near the latch, she touched the release and the gate swung open, making a horrendous creaking racket that brought out a rash of goosebumps along the backs of her arms.

Before she could do more than take a single step away, the glass door slid open with ominous silence and a man burst out of the house, seizing Riley by the forearm in a vicious grip, sending a bolt of pain up into her shoulder.

It was Anton Forst.

"You are trespassing on private property," Forst said, his voice cold, eerily controlled, with a brusque German accent.

Riley's mind spun, scrambling for a suitable response, but before she could form a solitary word, another man came through the door and the sight of him knocked every thought from her head and the breath from her lungs.

It was Rick.

58

Riley froze, utterly astounded, staring at Rick in the doorway. He was there, real, not a figment of her wishful thinking. A wave of supreme joy welled up, threatening to overwhelm her, but some inner instinct quelled the urge to throw her arms around him.

Instead, troubling doubts moved in, clouding her elation. Rick studiously ignored her, all his attention on Forst who was looking back at him, a dark scowl creasing his brow.

"Get back inside," he ordered, his voice a low, surly growl.

"I thought I heard someone knocking," Rick explained.

"Leave it! I'll handle her."

Riley picked up the lifeline Rick had thrown her. "I'm sorry," she said. "I did try knocking, and when no one answered, I thought I might find someone on the patio."

"Who are you?" Forst demanded. "What do you want?"

Riley swallowed, her mind blank. And then, from nowhere, a flurry of words tumbled out of her before she even had time to think them through.

"I heard in the village that a writer lives here," she said. "An expert in music theory. Such a fascinating topic, and I really wanted to meet him and discuss—"

"You were misinformed," Forst told her.

Riley bowed her head apologetically. "I'm so sorry, I…"

Forst was still holding her by the arm, and the look on his face sent a chill down Riley's spine. She realized how vulnerable she was and felt a sudden need to create the impression that others knew her whereabouts.

"I belong to a symphony orchestra," she said. "We're in the area for a music conference, and a colleague dropped me off here on his way to a meeting. I really hoped I wouldn't be disturbing you."

"You are disturbing me."

Still, Rick displayed no sign of recognition, only stared at her with a detached and slightly contemptuous expression. Riley took note of the patch on his head, the bandaged wrist and finger.

"I'm sorry," she said once more. The best thing she could do now was put some distance between herself and the menacing bald man. "I'll go."

Giving her arm a hard squeeze, Forst spun her around and released her toward the driveway. "Call your friend," he said. "Tell him you are walking back. Have him pick you up on the road. I don't want either one of you on my property."

Rubbing her arm where the steel-like fingers had bitten into her flesh, Riley hurried along the lane leading away from the house. She'd have to circle and find her way back to the academy without giving Forst any indication that's where she'd come from.

Amazed that he'd seemed to buy her story and hadn't pressed for her name, Riley felt a rush of gratitude and a resurgence of delight at seeing Rick alive and nearby.

What on earth was he up to?

59

Rick stood in the hallway, bracing himself against the textured plaster of the wall. He felt sick and his legs trembled like a school kid waiting to see the principal. Part of the blame lay with the illness and malaise he'd been fighting since the accident, but most of the reason for his shaky condition stemmed from seeing Riley appear so suddenly and so perilously on the doorstep.

His heart had leapt with fear for her and he'd moved fast to draw Forst's attention away from her initial reaction. Any doubts he may have harbored about bringing her into their little ring of spies died in that moment as he watched her instantly rally and convince the surly Forst of her innocent intentions.

She was a trooper.

The surge of adrenaline had left him feeling weak and looking ill. It meshed well with his playacting of the last several days. After his disastrous attempt to leap out of the car and its subsequent collision, Rick had remembered only brief, disjointed flashes as he drifted in and out of consciousness. The first solid memory he had was waking up in this strange house and wondering why he wasn't in a hospital.

A creeping feeling of horror had filtered over him, at least partially inspired by Stephen King's story, *Misery*. The impression deepened when he tried to get out of the house and was rounded up like an escaping prisoner and returned to his bed.

During his foray, Rick had gleaned some interesting clues about his situation. His keeper, a bald man he came to know as Forst, called him by another man's name—Salih. Rick deduced that had been the driver who'd picked him up at the airport, that somehow in the wreckage, their identities had become scrambled.

He'd had enough sense to keep his mouth shut, waiting to see how things shook out, feigning a deeper feebleness and confusion than he actually felt. During that first remembered encounter with Forst, Rick had learned that Salih was some kind of criminal, or at least wanted by the police. He learned that Forst and a group of unnamed accomplices were planning a heist or attack of some kind, and that it was imminent.

He learned Salih had a special role in their enterprise that somehow involved a canister and a key. Forst had pressed him about the key many times, demanding to know if Rick had it in his possession, and Rick continued to assert that he did.

He had no idea where the key was.

He was only relieved that Forst never asked to see it for himself.

During his recovery, while he was debilitated in actual fact as well as fiction, Rick determined to discover the target, the timeline, and as many details about the planned operation as he could before escaping to notify the authorities. This was difficult as Forst seldom left him on his own for any length of time.

On one occasion, however, the man had been gone from the house for an entire afternoon and the doctor who sometimes tended him left to see another patient. Rick had used the time to pick the lock to the basement door and explore the rooms below. He found abundant evidence of forgery activities geared toward some kind of high-level identity theft and human smuggling operation.

He'd almost decided to leave right then and contact Wright who might be able to arrange a crackdown before Forst and his people could bug out. Instead, he chose to stay and find out more about the impending attack.

And because he had, Riley had almost come to harm. Rick was certain she'd come poking around the house because of him, and now that she'd seen him there, what would she do? Who would she tell?

Based on what he'd discovered during his time in the house, another troubling question came to Rick's mind regarding Riley and her vulnerable position at the academy.

Who could she trust?

60

— · —

FORST STRODE ACROSS THE muddy yard to the edge of the garden and watched the pretty woman disappear around a bend in the lane. It wasn't too late to go after her, stop her.

Silence her.

Suspicion prickled his palms and tingled along the hairs on his arms. He didn't entirely believe the woman's story, but hoped he'd successfully sold her his own—the image of a curmudgeonly writer who valued his privacy above all else.

The sun hung low in the sky, its orange glow filtering through a lacework of branches on the western horizon. Birds sang their last trilling notes of the day and the evening grew silent and somehow heavy, full of portent, though he couldn't fathom a meaning from it.

Digging his phone from his pocket, he found Paula Hill in his recent contacts and pushed the call button.

"I just found a woman snooping around the house," he told her when she picked up. "Claimed someone told her a musical genius lived here and she wanted to pick his brain."

Forst felt a small, cold silence before Hill said, "Who was she? What did she look like?"

"She didn't give her name," he told her. "Said she was part of a symphony or something, here for a music conference."

"What did she look like?" Hill repeated.

Forst thought. "About mid-thirties, maybe. Long auburn hair, hazel eyes. Quite lovely."

Hill cursed. "I believe you just met our resident meddler, Riley Forte. The woman prying into the agent's death."

"What? How did she end up here?"

"How, indeed. What did you do with her?"

"Do with her? I told her to get the hell off my property."

Hill cleared her throat. "Are you sure that was wise? Maybe you should have...detained her."

"And have Wright's people nosing around here looking for a missing recruit?"

"No, you are right. Killing her would have been a mistake. Cincher has an inordinate fondness for the woman. Unless he orders it, we should—"

"Forget her!" Forst shouted. "We focus on finishing the mission. This woman knows nothing. I'm confident there can have been no leaks. Raul is the only one who—"

"Raul hung himself in his jail cell this morning."

Forst digested the news. "As I say," he pointed out, "no leaks. All the pieces are coming together. I have access to the Sammelplatz through Julia. Cincher said one canister will do the job. And Salih is carrying the key."

"Fine," Hill said. "We'll meet Friday morning to settle last minute details and put everything in place."

"Agreed."

Forst ended the call and stared off across the stubbly field. Slapping a hand to his neck, he came away with a smear of blood amid squashed bits of black, all that remained of the pesky mosquito who'd bitten him.

When this was over, he'd find a way to do the same to the bothersome Hill.

61

"Nate," Riley said, her voice trembling, her throat thick with a mix of overwhelming emotions so that she could barely speak. "Nate, brace yourself for some wonderful news."

"Okay. I'm braced and ready to receive."

"Rick is alive, Nate. Oh, I just can't believe it. He's alive!"

A long pause followed. "I can't believe it, either," Nate said at last. "Are you sure, Riley?"

"I saw him. I heard him. I could almost touch him."

"You better back up," Nate said, "and tell me what happened."

Riley caught him up with her visits to the *Hof* and what she'd learned there, ending with seeing Rick come through the door and astonishing the life out of her.

"He acted like he didn't know me," she said. "But he told Forst he heard knocking. I'm almost certain he was covering for me, giving me a way out of the situation."

Another pause. "Riley, are you really sure you saw Rick? It wasn't just someone who looked—"

"I saw him, Nate." Riley felt a measure of her joy flatten, like a popped balloon. "I'm not mistaken," she insisted.

Nate said quickly, "I'm sorry, Riley. I don't mean to imply that you're wrong. It's just…I'm struggling to wrap my head around this. When I got the news of Rick's death, I just couldn't accept it, but then somehow I must have. Because now it's hard to believe he's still alive."

Riley realized she'd gone through a similar sequence. "I guess if I hadn't seen it for myself," she confessed, "I might wonder too."

Another moment of silence passed, then Nate said, "Why didn't he recognize or acknowledge you? Could he be suffering from amnesia? You said he had a bandage on his head."

"Maybe," Riley admitted. "But I think he was deliberately acting like we were strangers. He didn't want Forst to know we're not. To me, it's clear he's under cover, and I didn't want to blow it for him."

"If that's the case, then a job well done." Nate hesitated, then said, "So, whose body was burned in the car accident?"

"Whose indeed? I tried calling Chief Wright to tell him the exciting news and ask that very question," Riley said. "But he was on a plane."

"I'll let him know," Nate said. "Unless you really want to be the one."

She did want to be the one, but decided to share the fun. "Yes, please bring him up to date."

"And Riley, speaking of planes. I'll be on one soon, headed your way. You've been dealing with a lot on your own—and doing a fantastic job—but I don't want you to feel alone out there."

Riley felt a rush of gratitude. "Thank you, Nate. I'll be very happy to see you."

"Sit tight," he told her. "I'm on my way."

NATE SAT AT THE kitchen table, staring at his phone, still reeling with Riley's news. It felt like Christmas morning. Like the best Christmas ever.

Rick was alive. His friend was not only still among the living, but apparently working undercover to bring some very corrupt people to justice and put a stop to their criminal enterprise. More than ever, Nate was itching to be there.

He wanted to be there to protect Riley, to be a part of the takedown, to join forces with his friends in standing against Olivero's traitor and foiling her plans, whatever they might be.

He pulled his laptop over from across the table, plowing through a field of toast crumbs and brushing them absently away. He opened the computer, connected to the internet, and scanned travel sites for the soonest possible flight from Seattle to Nuremberg.

With a sharp pang of disappointment, he saw the earliest flight would leave Seattle almost seventeen hours from now. Too long. The smaller airport at Nuremberg offered fewer options, but he found multiple flights into Munich departing much sooner.

He booked one and made a reservation for a rental car. Flying into Munich would leave him with a three hour drive to reach Riley, but at least he'd be moving in the right direction, making progress, not just sitting and waiting.

Right now, he couldn't bear to sit and wait.

Jumping up, he hurried to the bedroom and started to pack.

63

RILEY'S RESTLESS MOOD OF yesterday intensified, strumming on every nerve ending she had. After a mostly sleepless night spent twisting her pillow into a wrinkled mass, she rose early and tried to swallow a few bites of breakfast, suspended in the unbearable limbo of waiting.

Waiting for Nate and Wright's team to arrive. Waiting to discover Rick's purpose and if he could accomplish it. Waiting to see if Hill would make a move against her.

Waiting to find out if she could endure the torture of waiting.

Entering Professor Martel's classroom, Riley chose a seat and sank into it gratefully. If anything could take her mind off the waiting, it would be his first lecture on cryptology, a subject she found fascinating and infinitely engaging.

The room held a musty, faintly chemical odor, like a library basement. Which was not surprising, since two of its walls were lined, floor to ceiling, with shelves full of books and stacks of yellowed paper. On the white board at the front of the room, Riley was pleased to see a message printed in blue marker, the writing sloppy but still legible:

Serve Lady Twist in a negative way

— — — — — — — — —

She recognized the strange note as a clue from a cryptic crossword, her favorite kind of puzzle. The word "twist" suggested an anagram and since "serve lady" contained nine letters, like the clue's solution, Riley knew to unscrambled them to arrive at a word meaning "in a negative way."

She solved the riddle in less than five seconds, and wished Professor Martel had included the rest of the puzzle on the board to occupy her mind. Not five more seconds passed, however, before Martel himself came rushing in, out of breath, several strands of his ginger hair rising off his scalp under the influence of the static electricity he seemed to carry with him.

"Lots to cover today," he said, smoothing his blue plaid shirt over the slight paunch at his belt line. "So, let's get started. How many of you solved the clue on the board?"

Riley glanced around at the rest of the class. She raised her hand, along with all nine of the other students.

"Wonderful," Martel said. "I chose to start our class today with a cryptic crossword clue because it's a fairly instructive way to illustrate what cryptology and cryptography are all about—hiding or disguising secret information in a way that can be deciphered by someone who knows how while remaining hidden to those who don't."

Riley smiled. She looked forward to being one of those who knew, who could divine the secrets of cryptic communications, starting with the card burning a hole in her laptop case.

"No one can really say when codes, ciphers, and secret languages began, but no one can deny they've been around for centuries. Methods for encrypting them, for breaking them, for passing and concealing them, have developed over time in some amazing ways. In fact, today it is possible to encode a message in human DNA, with the sender creating a unique strand that only the intended recipient can isolate and read from millions of other strands."

Martel stood rubbing his hands together, clearly enthusiastic about sharing his area of expertise.

"The history of codes and ciphers is rich and intriguing. I could tell you about protocryptographic practices in ancient Egypt. Cryptologies used in Mesopotamia and Babylon. In India, China, and Arabia. And in my history class, I will do exactly that."

Gazing around at his students, he caught Riley's eye and gave her a tiny nod. "Today, however, we will focus on some basic background using fictional characters who we'll call Alice, Bob, and Eve. These three have become the industry standard for discussions about cryptography."

He paused. "Let us say Alice wants to send Bob a message, for his eyes only. But she knows Eve is intent on intercepting the message. So Alice gets the idea to send the message in a secret language, unknown to Eve. She takes her basic message, encrypts it using a key, and sends it to Bob."

Martel began pacing at the front of the classroom, his face animated, hands making the motions as if he was writing the note himself.

"Now, even if Eve sees the message, she won't understand it. The meaning will be hidden to her. But when Bob gets it, he uses his key to decrypt it and—voila!—he knows what Alice wanted to tell him."

The man sitting next to Riley raised his hand. "But how does Bob get the key?" he asked. "If Alice sends Bob the key, wouldn't Eve just intercept it the same way she intercepted the message?"

"Ah! You've hit on the age-old problem of key distribution. A beguiling subject, and one for another day. For now, let's assume Alice and Bob met personally and they now both have a copy of the key. They can send messages back and forth, encrypting and decrypting at will, and no one else can interpret their communications." He paused. "Or can they?"

Martel stopped pacing and again checked his audience to make sure they were following. "Let's say Alice and Bob were using a simple shift cipher, just shifting each letter of the alphabet by a set number of moves. How could Eve crack the code?"

"Easy," said a woman at a table across the aisle from where Riley sat. "There are only 26 possible combinations. She could simply try each one until the message clicked."

"True," Martel conceded. "She could use that brute force attack and arrive at the solution. But is there a more efficient way?"

Martel looked at Riley, as if expecting her to answer, so she said, "You could look for patterns and the frequency of letter occurrences, solve it like a cryptogram."

"Yes, you could. That's because a simple shift code leaves a very legible fingerprint. If the message is written in English, E is by far the most commonly occurring letter, followed by T and A, and so on. Using frequency analysis to interpret the message will often yield a faster solution than a brute force attack."

Riley thought about her many failed attempts to solve the cipher she'd picked up at the dead drop. She raised her hand. "But what if the message looks like a simple shift code, but can't be cracked using that method?"

Martel gave her a delighted grin. "I'm so glad you asked. Let's say Bob and Alice discover that Eve has been intercepting and deciphering their secret messages. They have been leaving indelible fingerprints, an easy clue for Eve to follow, so they need to lighten the prints they leave. They can do this by flattening the distribution of letters—making it harder for Eve to solve—with a polyalphabetic cipher."

"Say what?" piped up a man sitting behind Riley.

"We'll walk through a simple example together," Martel assured him. "What message should we have Alice send to Bob?"

Various suggestions popped up around the room.

"Can you hear me now?"

"What hath God wrought?"

"Three may keep a secret, if two of them are dead."

"For simplicity's sake," Martel said, "let's keep it short. He wrote on the board.

WHAT HATH GOD WROUGHT

"Now, let's convert the alpha to the numeric, assigning each letter a value according to its place in the alphabet." He added the numbers beneath their corresponding letters.

WHAT HATH GOD WROUGHT
23 8 1 20 8 1 20 8   7 15 4   23 18 15 21 7 8 20

"A simple shift code would move all the letters the same interval," Martel continued, "resulting in the type of linguistic fingerprint we talked about, and making Eve's task a matter of analyzing the frequencies. But a polyalphabetic cipher uses a key word to twist that fingerprint and make it harder to read."

Riley liked seeing his eagerness. It always seemed easier to her to learn from someone who taught with passion. He turned from the board and swept his gaze over the classroom.

"What shall we use for our key word?" he asked. "Let's make it five letters."

A woman in the front row pointed to the globe beside the white board. "How about globe?"

Martel nodded. "Let's do it. We'll assign numbers to the letters in globe."

G L O B E
7 12 15 2 5

"Remember, both Alice and Bob know the key word. So Alice uses it to encrypt her message by repeating the key word along the length of the message. Like this."

W H A T	H A T H	G O D	W R O U G H T
23 8 1 20	8 1 20 8	7 15 4	23 18 15 21 7 8 20
7 12 15 2	5 7 12 15	2 5 7	12 15 2 5 7 12 15

"And then adding the numbers, like this."

W H A T	H A T H	G O D	W R O U G H T
23 8 1 20	8 1 20 8	7 15 4	23 18 15 21 7 8 20
7 12 15 2	5 7 12 15	2 5 7	12 15 2 5 7 12 15
30 20 16 22	13 8 32 23	9 20 11	35 33 17 26 14 20 35

Martel faced his students and asked, "How many of you are accustomed to using the military or European system of telling time? The 24 hour format?"

Again, everyone raised a hand and Martel said, "That system uses a mod 12, a closed loop of 12 numbers, so if you want to express what Americans call 4:00 pm, you go the limit of the loop to 12:00 and add the 4 to get 16:00. Reverse the process to figure out that 19:00 European means 7:00 pm. Nineteen minus twelve. Got it?"

He turned to see everyone nodding, so he continued. "With our polyalphabetic cipher system, we're using a mod 26, right? So, for those numbers over 26, simply subtract 26 to arrive at the proper number. Thus, we have:"

```
W  H  A  T     H  A  T  H     G  O  D     W  R  O  U  G  H  T
23 8  1  20    8  1  20 8     7  15 4     23 18 15 21 7  8  20
 7 12 15 2     5  7  12 15    2  5  7     12 15 2  5  7  12 15
30 20 16 22    13 8  32 23    9  20 11    35 33 17 26 14 20 35
26                   26                   26 26             26
 4 20 16 22    13 8  6  23    9  20 11    9  7  17 26 14 20 9
```

"And now we can swap the numbers back to letters and send our encrypted message."

```
4 20 16 22    13 8 6 23    9 20 11    9 7 17 26 14 20 9
D T  P  V     M  H F W      I T  K     I G Q  Z  N  T  I
```

"Cool," said the guy sitting next to Riley. "And Bob will reverse the process to decrypt the message?"

"Correct," Martel said. "Bob will repeat the key word across the cipher and subtract, adding 26 to any negative results. This technique flattens the distribution frequency and makes it a lot harder for Eve to crack."

"But she still could," Riley suggested.

"Of course," Martel agreed. "But it would cost her time. That's the strength of the polyalphabetic cipher. By the time Eve decrypts the message, it may no longer be relevant."

"Are there methods for sending codes that no one can crack?" Riley asked.

"The answer to your question is rather fluid," Martel said. "Since the science of both encryption and decryption is developing on a continual basis, the safe answer is no. The horizon of what can be done continues to expand. However, the one-time pad is a pretty good bet for sending an unbreakable code."

The woman who'd chosen globe as the key word spoke up. "How does the one-time pad work?"

"That," Martel said, "is a topic for another day. Sadly, we are out of time. This concludes our lecture for today. I expect to see all of you back here next week."

64

RILEY STOOD, WANTING TO speak with Martel and thank him for the intriguing lecture, but a few of the other students had similar thoughts and beat her to it. As the immediacy of the lesson faded, giving way to her prior anxieties, she felt too restless to wait her turn. She'd thank him later.

She wanted to apply her new-found knowledge to the cipher from the dead drop. Retrieving it from her room, along with a notepad and a sharpened pencil with a good eraser, Riley started down the wooded trail. She wanted to be alone and uninterrupted.

In her wanderings, she'd noticed a hexagonal, gazebo-like summer house on one of the lesser-worn paths. It was enclosed, rather than open to the elements, with thin wooden screens dotted with tiny openings for airflow.

Peeking inside, she'd seen it was furnished with a sofa, a desk and chair, and a large fluffy rug, all of it slightly dusty but serviceable. No electricity for lighting, but she could open the shutters on the two windows and get enough sunlight to accomplish her purpose. It was just the sort of secret place she wanted for her project.

But as she approached, she heard faint noises coming from within the structure. Moving silently, she crept closer, curious to know who was inside. The small holes punched into the siding made it easy for her to peer in, and what she saw provided an immediate explanation for some of the concerns she'd had since arriving at the academy.

Her roommate, Colette, lay on the rug, entwined with Gideon, the martial arts instructor. He was propped on an elbow, gazing down at her with a look of such tenderness it brought a sting of tears that Riley blinked away. Colette stroked Gideon's golden hair, touched his cheek. The two were lost in each other, clearly in love.

A forbidden love.

Romantic relations between instructors and recruits was strictly prohibited. If they were caught, Colette would be subject to expulsion and Gideon could lose his job. Which might explain Colette's general animosity and suspicion toward Riley if she thought she'd been installed in their room to spy and inform. Which also explained Colette's escape into the night, probably to rendezvous in this very spot. And it also explained Gideon's changed attitude toward her, especially when Riley told him she'd seen him in the night.

Careful not to step on dry twigs or leaves, not wanting the couple to know their privacy had been invaded, Riley stole away from the summer house. She turned down another path where she'd seen a picnic table inside a small, open-sided shed. Brushing dirt and pine needles from the table, she settled onto the bench and opened her notepad, spreading the card beneath a small stone acting as a paperweight in the feathery breeze.

Of course, in order to decrypt the message as she'd just learned in class, she needed the key word. If the message in the dead drop had been meant for her, and she supposed it was, the sender should have somehow delivered her the key word as well.

Unless he deemed it to be obvious.

Had Ilya been the one to encrypt and leave the message in the dead drop? Or one of the instructors? What could any of them assume would be obvious to her?

Music? Piano? Mozart?

Riley almost laughed aloud when the truly obvious occurred to her.

Her name.

She wrote the alphabet across the top of a page in her notepad and the corresponding numbers, 1 through 26, below them. Converting Riley to numerals, she got 18 9 12 5 25.

Applying a number to each letter of the cipher, she then repeated the sequence of 18 9 12 5 25 beneath them as Professor Martel had demonstrated. Scribbling furiously and doing the math in her head, she produced a new set of numbers and converted them to letters. The resulting message read:

REMEMBER HOW WE MET MY DAMSEL IN DISTRESS

Riley's blood chilled in her veins. She knew immediately the message was not from Ilya or anyone else at Olivero. The man she knew as John had placed it for her to find. Just as he'd given her the coin after fooling her with a bogus bike injury and hitching a ride.

She shuddered, clenching her fists on the tabletop. She hadn't recognized him, hadn't been aware of his presence, though he'd clearly been watching her. The fact that he could move around her with impunity, beneath her radar, making contact whenever he desired, frightened her to the core.

Was he connected with Hill's scheme, pulling her strings? It seemed likely, and the notion disturbed Riley even more.

Looking around her at the deepening shadows and gently swaying branches, she suddenly wondered if he was there now, watching her, enjoying her consternation, her fear. She saw no one, but felt exposed and vulnerable, all the harmless forest noises now seeming to signal danger. Rising from the bench, Riley hurried along the path, wanting to be inside a room with a locked door.

As if that could stop him getting to her.

65

RICK FINISHED RINSING THE last of the breakfast dishes and stacked them in the drainer. The fact that Forst had removed the wrappings from his wrist and finger and put him to work washing dishes showed he was no longer being treated as an invalid. More than ever, Rick felt a sense of urgency in the air. Whatever Forst and Hill planned to do, it would happen soon.

Swiping the damp dishcloth over the wooden kitchen table, Rick rubbed away the dabs of jam and scattered crumbs from the crusty bread rolls he'd come to love. The kitchen was still fragrant from the dark, rich coffee Forst liked to brew, and stripes of orange sunlight fell across the wide planks of the hardwood floor, warming the room.

A murmur of voices came from the salon where Forst sat with Hill. Rick stepped closer, hoping to pick up on their conversation, but the sound of Forst's heavy boots moving toward the kitchen sent him back to scrubbing at the table.

The German surveyed his work and nodded. "Clean enough," he said. "Come, we have much to discuss."

Rick followed him into the living room where Hill sat perched on the edge of a leather armchair, her blonde hair tied back in a multi-col-

294

ored scarf. She regarded him coolly, her gaze lingering on the bandage still taped in place on his forehead.

"I'm fully functional," Rick assured her. "Let's get busy."

He sat on the sofa, next to Forst who was shuffling through the layers of paper on the low table in front of them. Rick had snatched a few opportunities to examine the documents on earlier occasions. He'd seen maps of the local area, chemical diagrams and specs, blueprints of an unidentified building, as well as technical drawings for some type of device. Altogether, the documents looked menacing and left him feeling very disturbed.

The titanium case resting beside the table, secured by two heavy-duty combination tumblers, increased his level of unease.

Forst found the sheet he wanted and raised it to the top of the stack. "These are the architectural plans for the Sammelplatz," he said. "They include schematics for structure, plumbing, electrical, and ventilation."

Hill nodded and Rick bent over the page, studying the lines and labels, a chill running through him as he realized the target location was above them on the volcanic mountain, a gathering place for private events. He wondered who would be gathered there, and what catastrophe Forst and Hill had planned for them.

"I made a trip up there last night," Forst said, "and hid most of the heavy equipment behind the hedge so we won't have to haul it."

"Glad to hear it," Hill said.

"We'll come in through here," Forst continued, pointing out a maintenance door to the basement level. "I made a copy of the key, I know the alarm code, and their security personnel will be focused elsewhere. We'll move down this corridor." He traced his finger along the paper. "And plant the device here."

He tapped the blueprint with a smirk of anticipation. "Four big industrial fans situated here, in the utility area, will facilitate the dispersal of the agent through the ventilation system."

Rick felt the skin at the back of his neck prickle at the word "agent." He realized they planned to disseminate a chemical gas throughout the target building. That explained the reports filled with chemical diagrams and the canister Forst had asked him about. He suspected that's what was inside the titanium case.

Forst rifled through the papers and brought another one to the top. "Here are the schematics for our detonating device."

"Where did you get it?" Hill asked.

"It was part of a Soviet biowarfare arsenal until the late 1980's. It was used to disperse pathogens through the atmosphere, but it has been modified and programmed to work for our special purposes."

He paused. "Cincher ordered a team to liberate it from an armory in Ukraine and his scientists in Czech updated it with the advanced technology. One of them is bringing it now." Glancing at his watch, he said, "It should be here within the hour."

Rick felt a stir of nausea in his gut. This was worse than he had imagined.

"We'll arm the device with the canister and set the timer for detonation, giving us a chance to get clear before the chemical hits the air."

Hill leaned forward. "What effects does this form of Sarin have on its victims?" she asked.

Forst motioned expansively toward Rick. "Let's hear it from the expert," he said. "Salih was on the team who designed the stuff."

Hill stared at Rick, waiting for his answer. He felt the nausea in his gut rise to storm level, sending a gush of acid up into his throat. He swallowed hard and shook his head. "Trust me," he said, "you don't want to be anywhere near when that thing goes off."

He thought Hill meant to press him for a more complete response, but Forst cleared his throat and continued outlining the plan. "The device has a double key system," he explained. "We insert the canister into this slot and flip switch one. That's when I insert my key."

He indicated the slot and switch on the diagram and tapped an opening labeled "Key 1" with his finger.

"We wait ten seconds, and flip switch two. Then," he said, looking at Rick, "it's time for your key."

Rick hoped he looked confident when he said, "Okay. I got it covered."

He still had no idea what, or where, the key was. On the one hand, that was a great relief to him. If he wasn't able to get away and alert the authorities before they forced him into motion, he'd foil their plan by default. They clearly depended on the key for the success of the mission, and he didn't have it.

On the other hand, he dreaded what they'd do to him when they found out.

Hill stood. "All right. I think the rest of it's pretty clear—we get out the way we came in and head to the exfil point." She looked at Forst. "You have all our new documents?"

"Almost finished," he said. "Don't worry. Everything will be ready."

"Good." Hill lifted her coat off the arm of the chair and shrugged into it as she walked toward the door. At the threshold, she turned back, smiling as she spoke the last words Rick wanted to hear.

"This happens tonight."

66

—·—

RILEY LEANED AGAINST THE rough bark of a towering pine tree and peered through the screen of tall billowing ferns giving her cover. The morning had started warm and sunny, but by the time she'd reached the gate at the end of the academy trail and let herself out, the sky had grown thick with dark scudding clouds and a brisk wind blew, stirring the tree branches into a wild dance. She smelled rain coming, felt its threat in the air, and shivered.

She was skipping out on her Tracking and Evasion lecture. Feeling a little like a delinquent high-schooler cutting class, Riley crouched and waited for Nate to arrive. He'd called from a rest stop on the autobahn and they'd decided to meet secretly outside the bounds of the academy. With Director Edwards once more out of town at an important meeting regarding The Knot, they'd decided the fewer who knew about Nate being there, the better.

Using an app on the phone Matsui had given her, she'd pinned her location outside the academy gate, and described the area to Nate. She had no doubt he would find her.

And he did.

Holding her in a long, tight hug, Nate said, "It's so great to see you, Riley. And to know you're safe."

299

"Safe? I don't feel at all safe. For all I know, John is watching us right now."

Nate pulled away and stared into her face, his forehead creased, his brown eyes troubled. "I know you're scared, and you have every right to be. But John is a busy man. He can't be watching you all the time." He smiled. "I mean, what are the odds?"

Riley laughed, knowing he was trying to lighten the mood and reassure her. It felt wonderful to have him there. She grasped his hand tightly. "Thanks so much for coming, Nate. I can't begin to tell you how much better I feel with you here."

"Good."

Cupping her elbow, Nate started along the forest path. "Let's find a better place to talk," he said. Glancing at the sky, he added, "Maybe someplace with a little shelter."

"The only shelter I know near here is the *Hof*," Riley said. "And that's best avoided."

"I agree. But let's move toward the mountain. Maybe there's a cave or an outcropping."

They walked for about ten minutes and came to a natural stone wall at the foot of the mountain. Strange twisting formations, tubular and hexagonal, clung to the steep surface, as if extruded from a child's Play-Doh toy.

Fascinated, Riley ran her hand across the rough stone. "One of the instructors at the academy told me about this," she said. "These hexagonal strands were formed by cooling magma after a long ago volcanic eruption."

"Oh no, not another volcano!"

"That's what I thought when I heard about it," Riley said. "But this one is long extinct. It's the least of our worries."

"Okay, then. Let's talk about the most of our worries. What is Rick up to? What is Hill planning? And, more importantly, what are we going to do?"

A bank of charcoal gray clouds moved in the sky, blocking the feeble sun, turning the day a few degrees cooler and adding to Riley's gloom.

"I'm afraid," she said. "I worry that my showing up at the *Hof* put Rick in danger. I didn't mean to jeopardize whatever he's doing. I had no idea he was there."

"Of course you didn't," Nate agreed. "But they've probably raised their alert level. Your visit may have accelerated their timeline."

"Or they may move their base of operations. If they do that," Riley agonized, "we'll lose track of Rick."

As she stared at Nate, a pebble bounced off the tubular formations and hit him in the side of the head, followed by a clatter of small stones raining down on them. Nate grabbed her by the hand and pulled her away as a boulder the size of a suitcase crashed down from above, smashing into the ground where they'd stood only moments before. It bounced once and tipped over on its side.

Riley found herself in Nate's arms, her face pressed against his chest, her breath coming in short gasps. He felt warm and solid. She didn't want to let go, but reminded herself he had a family at home, waiting for him to come back to them. Loosening her hold, she stepped away and worked to catch her breath.

"Are you all right?" Nate asked, brushing her hair off her face and peering into her eyes. "Are you hurt?"

"N-no. I'm okay. Are you?"

Nate slapped his hands against his pants, sending up a cloud of dust. "I'm fine, but—"

"Shh," Riley warned, covering his mouth with her fingers. "Do you hear that?"

Straining her ears, she listened. From somewhere above, she heard the sound of hoof beats, growing fainter as the horse moved away.

"What the hell! Someone pushed that rock down on us," Nate said. "They meant to kill us."

"Or scare the crud out of us."

Riley could think of only one person who rode a horse around the academy grounds and lived in this direction. She told Nate about Gideon.

"But why would he try to take us out?" Nate asked.

"I'm not saying he did. I can't think of any reason he would, but we just don't know enough about anyone here. I don't know who to trust." She paused. "The only person here, besides you, that I feel certain about is Matsui."

"Who's Matsui?"

"She's our resident bomb expert. And I think I can call her a friend."

They were silent for a second or two, with only the sound of the rustling boughs to disturb their thoughts. After a moment, Nate put his hand on her shoulder, giving her a comforting squeeze.

"Look, Riley, as you say, we just don't know enough about the situation to make a sound action plan. Wright has scrambled a team of agents and they'll arrive at the airport in Nuremberg any time now. Why don't I go meet them and bring them up to speed."

"What about me? Shouldn't I go with you?"

Nate hesitated.

"I would love to take you with me," he said. "But I suspect your sudden absence would tip Hill to something going on. Go to class, Riley. Attend your trainings as scheduled. Stay where you have safety in numbers. I'll bring the cavalry as soon as I can."

They hurried to the gate and Riley stepped to the keypad, ready to enter the code, but Nate drew her back. "Wait a minute," he said.

Reaching into his pocket, he pulled something out and grasped Riley's hand. She saw he had a watch, which he fastened around her wrist.

"It contains a tracker, Riley. Don't take it off."

They hugged briefly, then as Riley turned to let herself in the gate, Nate said again, "Don't take off the watch." He paused. "I don't want to lose you."

He brushed his finger against her cheek, and then he was gone.

67

LIESL FOUND JULIA ON a bench beside the trout pond, watching a Romanian couple across the water cast their lines. The darkly clouded sky and impending storm had driven most of the guests indoors, but Liesl knew many anglers preferred a rainy day. Half a dozen people scattered the shore, tending their rods.

Sinking onto the slatted wooden surface next to her sister, Liesl leaned over and gave her a brief squeeze around the shoulders. Neither spoke. The freshening wind whipped the tree branches overhead, sending showers of dried needles down on their heads and a chill along Liesl's spine. She would not have chosen to come out in this weather except that she really wanted to speak with Julia.

The peace talks between leaders of the adjacent eastern European nations seemed to be progressing well, yet Liesl felt an increasing tension in the air. She couldn't shake a premonition that something awful was in the works, building to a breaking point. And when it happened, it would destroy her job, her family, her life.

As much as it made her feel like a lousy sister, Liesl wished that Julia would stay in the apartment during events. She was grateful Anton Forst hadn't made an appearance but even so, it made her nervous to see Julia circulating among the guests. Her sister's behavior could be brash, almost vulgar at times, and any negative incidents would reflect poorly on the Sammelplatz, and on her own job performance.

But how could she express her concerns to Julia without offending her? She seemed all too ready to bristle at everything Liesl said or did.

"It's pretty, isn't it?" Liesl commented, waving her hand toward the rippling pond and the swaying trees beyond. "Even in the rain."

Julia's eyes were closed, her face lifted to catch the light smattering of droplets. "Especially in the rain," she said.

A moment passed, then Liesl spoke again. "We should get inside before the storm hits."

"You go. I want to feel the wind and the rain, let it soak me to the skin."

And then you'll come dripping in, trailing mud and looking like a drowned rat. Moving among the guests in your wet T-shirt and making me look bad.

Liesl clamped down on her acid thoughts, saying instead, "I wish you wouldn't. You could catch cold."

Julia said nothing.

A gust of wind lifted Liesl's hair, blowing it across her face, plastering damp strands against her mouth. Irritated, she brushed them away. "My job depends on this summit going well," she said. "And your home depends on my job going well."

Julia turned a hard-eyed glance in her direction. "Do I embarrass you, dear sister? Maybe I should pack my bags and leave."

"No, Julia. I don't want that. I'm just...I don't want anything to jeopardize my position here."

Julia's eyes narrowed. She turned her face back toward the pond where the fishermen were reeling in their lines and gathering their things.

"Don't worry," she said. "I promise I'll be good. In fact, I think you'll be drop dead amazed at how very good I'll be."

Julia rose from the bench and strode off toward the Sammelplatz, leaving Liesl to look after her, more worried than ever.

68

RILEY COMPLETED HER EVASIVE driving exercises and ate lunch in the cafeteria.

The glowering clouds continued to build and hover, holding back their fury with a heavy, ominous tension that mirrored her own. It seemed to her that Nate had been gone for agonizing ages and she longed for him to return with Wright's team, letting them take command of the situation.

After lunch, she went to her room where she was supposed to spend an hour studying and memorizing. Unable to even sit, she kicked off her shoes and stood at the window, staring out over the grounds, watching the tall pines at the edge of the forest bend and toss in the swelling wind.

The door clicked open and Riley turned to see Colette enter. Her roommate's expression held both resentment and guilt, and Riley wondered if the guilt stemmed from her secret forbidden romance or because she and Gideon were somehow allied against her.

Had Gideon been the one to send the stone hurtling down the mountainside? And if so, why?

Riley's unease, building inside her and twined with the unbearable strain of waiting, brimmed over and broke. Fighting a wave of anger, her hands clenched into fists at her side, she stepped close to Colette, struggling to keep her tone even as she said, "What is your problem with me?"

Her roommate glared. "What are you doing here?" she demanded. "Did Hill send you to spy on me?"

Surprise drained some of Riley's anger. Her hands relaxed but she didn't step away. Maintaining close eye contact with Colette, she said, "What are you talking about? Wright himself sent me."

Colette's eyes widened, her beautiful bird wing eyebrows rising on her forehead. "The Chief sent you to spy on me?"

"No, Colette. No one sent me to spy on you."

A flush of heat rose in Riley's face as she remembered that she had, indeed, spied on Colette and undoubtedly uncovered the secret she strove so hard to hide.

"What makes you think Hill wants to spy on you?" Riley asked.

The woman's generous lips thinned as she pressed them together. "She's always watching me. It's creepy. She reminds me of—"

Colette broke off, but Riley pressed her. "She reminds you of what?"

Shaking her head, Colette said, "No, it's impossible. That was long ago, and the face and hair are different. It's just...her voice."

"Who does she sound like?"

Colette collapsed into a sitting position on her bed. Riley followed suit, dropping down onto her own. "Come on, Colette. I mean you no harm, and I share your feelings about Hill. She is creepy."

Her roommate was quiet for a long moment. Finally, she said, "When I was a young girl in Marrakesh, there was a lot of civil unrest. It was a turbulent time. There were many Islamist terrorist cells recruiting among my people." She paused. "They got my older brother. And...and I followed."

Riley sat stunned, a slow pang of sympathy shivering through her. "How old were you?" she asked.

"I was eleven. A woman taught us, showed us what to do. She fed us and cared for us like a mother."

"What about your own parents?"

"Our mother died when I was born. Our father was...a busy man. He left us to our own devices, and so it felt good to have someone looking after us."

"This woman," Riley said, "something happened with her, didn't it? Tell me."

Colette looked down, shame written in her face. "This woman, Rizeen, became obsessed with me. Wouldn't let me out of her sight, always watching, stroking my hair, bringing me gifts. It got to the point where she was jealous of Patrice, my brother, spending any time with me."

"And her voice is like Hill's? Is that what you meant?"

She nodded. "Yes, it's the same voice. I grow more certain every time I hear it."

Colette bit her lip and several long seconds passed before she spoke again. "She sent my brother into the marketplace with a bomb strapped to his chest. He died buried under a mass of destroyed melons and innocent people."

"Oh, Colette! I'm so sorry."

Riley didn't know what else to say, how to comfort the woman. Nothing could be adequate. She simply waited, and after a moment, Colette continued.

"The authorities closed in and Rizeen had to flee. I was taken into custody. Shortly after that, my father died of a heart attack. I was released into a foster home and my new life began, a life I have dedicated to fighting terrorism and upholding freedom." She paused, lifting her chin defiantly. "That is why I am here."

Riley's chest felt tight. She said, "Colette, there is something I must confess. Truly, I am not here to spy on you, but I do know about you and Gideon."

Colette raised her head, wariness back in her eyes.

"What you do is your own business," Riley assured her. "I have no intention of telling anybody about your relationship with Gideon. And the last person I would ever tell would be Paula Hill."

"Why is that?"

Anger and hot indignation boiled in Riley's chest, born of Hill's treachery and deceit. "Because Hill is a t—!" She stuttered to a stop, biting back the words.

"A what?" Colette stood, peering at her intently. "You know something about her," she said. "I want to know it, too."

Riley said nothing.

"You were about to say that Paula Hill is a terrorist," Colette concluded, her face pinched and white with grief. "And now I know for sure."

Before Riley could so much as stand from the bed, Colette was out the door and away.

RILEY STARED AFTER COLETTE, heard the door of their room thud shut behind her. The word she'd stifled had been traitor, not terrorist, but Colette's ears were tuned to her own agenda. And maybe Paula Hill actually *was* the woman who'd sent Colette's brother to his death, transformed now with a new face and a new identity.

So many things were not what they seemed.

Stooping, Riley pushed her feet into her sneakers and tied the laces. She had a bad feeling about what might happen when Colette confronted Hill, and it would be partially her fault. Grabbing her jacket, she slipped her arms into the sleeves as she moved out into the hallway, looking and listening.

Where had Colette gone? Up the stairs to Hill's office? Across to the classrooms? Riley hurried down the corridor and stared out the big windows in the lobby, catching a glimpse of Colette's buttercup yellow blouse disappearing around the corner of an equipment shed.

A stiff breeze lifted Riley's jacket as she ran out the door, sending it billowing up, flapping like a mad bird. She pulled it down and fastened the zipper as she ran toward the shed amid a spatter of raindrops. Reaching the corner where she'd seen Colette, she peered ahead but saw no one. Only two buildings lay in this direction, set back near the edge of the forest, and Riley was not familiar with either one.

Choosing the one on the left, Riley cautiously opened the door and slipped into a small, darkened antechamber. Flashes of light penetrated through the crack in a set of swinging doors, as if a movie played on a big screen beyond. As Riley carefully pushed open the doors, she saw that's exactly what was happening, but a specialized type of movie.

A virtual experience.

She was in a driving simulator. The images on the wrap-around screen moved through an urban environment, past crowds waiting to cross the street and taxis cutting across traffic. The sharp, erratic action threw darts of light and shadow around the enclosed space, creating a surreal effect that made Riley's stomach feel queasy.

Assistant director, Paula Hill, stood facing Colette beside the empty driver's capsule. No one else was present. The city sounds of the simulator drowned out their words, but their gestures and facial expressions, punctuated by the jerky projections of light, spoke clearly of pain, rage, and something beyond.

Riley thought she recognized maniacal obsession on Hill's face.

Pressing against the back wall, Riley watched them argue, wondering if she should intervene or let it run its course. Wright had ordered her to steer clear of Hill, but he couldn't blame her for trying to help if—

Too late.

Shocked, Riley watched as Colette sank to the floor, a bright scarlet stain blooming across the gold of her blouse. Hill's arms were around her, her blonde head, wreathed by a multi-colored scarf, bowed. Even over the urban soundtrack, Riley heard the woman's raw sobbing.

Stunned, Riley turned to go for help, but the motion must have caught Hill's eye. The woman stood and Riley saw the blade in her hand, dripping and glinting in the light of the screen. The whites of her eyes shone bright, sharp as bone in moonlight. She gave a guttural growl, stepping forward, and Riley bolted, pushing through the swinging doors and out into the rising storm.

Instinct sent her running for the refuge of the forest. It was not the first time she'd fled from a killer amid pines and birch. The gathering gloom would be her friend, hiding her as it had in those long ago childhood days playing Spy Catcher.

As it had when she'd run from John.

After five minutes of frantic dashing, Riley realized she was heading toward the *Hof* and knew it was the right thing to do. Until help arrived, there was no going back to the academy, and even after Nate returned, bringing Wright's team with him, logic would send them to the *Hof*.

She did think of circling back to Colette, of trying to help. Maybe she was still alive. But the girl's silent fall, the spreading lake of blood beneath her, and her own common sense told her it was no use. There was no going back.

Only forward.

The rain came down harder now, lashing across her face, pasting her hair across her eyes as she stumbled among the trees, putting her hands out to feel their sodden trunks. Ferns and briers snatched at her feet, tripping her up as she searched for the trail, the clearer path, in the gloaming forest.

Fear clung to her, stealing her breath, dogging her footsteps. Her theory about Hill's wicked intents had become fact before her eyes.

And it wouldn't end there. Riley felt a dawning dread, a certain knowledge that the dark night had just begun.

She raced along, slipping on pine needles, filled with a frenzied desire to reach the *Hof*, to warn Rick and get him out of there before anything worse happened. Twice, she fell, scraping the palms of her hands on rough bark, banging her knee on a jagged stone. But she hardly noticed the pain, scrambling up to hurry on, buffeted by gusts of aggressive wind.

Reaching the gate, she punched in the code, her hands slimed by mud and shaking so badly she had trouble hitting the right buttons. And then she was through and running again, the trail beneath her feet more steep than she remembered and littered with loose stones and entangling vines.

At last, the *Hof* appeared out of the gloom ahead, crouching under the beating storm like a sullen cat, yellow light showing through the slitted shutters of the kitchen window. Riley slowed her steps, moving furtively along the path, watching for movement inside and out.

Working her way closer, she edged up to the window and peered through the crack like she had on that first night. As before, a fire burned on the grate and Riley wished its warmth would extend to where she stood, shivering in the cold and rain.

Shifting her gaze, she saw Rick at the kitchen table, frowning down at a scattering of bags, bottles, and spools of wire, his lip caught between his teeth as she'd seen him do when deep in thought.

No one else was in the room.

70

Rick stared at the detonating device, at the wired connections and digital countdown timer, running scenarios through his head until he felt like his brain was on fire. Before disappearing into the basement, Forst had tasked him with arming the device, setting it with small charges designed to disperse the contents of the canister into the ventilation system at the Sammelplatz.

He couldn't refuse without blowing his cover. Forst would be sure to check his work, confirm the wiring and efficacy of the charges. Rick reminded himself that he didn't have the necessary key to activate the timer and start the device on its deadly mission. That was his failsafe.

But he had another problem. The man he was impersonating had apparently been skilled in the art of explosives. Rick was not. He'd taken the basic courses with Matsui at the academy, and before that, with his work as a Seattle police officer, but he had little hands-on experience.

He wasn't sure he could pull off the job laid out on the table before him.

As he feverishly considered what to do, he heard a noise at the door, a faint tapping on the thick, leaded panes. A face peered in at him, the glass distorting the image, making it unrecognizable. Unsure whether to summon Forst or answer the quiet knock himself, he crept to the door and opened it a crack.

Riley.

Rick felt a rush of relief. Glancing behind him to make sure the basement entrance was still securely closed, he opened the door and crushed Riley in a brief hug as cold needles of rain fell on his face.

Keeping his voice low, he said, "I've never been so glad to see a person."

"You can't begin—"

"No time, Riley. We have an urgent situation, and I can't tell you everything now. Just enough to be getting on with and we'll save the rest for later." He released his grip on her and stepped back. "This crew is planning a chemical attack on the Sammelplatz at the top of the mountain. Tonight."

Riley's eyes widened, and he gestured to the implements on the table. "They're placing a dispersal device in the ventilation system. And Riley," he added, "it will be armed with Sarin gas. Everyone in the building will be dead within minutes."

"Oh no, Matsui told me there's an international peace summit happening up there now. Leaders from several eastern European countries meeting to work out their tenuous relations."

"Tenuous now," Rick said. "Utter chaos, if this attack goes off. You have to get away from here and alert the authorities."

"But Rick, we don't know who we can trust. Edwards is out of town. Hill's a traitor. The head of the local crime unit colluded with these people to make me think you were dead."

"I am dead, as far as they're concerned. They think I'm a fellow terrorist by the name of Taz Salih."

"How did that happen?"

Rick felt a frantic need for her to be gone. "Not now, Riley. Go. Call Wright. He'll know what—"

Behind him, he heard the heavy tread of boots on stairs and the metallic click of the basement door lock releasing. Reflexively, heart pounding in his eardrums, Rick turned his head and stared.

Anton Forst entered the kitchen.

71

RILEY'S HEART FLEW INTO her throat at the sudden metallic clank of a door opening. Her gaze flew across the broad floor boards of the kitchen and blood sizzled in her veins as she watched a bald head emerge from the basement. Muscles tensing, she turned to flee but before she could spring away, Rick seized her in a rough grasp.

"Look what I found," he said, pulling her fully into the room and wrapping his arm around her neck in a choke hold. "She came snooping around again."

The bald man came close, though he stayed out of kicking range. His thick eyebrows drew together as he glared down at her. "*Ach,* Cincher's pet," he said. "The wanna be spy, playing a spy game."

Cincher's pet? Riley struggled to order and digest all the shocking and distressing pieces of the puzzle that were falling into place all too fast. Her knees felt like spent rubber bands and she leaned against Rick, drawing on his support even as he held her throat in the crook of his arm.

The man called Forst snorted, his lip curling. "We don't have time to deal with her now." He made a dismissive gesture as if brushing off an irritating fly. "Kill her."

Riley gasped, but Rick's arm tightened, cutting off her cry. "All right. If you say so," he agreed. "But...I don't think Cincher will be pleased."

Forst growled out an angry curse. He circled her, his hand rasping against his stubbled chin as he considered his options. Riley's heart beat painfully in her chest and she needed to draw in more air than Rick was giving her. Her vision started to dim, fading slowly to black at the edges.

"Tie her up and leave her," Forst ordered. "I'll call Cincher and let him know. He can decide what he wants to do with her."

Rick's hold loosened and Riley inhaled sharply, weak with relief. He marched her into a room opening off the kitchen, a bedroom. Using neck ties from a collection hanging in the *Schrank*, he tied her hands behind her back, stuffing another into her mouth and cinching it hard.

Forst appeared, watching from the doorway. When Rick finished, he said, "Let's wrap up those charges and load the van."

Rick pushed Riley onto the bed and brushed his hands down his pant legs as if he'd just completed an arduous task. "Sure," he said. "I'm ready."

"Good." The bald man gave a crisp double clap with his hands. "It's time to go."

72

FORST LEANED AGAINST THE door jamb, watching the woman squirm on the unmade bed. Her hair, soaked by the rain to a dark chestnut, lay tangled against the pillow. He imagined it wet from perspiration after a vigorous romp in bed. In his mind, he removed her rumpled sweater, the soggy jeans, her underthings.

He left the knotted neck ties in place.

Glancing at the table, he saw Salih still painstakingly measuring, mixing, coiling wires. "You're taking too long," he complained.

The chemist turned a sullen gaze on him. "I like to be precise."

"What's to be precise about? It's a simple job. I could do it in my sleep."

Salih glared, opening his mouth to grumble some more, and suddenly Forst had reached his limit. "Leave it!" he said. "Start loading the van. I'll finish the detonator."

He sat at the table and assembled the charges needed to disperse the chemical agent, deftly connecting them to the detonating device. He wrapped it carefully in a plastic tarp and placed it in the carrier beside the titanium case holding the canister of deadly gas.

In the barn next to the house, a considerable pile of additional equipment—including gas masks, more plastic tarps, and a portable

320

toolbox—waited to be loaded into the van. The storm had picked up energy, hurling rain from the skies and whipping the trees into a frenzy. He didn't fancy carrying out the mission in that mess and wished Cincher had consulted the weather forecast before picking his timeframe.

"Take this," he told Salih, handing him the carrier. "Make sure nothing gets wet. Use the tarps."

The chemist scowled but said nothing. Covering the carrier with a sheet of plastic and flinging the door open, he stepped out into the storm, disappearing in a sheet of rain. Forst hurried across the kitchen and shut the door, cutting off the deluge. Wiping his bald head dry with a dish towel, he smoothed the shirt over his chest and crossed to the bedroom.

Cincher's pet stared at him, her eyes wide and almost luminescent in the light spilling in from the kitchen fire. Her mouth moved, producing only a muffled moan which he found amusing. Moving closer, he placed one knee on the soft mattress and shifted his weight onto it, creating a void that forced her to roll in his direction.

"I'm beginning to understand why Cincher is so taken with you," he said.

She glared, mumbling loudly, trying to form words against the wad in her mouth. Why had Salih gagged her? There was no one near to hear her cries. Grasping the silk fabric, Forst slipped it off her head, freeing her tongue.

She grimaced, working to restore moisture to her mouth. "Your plan will fail," she finally managed. "The police are on their way here now."

Forst laughed. She really was delightfully playful. "That's not true, Riley, but ten points to you for trying."

Squirming all the more, she said, "You are vile! Pitiless." She locked eyes with him, her intense gaze generating an energy that both disturbed and thrilled him. "I don't understand what made you that way," she said.

Sitting beside her, he leaned close and whispered. "Do you really want to know? I confess I find the idea of sharing myself with you very intoxicating."

She recoiled at his breath against her ear, and he saw goose flesh forming along her arms. "I see you are stimulated by me as well."

Nostrils flaring, she turned her face away. Forst knew he shouldn't be taunting her like this, shouldn't be playing with Cincher's pet, but he really couldn't restrain himself. Caressing her cheek, he began crooning, a tuneless melody, enjoying the fine texture of her skin. And in that moment she did something he should have expected, but truly hadn't.

She bit him.

She turned her face and fastened her teeth on his thumb, grinding down through the fleshy pad and clear to the bone.

He screamed. Furious, hurting, feeling betrayed, he raised his other hand and brought it down hard, backhanding her across the face. Her head snapped back, falling limp against the pillow.

With a feral growl, he gripped her by the upper arms, smearing her jacket with his blood. Before he could roll her over, the outer door banged open with a crash. Looking over his shoulder, he saw that Hill had arrived and stood dripping, glowering at him with narrowed eyes.

Rising from the bed, he went out, pulling the door shut behind him.

73

Woozy, her cheek smarting from Forst's vicious blow, Riley rolled onto her side and used her fingers to pry at the knots Rick had tied. He'd left her a measure of slack, something to work with, but the task was still challenging and her hands were cramping with the effort.

Pausing to rest, she saw that the door Forst had pulled shut had not latched, giving her a four-inch slice to peer through. She made out a corner of the wooden table, still spread with spools of wire. A wedge of fire flickered on the grate, illuminating the movement of two figures, partially revealed through the crack.

Forst and Hill.

They were speaking, and she strained to hear what they were saying, a job made easier as their voices rose in anger.

"...brought this problem on us," Forst was shouting. "You are the link that brought her here."

"So, let's deal with it," Hill returned, matching his pitch. "She has to die, Forst. We both know it, and Cincher must know it, too. He'll thank us, in the end."

"Somehow, I doubt he will." A pause, and he lowered his voice. Riley struggled to hear his next words. "I agree, she must be eliminated. But I'll take that order only from Cincher himself."

324

Riley heard a hissing intake of breath. "There was a time when you killed without an order from Cincher," Hill said. "I have the photos to prove it, and I'll use them if I have to."

An ugly silence followed. Rain drummed against the window, a ragged rat-a-tat that shook the panes. Footsteps sounded across the floor, lighter than Forst's step, and Riley heard a disdainful snort as the stripe of light widened across the darkened bedroom floor. Hill stood framed in the doorway, her features obscured, her head haloed in light from the kitchen behind her.

"You're pathetic," she said. Riley wasn't sure if the insult was directed at her or at Forst.

A beat passed, and when she spoke again, her voice had sharpened, taking on a more distinct accent. One with a middle eastern tone. "Here you stand, a man quailing before a pretty woman. You don't have the strength of character to do what needs to be done."

The scene from the simulator flashed in Riley's mind—the spreading bloom on Colette's golden blouse, the surreal shifting of light and shadow, the shimmer of blood on the knife.

The same knife Hill raised now, clutched in her fist.

She staggered forward and as she came, her darkened features solidified, like the floating die of a Magic 8 Ball coming to the surface to answer a fervent question.

OUTLOOK NOT SO GOOD.

Stopping beside the bed, Hill stared down, her eyes burning into Riley's with a lunatic gleam. "You took my Colette from me." Her voice was quiet, almost a whisper, but it cut through the dimness of the room like a javelin. "You killed her."

And then, rising to a shriek, she repeated, "You killed her!"

The knife slashed down in a swift arc. Riley rolled away as it plunged into the mattress with a sickening ripping sound. Forst grabbed Hill from behind and they fell onto the bed, wrestling, their flailing arms and legs sometimes lashing out at Riley where she curled protectively against the wall, hands still fastened behind her.

The struggle continued for what seemed like hours, punctuated by grunts and yowls as the two rolled back and forth on the sagging mattress. In the dark and from her limited perspective, Riley couldn't discern what was happening but it ended with Forst rising to his feet, the knife in his hand, and Hill's blood pumping out onto the mattress.

He stood panting, his head angled toward Riley though she couldn't see his eyes in the shadow. In that instant, the outside door burst open, letting in the sounds of the storm.

"It's getting bad, Forst," Rick shouted. "We have to go now."

The panting shadow hovered over her, motionless. If he considered her a witness to the murder he'd just committed, he would certainly silence her now. He still held the knife and she was still bound, cornered against the wall.

Rick could help. If she screamed, he would come. He—

Forst turned and left the room. Riley heard the howling wind, the insistent patter of rain, the sound of boots on floorboards. And then silence.

She was alone with a dead woman.

74

NATE PULLED UP TO the Arrivals curb at the Nuremberg airport and leapt out to meet the cluster of eight men dressed in tactical gear. A cold piercing rain fell in unrelenting forays, but the men hardly seemed to notice, accustomed to harsh conditions of every kind. Nate knew some of them even welcomed it as a kind of spice to heighten the flavor of their missions.

As he approached, the man in charge gestured toward the row of parking spaces. Turning his head, Nate saw two black Mercedes-Benz G-Wagens.

"We'll follow you," their leader said, a trace of Australian accent in his voice. He walked forward and extended his hand. "I'm Ziegler."

"Nate Quentin." Nate shook the rain out of his collar and asked, "Is there someplace dry we can talk so I can bring you up to speed?"

Ziegler clapped him on the back. "Autobahn sounds about right for bringing us up to speed. We'll let you talk on the way."

One of the men tossed Nate a handheld radio and the group moved to the vehicles, clambering in as their engines fired up. Nate climbed back behind the wheel of his rental and led the way. The rain was coming down in sheets now, sluicing over the windshield faster than the wiper blades could clear it.

This worried him. The last thing Nate wanted to do was wreck on the way, postponing the help Riley so desperately needed.

Keying the radio, he began filling in as many details as he could about the situation they were heading into and the risks involved. As he talked, he realized one very disturbing fact.

He didn't know nearly enough.

75

RILEY LAY FROZEN, CURLED against the rough, bone-chilling plaster of the wall. She ached, shot through with horror and exhaustion. Beside her on the bed, the dead woman sprawled, face hidden in shadow, one arm flung outward as if reaching for Riley, almost touching her.

Riley shrank away. Closing her eyes, she tried to swallow down the nausea, grab hold of her panicked thoughts. Nate felt impossibly far away, in another world. Petrified in this moment of terror, thoughts of Rick and the peril that lay at the top of the mountain refused to register, swimming away from her mental grasp.

The notion that this was real, was happening here and now, overwhelmed her. She bit back a sob and lay listening to the storm, struggling to calm her pounding heart.

Gradually, she became aware of another sound, masked by the shriek of wind and beating rain. A low moan, repeated at intervals. Riley stared in dread at the reaching hand, saw the fingers twitch.

Hill was alive.

Horrified, Riley wrenched desperately at the knots still binding her hands. Working the fabric loose, she pulled free, whimpering with relief. She wriggled closer to the injured woman and raised her blouse, searching for the source of blood soaking the bedsheets.

In the dim light, Hill's abdomen appeared to be smeared with tar, blots and dollops of a black viscous substance. Riley found the wound and pressed the necktie into it, slammed by a sharp pang of regret that she hadn't done this for Colette—only for her killer.

Adding a corner of the blanket to her compress, Riley applied as much pressure as she dared. Her gaze went to Hill's face and she was startled to see the woman's eyes open, fixed on her own with a terrible sort of intensity.

She spoke, her tone low and gurgling. "Cincher's pet...his plaything. Now...and forever."

"Don't speak," Riley said. "Save your breath."

Hill laughed, coughing out a spray of blood. "He has a remarkable...power. He will bind you to his will...as he did me." She coughed again, weakly, her voice fading. "As he does everyone."

She shuddered, and the terrible eyes rolled back in her head. Grasping Riley's forearm with surprising strength, she groaned and struggled to speak again. "You will never be free of him, but I..." She paused for breath, choking on blood, coughing more of it onto the spattered bedclothes.

"I, at last...."

A violent gust of wind shook the window panes, as if rattled by Hill's departing spirit. Riley looked at the woman's face, her eyes still staring, but sightless now. The grip on her arm loosened and she peeled the fingers away, placing the hand on Hill's chest.

Riley shifted off the bed and stood, stretching the kinks out of her muscles, catching her breath, ordering the thoughts which now entered her head. Unzipping the inside pocket of her jacket where she'd kept her cell phone safe from the rain, she tried raising a signal.

One tiny bar showed on the screen, and she dialed Nate's number. But in the storm, or because of the rural location, she couldn't get the call to go through.

Unwilling to wait for Nate and his troops to appear, she moved into the kitchen, searching for paper and pen. She found a grubby-paged notebook and a dull pencil in the drawer of the kitchen desk.

Sitting at the table, she wrote down everything Rick had told her about the planned attack at the Sammelplatz, underlining that it included the dispersal of a chemical agent and that it was happening now.

As she scrawled the notes on paper, a strange feeling of déjà vu crept over her. She remembered Nate doing much the same thing when they'd first met—leaving a hastily written improvised report at a crime scene on the first case they'd worked together.

Not that their association had been in any sense official at the time. And it still wasn't.

Yet here they were.

Leaving the note on the table, held in place by a spool of red-coated wire, Riley swept out into the storm and set her face toward the mountain.

76

RICK GRITTED HIS TEETH as the van squealed, skidding on the wet pavement of the narrow, twisting road leading up to the Sammelplatz. He'd been horrified to see Forst stumbling out of the bedroom back at the *Hof*, his shirt smeared with blood, Riley lying motionless on the bed behind him.

But the fact that Hill wasn't accompanying them as planned, suggested the blood belonged to her. Not Riley. Rick clung to the notion that Forst wouldn't harm Riley as long as Cincher wanted her alive.

That had to be true.

A bolt of lightning split the sky in front of them. Rick's grip on the dashboard tightened as he stared out into the wicked night. Sheets of rain slashed down and visibility out the windshield was horrific, creating the real possibility that Forst might steer them wrong and send the van plummeting down the mountain at any moment.

"This is madness, Forst. We need to wait until this typhoon passes."

Forst spared him a half-second glare. "You know we can't do that," he said. "It has to be now. This is the beginning. Everything that comes after, depends on what happens now."

Rick shuddered. He'd barely discovered what Forst and his crew had planned for now. He couldn't imagine what they anticipated would happen as a result of this first domino tipping.

He had to stop it happening. And he would. He didn't have the vital key they depended upon; therefore, he would succeed in toppling their mission. Or at least delaying it long enough to wreck the train of events to follow.

He hoped.

The knowledge that such a success would most likely be at the expense of his own life hovered at the edge of his consciousness, but he pushed it aside. He couldn't let that figure into his choices. There was too much at stake, too many lives at risk.

They veered around a bend and Rick braced himself against the dashboard, cringing at the scream of the tires. Suddenly, in the watery view ahead, a tree loomed out of the darkness, blocking the road.

Forst slammed on the brakes and the van slewed, its rear axle sliding around to the right where the edge of the road waited to swallow them. Rick's grip tightened and he glanced at Forst, saw his face, white as bone, in a sudden flash of lightning.

"What the hell...?"

A rough-barked pine lay across the pavement, fallen in the storm. With a thick trunk, more than twelve inches across, moving it was not an option. Cursing, Forst put the van in reverse and Rick's heart lurched as he felt the rear wheels spin in the loose earth near the brink.

"This is the only road up to the Sammelplatz," Forst said. He slumped in the driver's seat, staring ahead, burning desperation in his eyes. "I'm going to try driving around it."

The van plunged into the shallow ditch running along the inner border of the pavement and bounced once as it headed for a break in the trees, the underside scraping on roadside rocks. Rick's heart sank as he saw that Forst might be able to get the van through the opening and back on the road.

But the rain-soaked soil was a quagmire, clutching the van's tires and sucking them down in an unrelenting grip. The engine whined as Forst repeatedly tried breaking the muddy hold. The van didn't budge.

Inside, Rick sat tense, waiting, with only the sound of the wind and rain beating against the skin of the van until at last, Forst spoke.

"Grab the gear. We're going on foot."

"What? In this?"

Forst sneered. "You would give up this easy? We're halfway there. Two miles—even in this—shouldn't stand in our way."

Forst opened his door and the storm roared in, spraying a mist of droplets clear across to where Rick sat, wondering how this crazy night would end and hoping he lived long enough to find out.

77

—·—

LIESL STOOD BEHIND THE reception desk and watched the summit guests mingling in the lobby, sitting in groups beside the massive stone fireplace, chatting, or pausing to watch the spectacular display of the mighty storm through the massive plate glass windows.

Wrapped in a shimmer of fulfillment, she took in the pleasant smiles, courteous nods, and congenial behavior with a feeling of gratitude.

The event had been a success, and tonight it would culminate in a celebratory banquet with dancing and a slide show she'd created from photos taken during the preceding days. The presentation was designed to highlight the special moments shared and the hope of a friendly future between the represented countries in attendance.

With the storm continuing to lash outside the windows, casting an occasional dash of brilliant lightning against the blackened sky, the warmth inside the Sammelplatz glowed in rosy contrast. Liesl felt almost able to relax and enjoy herself.

Julia had disappeared from sight after their talk beside the trout pond, and the summit's last arriving guest, a newly-appointed minister, had made it safely inside before the worst of the rain crashed down.

335

Max had told her the exciting news that he and her parents were going to watch a movie—with popcorn—after dinner. A film of his own choosing. Liesl guessed it would involve a super-hero of some stripe, as that was his latest passion. Her mother would enjoy the movie, squeezing Max's hand during the good parts, and her father would snore along beside them, vigorously denying it afterward.

Liesl felt a surge of relief. Her final exam was nearly over, and it was beginning to look as if she might ace it. She straightened her spine and smiled at a passing ambassador's wife.

She was weathering the storm.

78

In the muddy courtyard, pelted by cold spikes of rain, Riley squelched through ankle deep slime. She felt small and ineffective. Anything she might do to stop the disastrous series of unfolding events would be like spitting into the furious wind that howled around her.

Yet she couldn't do *nothing*. She figured the road to the mountaintop resort ran for perhaps four miles. Under these weather conditions, it would take her more than an hour to get there on foot. Useless.

Running to the barn, she pushed open the door, hoping to appropriate an operational vehicle of some sort, but found only a rusty bicycle with a flat rear tire.

Behind her, the sky lit and she turned to see a massive fork of lightning splitting the darkness. A sudden boom of thunder followed, making her jump as it rumbled away in a sullen diminuendo.

Riley let out a shriek of frustration. Determined to make it to the top, to help Rick, to warn the building's occupants—anything and everything she could do to aid in thwarting the attack—she started up the mud-slicked road, moving as fast as she dared in the riotous storm.

She knew the chance of encountering someone on the way up and hitching a ride was impossibly slim but hope still swelled within her.

With her ears tuned to the sound of an approaching vehicle, she almost missed her opportunity when it came.

In the gloom ahead, a familiar form took shape even as the sound of hoof beats registered. Gideon appeared on the magnificent Maximus, piercing the darkness with a torch wielded like a golden lance. He saw her and pulled up on the reins, turning the horse in her direction.

"Have you seen Colette?" he shouted into the buffeting wind.

Riley faltered, feeling as if a stone pressed against her breastbone, composed of guilt, sorrow, and aching regret. The scene from the simulator came back to her in sharp detail, bringing the same sick feeling. She didn't want to tell him where to find Colette.

Besides that, she desperately needed help and he could provide it. There was nothing either of them could do now for Colette, but he and Maximus could get her to the Sammelplatz. Together, they might save a lot of lives.

Feeling horrible about it, Riley nevertheless judged it better to break the news of Colette's murder later, after the crisis was over. Skirting his question, she raised her voice against the wind and shouted, "We need to get up to the summit! Immediately. Many lives depend upon it!"

He scowled down at her. "What are you talking about?"

"Terrorists are headed there now to unleash a chemical attack. I need your help to stop them."

To his credit, Gideon didn't waste time on more questions. He reached down and gripped Riley's hand, pulling her up into the saddle. She wrapped her arms around him as the horse leapt forward, taking comfort from his warmth, his solid presence.

The storm continued to beat down as Maximus carried them on, slipping once or twice on wet pavement, skittering when bursts of thunder echoed in the sky. Halfway up the mountain, they came upon a large pine tree which had cracked at the base of its trunk and lay across the road, blocking it.

Mired in the mud beside the pavement, was Forst's van. Abandoned. Gideon pointed to a set of deep indentations where someone wearing boots had climbed the slight verge onto the roadbed.

"They had to go on foot," he said.

"We can overtake them!"

"And then do what?" Gideon countered. "Are you armed?"

"No."

Crestfallen, Riley considered his point. She hadn't thought beyond just getting there.

"We need to arrive ahead of them," Gideon said. "Warn everybody, put up a defense, lock them out."

"Can we?"

"I think so, *ja*. I know a shorter path."

Gideon turned Maximus off the road, and they threaded their way through the dripping trees and sagging ferns, led by the light of the torch. The fierceness of the wind eased off and the rain quit its steady downpour, coming instead in spates—frenzied one moment and gentle the next. The clouds which had shrouded the moon scudded aside and a weak silvery light frosted the landscape.

Their path narrowed to a rocky trail, falling sharply away to their left, stone walls rising high above them on the right. Looking down, Riley was surprised to recognize the spot where she and Nate had talked as the boulder hurtled down on them from above.

A chill ran through her as she realized she now had her arms twined around their prime suspect. Both Gideon and the horse seemed familiar and comfortable with the narrow ledge of the trail.

As if they'd been there many times before.

A fresh stab of fear penetrated through the cold and damp, through her worry over the attack at the top of the mountain. She was here, alone and vulnerable, with a man she hardly knew and who might—for some unknown reason—want her dead. He claimed they were headed up to the Sammelplatz.

But were they?

Gideon seemed to sense her unease. Craning his neck, he asked, "Are you okay back there?"

Riley swallowed, working to make her voice sound normal. "Yes. Are we almost there?"

He laughed. "Like a child you are, Riley."

Heaven help her.

She'd already admitted to him she didn't have a weapon. As a martial arts expert, his hands and body were his weapons. He could easily overpower her, break her neck, and throw her over the precipice. It would look like she got lost in the storm and fell.

Feverishly, Riley debated within herself. Did Gideon wish to harm her? Should she trust him? She came up with several reasons not to—the boulder incident, his hostile behavior toward her on occasion, his ability to hide the truth, demonstrated by his relationship with Colette.

And simply the fact that so many things here were not what they seemed.

About the only thing that counted in favor of Gideon was her gut. She instinctively wanted to trust him. Wright said she had good instincts.

But was that true?

It was not that long ago that she'd liked and trusted the man who'd killed her family and held a knife to her throat. Clearly, her instincts were not infallible.

Trying to free her mind of panic, Riley stilled herself in the saddle and listened. The sounds of the storm abated as they moved along the trail, but a new sound was arising, growing louder with each second. A rushing, as if torrents of water gushed down the mountain.

Gideon's muscles tensed beneath her arms. The earth shifted below them. Maximus whinnied and shied.

Riley watched, awestruck, as the ground in front of them churned into liquid.

The mountain was moving.

79

NATE SLOWED THE RENTAL car and squinted past the thumping wipers into the rain-lashed night.

He and Wright's team had arrived at the academy to find it in a state of chaos. With the director out of the country, the assistant director nowhere to be found, and the senior instructors shocked by the discovery of a body in the driving simulator.

A student had been stabbed to death.

Riley's roommate.

And Riley was missing.

Pain closed in around Nate's stomach, acid boil caused by anxiety. He never should have left her alone here. If he'd brought her along—as she'd suggested—she be here now, by his side.

Instead, Matsui Haruko rode beside him. She had insisted on coming with him to find Riley and rescue Rick, and Nate was grateful for her calm spirit and competent companionship.

She spoke soothingly, her voice clear and precise, her face earnest and creased with concern as Nate searched the darkness for a turnoff leading toward the *Hof's* location as Riley had described it to him.

He hoped to heaven she was okay.

"We got a road coming up on the right," Matsui told him.

"Let's take it."

The area was sparsely populated and roads were few, so Nate figured chances were good they'd found the right one. He turned, and the two G-Wagens followed.

They pulled up in a courtyard empty of vehicles, triggering a motion-activated lamp that cast a cone of light over the muddy drive. This was it. The *Hof*.

Ziegler gave a signal and four of Wright's men split and circled the house, two in each direction. The other four approached the front with Nate and Matsui. Repeated pounding brought no one, but the door was unlocked and they pushed inside where the team split, two men clattering up the staircase, two remaining to scan the downstairs area.

Nate entered a wide hallway with a living room opening up on the left, filled with brown leather furniture and flanked by an enormous double window drenched by the rain. The kitchen was on the right, the embers of a dying fire glowing in the grate.

The table and counter were littered with a hodge-podge of items and Nate's eye swept over and past them to the doorway beyond where one of the team had just entered. A second later, Nate heard the words he dreaded.

"Got a body!"

Closing his eyes, he fought down a wave of nausea. Please don't let it be Riley. He couldn't live with that grief.

With that guilt.

The other downstairs man pushed past him and went in. Nate forced himself to follow. Matsui waited in the kitchen.

He stared across at the bed against the wall. It was bathed in blood, bedclothes twisted into crimson-capped mountains, the pillow smeared and stained with red.

The body sprawled across the length of the bed, one leg hanging off, one hand outstretched toward the wall. Blonde hair, rusty with drying blood, lay tangled against the sheets.

It wasn't Riley.

Nate let go of the breath he'd been holding. It hissed out of him in a long, drawn-out sigh. He heard boots on the stairs as the other two came down, and then Matsui gave a shout.

"Take a look at this!" she said.

Nate left the bloody bedroom and saw Matsui bent over the kitchen table, reading from a sheet of paper held in place by a spool of wire.

"It's addressed to you," she said, nodding to Nate.

Nate stepped forward and read the note:

Dear Nate,

I've learned what Hill and Forst are planning—an attack on the peace summit taking place at the top of this mountain, at the Sammelplatz.

They are detonating a device designed to disperse Sarin gas throughout the building, killing everyone inside. Those in attendance include ministers, presidents, and other leaders of eastern European nations involved in peaceful negotiation.

Rick is working undercover to foil the operation. He is with them now. The attack is happening tonight. I couldn't wait. Have gone to help. Sorry.

Riley

The anxiety he'd just released came rushing back. Riley was out there in one storm and running headlong toward another—one certain to be more dangerous. More deadly.

Even as he worried, he felt a twinge of admiration, a touch of wry humor as he recognized what she'd done. The first time they'd worked together, they'd processed a crime scene under disastrous circumstances and left a written report for those to follow.

He wondered if she'd thought about that while writing this note to him. He wondered if it had strengthened their connection for her as it was, right now, for him.

He had to find her.

"Let's go!"

Ziegler barked the order and the men returned to the G-Wagens. Nate folded Riley's note and put it in his pocket as he and Matsui ran to the rental car.

"Ditch the weeniemobile," Ziegler shouted. "If we have to go off road, you'll be stuck. Climb in."

Matsui changed direction and jumped into one of the G-Wagens. Nate clambered into the back seat of the other—Ziegler's vehicle—forcing one of the men into the undesirable middle position, which he bore with stoic disregard. They tore out of the courtyard and back to the road heading up the mountain.

The storm was waning, the wind dying, the rain spattering down in random flurries. Ziegler cut the rate of the windshield wipers and adjusted the headlights. Nate stared ahead and to the sides, watching for movement, for any sign of Riley.

They rounded a bend and Ziegler jammed his foot down on the brake, sounding his horn at the same time to warn the vehicle behind him. An enormous pine tree lay across the road, completely blocking passage.

Ziegler jumped out of the car and his men followed suit. As they stood in the dark, examining the situation and debating their options, Nate heard a distant rumble. He strained his ears, listening, as it grew in volume and intensity. Matsui, standing next to him, grabbed his arm as the ground beneath their feet began to shake.

"Brace yourselves!" Ziegler shouted.

80

—·—

RILEY'S HEART SLAMMED IN her chest. She felt it beat against Gideon's back as she clung to him.

"What's happening?" she shouted.

In the squall of noise, she barely heard his answer.

"Avalanche."

The sudden accumulation of pelting rain had combined with water-saturated rock, soil, and debris to create a mudslide and send it barreling down the mountain.

Astonishment struck Riley full force. She'd lived through something very like this when Mt. Rainier had erupted, the intense heat of the pyroclastic event turning massive amounts of snow into a river of mud that wreaked havoc on her corner of the Pacific northwest.

And now, she'd traveled across the entire United States and the Atlantic Ocean to experience the same peril here. You really cannot run away from your terrors.

And she was terrified.

A torrent of motion, not more than five meters ahead of them on the trail, marked the border of the mudslide. Riley watched in horror as a rubble of loose, slimy earth filled with rocks and tree branches

347

churned past in thundering fury, wiping out the path and everything in its trajectory.

The ghastly raucous noise quivered in the air, vibrated in the ground beneath them. It grew to a monstrous level. Riley longed to cover her ears but didn't dare take her arms from around Gideon.

Maximus shied and reared, circling in panic on the narrow trail. The well-muscled martial arts instructor stayed in the saddle and Riley's grip on him never loosened.

And then, as the awful clamor reached a climax, the horse reared again and shook his hindquarters. Riley slid off and Gideon came with her. She hit the ground and rolled away from the stamping hooves, right to the crumbling edge of the path.

And partway over.

Grasping desperately for something to hold onto, to stop her slide into the dark void, she found an outcropping of rock and clutched its slippery surface, dread filling her as she felt the relentless pull of gravity.

She screamed, but the sound was swallowed in the rage of the avalanche. Her fingers, aching with the strain of holding her, slipped closer to the edge. And then, as her terror mounted to new heights, the racketing noise faded into a series of ghostly echoes and she screamed again.

Instantly, Gideon appeared above her. He fastened his hands like a double vise on her forearms and bracing his boots against the rock, he pulled her onto the crumbling ledge. They lay panting, trembling, covered in mud and pine needles.

"What happened to Maximus?" Riley asked. "He didn't...?"

"No, he didn't fall. He'll be halfway home by now, having a bit more sense than the two of us." Gideon paused to suck in a deep breath. "Because we are going on, aren't we, Riley?"

She lay staring up into the clearing sky, at the stars hidden and then revealed by the ragged, sailing clouds. "We have to," she said. "But how can we? The way back won't work, and the way forward is obliterated."

Gideon gave a soft, humorless laugh. "You're overlooking our last option."

"Which is...?"

Gideon raised his arm, pointing straight at the sky. "Up," he said. "We go up the cliff face."

Riley gasped, a flash of terror slicing through her. She'd only just felt gravity's terrible power and she knew her limitations. "But, we don't have any gear or the proper shoes."

"No, we don't."

Gideon rolled over and rose to his feet. He gazed up the stone side of the mountain. "You don't have to do this, Riley. You're just a trainee. Go back. Be safe."

Riley rose and stood beside him. "You don't have to do this either. You're just a trainer."

His beautiful face lit with a smile. "You're right. I don't have to do this," he said. "But I'm going to."

Riley pushed away her doubts, her second thoughts, her fears, and even her worries over the condition of her precious fingers.

"So am I," she said.

81

RICK TRAILED A FEW steps behind Forst, his boots sliding a bit on the rain-glazed pavement. The storm was petering out and their journey on foot had presented fewer challenges, and fewer delays, than he'd hoped for.

The Sammelplatz loomed directly ahead, less than a football field away.

He and Forst had heard the riotous torrent of noise and felt the trembling ground, pausing to take it in, staring wide-eyed at each other, knowing what it meant. But as it hadn't affected their route, Forst had shrugged and pressed on.

Rick felt an added tightness across his chest as his worry over Riley returned. He didn't actually know what had happened in the bedroom at the *Hof* but he'd seen both Forst and Hill go in, and only Forst came out. He'd concluded that the blood covering Forst's shirt and hands was Hill's, and Hill's alone.

But was it?

He'd left Riley's bonds loose so she could get herself free and go for help. So where was she now? He fervently hoped she hadn't been caught in the avalanche. The thought sickened him.

350

He followed Forst as he skirted the front of the event center, hugging the bushes and staying low as they circled around to the gray metal maintenance doors. Digging into his pocket for the key, Forst said, "We're down a man—or should I say woman? Herr Doktor Müller will have to do his bit without her help."

"Where is he?" Rick asked.

"Out there," Forst said, motioning vaguely into the night.

Once inside, the security system began a steady beeping and Forst punched a sequence of numbers into the keypad, silencing it.

"How did you get the code?" Rick asked.

Forst gave him a hostile glare. "Don't worry about it, Salih. Just focus on doing your part."

Moving down the dimly lit corridor, they entered a large room filled with the whoosh and hum of industrial machines. Forst halted and shook the rucksack off his shoulders. From it, he drew two gas masks and handed one to Rick.

He pointed to the far side of the room where a line of four sturdy fans, each of them five feet in diameter, fed into large ventilation ducts, supplying the building above with fresh, moving air. Forst motioned for Rick to open the plastic-wrapped carrier which held the detonating device.

"This is it," he said, smiling grimly. "Hook us up."

82

—·—

RILEY CLUNG TO THE rain-slicked rock, fingers searching above her for a new handhold, a crack or indentation she could use to pull herself another agonizing foot or two up the side of the cliff.

The tubular formations of petrified lava that dotted the mountain provided welcome moments of relief, acting almost as handles. A godsend, and Riley sent her thanks heavenward. But the ready-made hand grips became increasingly scarce the higher she went.

A few meters above and to the right, Gideon scaled the stone and seemed to be having an easier time of it. She heard a rattle of loose pebbles and a grunt from him as he slipped and caught himself.

"Almost there, Riley. I know you can't see it yet, but we're only four or five meters from the top."

Which meant six or seven for her.

Chewing her lip, she struggled for courage, but Christopher wasn't there to belay her. She wore no harness, wasn't clipped into any lines. And despite Gideon's assurance, she couldn't see her goal in sight.

Legs shaking, fingers growing numb with cold, Riley fought to swallow the lump of dread rising in her throat. Inside her ribcage, her heart pounded out a wobbling presto beat as despair settled over her.

She wasn't going to make it.

The courageous line of her progenitors, carried on by her mother and father and those before them, was ending here. With her.

She didn't dare look down, but she knew that when her feet and fingers gave out and she plummeted, the fall would likely kill her. And she'd be leaving no one behind to carry on the tradition.

The unbearable ache of it filled her chest.

How could she progress, moving smoothly upward from one hold to the next, when her heart was juddering so violently inside? It was impossible to reconcile the two extremes and make them work together.

It was her unattainable staccato passage.

The realization wrenched a cry from the core of her being and she clenched her teeth against it. But the sound of her own anguish and the notion that it might be her last utterance, broke something free inside her.

A heat, a vehemence, a rushing internal torrent to parallel the avalanche she'd just lived through, streamed like fire along Riley's veins. Her heart still hammered wildly against her ribcage and her legs still trembled, but a new energy flooded into her fingers, driving away their numbness.

And the surge brought something else for her.

Hope.

"Come on, Riley!" Gideon called from the top of the cliff. "I made it. You can, too. You're almost there."

With her pulse beating in her ear drums, Riley moved her hand along the rough stone and found purchase, hoisting herself another foot up the vertical climb. And then another after that.

And another.

Moving now with more confidence, feeding herself strength, she stretched and gripped and pulled her way up until Gideon's face appeared above her. As before, he grasped her arms, securing her and helping her cover the last burst of the journey.

A friend. An ally.

Someone she could trust.

"Take a moment," Gideon told her. "Rest."

Riley sat, catching her breath and letting her heartbeat return to normal. But the Sammelplatz was in view now and she couldn't bear to sit immobile when everyone inside was at risk.

Leaping to her feet, she grabbed Gideon's hand and squeezed hard. "Let's go!"

83

SAVORY SMELLS WAFTED ON the air amid the sounds of a busy kitchen crew. Liesl sniffed, pleased with the mouthwatering aromas of garlic, tomatoes, herbs, schnitzel, and gravy. She watched the first of the magnificently dressed guests arrive for the banquet and find their place cards at the round tables.

She moved through the great hall, checking centerpieces and place settings, pausing to chat with Dr. Vlasov and his wife. They were thanking her for a lovely week when Gunther caught her eye from across the room and motioned her over.

His face held no expression, but Liesl heard strain in his voice as he said, "You need to come with me."

He led her to his office in the corridor behind the kitchens. Liesl followed him inside and stopped short, astonished at the sight of two strangers. A man and a woman.

Both were sodden and filthy, with bedraggled hair and assorted cuts and scrapes. The woman's clothes and fingernails were stained with blood.

"They may not look like the most reliable sources," Gunther admitted, "but I think we need to pay attention to what they have to say."

Dismayed, feeling the successful completion of the summit slipping away, Liesl said, "Very well. What are they saying?"

Gunther nodded to the grubby woman who stepped forward with an air of anxiety. She wasted no time on greetings.

"We have strong reason to believe this facility is under attack," the woman said. "Terrorists with a chemical weapon are on their way here, or may possibly be here already."

"You need to get everyone out," her companion added. "Now."

Liesl stared, incredulous. "How can you know this?" she demanded.

"Please," the woman said, "there's no time to explain. You have to evacuate."

Evacuate! No, that would certainly put an indelible black mark on her audition. These people, lunatics by the look of them, had to be mistaken.

Gunther said, "I'll alert my staff and initiate the procedure."

"No," Liesl said. "I don't know who these people are or where they get their authority, but I am not evacuating my guests out into a storm."

"Sarin gas," the strange man said, "will kill everyone in the building within seconds."

Max! Her parents. Julia. Expelling the summit attendees into the rain and cold would count poorly against her. But not as poorly as getting them all killed. And the thought of Max...

"Very well." Heart sinking, she turned to Gunther. "Take care of the guests. I'm going after my family."

Rushing to the apartment, Liesl found Max and her parents in the living room, curled on the couches and watching an action scene rife with special effects and a booming soundtrack. Grabbing the remote control, she hit the power button and the room went suddenly quiet.

"Mama!"

The expression on Max's face—half delight at seeing her, half exasperation at the interruption—would have brought a smile to her face at any other time. Now, it only spurred a sense of urgency that made her realize she'd really begun to believe the strangers' crazy story.

"I'm sorry," she said, keeping her voice calm. "You can watch the movie another time, Max. Right now," she turned a pointed look on her parents, "we need to go outside. Get your coats and follow me."

Max's eyes were round with curiosity. "Why, Mama? What are we doing outside?"

"Come, and I will show you." Liesl moved toward the hallway. "Julia!" she called.

When her sister didn't answer, Liesl ran to the small den Julia used as a bedroom. It was empty.

Meeting her family at the door, she said, "Julia's not here. Did she say where she was going?"

Her mother looked contrite. "I'm sorry," she said. "I didn't even know she was gone."

There was no time to straighten it out now. Liesl herded Max and her parents into the corridor and down the stairway into the crowded lobby. She frowned, not understanding what was happening.

People were milling around, shouting in confusion, worry and fear in their faces, but no one was leaving.

"Wait here!" she told her parents. Pushing through the growing throng, she found one of Gunther's men. "What's going on?" she asked. "Why is no one evacuating?"

He pointed toward the big glass doors but Liesl's view was blocked by the crowd. She squirmed her way forward, gasping as she saw and understood the problem.

The doors were wrapped with heavy chain and padlocked.

They were trapped inside.

84

—·—

RILEY HURRIED DOWN THE harshly lit hallway, Gideon at her side. The kitchens opened onto this wing and a medley of delectable aromas hung in the air, reminding Riley she hadn't eaten since her early lunch and she'd burned off about a week's worth of calories since then. She was starving.

But the thought was fleeting as they rushed beyond the kitchens, searching for the passage down to the maintenance level.

"Found it!" Gideon said, holding the door for her. They pounded down the concrete stairwell, their steps echoing frenziedly in the empty chamber.

"Rick said they were using the ventilation system to disperse the chemical," Riley said as they reached the basement and she saw corridors breaking off in three different directions. "Which way?"

"Let's split up and start looking."

Riley moved off down the hallway to the right, padding swiftly in her sneakers. In contrast to the upper corridors, the light down here was dim and filled with shadows cast by pipes, utility boxes, and machines that roared and hummed so that she didn't hear the voices until she was almost upon them.

The end of the corridor opened into a large space filled with equipment and cartons labeled for storage. Peering carefully around the corner, Riley saw Rick and Forst standing before a bank of industrial-sized fans. They both wore gas masks.

Forst was snapping a canister into place inside the ominous-looking device Riley had seen on his kitchen table. She guessed it was the dispersal unit.

She'd arrived too late.

Running forward, she called out, "Stop!"

Forst swung toward her and drew a pistol from his jacket pocket, pointing it at her.

"You are seriously starting to annoy me, Ms. Forte."

"Likewise, Mr. Forst."

His hand moved to a toggle switch on the dispersal unit and he flipped it, watching her face as he did so. A green light came on. "The device is now activated," he said. "There's nothing you can do to stop it."

Riley held his gaze, step by step moving closer. He kept the gun in his right hand, aimed in her direction. Smiling, he inserted his left index finger into a round opening on the face of the instrument. Riley heard a click as another green light indicator came on.

Forst pulled his finger from the device and sucked it briefly before wiping it on his shirt. Watching her again, his expression taunting and full of malice behind the screen of his mask, he toggled another switch and one more round of glowing green appeared on the instrument panel.

"Okay, Salih." He nodded to Rick. "That's your cue."

Riley turned her gaze on Rick. He didn't move. Forst joggled the pistol impatiently, making Riley cringe.

"It's on you, *mein Freund,* we need your key. It all hangs on this."

Still, Rick remained motionless, simply glaring at the man and his gun. Forst shifted the pistol from Riley to Rick, leveling it at his chest.

"Your finger," he commanded.

Riley stared, suddenly understanding. The detonator used a very sophisticated version of a fingerprint reader. She remembered Martel, her cryptology professor, telling the class about technology under development that would allow a message to be passed in a strand of DNA. A message that might include a password.

Or a key.

She guessed the machine harvested a drop of blood for DNA analysis and needed to pair it with a pulse. Otherwise, Forst would just shoot. And she understood something else.

The moment Rick put his finger in the device, his cover would be blown.

85

—·—

NATE SWAYED AS ZIEGLER steered sharply around a curve. He'd been relegated to the middle seat as the G-Wagens continued their journey to the top of the mountain, and there was nothing for him to hang onto as the vehicle bounced and swerved through the darkness. He tightened his core to keep from careening over onto the laps of his fellow passengers.

The road was bumpy, littered with branches and debris, but once Wright's mighty men had pushed the pine obstruction off to the side, their progress had been steady. Less than five minutes passed before they were turning in at the gate to the Sammelplatz.

The place was lit up, and Nate saw crowds of people moving inside beyond the huge plate glass windows. Though they wore festive clothing, he got the impression they weren't celebrating.

They were panicking.

He realized they knew. They knew they were under attack, but why weren't they coming out of the building into the fresh air, away from the effects of a chemical strike?

And then he saw.

The exits had been disabled, wrapped with heavy chain and padlocks. The terrorists' intended victims were trapped inside the big glass bubble, like fish in a tank.

"Ladders!" Ziegler shouted to his team. "Scout out the gardening shed, maintenance huts, every outbuilding. We need ladders, rope, whatever you can find to help these folks get out safely."

From the second floor and above, a series of balconies jutted from the building, and Nate watched as people pushed out onto them, nearly spilling over the rails.

More people than they were designed to hold.

"Step back!" Nate shouted, waving his hands. "Don't crowd, don't panic."

He didn't think anyone could possibly have heard his warning over the wild commotion, so he was surprised to see people stepping back into the rooms beyond the balconies. Whether by his voice, or someone else's, the crowd seemed to be calming, becoming more orderly.

He looked up and saw many of their faces turned out, toward him and Wright's team of men, beseeching their help. Nate's heart leapt in his chest. He felt a fervent need to do all he could for these people.

Turning, he sped across the soggy grass, feeling mud squelching between his toes and paying it not the least concern.

He had to find a ladder.

86

—·—

RICK KNEW HE WAS a dead man.

He suddenly understood the key and knew he could no longer hide the fact that he didn't have it.

He'd read reports about such locking devices, triggered by a specific strand of DNA and a pulse. Once his finger was in the device, Forst would recognize him for an imposter. There would no longer be a reason to keep him alive.

Forst's anger at the betrayal would be enough to kill him.

Still, Rick took perverse and devious pleasure from being the one to foil the attack and destroy the plot against peace. He caught Riley's eye, saw the fear she was doing a pretty fair job of hiding. Her chin was held high, eyes steady. Only a slight tremble of the lip, a tiny flair of her nostrils, let on how frightened she was.

He held her gaze, smiling briefly. Then he inserted his finger into the key hole. He felt a quick jab of pain as the lancet drew a drop of blood.

Nothing happened.

The final green circle remained unlit. And then, with a beep, it flashed red.

Forst cursed. "You're doing it wrong," he said. "Try it again."

Rick breathed deeply, enjoying the moment, despite its possibly being his last. He pulled his finger free and reentered it, setting off another beep and wink of red light.

Forst screamed in fury. "You said you had the key! I cared for you like a mother for the last week because I thought you had the key." He raised the pistol, hand shaking.

Rick looked straight down the barrel. "Maybe it's you," he said. "Maybe you're the one who's doing it wrong."

Inside his gas mask, Forst's face went a deeper shade of red. He took a step forward. "It's you!"

"Or a glitch in the technology," Rick suggested. "It could be faulty wiring."

He'd drawn the man close enough, and thought about making a grab for the gun. But before he could put his desperate plan into action, a piercing shriek filled the room. Rick looked beyond Riley to see another woman, face white, hands pressed to her cheeks.

"Anton Forst," she screeched. "I *knew* you were a bad man!"

87

Liesl stared at Forst, at the gun in his hand, at the gas mask he wore, and felt faint. Her knees wobbled and she would have fallen if the bedraggled woman who'd come to warn her about the attack hadn't rushed to her side, bracing her up.

"Where's Julia?" she shouted. "What have you done with Julia?"

No one answered her.

After finding the exterior doors sealed, Liesl had hurried her parents and her son down into the bowels of the building, looking for an unblocked door or window to get them out. She was able to open the big set of steel doors and send her family into the night, with instructions to shelter in the stable and wait for her there.

She wanted so much to go with them. But she was responsible for these people, for the Sammelplatz. And for Julia.

Hearing voices, she'd rushed toward them, hoping to find her sister. Instead, she'd found...this.

In horror, she stared at the device resting on a ledge just outside the ventilation ducts. Attached to a gas canister and placed next to the fans, she understood the purpose of the device. A shiver coursed through her.

But also, a thrill of hope.

The device wasn't working. It wouldn't deploy the chemical. Three green lights and a red meant something had gone wrong.

Or, from her perspective, right.

The two men in gas masks were arguing, blaming each other for the device's failure, and Forst looked ready to shoot the other man. As Liesl wondered what she should do, she heard footsteps coming down the corridor and looked up to see Julia.

"Oh, thank heaven!" she said, running to take Julia's hand. "I've been—"

Julia swept her aside. "It didn't detonate," she announced coldly, coming to stand before the two men at the dispersal device, "because one of you is a traitor."

Liesl's knees faltered again, and this time she sank to the floor, staring at her sister's stony face, almost unrecognizable in the gloom of the basement. "I don't understand," she moaned.

Julia was pointing a gun, moving it slowly and deliberately from one man to the other.

"Julia! What the hell?" Forst said, his tone full of anger and confusion.

"What the hell? I'll tell you what the hell is," Julia said. "Cincher wasn't sure you were up to the job, and it looks like he has you pegged, Anton."

Liesl watched in bewilderment as Julia sneered and motioned for Forst to drop his weapon. He lowered it to the ground and kicked it into the shadows.

"As you know, Anton," she continued, "Cincher doesn't take kindly to betrayal."

Liesl saw Forst's eyes, inside his mask, go wide. He shook his head vehemently.

"No! I didn't...I wouldn't."

Julia indicated the malfunctioning machine in front of them. "It certainly appears as if one of you has failed him."

Liesl screamed as Julia steadied her aim and pulled the trigger.

88

RILEY GASPED AS THE woman fired the gun. The sound was painful, deafening in the enclosed space of the basement. She clenched her fists in agony, squeezing her eyes shut, unwilling to open them and see Rick slumped on the floor, dying.

Just as she was getting used to him being alive again.

"Riley!"

Forcing her eyes open, she turned to the sound of Rick's voice and saw it was not him, but Forst, crumpled on the cold concrete. Rick pulled off his mask and stepped toward her, but the woman with the gun used it to motion him back.

"Throw me the mask," she ordered.

Hesitating only a second, Rick tossed her the gas mask and she tucked it under her arm. The Sammelplatz woman, still curled on the floor, whimpered, "Julia, what's going on? Why are you doing this?"

The woman with the gun ignored her. Keeping her pistol trained on Rick, she stepped up beside the detonation device, gazing down at it with an eerie smile.

"You should have kept the mask," she told him. "Because I've got the override key."

She inserted her finger into the second key hole, triggering a beep as the final green circle shone bright. The digital countdown timer blazed to life.

9:56

"Enjoy your evening."

She strode across the open space and disappeared into the corridor. A second later, Riley heard the slam of heavy metal doors, signaling her exit from the building.

Rick ran to the darkened corner where Forst had kicked his gun. Riley moved cautiously to the set of steel doors. She heard the scrape and clang of metal on metal and tried to push the doors open. They budged only a few inches before catching against an obstruction.

Trapped inside, and with no time to waste, she hurried back to the device. The numbers flashed by with dismaying swiftness.

9:18

"Your phone, Riley!" Rick said, his voice thick with urgency. "Do you have a phone?"

She'd forgotten her cell phone, zipped away in the inside pocket of her jacket. With shaking hands, she retrieved it. The screen was cracked, a spiderweb of tiny fissures spreading across its face. It had taken a beating during the night's events.

Holding her breath, she pressed the button to wake it and sighed with relief when the screen lit and three bars showed in the top right corner. She retrieved Nate's number from her stored calls and tapped to reach him.

"Riley! Where are you?"

She switched the phone to speaker mode so Rick could hear too. "I'm in the basement of the Sammelplatz," she told him. "And

Nate…I'm looking at the dispersal unit. It's active and counting down. We have eight minutes and twenty-six seconds."

"Can you get out of there?"

"No. We're locked in. What do you know about disarming a bomb?"

"Not much," he said. "But give me a second and I can hook you up with an expert."

"A second is about all we have, Nate."

"Right. Hang tight."

She held the phone out to Rick. "You do it," she said.

He refused to take the phone. 'You're the one with the magic hands. You should be the one to disarm the device. I'll assist. Like your scrub nurse."

The Sammelplatz woman had risen from the floor and stood watching, her mascara-smeared eyes red and frightened. She stepped forward. "I can help. Please, let me help."

"What's your name?" Riley asked.

"Liesl. I'm Liesl."

Riley gave what she hoped was a reassuring smile. "We'll get out of here alive, Liesl," she said. "It's going to be okay."

Rick nodded and spoke softly to Liesl while Riley listened to the confused tumult of noise on Nate's end of the connection. Quite a lot more than one second passed before he came on, saying, "Here's Matsui."

"Hey, Riley. Send me a picture." Matsui's voice sounded bright, almost carefree, as if requesting a photo from a vacationing friend. "I need to see what you're dealing with."

Riley snapped a photo of the device, noting that the timer now read 7:56.

"Do you see the flat metal plate?" Matsui asked.

"Yes."

"Open it."

Riley stared at the little screws securing the corners of the panel and felt a moment of panic, but Rick handed her a small screw driver and she realized he was standing over an open toolbox. He hadn't wasted time while waiting for Matsui. Liesl knelt beside him, sorting the jumble of implements into useful order.

Taking a breath, stilling her hands, Riley removed the screws.

"Okay, it's open," she told Matsui. "I'm looking at six wires twisted together on the left side of the panel."

"Careful, Riley. You'll need to separate them."

Riley swallowed hard. Steeling herself, she began gently pulling the wires apart so that they no longer touched at every point.

"Done," she said.

5:13

"Send me another photo."

Riley did as asked and waited for her next instruction, taking the pair of wire cutters Rick passed her.

A moment later, Matsui said, "Cut the red wire. But make sure you don't contact any of the other wires. Pretend you're playing a game of *Operation*."

Heart hammering in her chest, blood rushing in her eardrums, Riley thought about the staccato passage. About keeping the motions of her right hand smooth, controlled, and connected in contrast to the frenetic activity around her.

She felt the bench beneath her, the keys under her fingers. She remembered her father and her mother. The heritage of courage they'd given her.

She remembered her God, trusting him to bless her hands and her actions.

She cut the wire.

4:23. And counting.

"The timer didn't stop!"

"It's okay. You still have to cut the green wire. Locate the green wire in the group to the right."

Carefully, Riley separated the tangle of wires on the right side of the panel, dread seeping into her as the seconds ticked by.

"I don't see a green wire," she said. "I have orange, yellow, black, and purple."

"Send me a picture."

3:07

"Okay, don't panic, Riley. The device is wired differently than I expected. It's a configuration I'm not familiar with. Give me a minute, and don't cut anything else until I figure this out."

2:59

Don't panic?

Riley locked eyes with Rick. He smiled encouragingly. "You're doing great." He paused. "No matter how this day ends, Riley, you are a hero. You stepped up to the plate and followed through with your swing. You can be proud."

Riley felt curiously light, a shimmer of wonder passing through her. How could it be that only an hour earlier, dying on the cliff had felt like the height of shame and now, the thought of perishing in horrible chemical induced agony didn't seem as awful?

It was an alchemy she didn't understand and there was no time to ponder it now. The clock was ticking.

1:09

"Matsui? Are you there?"

Nate's voice answered. He sounded hearty but Riley heard fear in the undertone of his voice. "She's here," he assured her. "Still working on it, but she's almost figured it out. You'll make it, Riley."

Three more seconds ticked by. Nate said, "Riley, I just want you to know—"

"Hold on, I think I've got it!" Matsui interrupted. "You need to cut the black wire."

0:11

Riley took a breath and gently manipulated the black wire, preparing to snip it, when Matsui burst out, "No! Wait. I'm not sure. I need to check one more thing."

Riley looked at the timer.

0:03

She cut the black wire.

89

—— ● ——

THE MAN CALLED CINCHER watched the last of the lightning play across the expanse of his window. The storm had been magnificent, but it was dwindling and his fascination with it faded, replaced with eagerness for a phone call, an update on the situation at the Sammelplatz.

On the one hand, he was disappointed that the operation had not gone as planned. It had been designed with a dual purpose, and had failed at its first aim—to send a DNA calling card incriminating the minister of one vulnerable eastern European nation as the instigator of the attack, setting the whole precarious region at each other's throats.

The ingenious detonating device created by his scientists, adapted from his trove of Soviet biowarfare paraphernalia, was designed to capture and record key DNA, a boon to terrorists who wanted to take credit for their work and leave no doubt about it.

That objective had been thwarted.

At the height of the storm, he'd received word from Inspector Zimmermann that the man who'd carried the inflammatory message in his blood had inexplicably burned to death on the side of the road. Forst had done that.

Forst had betrayed him in other ways, as well.

But never again.

On the other hand, the Sammelplatz plot had succeeded as a test run for the woman now called Julia. She'd infiltrated, played her part convincingly, and proved she was capable of the mission for which he'd created her. It was almost time.

As a bonus, his Riley had been drawn into action and even now lay bound and gagged at Forst's base of operations, awaiting his pleasure.

What should he do with her?

His phone buzzed. "Is it done?" he demanded.

"It is done. Forst is dead, the device is set to detonate at any moment, and the exterior ground floor exits are secure. Evacuation is underway, but only a fraction of the targeted will be able to escape before the chemical is dispersed."

"All the better," Cincher said. "Those who survive will carry the sad tale home and tell it with more conviction than a dispassionate reporter."

"The woman tried to interfere," Julia added, "but she couldn't do anything. It all worked out very neatly."

"The woman? Do you mean your 'sister?' Are you talking about Liesl?"

Julia laughed shortly. "No, my 'sister' was even more pathetic than I imagined. I'm talking about the snoop, the one Forst caught sneaking around the *Hof.*"

A shock of surprise thrummed through Cincher's chest. Riley...at the Sammelplatz?

A searing regret tore through his chest, an ardent wish that Forst was still alive.

So he could rip the beating heart from his chest.

90

RICK HELD HIS BREATH, staring at the tangled mass of multi-colored wires at the core of the device.

He heard the *snick* as Riley clipped the black wire.

The timer froze.

0:02

He let his breath out in a long sigh mixed with incredulous laughter. Beside him, Liesl sank onto the concrete floor, mumbling her thanks to God in fervent German.

Riley dropped the wire cutters into the open toolbox and stood with her hands pressed to her chest, little moans escaping her lips as she vented her anxiety.

They'd done it. It was going to be okay.

He heard a thump and clank from the corridor, followed by the scrape of a metal door opening. Outside help was coming. Someone was freeing up the exits.

He stepped forward, ready to gratefully greet their rescuer, and was astonished to see the woman called Julia returning, forcing him back with a wave of her pistol.

"It appears I wasn't quite finished here." Pointing the gun at Riley, she barked, "You! Come with me."

Rick looked sideways to where Forst's pistol rested on the ledge beside the disabled detonator. He edged toward it.

A shot rang out. Chips of cement burst like shrapnel and Rick felt their sting in his arms and face.

"Don't even think it," the woman snarled.

"Julia!" Liesl, still slumped on the floor, held her hands up, pleading. "Why are you doing this? I don't—"

"Shut up!"

Julia swung the gun down, pointing it at her, and Liesl clamped her lips together, shaking her head as tears traced down her cheeks. The barrel of the gun veered back toward Riley.

"Let's go," the woman commanded.

Helplessly, Rick watched Riley walk to meet her. The woman locked an arm around her waist, using her as a shield as they made their exit.

Before he could do anything more, they were gone.

91

THE SOUND OF THE steel doors scraping shut was like fingernails on a chalkboard, making Riley cringe. As if that was the worst thing happening to her right now.

"Lock it," Julia ordered.

She watched, eyes narrowed, while Riley fed the heavy chain through the door handles, shivering at the touch of the cold metal links, and secured it with a sturdy padlock. When she finished, the woman prodded her in the back and they half-walked, half-ran to a jeep hidden in the shadows.

"It turns out, Cincher would be very peaved with me if I left you to die," Julia said as she opened the driver's door and motioned Riley inside. "Whatever plans he has for you, they're not finished."

She slammed the door and before Riley had a moment to think, the woman clambered into the passenger seat. "If I were you," she continued, "I'd be apprehensive about that. Very apprehensive."

Handing Riley the ignition key, Julia rested the gun on her left forearm, firmly aimed toward Riley's gut. Riley started the jeep and drove as the woman directed her down the mountain.

Glancing at her watch, she saw it was nearly half past one o'clock. The moon was high in the sky, and with the storm clouds blowing away like rags in the diminishing wind, it shone bright on the wet pavement, turning it the color of pewter.

Riley recognized the spot where the pine tree had come down, blocking the road. But it lay parallel now, resting in the roadside ditch beside its splintered stump. She drove past it and down to where the road flattened, passing through thick forest on either side.

"Take the next left," Julia told her. As Riley made the turn, she read the sign. *Flugplatz.* Around the bend, the forest thinned, giving way to an open field. Riley's heart thumped with dread as she saw the little tower flanked by a long strip of asphalt. The tower windows were dark, unmanned.

A little plane sat at one end of the runway, bright orange chocks beneath its wheels. Julia directed her to drive up beside it.

They left the jeep and Julia motioned her to the little plane. It was white, with a blue nose bordered by slim scarlet striping. The wings were fastened with struts, above the windows. For better viewing from inside, though Riley didn't think they were going on a sightseeing tour.

Julia ordered Riley to remove the chocks and throw them aside. Opening a door in the side of the plane, she unfolded a set of three steps. She gestured for Riley to climb in, but stopped her before she mounted the steps. "Your phone, Riley. Give it to me."

Surrendering the phone felt like severing a lifeline. A very real lifeline, as it had already saved her once that night.

Riley felt an almost physical tug in her chest as she handed it over. Julia cocked her arm and hurled the phone into a clump of long grass beside the runway.

They boarded.

Riley could only guess how many passengers the plane was designed to carry. Most of the seats had been removed, leaving open floor space down the right side of the cabin. Only three passenger seats remained, stretching single-file along the left side of the plane.

"Buckle up," Julia said, giving her a shove toward the middle of the three seats. She waited while Riley fastened her seat belt, then handed her a headset with a mic. "Put it on."

Riley placed the padded cups over her ears and watched Julia move forward and take the pilot's seat, donning her own headset. She rested the gun on the co-pilot's seat beside her and fired the plane's engine.

She didn't radio for any instructions or permissions, and Riley guessed this was an unscheduled, unauthorized flight. Julia clicked the radio and a double row of lights flared up, illuminating the runway as she began steering down its length.

Riley's heart hammered as the lights flew by and the plane accelerated. Her breath was coming in shallow gasps and she closed her eyes, concentrating, working to pull in a deep, assuring lungful of air.

A burst of downward tension signaled their defiance of gravity as the plane lifted into the night. The sensation of losing control that she fought against every time she flew almost overwhelmed her. Every vestige of control seemed stripped from her now.

She was adrift.

Her ears closed and she worked her jaw, trying to relieve the pressure differential. As she yawned and stretched her mouth, Julia spoke into the headset mic.

"Do you know why I learned to fly, Riley?"

Riley shook her head, but realized there was no rear view mirror. Julia couldn't see her.

"I have no idea what motivated you," she answered.

"It was because Cincher killed a pilot. A woman who ran drugs for the biggest cartel out of Brazil."

Several seconds passed with just the deafening noise of the plane as it bumped and shuddered through the atmosphere. Finally, Riley said, "Okay."

"Before Cincher, I was nothing. A college dropout from a dysfunctional family. And butt-ugly, to boot. Cincher re-created me. He gave me power. He made me beautiful."

Riley said nothing.

"He rescued me from a life of desperation and remade me to fulfill his own purposes. I took the pilot's identity, I used her connections to access the upper echelons of the cartel, and I delivered the entire operation into Cincher's waiting hands."

She seemed to expect Riley to respond, so she said, "Impressive."

"I had to learn how to be somebody else, Riley." Her voice crackled over the headset but even so, Riley heard the strain in it. "I had to learn how to fly. I had to learn how to kill. I had to learn how to do drugs, and I had to learn how to get clean again."

Her voice grew louder and took on a new, harsh edge. "I went to hell and back for that man," she said. "And I'd do it again."

A brief pause. "I *am* doing it again."

Fear crept along the back of Riley's neck, raising the little hairs there. She sensed utter bitterness and despair in the woman. She sounded like someone reaching the end of her tether, and she held both their lives in her hands.

"Are you wondering why I didn't tie you up or smack you silly with the butt of my gun?" Julia asked.

Riley said nothing.

"It's because I know you won't do anything stupid up here, five thousand feet above the ground. You won't jeopardize your own safety. You know, if you mess with me, we're going down."

A moment passed. The plane bounced and juddered. The engine roared.

Julia's voice came back over the headset, softer now so that Riley wasn't sure she'd even heard the whisper. "I almost wish you would."

Stiff in her seat, Riley considered her predicament. The ice-glaze of terror encased her limbs, yet a flame burned in her gut, driving her to do something while she still had time.

With quiet fingers, she unfastened her seatbelt.

92

Moving slowly, carefully, Riley crept toward the front of the plane, believing that Julia wasn't able to see her movements. She planned to grab the gun and force Julia to land the plane, but she knew it was risky.

Beyond risky.

Even if she succeeded in obtaining the weapon, she sensed that Julia's current mental state might send her into a nose dive. Figuratively and literally.

Still, she couldn't just sit and wait to be delivered up to this Cincher, the man she suspected might be John. The man who'd almost killed her once before. She had to act, to take advantage of every opportunity.

Like the one in front of her now.

Moving with achingly small motions so Julia wouldn't sense movement and turn, Riley edged toward the co-pilot's chair. The very second she poised to seize the pistol, Julia reached out a hand and snatched the gun. Twisting in her seat, she lunged forward, swinging out with her left fist, catching Riley just below the ribcage, driving her back.

Riley stumbled and went down onto the floor of the plane. Julia stood over her, aiming the gun down, straight at her face.

No one flew the plane.

Acting now in full adrenaline fight mode, Riley kicked out and connected with Julia's shin, destabilizing her balance so that she fell forward. Riley rolled to avoid her, but Julia grabbed a handful of Riley's sweater and yanked, pulling her back.

They tussled, scrapping on the floor like a pair of high school wrestlers, rotating with first one on top, and then the other. Riley hardly knew where the pistol was anymore. Didn't care.

The plane listed, tilting slightly sideways like a ship in swell, and Riley hurtled over the top of Julia.

The gun went off.

Riley heard the shot and a metallic *ping* from the instrument panel. A chatter of sparks flew from the bank of buttons and gauges, and then a loud *bang* slammed her in the eardrums as something in the engine compartment exploded.

Flames erupted from the nose of the plane, flaring orange as Riley stared, instinctively shielding her face. Black, oily smoke streamed over the windshield, leaving a grimy film. The cabin filled with a sickly, resinous odor.

The engine began to stutter, churning out noise and chilling silence in alternating bursts. An alarm blared, its strident rhythmic shriek ratcheting up Riley's terror. A few seconds later, it was joined by a deep, sonorous buzz.

Bam!

The plane thumped and bounced. Riley looked out the windows, saw feathery pine boughs going by in a blur. The wings and belly of the plane scraped along the tops of the trees, the buffeting increasing as they fell lower in the sky.

Riley pulled herself into one of the seats and groped frantically for the seat belt.

"We're crashing," she shouted, finding the belt and snapping it into place. "Get in a seat!"

A horrific screeching filled the cabin and the plane jolted, the wing hitting something that spun it a quarter turn. Riley watched Julia stagger into the seat in front of her and scrabble for her own seat belt.

Suddenly, the battering of the trees ceased. Riley stared out the windshield. No more woods.

Instead, she saw water.

They splashed down, sending a foaming torrent up and over the windshield. The crushing impact hit Riley like a full-body hammer blow as the plane tossed and flipped.

Everything went black.

93

THE SOUND OF DRIPPING water woke her.

Moaning, Riley struggled to open her eyes. Pain emanated through her, and she grew aware that the worst of it came from pressure cutting across her hips. The seat belt.

She was upside down.

Water continued to drip into the growing puddle on the ceiling of the sinking plane, its tempo increasing as the puddle grew. Riley lifted the metal flap on her seat belt but the buckle wouldn't release.

She was trapped.

Struggling to keep panic at bay, she wrenched at the fastener, working it back and forth, up and down, any which way. But to no avail.

With desperate regret, she looked at the orange-handled belt-cutter velcroed to the pilot's dashboard, far out of reach. She had nothing she could use to cut the belt.

She realized the pool forming at the bottom of the plane was tinged red, the shade darkening with each second that passed. Julia hung limp and silent from the seat in front of her. And she was bleeding.

Squinting into the deepening gloom, Riley saw that patches of the plane's skin had shredded into knife-like shards. Stretching, she found one of the sharp projections within reach and tugged to work it loose.

The metal sliced into her fingertips, adding her own blood to the rising tide. But at last, Riley freed a jagged splinter and used it to saw through her seat belt, accompanied by whimpers from Julia as she began to regain consciousness.

The last of the fibers frayed away and Riley fell head first, splashing into the bloody pool. Water poured in more steadily now, rapidly displacing the air. Riley felt suffocation closing in.

She scrabbled to Julia's seat and pulled up on the metal flap, relieved when Julia tumbled promptly into the water.

"We're sinking. We need to get out now!"

Julia didn't move. Her eyes remained closed, her face ghostly pale in the waning light. Riley's hands moved over her, finding a shank of metal jutting from Julia's thigh. The source of the blood.

As she touched it, Julia's eyes flew open, a wild scream tearing out of her. Before Riley could form even a fraction of a plan, the cabin suddenly shifted radically, turned by the rush of water through a broken window.

The plane flopped over, upright now but sinking like a stone. Riley gulped in one more lungful and then she was under. She grasped Julia, her hands digging into the woman's armpits, and began tugging toward the open window.

The time, the effort, they were all draining her oxygen supply fast and each second took her farther from the water's surface. Despair hit Riley like a bowling ball to the gut.

They were almost to the window when the bubbles from Julia's mouth diminished, then stopped altogether. With a mixed rush of relief and guilt, Riley dropped her abductor and pushed through the broken window, kicking hard in the black enveloping water.

Her lungs cried out, screaming for air. Riley knew from a years-ago scuba training that there's a point when breathing becomes involuntary. That the body will gasp desperately for oxygen, even when the mind knows it will bring drowning and death.

Above her, faint illumination shimmered. Moonlight, drawing closer with each kick.

But not close enough.

She sensed the end, her limit. She pushed it off, shoved it away. Just one more second.

Two more.

And then she burst free from the dark hold of the water and sucked in a lungful of blessed air.

94

NATE KEPT HIS FOOT pressed down on the accelerator, pushing the G-Wagen on loan from Ziegler along the dark country lane. Matsui sat in the seat next to him, leaning forward, staring raptly out the windshield as if Riley might appear at any second.

In the back seat, Rick and Gideon monitored the tracking device, giving constant updates on Riley's movements. The speed of her travel told them she was on a plane, and Nate sent up a prayer of gratitude that he'd been able to place that watch on her wrist.

Otherwise, she might be lost to them forever.

"She's slowing down," Rick said. "She's...wait. What?"

"Speak!" Nate said. "What's happening?"

Gideon said, "The dot stopped moving."

"Okay," Nate said. "That's good. We can close in on her location."

"Yes," Rick agreed. "But either this thing is broken or we better put on a real burst of speed, because it shows Riley in the middle of a lake."

"What the...?" A chill passed down Nate's spine. "Did her plane go down?"

No one wanted to answer the question. After a moment of silence, Rick said, "It's Riley, guys. We'll get her back. We have to."

"That's how we felt when we thought *you* were dead," Nate told him.

"And look what came of that." Rick said. Nate felt his friend's hand close over his shoulder, giving it a squeeze. "Let's go get her."

"How far out are we?" Nate asked.

Gideon spoke up. "Looks like...about twenty-six kilometers."

"I'm too rattled to do the math," Nate said. "What's that in miles?"

"Sixteen miles and change," Matsui said. "At your current rate of speed, and assuming you don't get stuck behind an early morning tractor driver, we should reach Riley in approximately eleven minutes."

"I can do it in eight," Nate said.

"Yes," Gideon replied. "But should you? The roads are still slick after all that rain."

"We don't want to end up in a ditch," Rick added.

"Okay, grandma. I'll keep that in mind."

"Just razzing you, Nate. Go as fast as you dare."

As he navigated the twisting road, Nate fought to steady his breathing and the wild pounding of his heart. The thought of Riley in danger filled him with a strange and painful bittersweet angst. Bitter, because it worried and enraged him to imagine her crashed on the water and sinking. Or held at gunpoint, hurt and scared.

Or maybe dead.

The tinge of sweetness swirling through the bitter came from caring enough to generate such agony.

"Okay, we're coming up on the turn," Gideon warned him. "When the road forks, go right."

Nate saw the turn and veered off. The G-Wagen roared down the muddy dirt road, sending up spatters of slime, streaking the windows with dirt.

He saw the shimmer of water ahead, like a plate of burnished copper in the dawning sunrise. He pulled the car to a stop and leaped out, running to the shore of the lake, squinting across its surface.

It was smooth, unruffled, placid.

Where was Riley?

He scowled at the lapping water, trying to ignore the wrenching pain inside his chest. Was she down there, beneath the serene surface, beyond his reach? Beyond his help?

Beyond.

"Over here!" Matsui shouted.

Nate sprinted toward her. A sodden mass lay at Matsui's feet, undefined in the muted light. But as he drew near, he recognized the spread of auburn hair, the fine white fingers at the end of an outstretched hand.

Riley.

"She's alive," Matsui said.

95

RILEY RESTED FOR THREE days after the plane crash, doing nothing much more than sleeping, playing the piano, and laughing with friends. Wright had ordered her to take as much time as she needed. She heard the worry in his voice and knew he was afraid the whole episode might have scared her off Olivero.

Had it?

She was still processing. Decompressing. Trying to untangle her thoughts and emotions about the experience and figure out what it meant for her future.

On the third day, she rose early, when dawn was only a pearl-gray strip along the horizon, waiting to blossom pink. She pulled on a pair of sweats and sat to tie her shoes, heaviness pressing on her heart as she avoided looking at the empty bed across the room.

Colette was gone, and she'd been the one to break it to Gideon after all. In the car after her lakeside rescue, she'd sat wrapped in a blanket between Nate and Gideon in the back seat of the G-Wagen. She'd thought she was fine, and then she'd suddenly dissolved into a sobbing mess.

In broken sentences, she'd thanked Gideon for helping her, for saving her life. And then she apologized for deceiving him. Telling him what had happened to Colette took every ounce of fortitude she could muster, and it had thoroughly deflated the celebratory tone of their triumphal return to the academy.

Gideon hadn't spoken a word to her since.

Riley let herself out into the damp, chilly morning and jogged to the main gate. She wanted to sit on a bench outside the village *Bäckerei*, anonymous and unnoticed, with a pastry and a cup of hot cocoa. No one hovering over her, worrying and catering. Just feeling the sun on her face.

And thinking.

She carried out her self-prescribed plan and afterwards strolled along the cobblestone street. The smell of wood fires burning followed her as she skirted beds of geraniums and walked past the old-fashioned pump on the village square. She paused to watch a neighborhood cat stalking a sparrow, and then crossed over to the bridge that spanned a narrow river.

Stopping midway, she leaned on the railing and stared down at the gently flowing current, listening to the soothing musical chatter of water over stone. Mesmerized by the sound and movement, she relaxed, almost sagging as tension drained out of her.

After a moment, she became aware of someone else on the bridge. The whiff of tobacco reached her and she glanced over to see a man, bespectacled and looking almost formal in hat and coat. He was bent over the rail, smoking a cigarette, the packet and lighter resting on the rail beside him.

"Ein schöner Tag, nicht wahr?"

"Genau, wirklich schön." Riley replied, agreeing that it was a beautiful day.

"Ah, you are American," the man said.

Riley blushed. She hadn't thought her accent so poor as to betray her after only a few words. As if reading her mind, the man waved his hand, dispelling his smoke along with her doubts.

"It was your clothing that told me so." He paused. "And your hairstyle."

Surprised, Riley raised a hand to her head. Her hair was pulled back in an elastic band. A simple pony tail. Who knew it could say so much?

Smiling, she resumed her study of the water below. When she turned a few moments later to make a polite comment, the man was gone. The box of cigarettes still sat on the rail and Riley snatched it up, peering along the lane, but he was nowhere in sight.

That's when she realized that what she'd taken for a simple packet of cigarettes was something more solid. A wooden box, inlaid with a design on the lid.

An intricately tied knot.

With shaking hands, Riley opened the box, a chill feathering along the backs of her arms as she saw what lay inside.

A curl of auburn hair, tied with a blue ribbon.

Her hair.

She remembered blow drying her hair shortly after reaching the academy and noticing a missing hank from the back of her head. When had John taken it?

No question it was John, the man they called Cincher. She cast her mind back to the trans-Atlantic flight and the elderly man who'd retrieved her boarding pass from the floor and ridden behind her on the plane.

She thought about the bogus bicycler who'd hitched a ride and left her a coin engraved with a knot.

And an image of the world.

He wanted her to know he could get to her anywhere. Any time he pleased.

But that wasn't always true.

He'd wanted her delivered to him three nights ago. The agent he'd sent, along with his little Cessna, had ended up at the bottom of a lake in Bavaria.

He didn't always get what he wanted.

And that was partly down to her.

96

Liesl walked down the staircase from her apartment to the lobby of the Sammelplatz with its enormous picture windows overlooking the Bavarian countryside. She didn't feel the giddy pleasure that had accompanied her on that short journey so many times before.

It seemed as if she never would again.

In her arms, she carried a large cardboard box packed with sweaters, jeans, and shoes. Behind her in the corridor, another carton waited to be carried down. Liesl's heart felt heavy in her chest, a sad and bewildering weight as she set the box on the reception counter.

The boxes contained Julia's things.

Or the woman Liesl had *believed* was Julia.

Doubt and confusion clouded her mind. She still couldn't understand how the woman had impersonated her estranged sister, fooling all of them. Dieter was helping her sort through it, gathering pieces of information from South America, tracing the path of her sister's disappearance and death.

Liesl shuddered over the irony that Julia—like the woman who'd stolen her identity—had died while piloting a plane. Both women controlled, if Dieter's conclusions were correct, by the same insidious man.

Although the impersonator hadn't actually been her sister, Liesl felt real grief over the woman's death. They'd shared some moments. She'd had real worries, genuine concerns, for the woman she'd bonded with as Julia. Her emotions now were a convoluted mess.

But she still had her parents to help her through it. And Dieter.

And Max.

Dear Max. Her throat grew thick and she swallowed hard, turning back to retrieve the waiting box. Heaven above, she was grateful to be keeping this job.

It had been a close thing. But in the final analysis, those making the decisions had measured the way she'd stayed to help when she could have fled with her family. She'd demonstrated responsibility under extraordinary circumstances and assisted in defusing a chemical weapon.

That counted for a lot.

The bedraggled woman—her name was Riley Forte—and her companions had given Liesl's supervisors a glowing report of her performance. More glowing than she deserved, really, but she'd gratefully bowed and accepted it.

Adding to that, some of the guests had captured her speech on video, passing it on up her chain of command. That had bolstered her position considerably.

After the device had been disabled and removed from the property, Liesl had rallied Gunther's staff. Together, they'd calmed and assured the summit attendees, gathering them in the banquet hall where Liesl had commended them for working together, supporting each other, and making it through the crisis.

A strong demonstration of the power of peace.

Liesl had then signaled the waiters to begin serving, and the feast, though considerably delayed, began. A few guests insisted on leaving, but most stayed and ate with gusto after their brush with death.

All in all, the event was considered a success.

Liesl carried the last box down the stairs and placed it on the counter, ready for pickup by the charity van. Thoughtfully, she climbed halfway up the flight of stairs and turned to look out over the marble-floored lobby with its massive fireplace, the groupings of leather furniture floating on islands of brightly-colored carpet. She gazed out the windows at the lush green of the forest, the rich russet and gold of the rolling fields below. At the cerulean sky with puffs of cloud and swooping birds.

Maybe she could get that giddy feeling back after all.

97

RILEY CLOSED HER EYES and breathed in deep through her nose. She let the air out slowly and straightened her shoulders, bringing her hands up to the keyboard, letting her fingers rest against the cool smoothness of the keys.

Deliberately relaxing, she let her mind wander to that moment on the cliff, in the storm and tumult of that wild night. She had really felt like that was her last moment, that she couldn't go on, that she'd used every bit of strength left in her.

What had changed? What had recharged her stamina and pushed her to stretch and climb and reach for the top?

She tried to recall the specific sequence of her thoughts, but the memory seemed veiled, covered with a gauzy layer allowing only glimpses into what must be a core motivation for her soul.

She only knew it had something to do with the challenge she encountered in this particular piece of music.

Opening her eyes, she began to play. The opening measures of the composition were simple and serene, a lovely calm before the storm. But as she advanced through the music, it crescendoed and picked up in tempo. Riley felt every note register inside her.

And suddenly, there it was before her. The staccato passage.

For a fraction of a second, she faltered, feeling the darkness waiting to envelop her. Hardening her jaw, she pulled in a harsh breath through her nostrils, a millisecond from gaping despair.

And then she was playing through it.

It was as if someone had cut the knot, releasing a weight from around her heart, letting it drop away into oblivion. She felt light, joyous.

Redeemed.

Her fingers flew over the keys, her left hand executing the difficult detached notes of the staccato passage while her right hand moved smoothly through the legato phrases. Working together in beautiful contrast.

She played through the stormy section and beyond as the music returned to the original tranquil theme but with added notes of depth and inner melodies that hadn't been present in the introduction. She played the final note and as the sound of it faded, someone applauded from the darkened corner of the room.

She twisted on the bench to see a figure step forward, a man. The features of his impossibly handsome face became clear as he left the gloom of the shadows and came to stand beside the piano bench.

Gideon.

"Have you been here the whole time?" Riley asked.

He dropped a hand onto her shoulder. "*Ja,* the whole time, Riley. I hope I can always be here the whole time." His hand tightened, squeezing gently. "You have an extraordinary gift."

She scooted over on the bench and he sat beside her. Several moments of silence passed while he sat, his head bowed, hands folded in his lap. When he spoke at last, his voice was strained with grief and regret.

"I'm sorry I've been angry with you," he said. "I've gone over that night again and again and again. I cannot get it out of my mind. But if I am being fair," he added, "I cannot fault you for what you did. What sense would there have been in telling me sooner?"

A jagged bolt of sorrow chewed through Riley's chest. "I'm so sorry, Gideon. So sorry you lost Colette."

He said nothing for a long moment. Riley felt him struggle against tears, refusing to let himself lose control in front of her.

"I loved her so much," he finally whispered. "I planned to spend the rest of my life with her. I wanted to make a family with her. I hoped..."

He groaned to a stop. Rising from the bench, he said, "I'm sorry, Riley. I just wanted you to know that."

He moved quickly to the door and was gone.

Riley sat for a long while, silent on the bench while she tried to sort through her thoughts and feelings. At last, she got up and went to find Nate.

He'd spent the morning video conferencing with Director Edwards and Chief Wright, debriefing them on his part in the disaster that was turning out to have international repercussions. Many of them positive.

Some less so.

Riley knew there would always be endless amounts of work to be done for people like them.

Like her.

She found Nate exiting the elevator as she came into the main building. He greeted her with a smile.

"Can we go for a walk?" she asked.

He caught the serious note in her voice and took her hand. "Absolutely."

They took the forest path, walking hand in hand on the route Riley liked to jog on fine mornings.

"I want you to know how glad, how grateful, I am that you came, Nate. That you were here for me. It means the world, and I couldn't have done it without you."

He squeezed her hand and pulled her to a gentle stop. "I love you, Riley," he said, his brown eyes honest and sincere, a slight frown creasing his forehead.

"I know you do," she assured him. "I feel it, and I know I can depend on you always. For help. For friendship. For everything important in life. And I want to be the same for you."

He said nothing, just continued to stare into her face.

Riley took a deep breath. "That's why I want to support you in your decision to try again with Marilyn."

She felt a stab of pain, but pressed on. "You are a wonderful father, Nate, and your family needs you."

He started to speak, but she rushed on. "I'll be fine. I have all of this," she gestured around her, "to keep me occupied. And once I get the chance to buckle down and learn what they teach at this place, I'll be able to take care of myself a lot better."

She smiled, holding his gaze. "I love you too, Nate. That's why I want you to have the best chance for a happy and fulfilled life." She paused. "I think they're waiting for you back in Washington."

She watched a series of expressions wash over Nate's face, some recognizable. Others not. He looked as if he meant to protest her suggestion, but in the end, he simply nodded and continued walking.

No longer holding her hand.

Riley's heart twisted painfully in her chest. She watched him leave later that night, waving goodbye as he drove off in the rental car, heading back to the Nuremberg airport.

Part of her heart went with him and she fought a wave of regret and misery. How long would it take her to get over her heartache? Had she made the best choice?

She'd sincerely tried to.

Nate had a place in life, a family, a noble profession. And she was finding her place in this new life at Olivero, new purpose. A way to accomplish something good and meaningful. She intended to stay and keep learning.

To keep living.

Hearing footsteps behind her, she turned to see Rick striding down the concrete walkway. He came to stand beside her.

"How'd your debriefing go?" Riley asked.

"Fine," he said. "Long. Been in there most of the day."

"Yeah, well. Lots to talk about."

"Yep."

They both stared down the lane. Riley knew he must be missing Nate almost as much as she was. After a moment, he said, "It's just you and me now, kid."

"And Gideon," Riley pointed out. "I think we should claim him."

"Okay. And Gideon," he agreed. "But if we take Gideon, we gotta have Matsui, too."

"Of course! Where would we be without Matsui?"

Laughing, they walked back toward the door of the academy and somehow, Riley knew she'd be okay.

Rick had survived death.

Anything was possible.

Thank you so much for reading
Staccato Passage
YOU'LL FIND MORE SUSPENSE AND EXCITEMENT
AS RILEY'S STORY CONTINUES
IN THE NEXT BOOK IN THE SERIES
Cincher's Waltz.
If you haven't yet read
Nocturne in Ashes,
the book where it all began,
why not start the adventure now!

Thank you for reading *Staccato Passage.*

If you enjoyed the book, I would love for you to leave a review to help other readers find and enjoy it, too. Thank you so much for taking the time to make that happen.

I invite you to visit my book page at Paraquel Press for more suspense-packed stories, or just scan the QR code below.

Be sure not to miss the next Riley Forte suspense thriller, **Cincher's Waltz,** available now.

And if you haven't read the first book in the series, why not start now? Grab your copy of **Nocturne in Ashes** and prepare to burn the midnight oil!

Also, don't forget to sign up at joslynchase.com and join the growing group of readers who've discovered the thrill of Chase! You'll get *No Rest: 14 Tales of Chilling Suspense,* as well as VIP access to updates and bonuses.

Thank you!

— · —

Author's Notes

Nocturne in Ashes

Staccato Passage is the second book in the Riley Forte series which started with *Nocturne in Ashes.*

Hints of happenings from *Nocturne* are scattered throughout *Staccato Passage.* For instance, references to the eruption of Mt. Rainier point to the central event impacting Riley, Nate, Rick, and the other characters involved in *Nocturne.*

Also, Riley met the man they call Cincher in the pages of *Nocturne,* with nearly fatal results. It was the beginning of an epic relationship, though neither of them recognized that at the time.

I didn't even recognize it at the time!

It is also in *Nocturne* that readers learn about the circumstances surrounding the death of Riley's husband, Jim, and her son, Tanner. Including who killed them, and why.

In *Staccato,* John mentions a meeting with a bear cub in the woods that didn't turn out well. You'll find the details of that encounter in *Nocturne.*

Readers of *Nocturne* will also have a very keen notion of why Rick dreads traffic jams on the freeway. I mean, don't we all? But his

407

aversion to them runs a little deeper than most. Or a lot deeper. His experience in *Nocturne* explains why.

Nocturne is where Riley met Nate. They formed a makeshift partnership to catch a serial killer and protect an isolated knot of people trapped in the catastrophic aftermath of Mt. Rainier's eruption.

In *Nocturne,* Nate and Rick were police detectives, partners who split up to track down separate leads in a serial killer case. The sudden volcanic disaster came between them—literally—just as Rick discovered the identity of their murderer.

He tried desperately, for most of the book, to reach Nate, knowing his partner was most likely spending time with the killer and unaware. Rick tried to connect physically, by phone, by radio, every method he could come up with—but was completely cut off at every pass. He never gave up, though.

In the end, Rick met Riley and they became fast friends. A friendship highlighted in *Staccato Passage.*

The Olivero Private Security Firm

I'm not sure if such a thing does, or could, exist. But in my mind, I see people of many nations coming together to fight for justice and support the values of the American Constitution. Not because those values are inherently superior, but because those values are inherently decreed by God and were adopted and drafted into the Constitution by the founding fathers.

America is not, and never was, a perfect union. But I believe her foundations were set as perfectly as those of any organization since the days when Christ walked the earth. They set a standard to be reached for.

Chief Devin Wright, in establishing his Olivero firm, is reaching for those standards and resisting the corruptions that inevitably creep into any earthly establishment. He recruits the best people he can find to support his mission. Men and women of honor, valor, and multitudinous skills.

Volcanic Mountains in Bavaria

From the house where I wrote *Staccato Passage*, in the Bavarian countryside, I can see a small mountain poking up from the mostly flat surroundings. It is the site of a village called Parkstein and there is a church at the top, which my husband and I hiked up to one day during the Covid crisis.

Everything was shut down, so we weren't able to get inside the volcano or the museum, but peering through a tiny window in a door set into the mountainside, we got a glimpse of the interior. One of these days, we'll go back and try again. I've heard the volcanic eruption simulation is pretty awesome.

I found a nifty video on YouTube (https://www.youtube.com/watch?v=bKx64hEYDt8&t=25s) that features a real look at the essence of Parkstein as it currently stands. You will see the tubular basalt formations mentioned in *Staccato*.

Not too far away, is a similar basalt mountain, which we also chose to hike one day. As did Anton Forst, in the chapter where you first meet him in *Staccato*. I published an article about the wildflowers along the trail, which you can find on my website, if you're interested. https://joslynchase.com/wildflowers-on-the-trail/

These mountains were formed during the Paleocene-Pliocene period, when a chain of active volcanoes produced liquid magma during the collision of Europe and Africa.

The Alps appeared as a result. But a number of fissure vents and cracks also began to form throughout central Europe, with magma pushing up through the earth's surface. Most of the volcanic substance cooled below the surface but erosion has worn away the layers of earth covering it, exposing these amazing hexagonal structures.

The basalt mountain which shelters the Olivero spy training academy at its base while supporting the Swanhilde Sammelplatz at its crown, is fictional. It was inspired by its factual sisters, Parkstein and the Rauher Kulm, a spark which grew to a flame when connected to Riley's harrowing *Nocturne* experience with Mt. Rainier in Washington state.

THE DNA ENCODED KEY

Yes, the technology now exists where this could happen. It's called DNA steganography, and though it may not work in precisely the way I described it in *Staccato Passage,* it comes near enough to make the idea plausible.

And frightening.

Cryptology and Cryptic Crosswords

In case you weren't able to solve the cryptic clue Riley's cryptology professor put on the white board, let me take a moment to explain.

I have a vague memory of coming across a cryptic crossword puzzle when I was a little kid and not understanding what it was. Considering it from the angle of a standard crossword puzzle, I concluded that it was stupid and abandoned it in disgust.

Many years later, I encountered this type of puzzle again and it has become my favorite of all puzzles. Each clue is a riddle, forcing you to think outside the box and stretch your brain. Each clue is a delightful play on words in some sense. Let's take a look at Professor Martel's clue:

Serve Lady Twist in a negative way

_ _ _ _ _ _ _ _ _

Riley recognized that the word "twist" suggested an anagram and since "serve lady" contained nine letters, like the clue's solution, she unscrambled the letters in "serve lady" to arrive at a word meaning "in a negative way."

Her answer: adversely

I published an article about cryptic crosswords and how to solve them. They really are super fun and a great way to exercise your brain and keep it agile. Check out my article at

https://joslynchase.com/cryptic-crosswords-are-the-cream-of-the -puzzle-crop/

As for the rest of Professor Martel's lecture, if you find the subject as fascinating as I do, you can go through a fun little tutorial at Khan Academy.

https://www.khanacademy.org/computing/computer-science/cryptography/crypt/v/intro-to-cryptography

If you're interested in seeing how Riley worked out the encrypted message she picked up from the dead drop, using her name as the key, this is what she did:

Step 1: Converted the encrypted letters to numbers according to their place in the alphabet.

Step 2: Converted her name in the same manner to get: 18 9 12 5 25

Step 3: Repeated the numbers of her name along the length of the encrypted message.

Step 4: Subtracted her name numbers from the message numbers.

Step 5: Added 26 to any negative results.

Step 6: Converted the numbers back to letters.

```
J N Y J L T N D   M N O   F Q   R D L   V K   I Z E B Q Q   H F   M U X S J N E X
10 14 25 10 12 20 14 4   13 14 15   6 17   18 4 12   22 11   9 26 5 2 17 17   8 6   13 21 24 19 10 14 5 24
18 9 12 5 25 18 9 12   5 25 18   9 12   5 25 18   9 12   5 25 18 9 12 5   25 18   9 12 5 25 18 9 12 5
-8 5 13 5 -13 2 5 -8   8 -11 -3   -3 5   13 -21 -6   13 -1   4 1 -13 -7 5 12   -17 -12   4 9 19 -6 -8 5 -7 19
26    26    26   26 26   26      26 26   26      26 26    26 26      26 26 26
18 9 13 5 13 2 5 18   8 15 23   23 5   13 5 20   13 25   4 1 13 19 5 12   9 14   4 9 19 20 18 5 19 19
R E M E M B E R   H O W   W E   M E T   M Y   D A M S E L   I N   D I S T R E S S
```

Pretty cool, right?

SPYCRAFT

I used several sources to gather information about spycraft while writing this novel. Here, I've listed several of those I used the most:

The Spycraft series on Netflix

WIRED, on YouTube

Spy Briefing, with Jason Hanson

Spy Secrets That Can Save Your Life, by Jason Hanson

Blowing my Cover: My Life as a CIA Spy, by Lindsay Moran

The Ultimate Spy Book, by H. Keith Melton

OLD WORLD TECHNOLOGY

You may have noticed a bit of old-fashioned flavor during some scenes in *Staccato Passage*. That's because such a flavor is actually maintained here in Bavaria in many ways. At least, in the smaller towns and villages near where we live.

People still use corded desk phones in places. There are still quaint cobblestone streets in use and village post offices where you can pick up a newspaper or a liter of ice cream while mailing a package.

On the other hand, there are some interesting "new" technologies in use that I've never seen or heard of in the States. The *Milchtankstelle* Matsui points out after picking Riley up from the airport is a real thing here. They are cute little shacks where you can fill your bottle with fresh, unpasteurized milk and pluck a jar of local honey from a vending machine.

And speaking of vending machines, there's a sausage vending machine near our house where you can plop in a few coins and pull out a *Wurst* or other assorted meats. And I heard an announcement on Bavarian radio the other day that they are introducing pizza vending machines that will cook your pizza to order and dispense it hot.

Curioser and curioser...

WHY STACCATO PASSAGE?

Riley is a classically trained concert pianist. So am I. At least, I've had the training. I lack the temperament and fortitude for a concert career, though I performed on a limited basis and taught private lessons for over twenty years.

I love classical music, and so does Riley. When I started the series, I decided that I wanted to include a musical term and element in every title. Thus, I produced *Nocturne in Ashes* for Riley's debut. A nocturne is a night song. And if you've read *Nocturne,* you've probably gained at least an inkling of an idea why I so named the novel.

And now that you've read *Staccato Passage,* I hope you understand how the title connects with Riley's story. Staccato notes are sharp, detached, crisp, separate. Some of the most impactful passages of music employ the contrast between staccato and legato, which features smooth, connected notes without a break in sound.

This is not an easy technique to master.

I liked the idea of the contrast, and as I wrote the story, I found it becoming an underlying theme for Riley's new life with her Olivero friends.

Thanks for reading! I hope you enjoyed *Staccato Passage*.

MORE BOOKS BY JOSLYN CHASE

**DON'T MISS THIS
JOSLYN CHASE THRILLER!**

Available at your favorite bookseller

in eBook and paperback

MORE BOOKS BY JOSLYN CHASE

Nocturne in Ashes

Staccato Passage

JOSLYN CHASE

Steadman's Blind

The Steadman Mysteries series

The Tal Bannerman Thriller series

The Cathryn Harcourt Mystery series

The Historic Suspense series

Rapid Pursuit

Crimes Upon a Midnight Clear

The Tower

The Devil's Trumpet

For a complete listing, visit Joslyn's Book Page

Watch the trailers on

Joslyn's YouTube channel!

PREVIEW OF CINCHER'S WALTZ

PROLOGUE

Bavaria, April 1945

Deep in the bowels of the mountain, darkness pressed like a blanket, shifting reluctantly aside under the glare of two powerful electric torches. Oberführer Guntram Protz led the way, holding one of the lamps high above his head as the group of six *Schutzstaffel* officers descended still further into what felt like a bottomless abyss.

Moisture slimed the walls and the odor of mold and fungus hung thick in the air. Protz shivered and tried not to think about the sorts of monstrous organisms that might grow and flourish in this eternal blackness. It frightened him to realize he may, in these moments, be inhaling the insidious spores of death.

His beam of light probed the rough-hewn limestone lining the passageway. No one spoke and Protz was glad of it. The noise made by their boots shuffling along the uneven floor echoed disturbingly in the narrow space, leaving eerie impressions on his eardrums. He imagined the sound of a human voice might make him flinch unforgivably.

He must appear resolute. This mission, assigned to him by the Führer himself, was of the utmost importance. He was assured that the long-running future of the Reich depended on its success.

Protz felt certain the four men bearing the wooden crate containing what Hitler had referred to as "the Party's greatest treasure" harbored doubts and fears about what they were doing. They must believe, as he did in his heart, that the war was lost.

Still, Hitler claimed to have a final ace up his sleeve, and orders must be followed. It was up to him, as this mission's leader, to set a stalwart example.

Straightening his spine, Protz pushed further into the darkness. He'd visited their target location once before, but it seemed so much deeper than he remembered. Scharführer Schmidt, the officer bringing up the rear of their procession, held the other torch. Its rays bounced over the damp walls, billowing and distorting, adding to the queasy feeling in Protz's gut.

At last, they reached the chamber. Protz produced a key and turned it in one of the door's heavy locks. Wordlessly, he stepped aside and motioned to Schmidt. The sergeant came forward and brought a key on a chain from beneath the collar of his uniform.

Inserting it into the second lock, he twisted it and the door clicked open.

Pulling it wide, Protz ushered the men inside. They carried the heavy crate to the center of the small chamber and lowered it gently to the ground. Protz stepped forward and laid a hand on the coarse-cut wood. Bowing his head, he murmured softly.

"It is done."

The group of officers stood silent, as if gathered around the altar in a profane underground chapel. The four who'd borne the chest breathed heavily, in spite of their efforts to muffle the sound. Their burden had been weighty, and they'd carried it a good distance through a difficult passage.

Protz would let them rest.

As the sound of their panting faded, Protz moved gently among the men, touching each on the shoulder as he passed, inching his way back toward the chamber's entrance. Quietly, unobtrusively, he removed a pair of earplugs from his pocket and twisted them into his ears.

Drawing his service weapon, he turned and fired, downing the sergeant first and stunning the others.

Even with the earplugs, the sound of the shot sent a blast of pain rocketing through his head. Three of the remaining men froze and he picked them off quickly, expertly placing his shots through the heart.

Or near enough.

The fourth man had the presence of mind to scurry behind the crate where he crouched like a cornered rat.

"Why, Oberführer?" He shouted the question from his hiding place, his voice querulous as well as frightened. "Why would you do this?"

A stab of regret brought out a grimace on Protz's face. He gave a single groan, then answered honestly.

"Hitler's orders."

"But why?"

Protz drew a breath that caught in his chest. "Only the Führer knows the full significance of this mission," he admitted, "but he told me himself that nothing now is more important than this. And it is absolutely imperative that it remain secret."

"I'll tell no one."

"I can't take that risk."

The sound of fabric rubbing against rough wood gave Protz a mere second's warning before the bullet ripped into the flesh of his right shoulder. He stifled a scream of surprise and pain. His shooting arm was now disabled.

It did not matter.

Beyond Hitler's intention of preserving his secret, he'd revealed to Protz a further design in killing the other members of the team. Hitler was a man who accepted the workings of the supernatural. Like the pirates of old, it was his belief that leaving a few faithful followers behind to guard the treasure was a prudent measure to take.

Crouching low, Protz crept to the body of his sergeant. Blood puddled on the pitted floor beneath him, soaking the knee of his uniform as he knelt to tug the key and chain from Schmidt's neck.

A river of pain flowed down his right arm and it dragged uselessly against his side. As he moved once more for the door, the soldier behind the crate fired another shot. The bullet ricocheted off stone and Protz felt a searing jolt beneath his left eye.

Time to make an exit.

He rushed for the door and swung it closed, fumbling the keys in the locks as he felt a thud from the other side. A surge of sorrow engulfed him. It would have been far more merciful to put the man down than to leave him in this pit with only four dead men for company.

He'd sent them all to hell.

Protz winced, comforting himself with the assurance that he'd only done his sworn duty. Picking up the torch he'd left shining outside the chamber, he hobbled back the way he'd come. His shoulder burned, his cheek throbbed, and his feet felt as heavy as cinder blocks.

He had so far to go.

Dread filled him as he approached the threshold leading up to the next level. The tunnel had partially collapsed, damage caused by the sharp, penetrating sounds of the gunshots.

Gritting his teeth, Protz shoved at the fallen boards and managed to push halfway through the blockage before the supports above him groaned, letting down another shower of dirt, rock, and broken wood and knocking him to the floor. Debris pressed into his chest and agony flared beneath his ribs.

No. This wasn't happening. He couldn't die here and now.

The mission wasn't complete.

Protz had pledged, before the Führer himself, to accomplish his orders, down to the last detail.

He must not fail.

Clamping his jaw against the pain, he threw aside the rubble and pushed himself up. Staggering forward, he clawed past the wreckage blocking the tunnel and forced himself to keep moving.

Strength flagging, he reached the open shaft leading upward. He ignored the ropes still hanging from above, used by his men to lower the crate. Mounting the wooden staircase built into the side of the shaft, he used his left hand on the rail to heave himself up, groaning with each step.

Ages and eons seemed to pass before he came to the spot where he'd concealed the other, smaller casket entrusted to his care by the leader of the Third Reich.

He retrieved it from its hiding place and stumbled up the final flights of stairs, bursting into daylight and gasping breath like a dying fish. With the casket beneath his left arm, he limped through a fringe of woods and into an open field.

He must get his wounds attended to as soon as possible. He had more to do and little time in which to do it.

On the far side of the meadow, stood a house and barn. Someone there could summon a doctor. As he lurched across the lumpy soil, gray mist seeped in around the edges of his vision. Protz ordered himself not to faint, not to fall.

Then, he disobeyed.

Sprawling among the tender shoots of spring, he gaped up into the sky, despair tugging at his chest, eclipsing the pain of his injuries. And then he saw it.

Hope.

A young boy, his blond hair tucked beneath a feathered cap, blue eyes shining like stars. The beautiful Aryan lad knelt beside him, staring down at Protz.

And then he held out a hand.

CHAPTER 1

Bavaria, present day

Sunlight filtered down through the leafy boughs in golden shafts, like conduits from heaven. Riley stopped moving and pulled in a deep, cleansing breath of pine-scented air as she savored the sight of the glorious beams.

She loved the woodlands of Bavaria. They reminded her of home—the pine forests of western Washington. Many of the sounds were similar as well. The trilling of songbirds, chattering of squirrels, and hum of insects. With one notable exception.

Riley had never heard a cuckoo calling out its distinctive tune in Washington state.

Here, in southern Germany, it was not unusual to hear the cry of a cuckoo ring out in the woods, and it never failed to startle and amuse her. No wonder the clocks were so strongly associated with this area.

Idyllic as the scenery was, Riley's experience of the place had not been without hazard. In fact, only weeks ago, she had almost perished in a gorgeous lake not far from where she now stood, near the town of Schwandorf.

Even at this moment, she had to move with stealth and caution as she engaged in a training exercise designed to test her evasion and survival skills, part of her curriculum at the ultra-secret spy academy known as Olivero.

Over the course of two days, her task was to traverse a twenty-five-kilometer stretch without being seen, evading "enemy agents" prowling the area, as well as members of the public who had free access to the land.

She had camped overnight, fashioning a shelter from a tarp and paracord, using only the few items she carried and what she could scavenge from the surroundings to meet her needs.

As recently as a year ago, she could never have predicted what her life had become. Born into an eminent musical family, Riley had been a concert pianist, accustomed to lavish receptions and grand recital halls. Her wardrobe had held nothing more utilitarian than a pair of jeans.

And then, one curveball after another had altered the course of her life, sending her on a new and wholly unexpected trajectory. Yet, as difficult as it was for her to fathom, Riley was glad—no, much more than glad—she was grateful for the change.

Her life had been on a downward spiral and nothing she did had worked to reverse the cycle. After her husband, Jim, and her young son, Tanner, died in a fire, her concert career had disintegrated. She'd been unable to perform, to focus, to overcome her fear.

And her guilt.

When Mt. Rainier erupted violently during the weekend of her comeback performance, ruining all her plans and placing her in the sights of a serial killer, what felt like the end of everything proved to be a new beginning.

A beginning that had brought her to this point.

Now she had the opportunity to add new skills to her musical abilities and serve in ways she'd never foreseen, though perhaps she should have sensed it coming. After all, her grandfather had been involved in operations during WWII while using his cover and connections as a jazz pianist traveling with the USO.

She had a valiant ancestor who'd gone down still playing on The Titanic and another who'd used his music-based network of associates to move freed slaves through the Underground Railroad.

Though she'd never been able to verify this, Riley suspected her own parents may have engaged in clandestine service to the United States. She remembered trips during her youth, to South America and eastern Europe, during which she'd sensed an undercurrent of something happening beneath the surface during the ostensible performance tour.

When Devin Wright, founder and CEO of the elite under-the-radar private security firm of Olivero, had reached out to recruit her as an undercover agent, it might simply have been destiny coming to claim her.

Now she was in her training residency at the academy, learning the skills she'd need to be effective while undercover on her own concert tours. Somehow, in the process of pushing through the challenges she'd faced over the last year, she'd shed the worst of her fears and found a new treasure.

She felt alive again.

Drinking in another breath of the fresh, sun-dappled air, Riley strained her ears for the sound of anyone approaching. In the thickness of the forest, noise was the first indicator to be aware of, manifesting sooner than sight.

Yesterday, she'd had to conceal herself in the trees and underbrush twice while strangers passed nearby. Today, she'd seen no one yet but she knew there were Olivero instructors and senior cadets out there looking for her, masquerading as the enemy she must avoid.

She covered another kilometer before stopping to sip from her water bottle. As she screwed the cap back down, a breeze lifted the hair off her forehead and carried with it the faint sound of a voice.

Riley stiffened, listening hard. Yes, someone was coming.

Slipping quietly into a clump of bushes, Riley knelt and stilled her breathing. As she watched, two men moved down the path she'd been traveling. Their heads swiveled, taking in both sides of the trail, and they exuded an air of urgent watchfulness, clearly searching for something or someone.

Most likely, her.

She was clothed in olive drab, her auburn hair tucked up in a cap of the same color except for a wisp of bangs that had escaped. She'd also smeared camo cream over her face to dull the pale shine of it. Even so, she felt frighteningly exposed as the men drew near.

She reasoned they must be from Olivero. If they caught her, she'd fail the exercise and have to repeat it. Not a good outcome, but not life-threatening.

So why did she feel so terrified?

It was probably nothing more than adrenaline pumping through her veins. She held very still. They passed her position in silence but before they left her sight, she heard them exchange words in a foreign language. French?

Olivero was an international organization with agents from all over the world, so the French should not have come as a surprise. And yet, it left her feeling uneasy.

Riley maintained her frozen stance for a long moment after they'd moved on. She remembered the whiff of noise that had alerted her to their presence and didn't want to return the favor.

But it was difficult. She was kneeling on something hard that dug painfully into her kneecap and it was with great relief that she finally shifted off her leg and rubbed it to disperse the pain.

Looking down at the flat, half-buried rock that had caused her discomfort, Riley noticed a patch of dull crimson showing through the dirt. Curious, she brushed aside the dusting of soil and saw some kind of a symbol etched into the stone and stained dark red.

Using a spray of pine needles as a broom, she swept the rock as clean as she could make it and stared at the unusual symbol. It made her think of a Viking rune, but she had no idea if the marauders had invaded this area and felt certain the etching couldn't date back to that period.

Her interest in the icon intensified. Pulling her phone from her backpack, she snapped a couple photos of the symbol and was busy zipping up the pack and heaving it over her shoulders when she heard more sounds warning of an approach.

She crouched and froze again, groaning as the rock pressed once more into her sore knee. Another two-man team entered her view, and she held her breath as they searched the trail.

Riley was happy to note that the first pair of searchers had left footprints which obscured and confused her own, but she cringed when she remembered how careless she'd been in yanking up the zipper and hoisting the pack, rattling its contents.

They must be aware that she was close by.

The men moved slowly and cautiously, taking an age to pass beyond her sight. And still, Riley maintained her hunched position. Reminding herself to be careful, she finally rose on shaking legs and prepared to step out from her cover.

And that's when she felt cold metal on the back of her neck.

CHAPTER 2

The man known as The Cincher peered down at the Neuschwanstein castle far below him, so tiny it looked like a child's dollhouse and the tourists milling about it appeared as a swarm of ants.

He liked this view, the feeling it gave him. He liked the control he felt in his hands as he worked the toggles of the paraglider, sending it one way or another at his command. He liked the multiple strands he could pull, like a master puppeteer working his marionette.

If he could exert the same kind of power over the weather, he could not have ordered up a more beautiful day for soaring over the Schwangau region of Bavaria.

Green fields stretched across the valley like emerald velvet, Forggensee and several other lakes sparkled up at him like sapphires nestled in the plush of a jeweler's showcase. The craggy mountains rose majestic, awe-inspiring in beauty and magnitude.

And the castles, man's contribution to the landscape, were impressive as well. The creations of kings.

A gust of wind rippled over his wing, lifting him a few feet higher in the azure sky. This was indeed rarified air, gossamer thin and so far above where most people ever ventured without the skin of an airliner tucked around them and a pilot at the panel.

Cincher glanced to his right. Two more paragliders appeared in his peripheral view, a man and a woman, close enough for him to see the woman's pretty features and the look of horror on her face.

Laura Mangeson had looked at him once with that exact same expression, such a perfect replica in every respect that it took him immediately back to the eighth grade.

Laura had fascinated him, spellbinding him with her gray eyes so liquid clear that looking at her was like gazing into a pristine lake lined with beautiful stones. And her skin, glowing fine-pored and smooth, unmarred by the blemishes that plagued the rest of his classmates.

Most of all, it was her air of innocence. Of purity. She was like an angel or fairy. Something not of this world. Something above the rest of them.

She had to be brought down.

They shared an algebra class and Cincher had been simply John in those days. He'd befriended Laura, sitting beside her in class, defending her from bullies in the hallways, saving a place for her at the lunch table. He worked patiently to gain her trust and adoration.

Then he made his move.

"If I fail the algebra test," he told her, allowing his eyes to tear up, "my dad will beat me so hard I won't be able to sit down for a week."

"But John, you've done the homework," she assured him. "You know the material. You'll do fine on the test."

"No, I won't!" He wiped angrily at his eyes. "I cheated on most of it. I copied the answers from the back of the book."

She stared at him, frowning. "The test's not until tomorrow. We could study together tonight."

"Too little, too late, Laura. I'm done for. Unless..."

"Unless what?"

He let his face close, shutting her out. "Nothing. Never mind. I'll figure it out."

His ploy succeeded. After pulling her in so close, she couldn't bear the cold shoulder he turned to her now.

She begged for a chance to help.

The next day, when Mr. Rhodes caught them cheating and sent them both to the principal's office, Laura had been the one in tears. Sitting outside Mr. Statham's office, waiting to be ushered in for reprimand and punishment, she'd reached for his hand.

Wanting, *needing*, his assurance that everything would be okay. That her image and reputation would remain unsullied. That he still admired and respected her.

He'd pulled his hand away, letting hers hang empty and bereft, and let his lips twist in a cold, triumphant smile.

That's when she'd given him *that look*.

Delicious.

His undeveloped, clunky maneuver all those years ago had worked. Since then, he'd honed and perfected his technique into a fine-tuned machine.

A machine he exulted in using.

He'd only during the last year come into his own as The Cincher, a title passed along by power-wielding masterminds in Dread Pirate Roberts fashion. He'd earned it, making a reputation for himself by manipulating a repertoire of terrorists, presidents, kings, financiers, drug lords, arms dealers, and serial killers.

Among others.

He attributed his spiraling success to his grand vision and his ability to keep his eye on the supernal prize. He shared his ultimate ambition with no one, for no one was worthy of it, but he let it distill on his soul like an elixir of the gods.

Since childhood, he'd studied, practiced, worked, and learned volumes about how to maneuver and exploit, finesse and defraud. But it was not enough.

Cincher craved something beyond. Something few men have reached for and only a minute handful have brushed their fingertips over. No one had ever grasped it in both hands.

As he intended to.

Self-aware enough to realize he was obsessed, Cincher didn't consider it a drawback. Obsession provided the sort of fuel that burned hot enough and long enough to keep the engine running until the finish line was crossed.

He embraced obsession.

There was only one other passion in Cincher's life which came anywhere close to matching this one. Only one other fixation he allowed to influence his pursuits and decisions to such a degree.

And that was his interest in the concert pianist, Riley Forte.

CHAPTER 3

The subdued morning chatter of her fellow cadets floated in the air like background music as Riley took a seat in the Olivero cafeteria.

Steam rose off her made-to-order omelet, carrying the delicious scent of onions and peppers to her nostrils and making her mouth water.

She popped a grape onto her tongue and bit down as Rick slid his tray next to hers and plopped into a chair.

"Tough break, Riley," he said. "And you were so close."

"Right? Another five kilometers and I'd have made it."

"Chalk it up to experience and hit it again. You'll get there."

Crouching in the bushes with all her focus on the trail in front of her, Riley hadn't caught on to the "enemy" sneaking up behind her. She'd been captured and returned to the academy to brush up on her technique before another trial run.

Rick Jimenez was the man most responsible for bringing her here, to Olivero. He'd been a cop when they initially met, and she'd been a mess wrapped in a disaster tangled up in catastrophe. By the end of their ordeal, Rick had recognized something unique in her and when he left the force to join Olivero, he'd swept her along with him.

"You know what the worst part of it is?" Riley asked.

"The MREs?"

Riley laughed. "Okay, so this is a close second." She scooted back from the table and pointed out the purple bruise on her knee. "Hurts like a son-of-a-gun."

"How'd you get that?"

"Kneeling on a rock while trying to evade a swarm of searchers." She grabbed the cell phone from her pocket. "And check this out. I found this crazy symbol etched into the stone. Does that mean anything to you?" She showed him the photos.

Rick studied the images. "Doesn't look familiar, but there's something about it that intrigues me." He paused, drumming his fingers on the table. "What do you think about shooting it over to Daniel?"

Formerly employed by the Defense Intelligence Agency, Daniel Escobar was one of Olivero's computer tech geniuses, stationed at the firm's headquarters near Seattle. Rick sometimes referred to him as "miracle man," and Riley was beginning to understand why.

Along with Holly, his wife and favorite co-worker, Daniel had pulled off some incredible feats when it came to mining and analyzing information. Holly was an expert researcher who doubled as a superb travel agent and logistics manager.

Together, they represented a formidable force for good.

"Great idea," Riley said. "I'll do it now."

As she finished sending the photo with a brief message attached, they were joined at the table by two more Olivero residents.

Matsui was a weapons instructor at the school. A former member of the NYPD Bomb Squad, she knew her way around explosives, wires, and detonators like Riley knew her way around a piano keyboard.

Gideon settled into the seat across from Riley and gave her a slow-spreading grin. The man was impossibly good-looking and when Riley had initially met him, coming out of the evening gloom on horseback, it had been like encountering a fairy tale prince.

Tall, blond, with exquisite bone structure and muscle tone, Gideon was the self-defense and martial arts instructor at the academy. He was German and spoke six other languages as well.

Although his gorgeous smile made her swoon a little internally, Riley's feelings for him didn't venture beyond friendship. Theirs was a different sort of relationship and they'd been through some critical moments together that had tested them both and formed a solid bond.

She would trust him with her life and had done so on previous occasions.

As she dug into her omelet, Riley's gaze traveled around the table, taking in the circle of faces that was becoming such a vital part of her life. She felt a growing fondness for each of them and realized how much like family they'd become.

She was glad. But at the same time, she felt a tug at her heart and the aching throb of the empty hole left by the loss of her husband and son. Her fingers went to the locket she wore on a length of nylon cord around her neck.

Jim had given it to her when Tanner was born. One side of the locket contained a fine fluff of baby hair. The other bore a photo of Tanner. Each year, on their son's birthday, Jim had updated the photo, and Riley had expected it to remain a family tradition, with a long procession of pictures documenting her boy's journey into manhood.

It broke her heart to know the six-year-old Tanner would never be replaced.

She wore the locket always, replacing the delicate chain it had originally graced with the sturdy cord, often tucking it inside her shirt for safekeeping. Closing her fingers around it now, she took comfort in the thought of her sweet boy and the good man she'd married, believing they waited for her in another place and time.

As she let go of the locket, she thought of Nate, another man who'd formed an important part of her recent transformation and become very dear to her. She missed him and knew things might have worked out differently between them if she had willed it. It had hurt, to turn him away from her, but she would not—could not—stand between a man and his family.

If there was any chance he and Marilyn could mend their relationship and make a loving home again with their daughter, Nate owed it to all of them to grab that chance and run with it.

She hoped it was going well between them. She really did. Yet a part of her, a tiny selfish piece, wanted him to come back to her.

She squashed that piece and pushed it away.

As she finished the last bite of her breakfast, Riley's phone chirped out with a merry ring tone. She was surprised to see the incoming call was from Daniel.

"Wow, I didn't expect to hear back from you so soon," she said. "It must be nearly midnight there. I didn't mean to keep you up so late."

"Then next time, don't send me something so damn intriguing, Riley," he told her. "Once I showed the symbol to Holly, there was no sleep for either of us."

Riley opened her mouth to repeat an apology, but his words overrode hers.

"And Riley—we found something you'll want to hear about."

CHAPTER 4

Bellevue Detective Nate Quentin sprawled across his bed, staring at the ceiling and listening to the rain pelting against the windowpanes. The line of cedar trees outside his window twisted in the wind, dancing with the light of a streetlamp to cast writhing shadows across the wall of his bedroom.

As restless as the trees, Nate couldn't settle or sleep. He thought about his current case, the murder of an experienced hiker in a state park outside Seattle. The killer or killers had attempted to make the death look like an accident, a fall from a cliff into the river below.

Clever, but not clever enough.

Nate's thoughts shifted to his new partner, a woman everyone called Mack. They were still working to sync their individual styles, but he believed they were shaping into a bang-up team.

Only one day into the investigation and they already had a decent lineup of suspects. It was going well. It wasn't the case or the noise of the storm or the shifting shadows that kept him awake.

He missed Riley.

He'd tried so hard to scrub her from his mind, to commit his affections wholly to his ex-wife and work to revive the good relationship they'd once had.

And it had been good. Some days, it had been very good. Like the day Sammi was born.

In fact, Nate hadn't realized the good days were over until they'd been over for a good long time. He hadn't noticed, too caught up in his work as a homicide investigator, too focused on solving the next case, nabbing the next bad guy.

He'd let so much distance come between them. He'd been stupid.

Easy now, to look back and see that he should have been much more vigilant. He knew the divorce rate among law enforcement officers was upwards of fifty percent. He knew, and he still let it happen.

Because it didn't happen all at once. It was an erosion process, and by the time he realized what was going on, the rift was too wide. He couldn't bridge the gap.

But now, he and Marilyn were trying again, giving it another chance. He really wanted it to work out.

He did, really. For the sake of their daughter.

But for his own sake?

Clenching his teeth, Nate flipped onto his side and moaned, giving up the fight to keep Riley from his thoughts. If he was honest, he feared she occupied too much of his mind and heart to believe that renewing his vows to Marilyn could ever be a success.

Punching the lumps out of his pillow, he squirmed into a new position and squeezed his eyes shut, trying to clear all thought from his brain so that he could drift into oblivion. But it was no use.

He wondered what Riley was doing now.

CHAPTER 5

Valéry Russeau watched the dirndl-clad waitress weaving among the tables, enjoying the plump bit of cleavage showing above the white frill of her low-cut blouse. The French women of his home-land seemed to him brittle and staid compared to the buxom bounty of Bavaria.

He gave the woman a smile and a wink as she placed the stein down before him, the amber liquid filled to the brim with foam running over. Like the bodice of her dress. He took a long swallow and used his sleeve to wipe the beads of moisture from his mustache as he listened to the men at the next table argue over the football score.

He had a call to make but wanted to quench his thirst and steel his nerve first. The Cincher may, or may not, be pleased with what he had to report. On occasion, the big boss got curious about the movements of a woman named Riley, a recruit at a nearby, very low-profile academy for private operatives.

Russeau thought it tickled some bizarre fancy of Cincher's to know what she was up to and sometimes to let her *know* that he knew. Considering the scope of Cincher's enterprises and the crime-fighting power brewing behind the gates of the academy, it felt akin to poking a tiger with a stick, but Russeau didn't call the shots.

A swell of relief washed over him as he remembered how he and Emile had lost track of Riley in the forest...and then found her.

And found something else, as well.

He finished his drink and left a five euro note tucked beneath the glass, enough to cover the beer and the small *trinkgeld* the waitress would expect. Making his way along the *Biergarten* path, he walked into a neighboring field and found some privacy among the rustling poplars clustered beside it.

Cincher picked up immediately. "Tell me about Riley."

Russeau explained how he and Dupond had trailed her on a training exercise, staying out of sight as she attempted to do the same.

"We watched her take cover in the bushes while a team of spy school cadets passed through."

"She evaded capture?"

Russeau paused half a beat. "It looked like she was going to, but the cadets circled back and busted her."

A low chuckle, and then, "She'll have to learn, won't she? Anything else?"

"Yes, sir. After they left, we searched her hiding place, in case she left anything behind."

"And did she?"

"No, but there was something hidden there. A stone with a symbol carved into it. It looked like your girl had scraped away the dirt, uncovering it."

"Photos," Cincher demanded. "Send them now."

"Of course."

Russeau sent the pictures. "That's all, sir."

He heard a grunt and then silence as the call ended.

CHAPTER 6

Cincher switched off the swirling jets and stood from the tub, letting the still-warm water trace through the curling hair on his chest. He snatched the fluffy towel waiting for him on the marble countertop and rubbed it over his head, feeling a rush of satisfaction.

The symbol in the photos stirred something deep within him. It was not familiar to him, but he felt like it should be, like it was something he was meant to find.

Instead, it had been Riley who found it. Strange indeed.

And intriguing.

Climbing from the tub, he dressed quickly, reveling in the fantasy of reaching his ultimate goal. Every day, he drew closer. He felt it near, and also the frustration of never quite reaching it. A bittersweet sensation both stimulating and infuriating.

Last month, his contact in Argentina had tantalized him with hopes which eventually came to nothing. For nearly half a year, he'd had a team in South Africa running down leads that never panned out. But now...

The symbol spoke to him. His gut told him this could be a solid brick on the road to his destination, to attaining the object of his desire. Before the hour was out, he meant to have his people on track, analyzing its meaning, discovering the path down which it pointed.

And then, he'd put Russeau on the trail. During the four years the man had worked for him, he had never failed to complete his mission.

Whatever the cost.

Cincher expected that track record to continue, unblemished, until he was through with the man.

Glancing in the mirror, he ran a comb through his hair, hardly noticing how it seemed thinner every day. Hardly caring.

He laughed out loud. It appeared that he and Riley were engaged in a race, and she didn't even know it. It bothered him little that she had a head start. If the matter turned out to be something trivial, its importance obsolete or irrelevant, he would simply have a delightful time dogging Riley's heels.

If, on the other hand, it proved to be as significant as he suspected, Riley would be wise to take care. She would have to be careful. Extremely careful.

If necessary, he would crush her.

IF YOU ENJOYED THIS PREVIEW,

ACKNOWLEDGEMENTS

I doubt any author can produce a book worth reading without support from many sources. I know I certainly didn't in writing *Staccato Passage*. I'd like to take this opportunity to thank some of those who've helped to make this book possible.

First, I owe thanks to pilot extraordinaire, Carl Rydalch, for taking my sister and I up in his four-seater Cessna, executing a series of touch-and-go landings and takeoffs, and answering my many questions about flying in a small, private plane.

Next, I'd like to thank my advance readers who took time to read the book before its release in order to point out any gaping plot holes, major gaffes, or embarrassing mistakes. Any such that remain in the book are entirely due to my own negligence.

The most important thing I look for from my advance readers, however, is simply their reaction to the story. Did it grab and hold their interest? Did they find it suspenseful, engaging, exciting? Did they have trouble putting the book down?

If their honest answers are yes, I know the book is ready for publication.

My team of advance readers includes Terry Giles, Leslie Rydalch, Priscilla Fleischer, Roseann Saxton, Ilona Johnson, Georgina Bradley, McKall Henrie-Valdez, Kelli Dyerly, Emily Bangerter, Manie Kilian, Carolyn Brock, Fred Masek, and Denzel Struchen.

I also want to acknowledge my gratitude for my husband's support, love, and never-failing encouragement. Thank you, Terry. I really couldn't do it without you.

I can't finish without giving thanks for my largest wellspring of constant and faithful support, my Savior, Jesus Christ. I am nothing without it.

About the Author

Joslyn Chase is an award-winning author of mysteries and thrillers. Any day she can send readers to the edge of their seats, chewing their fingernails to the nub and prickling with suspense, is a good day in her book.

In 2025, Joslyn's thriller novel *Staccato Passage* was a semi-finalist for the *Adventure Writer's Grandmaster Award* and "A Band of Scheming Women" was a finalist for the *Derringer Award*. The first book in her Riley Forte series, *Nocturne in Ashes*, was also a finalist for the *Readers' Favorite International Book Award*. In addition, "Cold Hands, Warm Heart," was chosen by Amor Towles as one of the *Best Mystery Stories of the Year 2023*.

Her short stories have appeared in *Alfred Hitchcock's Mystery Magazine, Malice Domestic's Mystery Most Devious, Thrill Ride Magazine, Fiction River, Mystery, Crime, and Mayhem, Mystery Magazine,* and *Pulphouse Fiction,* among others.

Known for her fast-paced suspense fiction, Joslyn's books are full of surprising twists and delectable turns. You will find her riveting novels most anywhere books are sold.

Her love for travel has led Joslyn to ride camels through the Nubian desert, fend off monkeys on the Rock of Gibraltar, and hike the

Bavarian Alps. But she still believes that sometimes the best adventures come in getting the words on the page and in the thrill of reading a great story.

Join the growing group of readers who've discovered the thrill of Chase! Sign up for Joslyn's readers' group and get VIP access to great bonuses—like your free copy of *No Rest: 14 Tales of Chilling Suspense*—as well as updates and first crack at new releases.

bookbub.com/authors/joslyn-chase

facebook.com/joslynchasewriter

goodreads.com/author/show/16850235.Joslyn_Chase

linkedin.com/in/joslynchase/

pinterest.com/joslynchase/

youtube.com/@joslynchase5955/videos